T0265825

PEOPLE OF
CAHOKIA

MORNING STAR:
Lightning
Shell

PEOPLE OF
CAHOKIA

MORNING STAR:

Lightning
Shell

W. Michael Gear and
Kathleen O'Neal Gear

A TOM DOHERTY ASSOCIATES BOOK · NEW YORK

LIGHTNING SHELL

Copyright © 2022 by W. Michael Gear and Kathleen O'Neal Gear

Maps, timeline, art, and ornaments by Ellisa Mitchell

A Forge Book
Published by Tom Doherty Associates
120 Broadway
New York, NY 10271

www.tor-forge.com

Forge® is a registered trademark of Macmillan Publishing Group, LLC.

Library of Congress Cataloging-in-Publication Data

Names: Gear, W. Michael, author. | Gear, Kathleen O'Neal, author.
Title: Lightning shell : people of Cahokia / W. Michael Gear and Kathleen O'Neal Gear.
Description: First edition. | New York : Forge, 2022. | Series: North America's forgotten past. Morning star | "A Tom Doherty Associates book."
Identifiers: LCCN 2022008309 (print) | LCCN 2022008310 (ebook) | ISBN 9781250767202 (hardcover) | ISBN 9781250767219 (ebook)
Subjects: LCGFT: Novels.
Classification: LCC PS3557.E19 L54 2022 (print) | LCC PS3557.E19 (ebook) | DDC 813'.54—dc23/eng/20220224
LC record available at https://lccn.loc.gov/2022008309
LC ebook record available at https://lccn.loc.gov/2022008310

Our books may be purchased in bulk for promotional, educational, or business use. Please contact your local bookseller or the Macmillan Corporate and Premium Sales Department at 1-800-221-7945, extension 5442, or by email at MacmillanSpecialMarkets@macmillan.com.

First Edition: 2022

Printed in the United States of America

0 9 8 7 6 5 4 3 2 1

We dedicate this book

To

Some of our most treasured friends

How do we say thank you?

In no specific order

This is for

Barb and Merlin Heinze

Meri Ann Rush and Johnny Dorman

And, of course,

Deb and Rick Tudor

You are the beating heart

Of

Thermopolis!

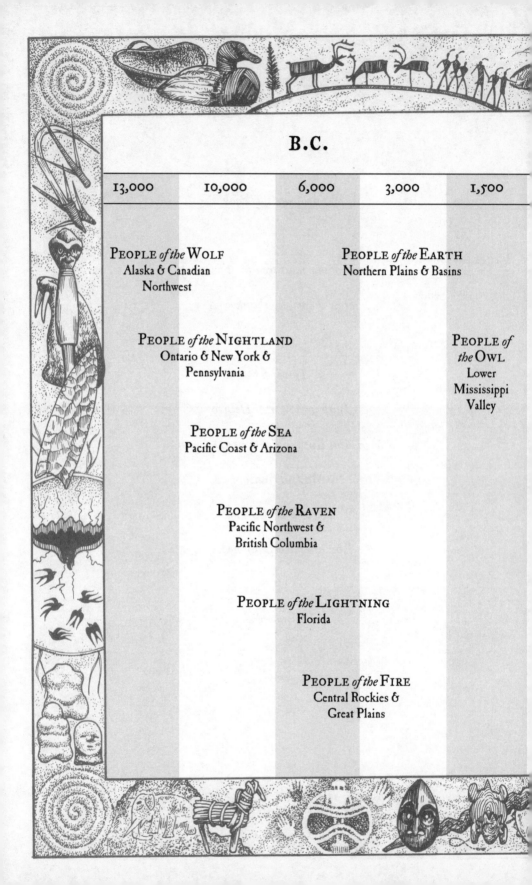

B.C.

13,000	10,000	6,000	3,000	1,500

PEOPLE *of the* WOLF
Alaska & Canadian
Northwest

PEOPLE *of the* EARTH
Northern Plains & Basins

PEOPLE *of the* NIGHTLAND
Ontario & New York &
Pennsylvania

PEOPLE *of
the* OWL
Lower
Mississippi
Valley

PEOPLE *of the* SEA
Pacific Coast & Arizona

PEOPLE *of the* RAVEN
Pacific Northwest &
British Columbia

PEOPLE *of the* LIGHTNING
Florida

PEOPLE *of the* FIRE
Central Rockies &
Great Plains

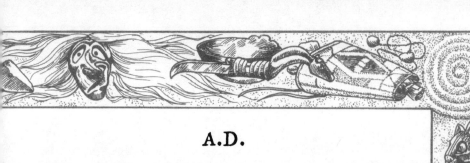

A.D.

0	200	1,000	1,100	1,300	1,400

PEOPLE *of the* LAKES
East-Central Woodlands
& Great Lakes

PEOPLE *of the*
WEEPING EYE
Mississippi Valley
& Tennessee

PEOPLE *of the* MASKS
Ontario & Upstate New York

PEOPLE *of the*
THUNDER
Alabama & Mississippi

PEOPLE *of the* RIVER
Mississippi Valley

PEOPLE *of the*
LONGHOUSE
New York
& New England

PEOPLE *of the* MORNING STAR
SUN BORN
MOON HUNT
STAR PATH
LIGHTNING SHELL
Central Mississippi Valley

The
DAWN
COUNTRY

PEOPLE *of the* SILENCE
Southwest Anasazi

The
BROKEN
LAND

PEOPLE *of the* MOON
Northwest New Mexico
& Southwest Colorado

PEOPLE
of the
BLACK
SUN

PEOPLE *of the* MIST
Chesapeake Bay

Serpent Woman Town

North

To the Sacred Cave

Marsh Elder Lake

Black Tail's Tomb

CAHOKIA

Evening Star Town

Avenue of the Sun

Avenue of the Moon

Canoe Landing

River Mound City

Horned Serpent Town

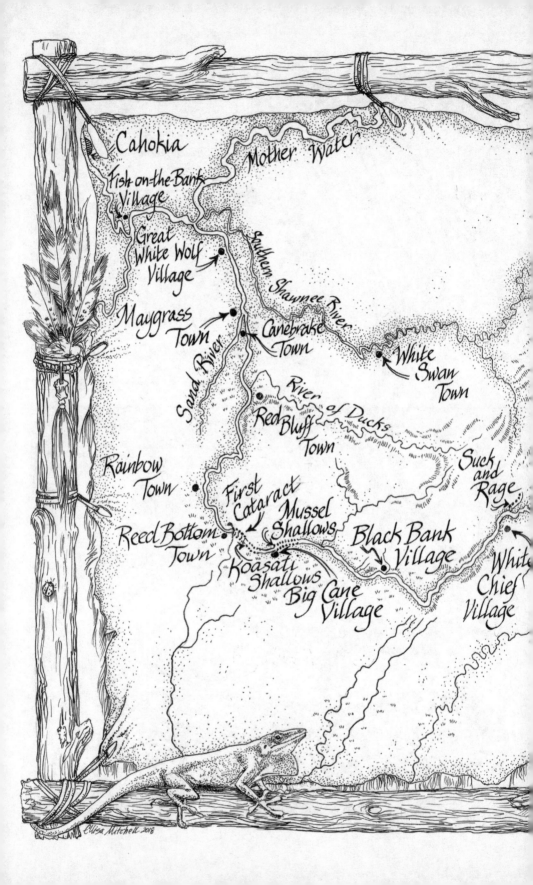

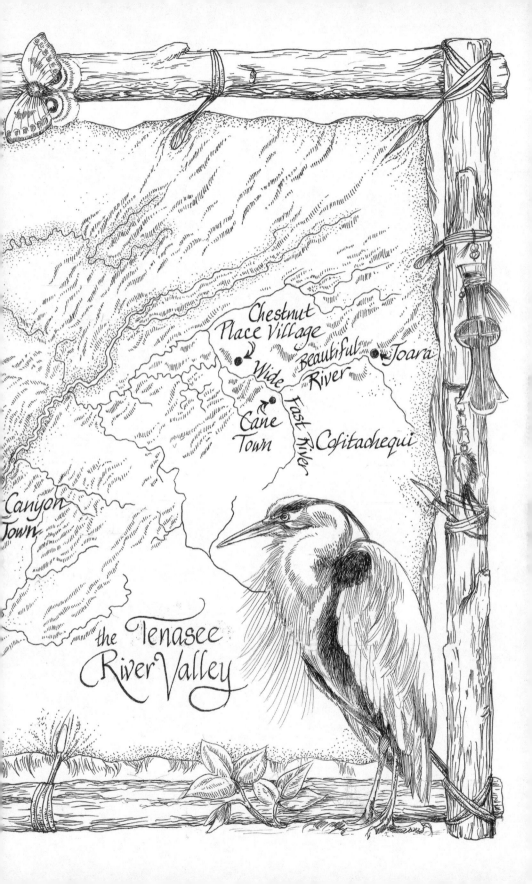

Chestnut
Place Village
Beautiful
River • Joara
Wide
River
Cane Fast River
Town Cofitachequi

Canyon
Town

the Tenasee
River Valley

PEOPLE OF
CAHOKIA

MORNING STAR:
Lightning
Shell

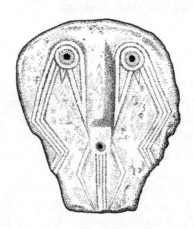

Dancing Barefoot on Obsidian

I am a lord of Cahokia, carried like one, born upon a panther hide–covered litter on the shoulders of eight blooded warriors. The trail we follow winds its way through the shadowed depths of the woods, beneath the towering trees and among endless vines as we make our way down the riverside trail. This is an ancient war and Trade route, a path trodden for countless generations as it descends from the high mountain divide. Hardly a path in the Cahokian sense, it is more of a rut, the bottom a mass of interlaced roots almost hidden in the leaf-covered black soil.

Up ahead, High Chief Fire Light and his squadron first, their weapons in hand, shields hung over their shoulders, walk in the lead. Fire Light thinks he's headed home, so he's more than happy to force his warriors to make good time on our way down to the banks of the Upper Tenasee. There we can obtain canoes for the trip downriver. Fire Light is an exile, but I have promised him clemency when we finally reach distant Cahokia.

More than once the warriors carrying me trip, cursing under their breaths as they struggle for footing on the root-thick trail. They do not look up, dare not meet my eyes.

They fear me.

And rightly so.

These days I am known as Lightning Shell, the witch of Cofitachequi. Perhaps the most feared witch in the entire world. I look as terrible as my reputation. The left side of my face is hideous—a mass of scar tissue, as if the skin had been scorched from cheek to brow. Must have been horribly painful, but I don't remember.

Out in public I wear a whelk-shell mask to hide the disfigurement. It keeps people from screaming and running away. The mask was carved from a large shell traded inland from the coast; in addition to a prominent nose, it has eye and mouth holes that allow me to see and speak. The forked-eye design emphasizes my allegiance to Sky Power, as do the lightning zigzags running down the cheeks.

The mask is but a part of my Power. You see, I was reincarnated, turned from the Wild One—the essence of "Thrown Away Boy"—into someone else. And yes, I know who I was before my rebirth: Walking Smoke, of the Morning Star House of the Four Winds Clan. My father was Tonka'tzi Red Warrior. Tonka'tzi translates as Great Sky, the honorific given to the secular ruler of the mighty city of Cahokia. But I am not the only one in my family to host a reincarnated Spirit.

So, too, does my brother. He was once known as Chunkey Boy. Chosen for the honor of hosting the spiritual essence of the Morning Star. When, during the reincarnation ritual, the living god took possession of my brother's body, Chunkey Boy's souls were consumed. His flesh, bones, and body became the host for the resurrected Spirit of the hero from the Beginning Times.

Years ago Cahokia consisted of a series of warring villages and clans. And then my grandfather, Black Tail, defeated and captured Chief Petaga in a bloody battle. The very day he defeated Petaga, a great star began to burn brightly in the daytime sky. Black Tail knew it had to be the Spirit of the Morning Star, beaming his approval. The moment Black Tail saw that star burning so bright in the middle of the day, he had his vision.

Through a complicated ritual—driven by the sacrifice of Petaga and most of his family and kin—Black Tail summoned the Spiritual essence of the mythical hero Morning Star down from the sky. When he did, Morning Star's Spirit took possession of my grandfather's body. The ritual was performed again, a generation later, when Black Tail's body wore out and he died of old age. That's when the living god's Spirit took possession of Chunkey Boy.

Power, you see, runs in my family.

Not that it seems to be doing me much good. I only need look back over my shoulder—though twisting my body strains the wound in my genitals and forces me to wince from the pain.

When I do, I can see my sister, Night Shadow Star, where she rides on the litter being borne down the trail behind me. She is carried by six muscular Cahokian warriors, their heads bobbing, sweat beading on their tattooed and sun-bronzed skin. I think my sister is the most beautiful and provocative woman alive. As she meets my gaze, something electric charges the air, a crackle of Power. My lust and her hatred, flashing, twisting, locked in desperate combat.

A faint smile curls her lips, one filled with promise and resolution. Her dark eyes seem to expand in her delicate face—looming and depthless portals that lead to her soul, and down, deep into the Underworld Power that is hers and her lord's.

Whereas I am possessed by the Thunderbirds, and was reborn through lightning, Night Shadow Star belongs to Piasa, the terrible Underwater Panther who stalks the dark and root-filled warrens in the bowels of the earth. Subservient only to Old-Woman-Who-Never-Dies, Piasa devoured my sister's souls. Made her a creature of the depths, of moss-filled tunnels, the homeless dead, serpents, and darkness.

"Which is why I will have you," I promise. It will be a conjoining of Sky and Underworld. The sexual union of brother and sister in a sacred abomination. A reconciliation of opposites that will mix her Power with mine and make me the most Powerful man alive.

Even more Powerful than the reincarnated Morning Star atop his earthen pyramid in far-off Cahokia.

Though we're no more than ten paces apart, her voice carries as if across a vast distance. "I will stand over your lifeless body."

The words send a chill down my spine. She has tried to kill me before. Back in Cahokia. In the river. As I was preparing to join with her in unholy copulation, she capsized the canoe we were in. Underwater, twisting in the current's depths, we battled. I was trying to choke the life out of her.

Cunning woman, my sister. She had lured me into the Piasa's lair.

But as the Spirit Beast rose from the depths to devour me, the Thunderbirds blasted the river with lightning. I remember the flashes of blinding white, the scream torn from Piasa as he fled the killing bolts cast down by the Sky World.

. . . And it was the last thing I remembered until I emerged from a lightning-blasted and burning temple nearly a year later and half a world away in Cofitachequi. As mysterious as the scar on my face, I have no clue how I got there, or where I might have been in those intervening months. That part of my life is blank, missing.

Night Shadow Star, however, was not finished with me. She traveled all that way from Cahokia, down the Father Water and up the Tenasee, just to kill me. But for Chief Fire Light's warriors, she would have succeeded. She struck me right between the legs, caught my stones and shaft square with the flat of her war ax. Would have crushed my head with the next blow had Fire Light's warriors not tackled her. She came that close!

Meanwhile, until my aching and weeping genitals heal, I will wait. Plan for the glorious occasion when I lower myself onto her ripe body.

One of the warriors stumbles, almost dropping me.

"Clumsy idiot," I growl. The sudden shift of the litter aggravates my wounded groin and bends me double with pain.

He starts to glance up, his instinctive response being to anger. Catches himself and makes a face as he avoids my eyes. Turns his attention back to the rutted forest path.

As I recover from the pain, I hear laughter, musically feminine and mocking. My sister revels in my agony. She should be cowed, worried, and terrified at what I'm going to do to her when my manhood heals. Though I love her and ache to drive myself into her, I will relish the moment she finally understands just how much my triumph means. I want to see the depths of defeat and the despair in her eyes. I want to break her and her Power so completely that all she can do is weep and plead for my touch.

Only then will she know the soaring extent of my victory.

From where we now wind our way down to the Tenasee River's headwaters, we are still months of travel and half a world away from Cahokia. I have plenty of time to heal and plan that mystical joining. I want it to be epic. Like the mating of Moon and Sun, or Earth and Sea.

And to think that some people say family relationships are complicated.

It all comes down to time and the inevitable.

I throw a glance back. Night Shadow Star's gaze is filled with resolve.

In the end, I will see tears streaming from those dark orbs.

One

On that summer afternoon, Spotted Wrist stood on the subterranean floor of a modest house bordering Cahokia's East Plaza. The dwelling lay perhaps three bowshots east of the Morning Star's great mound and palace. The room was foul with flies, the insects swarming the dead woman's corpse.

Willow Blossom had been Spotted Wrist's agent and part-time lover. Now her body sprawled beside the cold ashes of her hearth. Blood had soaked into the clay floor and dried into a black crust. Despite the circling flies, he could see the telltale froth where bubbly lung-blood had blown out of a wicked puncture wound in the woman's side.

Taking distant towns in the far north might have been child's play compared to navigating the politics of great Cahokia with its five rival ruling Houses, let alone governing the subordinated Earth Clans, who in turn kept a lid on the ethnically diverse, often antagonistic, dirt farmers with their generations-long vendettas and hatreds. The entire city was like a sealed pot boiling on the fire. One never knew when the pressure of the steam would build until the whole thing exploded into a thousand shards.

So, is this political? Did someone murder Willow Blossom because she was my agent? Is this a message? Some warning?

Cahokian politics were like a venomous spider's web of intrigue, plotting, and—as Willow Blossom had learned—murder.

And then, at the pinnacle of it all—up there in his five-story-tall palace atop the most prominent earthen pyramid in the world—lived the reincarnated god known as the Morning Star. The living miracle that had drawn entire peoples to pick up their belongings and journey to Cahokia, where they could share in the wonder of a living Spirit Being who walked among them.

It was one thing to revel in the miraculous, and another to deal with a living god on a daily basis.

As Spotted Wrist studied the woman's corpse, a shadow darkened the door. He glanced up as Clan Matron Rising Flame—a slim woman in her late twenties—lowered herself to the stepping post set in the floor. The clan matron wore a fantastic blue-, green-, and red-painted bunting cape; a fine dogbane skirt was belted at her narrow waist and displayed the muscular legs that betrayed her obsession with stickball. Her hair was pulled tight in a bun and held with polished copper pins crafted in the shape of eagle feathers. Her brow was furrowed, sharp eyes fixing on the corpse.

She waved at the flies, and said, "Your squadron first said you'd be here. Willow Blossom?"

"The very same, Matron. Been dead for a couple of days. These sunken-floor houses, the dirt is dug out, the trench walls put up, and the earth is piled against the house sides for insulation. Despite being mid-summer, on that cool dirt floor, she's only now starting to bloat. A litter bearer found her this morning. Came to my palace since it was the last place he and his team had carried her from."

"Think she was killed that night?"

"Probably. She's wearing the same shawl and skirt she had on when I last saw her. That timing would be about right given the size of the maggots in her wound, mouth, and eyes."

"Who do you think did this?"

"I was asking myself that same question when you arrived. So, was Willow Blossom's murder political? Or just a random event? As if, perhaps, she had returned home to find an opportunistic thief in her house? Thinking of a thief, Seven Skull Shield would want her dead. Or was she a poor victim of circumstance? In the wrong place at the wrong time?"

"None of her things have been taken." Rising Flame took note of the fancy bedding and the fine cookware Willow Blossom had absconded with when she moved from Night Shadow Star's palace.

"Might be a crime of passion. Her husband, that rope maker, Robin Feather? He might have finally caught up with her. Stuck her in the side with something sharp to repay her for running off with that foul Seven Skull Shield. Old Robin Feather's got a reputation for killing women who betray him."

"Shouldn't be too hard to run Robin Feather down. He's well known on the canoe landing." Rising Flame bent close, studied the roiling ball of maggots wiggling in Willow Blossom's wound.

Spotted Wrist narrowed an eye. "My best guess is still Seven Skull Shield. Willow Blossom played him, used him to get into Night Shadow Star's palace. Then she betrayed him to me. I ever tell you the story behind that?"

"No."

He gestured dismissively at Willow Blossom's fly-crawling corpse. "The only thing she ever wanted was wealth, status, and luxury. And she knew that I'd give anything to get my hands on Seven Skull Shield. The man's nothing more than a foul bit of walking human trash. Clanless! And that night up at Morning Star's palace, he humiliated me . . . and you . . . in front of half of Cahokia."

"As if I'm ever going to forget." Rising Flame straightened, studying Spotted Wrist with emotionless eyes.

He hated it when she looked at him that way. What, in the name of pus, was she thinking?

Spotted Wrist batted his irritation at the column of buzzing flies. "I'll never forget the thief's words: '*What's wrong? Can't find a woman who wants you?*' They burn like fire in my memory. Like a slap to my face. And then Willow Blossom shows up, and guess what? The thief is in love with her. Better yet, she is bedding him when my warriors charge in. Wraps herself around him like a cocoon. He can't even pull out of her while my men grab him." He chuckled. "How sweet revenge can be."

"You put Seven Skull Shield in a bear cage and beat him half to death. I'd call that sweet." That emotionless look turned even more distant. "But then you lost him. Let his friends slip in and rescue him. Whisked him right out from under your nose. They played you like a fool."

Spotted Wrist ground his teeth, slashed at the flies. "Blue Heron was behind that."

"So you torched her palace, and her inside it. Except when the ashes were searched, no one could find her charred remains. We know that she sent her household staff out to warn her allies. She might have fled, too. For all we know, your men burned an empty building."

"It wasn't empty!" Spotted Wrist roared. "My squadron second barricaded her inside. He was talking to her through the door until the fire got too hot. The *only* way she could have escaped that death trap was through the front door when it finally burned to ashes. And no old woman came staggering out through that flame and smoke."

Rising Flame had no give in her eyes. "Why couldn't you find her corpse? Or the body of her *berdache*, Smooth Pebble? Remember her? The woman who runs Blue Heron's household? The only corpse was that guard your men murdered. He was found half-burned on the veranda. Blue Heron's and Smooth Pebble's bodies were not among the ashes."

"It's obvious," he scoffed. "Like a cremation. The fire was hot enough, it rendered them down to fine ash. Maybe so fine they were kicked apart as my warriors searched the scorched wreckage."

Rising Flame paused for effect. "I think they escaped."

"If she escaped, why has no one seen her? This is Blue Heron we're talking about. One of the most vain, arrogant, and recognizable nobles in the city. She is a lady. She has standards. Not the sort to vanish into the crowd. A woman of her rank would be talked about, especially if she went to ground among one of the Earth Clans. I have eyes in the few warrens where she might have taken refuge. I even know for a fact she's not hiding in Columella's palace."

"Oh?"

He smiled grimly. "If Blue Heron were alive, she couldn't resist the temptation. Like a moth to a flickering flame, she couldn't help but take a hand, make a move in the game. The moment she tried to meddle, to stir the political pot, we'd hear. You'd hear. But cock my ears all I might, the silence is unambiguous."

Rising Flame's lips twitched. "Assuming we're not standing over her handiwork right here."

Spotted Wrist rubbed a hand over his face, glanced down at the corpse. "Next thing, you'll be telling me that maybe Blue Heron killed Willow Blossom to get even with me?"

"Unlikely," Rising Flame told him in that monotonous voice that was driving him half-insane. "Look at her. Willow Blossom didn't fight. Her clothing isn't disheveled; the shawl is still draped around her shoulders. Look at her hands. No sign she scratched at anyone, or even put up a fight. She didn't think that whoever killed her was a threat. Which, if you ask me, excludes Blue Heron, Seven Skull Shield, her old husband Robin Feather, and even your random robber that she might have walked in on."

Spotted Wrist felt his heart begin to pound. "Are you forgetting whose side you're on?"

The way she held his gaze wasn't reassuring. "My side is all about winning, Keeper. For the moment, your squadrons control the city. But this thing is still a long way from decided. Lady Columella has all of Evening Star House's squadrons called up. They're in defensive positions atop the bluffs on the other side of the river."

"Not for long." Spotted Wrist gave her a knowing grin. "Another couple of days, and I'll have bartered for enough big Trade canoes to paddle my squadrons across. Some upriver, some down. Columella will have to split her forces, following along the bank in hopes her squadrons can be in position in time to stop my landing. You know the western shore, tree-lined, cut by ravines where creeks empty into the Father Water. No way they can defend the entire western bank. In the end, I'm going to flank her."

"You talk as if this deed is already done," she replied, leaning her head back as she stared past the occasional buzzing fly at the roof poles and ceiling.

"I'm the Hero of the North," he told her easily. "Compared to the hard nut of Red Wing Town and the Upper River, Matron Columella's Evening Star House is like a soft plum. Rich, juicy, and easy to squash."

"Then I hope you don't choke on the hard pit." Her expression remained stoic, the tattooed stars on her cheeks barely visible in the dim light. She seemed unconcerned at the flies all around her. "You had better be right"—with her toe, she indicated Willow Blossom's dead body—"because your competence in political matters has me concerned."

"What's to concern you?" He slitted his eyes, the old call to battle coming to a boil around his heart. "Within the week, Evening Star Town will be mine. The *tonka'tzi*, old Wind, is my prisoner, which paralyzes the Morning Star House. Blue Heron is dead, and her allies in River House are in hiding. North Star House and Horned Serpent House are allied for the first time in a decade. I've got Cahokia by the balls."

"Really?" A faint smile bent her lips. "Aren't you forgetting something? Got the Morning Star by the balls, too, have you?"

"The living god?" Spotted Wrist shrugged it away. "What does he care? He's up there, sitting in his palace, bedding gullible young women and enjoying his feasts while embassies from half the world shower him with gifts and fawn at his feet. As long as we keep a lid on the city, keep the peace, and don't rile his enjoyment of godhood, what does he care?"

The frown deepened on Rising Flame's forehead. "It's always been said: 'The Morning Star plays a deep game.' You have to ask, why has he been silent? Not a single summons. Why did he allow us to go as far as we have? What's his stake in this latest shuffling of the Houses? What does he want?"

"I already told you: feasts, women, adulation, and luxury. He's a reincarnated god. The only thing he's complained about are those copper plates stolen from that Koroa embassy, and he replaced them with better pieces. With time, he'll forget about them, too."

"Something's not right," Rising Flame insisted, her gaze now fixed on the dead woman on the floor. "I'm missing a critical piece. And it's not just the Koroa copper."

Two

What a stunning vista. From an outcropping of granite bedrock that cleared the trees, the warrior once known as Fire Cat Twelvekiller, war chief of the Red Wing Clan, looked back to where thickly forested valleys converged. He stood on a height, just up from where the trail crossed a gap in the mountains. He could see where the valleys met three days' hard march to the south. The town of Joara was situated down there in that haze-filled basin. Not that he could make out the mounds, temple, and palace given the trees and distance. But he knew where Joara was: There, where the ridges tapered into the bottoms and the drainages met.

Off to the east—like a rumpled blanket—the forest-covered uplands faded against the misty blue horizon. This was mountain country carpeted by oak, maple, hickory, gum, and conifers. And though he had traveled the trails along the rivers and stared up at the peaks, Fire Cat had never seen the terrain from such an elevation. He gazed out on the thickly treed mountains, their upper slopes broken by rounded outcrops of pale granite and occasional cracked sandstone and shale. Dotted here and there with darker stands of pointed red spruce and the occasional pine and cedar, the muted greens were a stark contrast to the deep blue of the sky, with its cottony patches of luminous white cloud.

Born at Red Wing Town, in the upper reaches of the Father Water, Fire Cat had never stood at the top of a mountain. Hadn't even seen one until his travel up the Tenasee valley in pursuit of Night Shadow Star. From his outcrop, however, he could see the top of the world—still higher above him—and longed for the chance to climb to that lonesome tor. From there he would stare out across the entirety of the known universe.

He would have. But for Night Shadow Star and his chafing worry.

Even here, seeing the world as did *Hunga Ahuito*, the great two-headed eagle that lived at the top of the Sky World. Fire Cat's stomach churned in indecision.

So, had he made the right choice? Was this really the way Walking Smoke's party of warriors had brought Night Shadow Star? He had made a desperate gamble based on the statement of an old toothless woman in Joara who had told him, *"The Lightning Witch, the one you call Walking Smoke, said he'd get Chief Fire Light a pardon in Cahokia. Wanted to get there fast. Took that woman with him."*

She referred to High Chief Fire Light of the Morning Star House, exiled from Cahokia, brother to the new Four Winds Clan Matron, Rising Flame. Chief Fire Light had been given the "honor" of helping to settle the distant colony in Cofitachequi. Settle: a euphemism for exile. In this case, Fire Light had been punished for stirring up political trouble in Cahokia.

"Poor fool," Fire Cat murmured.

Walking Smoke would as soon cut the Cahokian chief's throat, attempt to scry the future in the man's spilled guts, and then eat his liver for supper. The chief and his warriors were only a means to carry Walking Smoke and the captive Night Shadow Star back to Cahokia posthaste.

But was this the right trail? Or were they back there? Headed west from Joara over the pass to the Wide Fast River and then down to the Tenasee? If so, Fire Cat, Winder, and Blood Talon should have encountered them on the way, seen evidence of their passing.

This *had* to be the right direction.

At the sound of moccasin-clad feet, Fire Cat shot a glance over his shoulder to see the burly Trader, Winder, step out from the tree-shadowed forest depths and onto the hard stone. The man was muscular, with a grizzled face that looked like it had gotten in the way of too many fast-moving fists. The big Trader wore a plain brown hunting shirt, belted at the waist; a pack hung over his broad shoulders by a single strap. Winder's hair was up in a simple bun, pinned with a wooden skewer. The tattoos on the man's cheeks were so blurred and splotchy as to be unrecognizable when it came to clan or people.

Which was just how Winder liked it.

"What have you found?" Fire Cat asked.

"We've got them," Winder told him with a grin. "Blood Talon found the place where they camped. Looks like eighteen men and one woman, and she was tied to a beech sapling for the night. Marks in the grass show where two litters were set. Blood Talon says from the feel of the ashes in the fire, they were here two nights ago."

Fire Cat's heart skipped. "Two days. That's not so much to make up. We might be able to catch them before they make the headwaters of the Tenasee."

"Might." Winder stepped up beside him, staring off to the south and east. "You can almost see all the way to the Salt Water from here. Almost."

"I would have liked to have seen that." Fire Cat gestured at the forested heights with their rounded peaks and the outcrops of weathered gray rock visible on the steep slopes. "It's enough to see mountains."

Winder absently pressed at the scabbed lump on the side of his head where one of Fire Light's warriors had whacked him with a tree branch. His sidelong gaze evaluative, he fixed his black eyes on Fire Cat. "You're a puzzle, War Chief."

"I'm not a war chief."

"You're not a bound man, either."

"I am." With a tip of his head, Fire Cat indicated the trees behind him. "Squadron First Blood Talon, back there, saw to that. He was in charge of one of Spotted Wrist's squadrons when they took Red Wing Town, murdered my children, enslaved my wives, and sent my mother and sisters with me to Cahokia to die in the squares."

"And after all that, you saved his life?" Winder's interest heightened.

Fire Cat concentrated on fixing the spectacular vista in his memory. To the day he died, he wanted to remember the beauty, the incredible tumble of mountains, ridges, green valleys, and the infinity of distant horizons fading into the sky.

"Power's a funny thing, Trader, and we're caught in the middle of it."

Winder stopped fiddling with the wound on the side of his head. "You don't need to tell me. You killed Night Shadow Star's husband, Makes Three, when the Morning Star sent him to destroy you. You're finally captured, given to Night Shadow Star so she can torture you to death, but you end up her slave. She crosses half the world to kill her brother, Walking Smoke, and he ends up hauling her back to Cahokia. Meanwhile the man Keeper Spotted Wrist sends to bring Night Shadow Star back to Cahokia, so the Keeper can marry her, is your blood enemy, but ends up being rescued by you. And we're still chasing Night Shadow Star? Is that a complex story, or what?"

Fire Cat watched an eagle soar over the trees below. "Tell me that Power doesn't use us for its own entertainment."

Winder's slight smile sobered. "She loves you, you know. Loves you in a way I've never known a woman to love a man. There is something epic about all this, a story for the ages."

"Assuming we can catch up with Walking Smoke and free my lady,"

Fire Cat rejoined. "Walking Smoke's Power comes from the Sky World. Night Shadow Star's Power is Piasa's. She belongs to the lord of the Underworld. Let's not forget, if this mysterious wound the old woman in Joara was talking about heals, Walking Smoke wants to rape his sister. Something about a twisted ritual that will make him the most Powerful man alive."

"Granted, Walking Smoke's a witch, and an evil wretch, but do you believe that bit about being the most Powerful man alive?"

Fire Cat shrugged. "He thinks that somehow the incestuous rape of his sister will allow him to kill Morning Star and take control of Cahokia."

"Epic, I tell you." Winder let his gaze search the hazy blue distance.

At the sound of feet, Fire Cat turned, glanced back at the trail as Blood Talon, dressed in a smudged smilax-fiber shirt, appeared from under the trees. "We've found them!" he cried, stepping onto the rock.

Most of Blood Talon's burns were healed into shiny pink scars; the man's thick black hair was tied in a simple bun, and he'd dispensed with the traditional Cahokian warrior's beaded forelock in the effort to look like a Trader. As if the balanced warrior's carriage could ever be discarded.

"Two days," Fire Cat said. "Winder already told me."

"They are making good time." Blood Talon hesitated, taking in the view. Cahokia born and bred, he, too, had never laid eyes on such a sight. Now he sucked in an awed breath. "Never thought I'd see the likes of this."

Winder slapped the man on the back. "Remember it. From here it's downhill all the way to the mouth of the Mother Water. You'll not see the equal of this again."

Fire Cat resisted the urge to take one last look as he trotted into the shadow of the mighty oaks, many with lightning-riven scars running down their bark.

Lightning. The thought sent a chill down his spine. Walking Smoke had taken lightning as his Spirit Power. Word was it had marked the left side of the witch's face, explaining why he wore his notorious whelk-shell mask.

Fire Cat could well believe it. He might be a heretic when it came to Morning Star and the whole crazy hoax surrounding his reincarnation. But Fire Cat had been there the day Night Shadow Star had dragged Walking Smoke's body down into the Father Water's murky depths. Fire Cat was perched in the canoe when the Thunderbirds blasted bolts of lightning all around, sundering the mighty river and whisking Walking Smoke away from certain death.

"Lady," he whispered under his breath as his feet shuffled across the leaf mat and he ducked around the vines winding their way to the upper story, "I'm coming. As fast as I can."

At their small camp, he slung the sack holding his weapons, armor, and chunkey gear over one shoulder, and, with Winder's help, lifted the ornately carved box of Trade. Then, with Blood Talon in the lead, they took the trail that led down to the valley beyond.

Three

The late-afternoon sun burned in the west like a white-hot orb. It cast shadows from the high palaces, the clan and society houses, and the charnel structure atop the Evening Star House burial mound. The temple to Old-Woman-Who-Never-Dies blocked the light and cast a dark shadow over the recorders' society house where it stood next to the round surveyors' society buildings. Interspersed among them all, and crowding the plaza, were the orderly camps of Evening Star House's military squadrons.

Beyond them lay the warehouses, the palaces, the society and charnel houses belonging to the various Earth clans. Mixed in were assorted peak-roofed temples before the town gave way to farmsteads with their domiciles, granaries, chiefs' palaces, tall society poles, stickball and chunkey courts. All of it stretching away to the west. Countless thousands of people, all under her dominion.

Pacing slowly, Matron Columella walked along the edge of the high bluff overlooking the Father Water. She couldn't see the expanse of city that extended westward. Her view was blocked by the tall mounds and buildings that surrounded Evening Star Town's great plaza. What she did have was a view of the Father Water, the mighty river that partially transected Cahokia, separating Evening Star Town from River City Mounds on the eastern shore. Beyond that—a half day's travel down the Avenue of the Sun—lay central Cahokia, with its great plaza dominated by the Morning Star's mound and temple. And a long day's travel beyond that, the Moon Mounds. All were part of the city. All seeming to hold their breath as events played out between her, Matron Rising Flame, and Clan Keeper Spotted Wrist.

Where it overlooked the river's west bank, Evening Star Town stood atop a high bluff, well above flood stage. At the base of the slope, the great river washed against the exposed shore. The water ran low, murky, swirling and sucking; this being midsummer. And the reports were that not much rain had fallen in the plains to the west, or in the forests up north. As a result, a lot of the sloping and sandy shore was exposed.

A fact that worried her as she walked beside the dwarf known as Flat Stone Pipe. The top of the little man's head barely reached her hip. People believed that Spirit Power manifested in dwarfs, and Flat Stone Pipe was one of the most remarkable men Columella had ever known. He was trained as an engineer, and his skill when it came to the complex art of mound construction was well known. More than that: along with being her lover over the years, and having sired several of Columella's children, Flat Stone Pipe ran a network of informants that spanned the city.

Now, he, too, was staring down at the low water, and remarked, "I'd say that's plenty of beach to land a squadron or two of Spotted Wrist's warriors."

Columella chewed on her lip as she lifted her gaze across the river and studied the canoe landing just below the thick-packed cluster of ramadas, warehouses, craft shops, granaries, and temples that was River City Mounds. In the middle of the clutter, atop the old levee, were the soaring roofs of the River House palace, its tall bald cypress world tree pole, and the steep-pitched roofs of the various River House temples and clan houses. They surrounded the elongated plaza with its famous chunkey courts. A haze of smoke, like a thin pall, rose from the city.

More to her annoyance, however, were the lines of large Trade and war canoes that had been pulled up on the canoe landing. The mismatched craft rested on charcoal-stained sand with their sterns lapped by waves. Nearly a hundred of them. Most commandeered by the three squadron firsts whose commands were camped in orderly lines just beyond the canoes and among the ramadas and stalls belonging to the river Traders. The place resembled a hive, packed with warriors who lounged around desultory fires and made life miserable for the river Traders seeking to land their goods.

"Three squadrons," Columella mused. "All Spotted Wrist's veterans from the north. Loyal to him. Maybe six hundred blooded warriors."

"Against whom we will field more than a thousand," Flat Stone Pipe told her as he ambled along on his short legs. "It's almost two to one, but our warriors are only trained. Not battle-hardened veterans. Everything depends upon the ground. Who has the tactical advantage. Were Spotted Wrist's squadrons to load up and paddle straight across, our people could mass, charge down the bluff, and overwhelm them as they tried to bail out of their canoes." The dwarf made a face. "My sources tell me he will do no such thing."

"Have you heard when he expects to move?"

"At the rate Spotted Wrist is accumulating war and Trade canoes, he could order an attack as soon as the day after tomorrow. Those three squadrons are smack in the middle of the canoe landing, and they're choking Trade. Essentially commerce is stopped, and I've heard of Traders camping up and down the river, waiting for the bunch of them to clear out.

"He can't put it off much longer. All those mouths over there have to be fed. Those warriors are draining what little food reserve was left in the River Mounds warehouses. Emptying the last of the baskets of corn, toting out the few remaining jars of acorns and hickory nuts. Not much left, and people are already growling. They can count just as well as Lord Three Fingers and that upstart, Broken Stone. We're still months away from harvest. The word is out up and down the river: Cahokia is low on food. Too many Traders are waiting out Spotted Wrist's army before bringing in food. What infuriates the people in River City Mounds is that where a basket of corn might have been Traded for a wooden-bead necklace last year, the Traders are now asking two. And getting it."

"You're right. Spotted Wrist can't put this off." Columella narrowed her eyes. "Is he still planning on dividing our forces?"

"That's what I hear." Flat Stone Pipe pointed a hand to the north. "Some of his forces paddle upriver. We have to send a couple of squadrons to shadow him." He turned on his heel, pointing south. "Same with Spotted Wrist's squadron that heads south. Our people have to race along the bank. They can't keep up."

He finished, now pointing straight across the river. "And we have to keep enough strength here to destroy that final squadron that might just paddle straight across."

"In the end, we lose," Columella said. She rubbed the back of her neck, feeling weary. Staring past the smoky haze hanging over River Mounds, she could barely make out Morning Star's distant mound-top palace through the afternoon haze. "What is the living god's game? Why has he allowed all this to happen? A usurper sits on the high chair in the River House palace, while Matron Round Pot and Chief War Duck slip through the shadows like wood rats, darting from place to place to avoid capture and being hung in a square."

Flat Stone Pipe's clever brown eyes fixed on Columella's. "After all our prayers asking to have those two eliminated, who'd have thought that we'd want them back, huh?"

"Power laughs," she told him. "We are made a mockery of. And through it all, the Morning Star is silent. Not a word is brought down his stairs, no messenger is sent. We are only told the *tonka'tzi*'s orders—and we know that Wind is being held under Spotted Wrist's guard."

"We're not beaten yet, Matron."

"We have three Houses against us, and Morning Star House is essentially neutered. A master war leader is preparing to attack us, and if he can execute even half of his plan, we will ultimately be defeated. I'm surprised you haven't told me to slip out in the middle of the night, take a canoe, and head downriver to try to find my husband and a nice place to spend the rest of my life in exile."

Flat Stone Pipe chuckled. "I like it better when your husband is gone Trading. I get more time in your bed." Then he sobered. "No, my love. It's not time yet for us to fade away lest we find ourselves hanging in a square. Like I said. We're not beaten."

Columella stopped short, the waffling breeze teasing her knee-length skirt and swaying the thin fabric cape over her shoulders. "Staying out of that square is going to take a miracle."

"You been smelling this bit of breeze? Notice anything about how heavy the air is?"

"I do. If it hadn't been so dry, I'd say a storm was coming in the next couple of days."

"And tomorrow night is the new moon." Flat Stone Pipe propped his hands on his hips. "It would take an act of desperation, and the conjunction of just the right events, to save us. I have an idea, but I'd keep that canoe ready just in case."

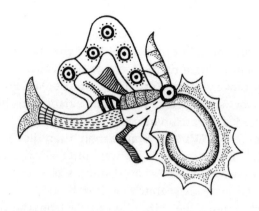

Four

Hollow thunder rolled across the high ridges and distant mountains. Then the air went still. It felt as if the forest were cowering in anticipation off the storm. Among the leaves, the chorus of insects turned mute, the chastening call of the fox squirrels gone as silent as the melodic calls of the now-cowed songbirds. Even the crows—those raucous jesters of the skies—had ceased cawing.

In the wake of the stillness, the wind hit like a hammer blow, tossing the treetops, whipping leaves into a roar. With it the lightning struck, lancing jagged, tortured patterns across the sky. Some flashed overhead, blinding the eye and piercing the ears with pain, so loud and close were they.

Where Night Shadow Star was borne down the streamside trail atop her litter, she winced as the first drops of cold rain hit her like thrown stones, each large drop splattering on impact. Moments later, the skies opened in a deluge. Sluicing down in sheets, the effect was like baskets of thrown water splashing down from the black and lightning-torn heavens.

"Get off the trail!" Night Shadow Star cried as she tried to huddle under the assault. But for her hands being bound behind her and tied to the litter, she would have lifted an arm in an attempt to shield herself. "Are you fools?"

The six warriors carrying her had hunched their shoulders, sliding in to get as far beneath the shelter of the litter's matting as they could. The onslaught burst into a misty haze as it blasted the tops of their heads. Her own misery was worse. Her bindings kept her flat on her back, so she took the full brunt. Cold water was pouring through her cape and skirt, sheeting over her bare chest, stomach, and legs.

Looking ahead, she could see Walking Smoke atop his litter. Her brother looked anything but miserable. Rising to his knees, he lifted his arms, hands open, welcoming the torrents. With each crack of the lightning, Walking Smoke whooped in delight, almost Dancing on his swaying litter as his porters struggled to keep their balance on the now-slippery footing. That they didn't drop him was a miracle, but then each and every one of them feared Walking Smoke more than they feared death and dismemberment in the squares. He was, after all, the Lightning Shell Witch. The man who saw across vast distances as he peered into the dark blood that pooled in his eviscerated victims' bodies.

"Find cover!" High Chief Fire Light called from the trail ahead. The chief's form barely visible in the downpour, he was waving his hands, trying to get everyone's attention.

"No!" Walking Smoke screamed. "Forward! Feel the Power! Dance with the lightning! I am alive!" Then he threw his head back, howling with the glee of a head-struck wolf.

"He's alive?" One of Night Shadow Star's litter bearers, Bluefish, asked. "I've got water running down around my balls. And it's rotted cold!"

"Try it up here," Night Shadow Star grumbled back through tight lips.

"Wouldn't trade places with you, that's certain, Lady," the Panther Clan warrior known as Made of Wood told her. "Wouldn't want to be up there in this rain, and I'm not too happy about what he wants to do to you when he heals from that whack in the stones you gave him."

"As for me," one of the warriors on the right, Singing Snail, said, "Lady, I'm just as happy that you wounded your brother with that war club of yours. Power has rules against incest. Now, granted, you're Four Winds Clan, of the Morning Star House. And your brother Chunkey Boy's body was taken over by the Spirit of the living god. But not even high nobles like you should discard the warnings of Power."

Shivers began to rack her limbs. "My brother's a twisted and evil witch. Why are you helping him?"

Water streaked down her head, running into her eyes, dripping off her chin in a stream. "Cut these bonds so I can get away before his shaft heals." If it could heal. She wasn't sure if Piasa's Power—filling the war club as it had—had permanently maimed Walking Smoke's genitals. As it was, he could barely urinate without breaking into tears, and his piss passed in drips and dribbles.

By Old-Woman-Who-Never-Dies, I wish I'd managed to hit him in the head instead of the testicles.

But that had been the only blow she'd been able to deliver before Chief

Fire Light's warriors had slammed her to the ground and clipped her skull with a war club.

Nevertheless, it had been enough to keep her from immediately being raped by her brother. She tried not to think of the other time—that long-ago afternoon after the Requickening ceremony when the Morning Star's Spirit had been called to take possession of Chunkey Boy's body. Her oldest brother's souls might have been overwhelmed, destroyed, or whatever, by the living god, but that hadn't lessened the impact on Night Shadow Star. Let alone the second violation as Walking Smoke had caught her, thrown her down in a storeroom. He had beaten her into submission before ripping her skirt off and forcing himself between her legs.

Madness and evil runs in my family.

She was shivering uncontrollably now, the cold leaching every bit of warmth from her numb flesh.

"Can't let you go, Lady," another of the warriors, Summer Ice, also of the Panther Clan, said as he and the rest slipped and slithered their way down the muddy trail. "The Lightning Witch would take our breath souls and body souls. He'd perform some abomination over us. Make it so we suffered alone, tormented, our souls screaming in horror and darkness."

"Got that right," Bluefish agreed. "The Lightning Witch flayed the last man to disappoint him. Stripped the skin from the man's body while he was alive. Left it hanging on a wooden frame outside the clan house. Like some perverted bird's hide, the skin of the arms all spread like wings."

"Wouldn't want to chance that," Summer Ice insisted with a hard nod of his head.

Another bolt of lightning split the sky, the blast so close and loud Night Shadow Star's struggling warriors almost dropped her. Coupled with the shivers racking her from head to toe and the slick mud underfoot, it was a miracle they hadn't fallen into a heap already.

Up ahead, Walking Smoke reached into his pack and pulled out the whelk-shell mask. Becoming the Lightning Shell Witch, he placed it over his hideously scarred face, tilting his head back so the rain exploded on the smooth mask's surface with its zigzags, nose, and lined chin.

"Heal me!" He thrust his arms up at the storm. "Make me whole!"

As Walking Smoke pirouetted, the struggling warriors bearing his litter splashed and staggered in the trail in response to his mad gyrations.

"Thunderbirds! Blast me with Power! Make me well so I can fulfill my destiny as the Wild One! When I do, I shall topple mighty Cahokia and throw the Morning Star's body at your feet!"

"Can he do that?" Made of Wood asked.

"Only if I d-don't kill him first," Night Shadow Star told him through clacking and chattering teeth.

She managed to toss a glance behind her. Half hoping to see Fire Cat and Winder appear out of the storm. But all that greeted her eyes was a muddy and water-logged forest trail churned and stippled by their passage.

For all she knew, Fire Cat had no clue where she might be. She didn't even know if he was still alive.

Piasa? Where are you when I need you?

But with lightning splitting the sky, her Spirit master would be hidden, cowering in the depths. Far from the Thunderbirds' deadly lightning as they pursued their war with the Underworld.

It is up to me. I have to kill my brother.

Five

Once Lady Blue Heron had been the Four Winds Clan Keeper and the most feared woman in Cahokia. Second in authority only to her sister, *Tonka'tzi* Wind, Blue Heron had been the master of a network of spies and informers that penetrated every House, Earth Clan, and even kept a finger on the pulse of the dirt farmers' communities.

Now she was a hunted fugitive—or would have been if Spotted Wrist or Matron Rising Flame ever figured out that she was still alive. The whole thing was intolerable. A fact that churned acidly in her stomach as she fingered the wattle under her chin and scowled at the room's occupants.

The triangular-shaped storeroom where she sat was packed with wealth: remarkable carved and engraved wooden boxes with shell and copper inlays; large seed jars filled to bursting with corn, acorns, and sunflower seeds; jars of hickory oil; fine textiles woven of dogbane and hemp; pots and bags of dyes; shelves crowded with ceramic and carved-stone statuary; sheets of flattened copper; sacks of saltwater shell Traded up from the Gulf; net bags filled with yaupon tea; ornate weapons; sacks of fine tool stones; and the list went on.

A Four Winds high chief would be blessed to amass such a fortune.

Instead, this was Crazy Frog's storehouse, hidden in the warehouse district of River City Mounds just up from the canoe landing. A three-sided, double-walled stronghold squeezed between buildings in such a way that the loot was not only easily defended—having only one way in—but for anyone searching for it, the place was nearly impossible to find.

Blue Heron shook her head at her predicament. Here she sat, a fifty-year-old ex-ruler, dressed in a rag, her graying hair in a bun pinned with a sliver of wood.

My, how the mighty have fallen.

Crazy Frog himself sat atop a stack of boxes in the rear. To look at him, nothing would have hinted that he was one of the most influential men in the whole of Cahokia. He was of average height, slight of frame, and wore a featureless fabric breechcloth. His unadorned hair was wrapped in a bun held in place by plain wooden skewers, and the tattoos on his ordinary face were so smudged as to be illegible. The only thing notable were his sharp black eyes, now watching the others in the room like some predatory weasel.

Blue Heron took the moment to study the man. Before she'd been replaced as Clan Keeper by that pus-licking Spotted Wrist, she'd formed an alliance of convenience with Crazy Frog.

Funny twist that, for the man was nefarious, into all manner of immoral doings along the canoe landing. He had a finger in most of River City's underbelly, including theft, intimidation, protection rackets, and the Trade in information and influence. Nevertheless, the scoundrel had been instrumental in saving Cahokia more than once. But his biggest passion was chunkey. He lived for the game, fielded his own players, and wagered incessantly on the matches played on the River City Mounds' famed chunkey courts.

Despite that, the man could have been mistaken for a dirt farmer. Totally forgettable. Which was exactly the way Crazy Frog wanted it.

Not that Blue Heron herself would have stood out on the street. Brown paint obscured the telltale starburst and Four Winds tattoos on her cheeks. There was nothing she could do to hide the scar on her throat, but the red had faded, and for the most part it mixed with the wrinkles.

She leaned uncomfortably against a waist-high stack of folded hair-on bison robes. Her hips ached, which, all things considered, was better than being dead. A condition in which, she hoped, that two-footed maggot, Spotted Wrist, still believed her to be. He had, after all, come within a whisker of burning her alive in her mound-top palace not so long ago. Amazing how coming so close to the final boundary could reorder a woman's priorities.

Across from her stood a big meaty man in his early forties. High Chief War Duck of the River House was nothing nice to look at. First off, his right eye was missing, a patch covering the grisly socket. In the man's youth a war club had left a disfiguring scar down the left side of his craggy face. His gray hair was done up in a warrior's bun, and a beaded forelock hung down almost the length of his nose. He wore a breechcloth that dropped to a point between his knees. Now he had his arms crossed; a smoldering anger lay behind his square-jawed expression.

In the rear, beside the door hanging—looking as if he were ready to bolt—stood old Blue Heron's erstwhile savior: Seven Skull Shield. The big thief wore a simple hemp-fiber hunting shirt belted at the waist with a rope from which hung a couple of leather pouches. Bruises and scabs were barely healed where his muscular arms were crossed. His hair had been pulled into an unremarkable bun; the man's too-often abused face looked deceptively mild. That, of course, was an act. Blue Heron had never known Seven Skull Shield to be anything but a foul-mouthed rascal, a common thief, shiftless, clanless, and as incredible as it might seem by looking at him, a shameless womanizer and seducer of vulnerable housewives.

How, by Piasa's balls, did he ever become my best friend? The very thought of it still left Blue Heron shaking her head.

To stand at eye level with the rest, the final occupant had climbed atop a couple of stacked boxes. Flat Stone Pipe had arrived just after dark, having been smuggled across the river from Evening Star Town and carried up to Crazy Frog's storehouse wrapped in a blanket. Sometimes being small was a useful asset.

Not that Blue Heron had ever underestimated the little man's remarkable talents when it came to clan politics. Thinking back, he might have been the most capable adversary she'd ever faced. But for him, Blue Heron would have replaced Matron Columella as the ruler of Evening Star Town years ago. A failure on Blue Heron's part, for which she was immensely grateful given the current circumstances.

But then, clan politics—as War Duck's presence proved—were a volatile and shifting sand upon which to plan.

"As we see it," Flat Stone Pipe was saying, "we have one chance. It will be tomorrow night. If my lady and I read the signs correctly, we should have a storm. And it's the new moon. Should be black as pitch. After midnight, a couple of hands of time before dawn, volunteers from our squadrons will paddle across the river. Just small groups of armed warriors. They will stay in formation, begin pulling the big Trade and war canoes off the sand and out into the river."

"And do what with them?" War Duck asked.

Flat Stone Pipe propped his hands on his hips and gave the high chief a challenging grin. "They'll turn them loose in the current. Let them float away. Then they'll go back after another one, and so on, until finally, someone sounds the alarm. At that time, the warriors will rush the camp. Attack in formation. Seek to cause as much confusion as they can, and immediately withdraw before Spotted Wrist can recover."

"And in the meantime?" War Duck asked.

"That's where you come in. If we're right about the storm, we want you, and those few agents you can trust, to be about the warehouses on the levee above the canoe landing. We need a diversion. Maybe set fire to a couple of warehouses. When you hear the commotion, start yelling, 'It's Columella! She's landed an entire squadron behind us! They're marching on River House! Quick! Send warriors! They're after Broken Stone!' Or whatever you think will get their attention. We want Spotted Wrist to think any fighting around the canoes is a diversion. If we can get him to send his squadrons into the city, our warriors can sneak back and shove more of his canoes out into the river."

War Duck was rubbing his finger along his scar. "Do you really think he will fall for this?"

Flat Stone Pipe shrugged his shoulders. "Part of any plan is the setup. What you can get an enemy to believe. We're going to give him reason to think an attack on River House is not only plausible, but imminent. With buildings burning behind him and calls of warriors on the march, we're hoping he responds with sufficient force that our people on the beach can get rid of enough canoes to delay his attack."

"How do you intend to feed him this information?" Blue Heron asked.

Flat Stone Pipe managed a solemn nod. "I think we can do it in a way that Spotted Wrist will find credible. He's a war leader first and foremost. He thinks in terms of battlefield tactics and deception. Just like he employed against the Shawnee, against Red Wing Town, and when he took military control of Cahokia. All planned perfectly. Right now he's not thinking of Evening Star House as an offensive threat. But he knows that High Chief War Duck, here, and Matron Round Pot are on the loose. He knows they are allied with Columella. We need to plant the notion that a fast raid to grab the usurper Broken Stone—and even Three Fingers—from out of the River House palace is taking place. Doing so would destabilize Spotted Wrist and Rising Flame's entire alliance. Spotted Wrist would see it as a slap in the face to his authority. The impression would be that he couldn't protect his own vassals. Even with three of his squadrons sitting right there within a couple of arrow shots of the supposed attack."

"I like the way you think." Blue Heron gave him a knowing squint. "If Spotted Wrist has any weakness outside of a dull brain, it's vanity."

"Got that right," Seven Skull Shield muttered from the door. "The man would have gone to war to kidnap Lady Night Shadow Star, and then he took me right out of her palace as payback for humiliating him up at Morning Star's."

"Thief, you never did know when to keep your mouth shut," Blue Heron told him.

War Duck continued to scowl and give Seven Skull Shield a narrow-lidded stare. Word was that he still suspected Seven Skull Shield of breaking into his palace, threatening Matron Round Pot with a potsherd, and extinguishing the sacred fire. All of which had led to his being deposed and on the run.

That was the thing about having an association with Seven Skull Shield. Life was never boring.

If there was any positive side to the thief's presence here, it was that he'd left his monstrosity of a dog outside. Sort of. Crazy Frog's wife, Mother Otter, had thrown a good Pacaha bowl at the beast when it had trotted in on its oversized paws and lifted a leg on her ramada pole. Farts had run as the pot shattered and rained shards down around him.

Though the dog looked more like a bear, Seven Skull Shield insisted that Farts was a Spirit dog possessed of remarkable Powers. Blue Heron thought the beast was nothing more than hair loosely pasted around a bark, an appetite, and a perpetually emptying bladder.

Seven Skull Shield shifted uncomfortably. "That's the plan? Your picked warriors sneak across the river in the middle of the night and shove as many canoes as they can into the river while War Duck and his people scream 'Warriors are attacking River Mounds!' up top? What happens if this all goes wrong? What if Spotted Wrist only sends out scouts? Keeps the rest of his warriors in their camps?"

Flat Stone Pipe gave Seven Skull Shield a sad smile. "Then, old friend, a couple dozen brave young men and women are going to be killed on the beach or caught and hung in squares to die of prolonged misery. Spotted Wrist, having all of his canoes, will launch his squadrons to paddle up and down the river and land where we can't control the shore. Then, by the end of another three or four days, Evening Star Town will be in his possession and all of Cahokia will be lost."

Six

Willow Stem Village sat on the third terrace above the East Fork of the Upper Tenasee, where the "South Trail" originated on its way to Joara. Not that the village was much, just a palisade surrounding a couple of low mounds that supported the chief's cane-walled house on one end and a conical burial mound on the other. A few dwellings, elevated storehouses, and an earth-covered council house were crowded inside the walls. As her litter was carried closer, Night Shadow Star could see scattered bent-pole houses along the palisade, some sided with bark, others with thatch. For each three or four houses, a communal granary was perched atop high peeled-and-greased poles.

The village was surrounded by fields filled with "the three sisters," corn, beans, and squash all planted together in a mutually beneficial tangle known to produce better harvests.

The people here, Mahica barbarians, came across as sullen and suspicious, bordering on downright hostile. So did their dogs, a pack of which had been chased away with thrown sticks, shouts, and kicks. All in all, not a friendly place for a band of Cahokians to approach on a warm summer morning.

But then, this was north of Cahokia's farthest holdings—the closest colony being Cofitachequi, a week's run to the south and east. Even so, as a town on a major trade route, supposedly the Power of Trade was honored here. Or so the young man who stepped out from the palisade gate insisted in his heavily accented Trade pidgin. Beanpole thin, he towered over Chief Fire Light. His only accoutrement appeared to be a long hardwood staff, stained dark brown and incised with geometric designs. He wore his hair in a high roach that added to his stature.

From atop her litter, Night Shadow Star looked around, catching hints of movement back in the cornfields. She suspected that Willow Stem Village's scouts had informed the local chief that a party of warriors was slipping and sliding its way down the still-rain-slick trail, and being a wise chief, he had scrambled his warriors to ensure that the newcomers acted in accordance with both prudence and the Power of Trade.

She was pondering whether to say anything when Chief Fire Light made a graceful bow, placing his right arm across his chest as he did. In accented pidgin, he informed the man, "Please tell your chief that we are not here to stay, nor do we require hospitality. Our only interest is in the procurement of a large Trade canoe capable of carrying our party down the Tenasee."

From one of the packs, Fire Light produced a stone chief's mace. The piece was finely chiseled and fashioned in the traditional turkey-tail design. Made of dark siltstone, the mace was as long as his forearm, incised and polished until it gleamed. This he offered for inspection.

The Mahica took it with interest, studied the workmanship, and tested the weight.

Night Shadow Star observed the puzzlement in the young man's face. Her days of Trade on the Tenasee made her wonder, too. The whole offer was clumsy and awkward. Surely Fire Light knew better. But then, being a Four Winds high chief, maybe he didn't.

A chief's mace—especially one made of polished black stone like that one—was indeed worth a great deal. But what it took to craft a large Trade canoe? That entailed a year's work for several men, and that didn't start until the right tree had been felled and limbed. Then it had to be left to season, all the while hoping the wood didn't split. Only when the log was sufficiently aged could the onerous task of burning, chipping, and scraping begin. Through it all, care had to be taken to keep from splitting the grain or burning through the hull. The fire had to be carefully applied to keep from warping the wood in any way.

Nor were all canoes created equal, at least not the good ones. Some, no matter how earnestly they were made—or how much Power was invested in their construction—still handled as sullenly as a floating log. Others glided lightly, buoyant, darting across the water as if blessed by Spirit Power.

"Will they take it?" Walking Smoke called from his litter. He was bent slightly, having complained that his balls had hurt more after the rain. "If they won't I might have to have a talk with their chief. See if he has any young daughters. No telling what sort of Power I might conjure from their blood. Shall I put on my mask so there is no question of just who I am?"

Fortunately he spoke in Cahokian, which the young man didn't appear to understand. What the fellow did notice was Chief Fire Light's sudden pallor and gulping swallow.

Before Walking Smoke could invite calamity, Night Shadow Star called, "Don't be an idiot, brother. The miracle is that he hasn't recognized you already, given the disaster that is your face. That scar is like a shouting announcement. Now, keep your stupid mouth closed while Chief Fire Light finds us a canoe."

"And why should I listen to you?" Walking Smoke craned around on his litter, his eyes glazed in pain.

"Because unknown tens of warriors are watching us from the cornfields. And *don't* the rest of you look. Eyes forward, fools!" Night Shadow Star barked. Then, in a derisive voice, she added, "Idiots! By Piasa's balls, it'll be a miracle if you make it onto the river."

The young man was watching the interchange intently, apparently very good at reading facial expressions. Now he fixed his eyes on Chief Fire Light. "Only one such canoe is here. It belongs to Six Toes. He is a Koasati Trader who is our honored guest. He has arrived at Willow Stem Village to Trade for mica and steatite that the Chalakee mine over east in the mountains."

"Then, where will we find him?" Fire Light asked.

The young man inclined his head. "In exchange for this trifle of stone, I will lead you to him and relay your request."

"That is a chief's mace!" Fire Light stiffened in indignation. "Worth a whole canoe!"

The young man handed it back, saying, "You might have better luck back in Cofitachequi." Then he spun on his heel and headed back for the village palisade gate.

Walking Smoke began chanting on his litter, raising his hands toward the sky, invoking some sort of ritual. Not that he looked imposing, still bent at the waist as he was.

"Wait!" Night Shadow Star called in Trade pidgin. She jerked at the bonds confining her to the litter, irritated by how they restricted her movement. In Cahokian, she snapped, "Brother! Lower your hands, shut your mouth, and by blood and thunder, stay out of this, or we're all dead."

"Do you doubt my ability to call the lightning, sister?" Even as he raised a hand to the heavens, a distant rumble sounded from the clouds that had formed over the peaks to the east. "Want me to bring down the Thunderbirds' wrath? I could sunder this pathetic excuse of a town into splintered wood and these people into charred meat. Want to see?"

"No. Because before you do, these people will kill you for the witch that you are." She gave him a mocking smile. "Not that I'd mind, but they'd kill the rest of us, too."

The warriors in their party looked anxiously at the now-gathering clouds as they obscured the mountains.

The young Mahica man had turned, waiting, his face blank and emotionless, though he had to be aware of the unease passing through the Cahokians.

In Cahokian, Night Shadow Star called, "Fire Light, stop acting like an arrogant Cahokian fool. Give the man a sack of corn from the supplies. Call it an act of goodwill. Smile when you do."

"But a whole sack is almost a week's rations!" Fire Light turned, shooting her a look of disbelief.

"Do it!" Night Shadow Star snapped. "I'll explain it to you later."

Walking Smoke, head swiveled her way, gaped at her. "You don't order my—"

She kept her eyes fixed on Fire Light and repeated, "Do it. And ask the young man to lead us to this Six Toes. It's a fair Trade and buys us the Mahicas' goodwill."

Chief Fire Light, looking skeptical, motioned to Field Snake, who fished out a bag of cornmeal. Taking the sack, he handed it to the Mahica, adding in pidgin, "Will this suffice to take us to the Trader known as Six Toes?"

The Mahica paused long enough to glance inside, nodded, and said, "Follow me."

As he led the way to a beaten path that headed down toward the thick line of trees along the river, Walking Smoke glared at her from atop his litter. "You take chances, Sister. Don't you ever rebuke me in front of my warriors again."

"You're a fool, Brother. Just because Sky Power has been forced to use you as a tool in its struggle for balance doesn't mean you're invincible when it comes to the ways of people."

"I could call down the lightning—"

"And blast the tens of warriors slipping along on either side of us?" As she said it, Chief Fire Light's warriors cast wary glances at the tall corn to the sides, now plainly hearing the parallel lines of warriors as they rustled through the stalks and leaves. As per instructions, they had their bows, quivers, and arrows cased, but war clubs hung from their belts.

"I am Lightning Shell!" he snapped, whipping his head back forward.

"You know why Power let me maim your balls and rod? It was to keep me alive so that I could get us back to Cahokia. You might be good at the evil uses of Power, at sacrificing and eating people, and seeing visions in their pooled blood and spilled guts, but without me, you'll never make it as far as the mouth of the Wide Fast, let alone Canyon Town above the Suck and Rage."

Walking Smoke ignored her, his head facing forward. But Fire Light's warriors sure cast wary gazes up at her, worry plain in their tense faces. The banging and cracking of lightning in the distance added to the tension.

Dropping down to the floodplain's first terrace, winding through cottonwoods and willows, the Mahica led them onto a cobble-covered landing just up from the swirling waters of the East Fork of the Upper Tenasee. Here the river was no more than a spirited stone's throw across; a thick screen of willows crowded the far bank, and the water ran deep and murky from the rains.

Under the spreading cottonwoods, a Trader straightened from the side of a high-walled canoe. The man looked the part: tall, his intricately tattooed upper body rippling with muscle, his legs rather thin and undeveloped. He wore his hair in an ordinary bun; a buckskin breechcloth clung to his hips. Set in a broad face with wide cheekbones, sharp black eyes took the approaching Cahokians' measure.

Five other men, dressed similarly, rose from a fire on the far side of the canoe. The rest of Six Toes' crew, no doubt. No way he could have paddled such a craft all the way upriver alone.

Nor was Six Toes' the only canoe on the landing. A full dozen vessels, ranging from small blunt-nosed dugouts to a shaped five-person craft with raised bow, were pulled up and tied off to the trees lest the river rise and carry them away.

As the Mahica raised his stick and called out a greeting, Chief Fire Light strode forward at the head of Walking Smoke's entourage. The warriors, thankful for the chance, lowered Walking Smoke and Night Shadow Star's litters, rubbing their shoulders and swinging their arms in relief. But all the while they were watching the brush where the encircling Mahica warriors now took position, their numbers still masked by the vegetation.

One thing Night Shadow Star knew: That one canoe wasn't going to carry their entire party downriver. In a deadpan voice, she said, "Oh my, brother, once again your leadership has proven faulty."

Walking Smoke wheeled around as he climbed to his feet. He stepped off the litter and winced, bending to cradle his crotch. Walking back, he raised a fist, as if to strike her. "Now it's your turn to keep your mouth shut. I am Lightning Shell."

"Really?" She arched an eyebrow. "For such a great personage, it seems you have to keep reminding people who you are."

Singing Snail, one of her bearers, barely suppressed a chuckle, only to have surly Summer Ice jam an elbow into the younger warrior's ribs.

None of the warriors bearing Night Shadow Star's litter wanted to be noticed by Walking Smoke. The rumble of distant thunder acted as a constant reminder.

As they spoke, Mahica warriors—simply dressed but carrying bows and war clubs—began to filter out of the willows. They stopped there, watching, silent, dark eyes wary and full of promise of violence should things go awry.

"What now?" Fire Light asked, eyeing the single big Trade canoe. "The Lady is right. It will only hold ten of us at most, including the five Traders."

"Leave the Traders," Walking Smoke told him. "Give Six Toes the mace. Tell him it once belonged to Moon Blade, that he carried it with him from Cahokia when he conquered Cofitachequi. He takes the mace, we take his canoe."

"Good luck," Night Shadow Star muttered from the side of her mouth as she tugged on the accursed bindings that kept her fastened to the litter. "Will someone cut me free so I can save our skins?"

From the expressions on the faces of her bearers, they were more than ready to do just that.

"Then," Six Toes said in passable Cahokian, "whatever mace we're talking about giving me for my canoe may or may not have belonged to Moon Blade? Is that what I'm hearing? That's a good thing, because my canoe is not for Trade. It was my father's, and I do not part with my family's heritage."

"But we're here under the Power of Trade," Chief Fire Light protested. "Isn't that how it works?"

Night Shadow Star burst out in laughter and called, "And you idiots think you will carry me back to Cahokia? You, High Chief? You've been an arrogant Four Winds noble all your life. You just ordered people around and things happened. Walking Smoke? Compared to a block of oak, the wood is smarter. Brother, you've been a spoiled monster all your life. Cut me free and let me sort this out."

Her bearers nodded, glancing back and forth.

The Mahica guide had been watching this unfold, and he now stepped back, his stick, staff, or whatever it was held at half-mast. The surrounding warriors were looking even more tense, fingering their strung bows.

Six Toes and his Traders, feeling the rising tension, looked ready to bolt for the safety of the willows.

"Hold!" Night Shadow Star ordered. "Everyone. Take a step back." To Six Toes she said, "We are in need of transport downriver. We have Trade. A black stone Cahokian mace that may or may not have belonged to Chief Moon Blade when he colonized Cofitachequi."

"Conquered, you mean?" Six Toes asked.

"That's as good a word as any," Night Shadow Star agreed.

"Wait!" Walking Smoke limped forward, still bent at the waist. "Why are we listening to my sister? I am Lightning Shell. The witch!" And with that, he reached into his belt pouch, pulling out the shell mask and slipping it over his face. "I give the orders!"

The Mahica guide may not have understood Cahokian, but the moment he fixed on the mask, he hastily backed away, his staff raised high. The surrounding warriors nocked arrows and raised their war clubs.

"*Stand down!*" Night Shadow Star bellowed. "All of you!" She felt her heart hammer in her chest. All it would take was a loosed arrow and they'd all die. "Brother, you are mere heartbeats away from death."

The way they fingered their cased weapons and stared anxiously at the surrounding Mahica, her warriors certainly understood the stakes.

She lifted her bound hands to Chief Fire Light, whose expression had become strained. Yes, he understood how close they were to being shot down. "Cut me loose, Chief. I can get you out of this, but only if you let me. Otherwise, cased as your warriors' weapons are? It'll be a slaughter."

Before Walking Smoke could react, Fire Light bent down, whipped his belt knife loose, and slashed Night Shadow Star's thongs. Painfully, she hobbled to her feet as Walking Smoke turned his angry invective on the almost trembling Fire Light.

As Night Shadow Star stepped past her brother, she knotted a fist, and with a backhanded swing thumped him in his swollen testicles. His howl came as pure delight to her ears.

It also shocked the Mahica guide, his warriors, and the Traders. Left them wide-eyed, as if the pure audacity of it reset the entire tenor of the negotiations.

Night Shadow Star inclined her head respectfully. In perfect Trade pidgin, she said, "My apologies for the misunderstanding. They are Cahokians. Which explains their rude and bumbling behavior. That broken wretch holding his cracked eggs is my head-struck brother. A simpleton. Last week he thought he was the Morning Star and that he could fly. If he claims to be Piasa next, or maybe Thrown Away Boy, just ignore him. He's harmless."

The Koasati were looking a great deal more relieved, their postures relaxing. The surrounding warriors, too, had stopped fingering their bows.

To Six Toes, Night Shadow Star said, "We have need of getting downriver. In addition to the mace, we have other Trade, exotic goods: yaupon, carved shell, and a couple pieces of copper. Fair Trade to carry us as far as Canyon Town. We can go on foot from there."

To the Mahica guide, she pointed to three of the larger dugouts, and said, "We would offer the rest of our Trade to the owners of those canoes and their paddles."

Over her shoulder, in Cahokian, she asked Fire Light, "What else is in that sack?"

"Shell bead necklaces, a couple of packages of yaupon tea, carved wooden boxes, black drink cups, fine chert blanks—but what are you doing?"

"Giving it all away to get us off this beach."

"Are you mad?" Walking Smoke's voice sounded strangled with pain.

"Just practical." Night Shadow Star walked to the sack, upended it, and spilled the contents onto the sand. It wasn't of the quality she'd have brought from Cahokia; only the best that a chief in far-off Joara might have been able to acquire. For the gasping Mahica, however, it would be enough.

"Very well!" Night Shadow Star cried and clapped her hands. "Now, let us be about Trade. What will it take to get those canoes?"

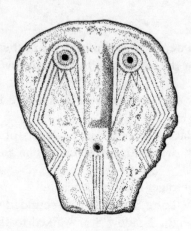

Humiliation

I crouch, bent double by pain, and bide my time on the litter. As if I didn't exist, Night Shadow Star stands with the Koasati Traders, laughing, chattering away like some head-struck songbird. The way she has the Traders rapt, their eyes gleaming with admiration and interest, she might be the one gifted with the Power to ensorcell. Not me.

To look at her, one would think she has been doing this all her life. The temerity of it! This is my sister. A high Lady of Cahokia's finest noble family, daughter of High Chief Red Warrior Tenkiller and sister to me and Chunkey Boy. Yet here she is, acting like some common-born clanless woman. Treating these two-footed vermin as if they were her equals. Listening intently, laughing at their jokes, acting lower than a dirt farmer's third wife.

Nor are Chief Fire Light's warriors much better. I had these buffoonish excuses for warriors cowed. What has happened to the fear that once filled their eyes? At my very approach they used to tremble, their gazes avoiding mine. I needed but hint, and away they would go, snapping to and leaving no stone unturned in their haste to do my bidding.

Now they shoot adoring glances at Night Shadow Star.

How has she done this to me?

But then, she has always been a worthy adversary. And perhaps she was right to stop me from calling the Thunderbirds to blast this place. I think back to that last night in Joara. I had laid my trap perfectly. Left that moron Casqui Trader as bait. Told him in no uncertain terms not to leave the clan house, no matter what.

Even so, it worked. I had Night Shadow Star. When she was distracted by the fire she'd set to burn me out of the clan house and by the Casqui as he finally fled the flames, I grabbed her from behind.

I take a moment to rub my nose, remembering how Night Shadow Star flung her head back to bash it. The eye-tearing pain as she head-butted me.

Trying to hold her had been like trying to wrestle with a cougar. The sister I had known had always been athletic, had loved stickball, shooting bows, even playing chunkey, but the woman I grabbed in the dark had been packed muscle. Strong enough to break loose and swing that gods-accursed war club of hers back between my legs.

Nothing, no other pain, had ever stunned me like that.

But for Fire Light's timely arrival, my beloved Night Shadow Star would have killed me right then and there.

And now the simpering sycophant has cut her loose?

I curb my rage, watching her and the Traders through slitted eyes. Most of the Mahica warriors have filtered off through the trees, figuring that the bumbling Cahokians are indeed leaving. A few of them—dressed in brown hunting shirts and with fabric wraps around their heads—have come to an agreement with Night Shadow Star by taking a chief's ransom in Trade for their ugly and ungainly dugout canoes, some paddles, nets, and fishing gear.

"The mace, the whelk-shell black drink cup, and the four pieces of copper, and your men stay behind." *Night Shadow Star is insistent as Six Toes frowns down at the heavy black-stone mace.*

His men sit on the canoe gunwale. One calls something in Koasati, and the others laugh, as if sharing some amusement.

Six Toes tells Night Shadow Star, "He says that by the time he and the rest can catch another canoe downriver, they will have several of these Mahica girls pregnant, which means they'll have to marry them. I, therefore, must ask for all your Trade, every last bit, to induce them to stay behind because some of these girls' parents are really, really ugly."

"All of it," *Night Shadow Star agrees.* "And we go. There are still six hands of daylight. We can be long gone downriver by dark."

Six Toes gives her an amazed stare.

"Lady?" *Chief Fire Light asks in Cahokian.* "All our Trade?"

"Trade is easy," *Night Shadow Star tells him.* "We can always find Trade."

Fire Light looks skeptical, but in the end he nods.

For once, I hold my tongue. It has occurred to me that for the time being, Night Shadow Star is doing my work for me. It doesn't matter that she's bartered away all of Chief Fire Light's wealth. If he hates her for doing so, that only strengthens my hand, brings him closer to me.

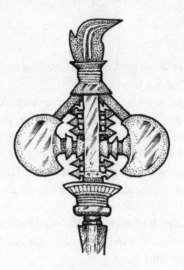

Seven

Blood Talon squatted on his haunches and used a stick to prod the sputtering fire. While the forest was still drying out, most of the easily collected firewood burned wet and hissing. Wreaths of the aromatic hickory and cedar smoke rose from the flames to brown the turkey carcass that sizzled and dripped where it hung over the heat.

The camp was little more than a clearing in the trail where a tornado had torn a swath out of the mature forest, splintered the mixed gum, oak, ash, and hickory, and scattered the remains of sundered trunks and broken branches in its wake. Blueberries, raspberries, currant and rosebushes, as well as man-high saplings had already begun the process of reclaiming the scar. But for the time being, it was one of the few places where the cloud-patchy sky was visible.

Not twenty paces to the south, visible through the tornado's gap, the crystal waters of the creek rippled and gurgled over rounded cobbles mottled with brown and green moss.

Winder crouched across the fire from Blood Talon, his eyes on the turkey as it cooked on the low flames.

They had stopped early—much to Fire Cat's displeasure. From the muddy tracks in the trail, they'd gained on Walking Smoke's party. Maybe as much as half a day. But Fire Cat's quick reflexes and fast shot with his bow had brought a tom turkey to a fluttering stop on the trail.

For all Blood Talon knew, Fire Cat might have continued on his way and eaten the turkey raw had he been on his own. But Winder had insisted that they cook the bird, that the three of them, already traveling on mostly empty bellies, would be better served to keep up the pace if they ate.

Blood Talon glanced down the trail where Fire Cat had disappeared, "to scout the route."

"The man is driven," Winder told him, apparently reading Blood Talon's thoughts. Then he added, "So, you were a squadron first for War Leader Spotted Wrist? You were there when Red Wing Town was destroyed and Fire Cat taken?"

Blood Talon poked the coals before adding another thick section of broken branch from the firewood pile. "I was. I led the first squadron over the walls that night. Seized Fire Cat and his wives in their beds. With my own hands I tossed his body into the canoe that took him and his mother and sisters back to Cahokia."

Blood Talon hesitated. "I watched as his children were killed, chopped up, and thrown in the river. Payment in kind for what the Red Wing Clan did to War Leader Makes Three."

"And after all that, Spotted Wrist still ordered you to bring Lady Night Shadow Star back to Cahokia? How did that happen?"

Blood Talon chuckled dryly, humorlessly. "Oh, a lot of ways. Spotted Wrist was desperate to marry Night Shadow Star for political purposes. Taking her to wife was the final triumph he needed to ally himself not just to Morning Star House, but within the Morning Star's family. That marriage would have made him royalty, and if he could plant a child in Night Shadow Star, so much the better."

"She didn't want the marriage, I take it?" Winder used an awl and sinew thread to repair one of his pack straps where it was coming loose.

"We came to the conclusion that she was obsessed with Fire Cat." Blood Talon smiled wearily. "We tried a lot of silly plans. I even tried to murder him. Fire Cat and I were supposed to have been training, sparring, and it would be an accident. A miscalculation with the war club. I would have been so sorry, almost weeping in remorse, and Night Shadow Star, bereft and mourning, would have acquiesced to Spotted Wrist in her grief. Or at least been distracted enough that we could have grabbed her in the middle of the night. Wouldn't have mattered if she were bound and gagged, Spotted Wrist could have married her. Even if we had to pry her legs apart and hold her in place, he'd have consummated the marriage, and it would have been done."

Winder accidentally poked his thumb with the sharp bone awl. Made a face and glared at the ball of his thumb. "Since Fire Cat is still alive, and so are you, I take it the combat never took place?"

"Oh, it happened." Blood Talon stirred the coals. "Fire Cat figured out exactly what I was about, and then he beat me. Beat me fair, and with enough control that he placed the blade of his war club here." He pointed to the curve of his neck where it met the shoulder. "Didn't even break the skin."

"Hadn't you heard the stories about Fire Cat beating the Itza in single combat? About his exploits?"

"We were still up north when all that happened. Sure, we heard. But remember, I was the man who caught him in his bed. Took his town. Sent him into slavery. I was the best Spotted Wrist had ever seen with a club and shield. As far as we were concerned, they were all crazy stories."

"And now?"

Blood Talon's heart skipped at the yawning inside him. How to put this in words? "Singlehandedly Fire Cat destroyed my pursuit. Capsized my canoe. Drowned my second and the rest of my men. Somehow I survived. Lost in the flooded wilderness until I was captured by barbarians and hung in their local equivalent of a square to be tortured to death."

He pointed at the still-healing scars. "Fire Cat rescued me when the barbarians would have burned me alive. He nursed me back to health, let me accompany him. Me, the man who brought him down and destroyed all that he was. Who would have murdered him."

"Sounds like more than I would have done. Any idea what might have possessed him?"

"Greatness." Blood Talon took a breath before adding, "I think he is the greatest warrior who ever lived. Yet he is a slave, a bound man in the service of Night Shadow Star when he could be so much more. Even now, after all this time in his presence, I struggle to understand."

"Consider yourself blessed." Winder reached for his pack, pulled out a wooden cup, and dipped water from a brownware bowl they'd filled. "He is a match for Lady Night Shadow Star. Maybe the only man alive who is her equal. He says he remains bound to her service; she tells him he's free. They are so in love they could care less."

"You've traveled with her. Is it true that her souls belong to Piasa? I've seen her do some spooky things but—"

"Oh, yes," Winder answered, a glinting certainty in his eyes. "At times, seeing her possession by the Spirit creature will send shivers down your spine. Power runs in that family. One brother's body is home to the Spirit of the Morning Star, the other is a terrible witch guarded by lightning and the Thunderbirds, and she's a tool of the Underworld. Piasa's weapon in our world. But even so, I know that she defied her master by taking Fire Cat to her bed. When you see her talking to her master, hearing his voice? Almost makes your hair stand on end."

"So, why are you here, Trader? Seems like the smart move would have

been to take some of the lady's Trade and scoot right back down the Tenasee to that cute wife I've heard you talk of."

Winder fingered his chin, stared at the browning turkey. "Oh, I'm as
caught up in this as you are, Squadron First. I owe an old friend who
serves Lady Night Shadow Star. Beyond that, she gave me a token that
binds me to her service for the time being." He gave Blood Talon a conspiratorial grin. "But most of all she's a way back to Cahokia, from which
I am as good as banned, and, well, after traveling with her, I have come
to love her. Not the way Fire Cat does—and not that I'd ever delude
myself into thinking she'd return it. My goal is to help her see this thing
through, see her and Fire Cat finally able to go off and love each other
as they deserve. It's . . . it's complicated. Sort of defies the use of mere
words."

"You know the odds are good that none of us are going to survive this.
We are chasing a band of Cahokian warriors led by a perverted witch
who skins his victims alive, cooks and eats their flesh, and wants to have
disgusting carnal relations with his Spirit-possessed sister."

Winder bit off a sour laugh. "Yes, a bit ominous, isn't it? Me, I want
to be a hero in what may be the mythic tale of our age. I was raised a
clanless orphan in Cahokia, living off garbage, charity, and what I could
steal. I wore rags, starved, and slept in abandoned warehouses, temples,
or wherever I could find a spot. I could have been happy being known as
the River Fox, but now I want my name repeated reverently, along with
yours, as the tale is told. As that man, I will be feasted, given access to the
finest Trade on the rivers. My reputation will be greater than any chief's,
second only to the Morning Star's." He paused. "And you, Squadron
First?"

Blood Talon poked the coals again, watching the end of his stick catch
fire. He snuffed it out in the damp soil and used it to poke the coals
again. Frowning, he got his thoughts in order.

"Trader, my entire life, since I was a boy, I trained for war. That was
who I was, all that I ever hoped to be. Right up until the day Fire Cat
tipped my canoe upside down. Since then, I have been face-to-face with
the man I was, and saw only a mask: an image of myself. When I look
past the mask's eye holes, all I see is emptiness. A void. Nothing where a
person should be."

Winder lifted his cup and drank, considering Blood Talon's words.
"That doesn't really answer my question."

"But it does," Blood Talon told him. "I now recognize the mask. I'd
know its features anywhere. I want to know who the man is behind it. I
want to fill in that emptiness with the kind of man I can be proud of. I
want to know who I really am."

Winder nodded, reached out, and thoughtfully wiggled the turkey's leg to see if it was cooked through. Pulled his fingers back from the heat and shook them.

"I have to tell you, Squadron First, you may have the toughest task of us all."

Eight

The storm—coupled with the black night—was a blessing. Where he sat by the fire, Clan Keeper Spotted Wrist listened to the pattering rain on the ramada roof and heard the runoff spattering onto the ash-stained sand behind them. Sometimes it was good to be the War Leader. True, the responsibilities never ended, and he was always on call, but on nights like this he would sleep warm and dry while his warriors made do with soaked blankets and sputtering fires.

Looking out at the darkness, all he could see of the canoe landing was the line of fires, flickering against the downpour, smoking, barely managing to burn. Some were obscured by the warriors hunched around them, capes over their heads to shed the rain. Their exhaled breath could be seen, backlit by the feeble flames as the warriors talked softly.

Spotted Wrist would have been nowhere else. His blood raced in anticipation of the morrow as it had on so many of those nights that preceded an attack. How many? More than he could count, right up to the triumph at Red Wing Town, and again, just weeks ago, when he marched his squadrons to take Cahokia itself.

And this may well be the last night I ever spend feeling like this. Surrounded by my squadron firsts, planning for the morning's action. Never again will I be the War Leader, sleepless in anticipation of battle.

Beyond them, the river was a black void, as if the rain-ringed and swirling waters sucked all the light away.

He need but look across that invisible barrier, and his objective was plain to see. Columella was no one's fool. Her squadrons were keeping watch, their line of bonfires illuminating the high bluff. She no doubt had warriors on patrol along her section of the river's shore.

Spotted Wrist told the men crowded around his fire, "Let her worry. Let her people lose sleep over it. As if I was green enough to launch a night attack across the Father Water while it is this dark and storming?"

Squadron First Flying Squirrel, of the North Star Squadron, shot a dismissive glance at the bonfires on the Evening Star Town bluff. "They've been on alert for days now. It must be taking a toll. All the better for tomorrow."

"You know where your beach is?" Spotted Wrist asked. "You understand your objective?"

"I know the beach. I just hope whoever they dispatch to stop me tries to keep pace with us as we canoe downriver. We'll have the current with us. They'll be worn out, scattered all along the west bank. My squadron, fresh, in formation, will just mow them down if any stand. But I suspect that against massed force, the majority will just flee, melt away. Some will run back to Evening Star Town with stories of disaster and panic."

"Same thing with my people paddling north," Squadron First Cut Weasel said as he propped his chin and stared at the flames. "We'll be off from the canoe landing with the first light of dawn. First to launch since we're headed against the current. I have three possible beaches that will serve. Which one I choose to land on will depend on whichever Evening Star squadron is trying to shadow me. If I have enough distance on them and they look tired enough, I'll take the first beach. If not, then the second. I doubt we'll have to paddle all the way to the third."

Spotted Wrist grunted. He could see it all in his head, as he'd seen so many of his carefully planned campaigns.

Heart Warrior—the squadron first in command of Forest Squadron, the hardened veterans of the Red Wing Town campaign—shot him a sidelong glance and asked, "You've heard the rumors that Columella has landed warriors upriver? That they are going to make an attempt to attack River City Mounds?"

"I am the Keeper," Spotted Wrist replied. "I hear all the rumors. Of course I heard. It doesn't make sense. I had scouts run up to the Cahokia Creek marsh and beyond. No sign of canoes landing. Not in numbers enough to warrant any concern. A large enough party of warriors to pose any kind of threat to our rear would have left sign on the levees and trails."

"It would be a masterful and bold move," Flying Squirrel said.

"What about all that movement we saw north of the city just before dusk?" Heart Warrior asked. "Like they were getting ready to move a whole squadron. And a lot of the canoes were paddled north during the day in ones and twos. Not more than a dozen were left on the bank over there at dusk."

"In the dark? On a night like this?" Cut Weasel gestured out at the pitch-black skies and rain. "Even if they could get their canoes lined out and their warriors loaded, they can't even *see* the east bank, let alone where to land. Not to mention that the current would scatter them up and down the entire eastern shore. But, all right, give them that. Say they could cross an entire squadron on a night like this. In the brush, marsh, and trees, how would they ever assemble? The whole lot of them would be stumbling, wading in the muck and mud, mired in the swamps, falling . . . it would be chaos, not an organized march."

"They would have had to cross and organize in daylight," Spotted Wrist told them. "Just like we'll have to do tomorrow."

But that left the nagging problem of what all those warriors were doing at dusk. The way they were assembling and marching north along the bank wouldn't have been any kind of training exercise. Not this close to Spotted Wrist's attack. From the high bluff, Columella and her commanders could count war canoes just as well as Spotted Wrist could. They knew the requisite number of vessels had been assembled.

So, what were you doing at dusk? he wondered.

Maybe trying to relocate at the last moment in an attempt to prevent Wolverine Squadron from landing above the city?

Spotted Wrist reached for his ceramic teacup where it warmed by the flames. "If they did move that mysterious squadron up north to counter your landing tomorrow, Cut Weasel, what are you going to do?"

"Paddle north for as long as I can get them to follow along the shore," Cut Weasel told him. "Once I have them so far out of position and scattered out, we turn, catch the thread of the current, and race back to the first beach. By the time any of them can flounder their way back, winded and exhausted, we're in formation to destroy them completely."

Spotted Wrist gave his squadron first a knowing wink. "It would really behoove Columella to just surrender. If she were to run, head off into the forest somewhere out west, it would keep her and her family from dying in agony in the squares."

At that moment, Spotted Wrist heard one of his warriors at the edge of the canoe landing call, "Who's there?"

"I am Clicking Boy! I have a message for the Keeper from High Chief Broken Stone. Take me to the Keeper. Now."

"What do you suppose this is?" Flying Squirrel wondered as he reached for his own cup of tea.

A warrior appeared out of the black rain, dripping, a cougar-hide cape from up north draped over his head and shoulders.

"Got a boy claims to serve the River House," the guard said. "Is that all right?"

"It is." Spotted Wrist squinted out past the ramada's protection where a skinny boy of maybe thirteen, wearing a soaked white-fabric cape and a simple breechcloth, stood shivering, his wet skin reflecting the firelight. "Ah, yes. I remember you. You tended the eternal fire in the River Mounds palace. What message from High Chief Broken Stone?"

The boy looked around wide eyed, his skinny arms crossed. Spotted Wrist figured that not all his shivers could be attributed to the cold. The kid looked scared to death.

"My L-Lord Keeper," the boy stammered, "my master, Ch-Chief Broken Stone, he has word. It's uh . . . well, he hears that warriors are infiltrating in from the north. That it's not a full squadron, but small bands of five or six. Dressed as dirt farmers, but with weapons. They're supposed to be in position to take the palace as soon as your warriors push off into the river in the morning."

"Strike behind my back?" Spotted Wrist asked. "Is that it? And they think what? That they can hold River City when I paddle my three squadrons back after I take Evening Star Town?"

"I . . . I wouldn't know, Lord. Just to tell you. My master sent me. Said he'd heard. That something was afoot, and you'd need to know. I-I did. So can I go?"

Spotted Wrist chuckled to himself, wondering if the boy could shiver hard enough to unhinge his bones. "Begone with you. Tell the good chief Broken Stone that I'll deal with any attack on his palace."

The kid whirled on his bare heel and vanished into the inky blackness. His guard, still clutching the cougar hide under his chin, asked, "Anything you need me to tell anyone?"

"Yes, pass the word. Just in case, be alert for any kind of action from the city. Not that I believe it, mind you; though it's the sort of thing an old fox like myself would pull."

Even as Spotted Wrist waved for the guard to go on about his duties, someone down the beach called, "Fire! Fire in the town!"

Spotted Wrist stepped out into the rain, shaded his eyes from the falling drops, and peered. Sure enough, one of the warehouses down at the end of the levee was in flames.

"What do you think?" Cut Weasel came to stand beside him.

"I think someone left a bowl full of hickory oil too close to a crackling fire."

A scream came from just inside the line of workshops and warehouses. "Help me! Someone bring water! The high chief's warehouse is burning!" And no sooner were the words out than a faint yellow glow from back in the buildings sent fingers of light and sparks up into the falling rain.

"Blood and piss," Flying Squirrel said, "Set enough buildings on fire, and dark of night or not, they'll have plenty of light. It will be behind them, War Leader. They'll see us plain as day. Backlit like they'll be, we'll just see silhouettes."

In that instant it all made sense. The moving squadrons, the relocated canoes. By Piasa's swinging balls, how had Columella managed to cross even a portion of a squadron? He couldn't just sit on the beach and let them burn the town.

"Alarm!" Spotted Wrist bellowed. "Squadrons! Prepare to defend yourselves. To arms! To arms! Prepare for attack from the town!"

Nine

Having set old Robin Feather's rope workshop on fire, Seven Skull Shield compensated himself, took two good basswood ropes for the effort of breaking in and dropping a hot pot of coals on a pile of fibers in the rear of the workshop.

Farts had enjoyed the sojourn as much as Seven Skull Shield. The big dog had been held hostage there, threatened with being brained before being tossed into the stewpot. Seven Skull Shield liked to think that's why the big Spirit dog had lifted a leg on the doorframe and most of the workshop's interior fixings.

Now, standing outside in the dark rain, coils of rope over one shoulder, his hand resting atop Farts' huge head, Seven Skull Shield took a last look back. The first flickers of yellow flame were eating through the thatch at the back of the house.

"Can't say I'm sorry. He really isn't a nice man. Dreadfully mean to his wives. Still, he does make the finest rope in the city."

Farts made a slurpy sound as he licked his block of a nose, tail waving back and forth.

"Would have been nice to put the torch to Spotted Wrist's palace back in central Cahokia, but we've got to concentrate on River Mounds. Now, let's see. Who else here in River City do we owe for inconveniences or slights rendered?"

That's when he heard a shout from over by the River Mounds plaza. Someone bellowed something that might have been a rain-muffled "Fire!"

Seven Skull Shield looked down at the dim shape of his ungainly dog. "The River Mounds palace? Surely you don't think that good old Broken

Stone, Three Fingers, and that rat-tail-chasing bunch of usurpers are thinking themselves invulnerable, do you?"

In the growing light from Robin Feather's crackling roof, Farts looked up, the dog's odd eyes, one blue, the other brown, seemed to gleam in his damp head. The tail slashed back and forth as if in agreement, flinging water all about.

"Well," Seven Skull Shield told the dog thoughtfully, "they most certainly wouldn't expect anything so rash. And what good is a deception if it doesn't decept? Or whatever pus-dripping word you'd call it?"

Seven Skull Shield grinned as he started off through the stygian-black passageways that led between warehouses and workshops. Seven Skull Shield knew the backways as intimately as he knew the lines on the palms of his hands.

Even as he led the way past latrines and storehouses, he could hear more and more calls in the rainy darkness. Sounded like a lot of people were panicked, which, was, after all, what Flat Stone Pipe had intended.

As he stepped out from between the Four Winds Clan House and Old-Woman-Who-Never-Dies' mound-top temple, Seven Skull Shield could see across the rain-misty plaza, past the world-famous chunkey courts and the World Tree Pole to the stairs leading up to the River House palace. The doors were open, people emerging, stepping to the edge of the high earthen pyramid as they stared off to the north.

Seven Skull Shield, Farts at his side, trotted across the chunkey courts, heedless of the tracks he made in the wet sand. If everything went according to plan, come morning Broken Stone would have a lot more to be incensed over than footprints in his chunkey court.

Especially if Seven Skull Shield had anything to do with it.

The calls from up on the mound were louder now, echoing. "Fire! Three of them."

"No, look. There's a fourth!"

"You think Evening Star House is behind this?" another called from the lit doorway.

"If it is, they're going to run smack into Spotted Wrist's warriors as they come charging up from the beach."

Seven Skull Shield told Farts, "See that guy in the doorway all silhouetted by the light from inside? That chubby thick-waisted fellow with the oversized headdress? Got to be Broken Stone."

Which gave Seven Skull Shield a notion. He trotted across the dark plaza, figuring the people who'd flocked into the rain would be fire-blinded after being inside. It would take a finger of time for their eyes to adjust to what little visibility there was.

Cupping his hands, Seven Skull Shield called up, "Keeper Spotted Wrist is under attack! He asks that Broken Stone call up his warriors. You are ordered to place Three Fingers in charge of one group, send them down the levee. Broken Stone is to lead the second group around to the Avenue of the Sun and then hook back to the canoe landing from the east. Keeper Spotted Wrist wants you to cut off any retreat when the raiders try to flee." Seven Skull Shield took a deeper breath, then thundered, "*Do you understand?*"

"Yes," the paunchy fellow called down. "How soon does he—"

"I said, Do. You. Understand? Go. Now. Or you will answer to Spotted Wrist for your failure. And take every able-bodied man with you! Do it now, by Piasa's blood!"

Broken Stone—it had to be him—paused only a moment, and turned back to the others, howling, "You heard him! Grab your weapons. Three Fingers, take the men you need. Hurry, or so help me, I'll let Keeper Spotted Wrist himself deal with anyone who lingers."

From the shadows, Seven Skull Shield figured it took less than a finger's time before the last of the men clattered down the ramp stairs, joined the confused chaos at the bottom, and finally vanished into the night.

Better yet, when he and Farts sprinted up those same steps, most of the women and slaves were congregated in the corner of the mound back of the two Eagle guardian posts, and all were chattering in excitement as they stared north and west at the six fires now burning brightly. Shouts and calls could be heard from the direction of the canoe landing and the warehouses.

When Seven Skull Shield burst into the palace great room, the place was empty. In the room's center, the eternal fire crackled merrily. He found jars of hickory oil in the usual places under the sleeping benches where they were built into the surrounding walls.

Farts immediately fixed on the large stewpot that rested next to the fire. Standing knee high—as the big corrugated-ware pot did—it was no challenge for Farts. The big dog stuck his head over the rim, sniffed, tested the temperature, and began slurping up mouthfuls.

Seven Skull Shield started with the big hickory oil pots in back, pouring them onto the cane wall that separated the great room from the storerooms, the high chief's, and the matron's sleeping quarters in the rear. He paused only long enough to grab a pine sap torch, light it, and toss it into the puddled hickory oil. Then he turned his attention to the beds along the back walls, dousing each liberally with oil.

As he did, he couldn't help himself. He burst into song, his self-proclaimed melodious voice rising: *"Her body was fair, with long lustrous hair! She lay in my bed, her sheath wide and red!"*

He managed to grab a burning brand from the fire by the still-unburned end, seared his fingers as he tossed it onto the bedding.

Then, on a lark, he considered the High Chief's litter—River House's high chair—an ornately carved thing with a raised seat covered with cougar hides. It took all his strength, but he toppled it off the clay dais on which it sat and dragged it over to the spreading fire in the bedding. With a heave, he lifted and upended the wooden litter onto the flames.

"My shaft, I recall, it stood hard and tall. At the very sight, she gasped in delight."

Seven Skull Shield upended another jar of hickory oil on the bedding across the room, figured better than to grab another brand from the fire, and snagged up a convenient elk antler that someone had been sawing on. Using the tines like a fork, he lifted out another burning chunk of wood and propelled it onto the next pile of bedding.

"She yipped loud as sin, as I slipped it all in."

"What are you doing?" A woman's voice cried in anguished disbelief.

Seven Skull Shield turned, glanced back at the door where a slave woman was gaping, her hands lifted in a gesture of dismay.

"I'm singing."

Wide-eyed with fear, she stared fixedly on the flames climbing the mat wall in the back, licking around the giant carving of the Four Winds clan symbol, and eating at the fine fabrics hanging from the cane walls. Then she saw the bedding in back: all in flames. Her mouth reminded him of a fish out of water, soundless as it popped open and closed. Her startled eyes widened further at the sight of Farts. The big dog was now standing with his front feet in the pot as he continued to slurp up whatever tasty stew was within.

"Don't look so shocked," he told her.

Seven Skull Shield used the elk antler to pitch another of the burning branches into an open box of textiles beside one of the beds. Looked like a collection of dyed dogbane capes. Expensive ones. Pity.

"A lot of people are surprised at first," Seven Skull Shield continued. "Yes, it's true: Such a clear and mellifluous sound, that vibrant harmony, can indeed come from a human throat. Not to mention the magic of the lyrics. To string words together with such fluid poetry? I want you to know, my singing has laid people prostrate more than once."

The flames were eating their way up through the war trophies that hung on the walls: old bows and war clubs, wooden shields, polished skulls and long bones, all long-dried and seasoned.

"You're mad!" The woman cried breathlessly, then she filled her lungs and screamed, "Help!"

"No more singing?" Seven Skull Shield wondered, and then, picking up a sack of beautifully crafted chunkey stones he thought Crazy Frog might cherish, he charged straight at the woman.

"Dog!" he bellowed. "Time to go!"

Farts—long accustomed to the call—started, half-panicked, and in the effort to extricate himself from the stew pot, tipped it onto its side; the contents flooded into the great hearth. Which was when Farts caught a back leg in the pot of water used to brew black drink. In the scramble to kick it free, he launched the decorated pot arcing into the fizzling flames. With a sizzling and hissing, the fire flickered and died, leaving only the leaping and garish inferno devouring the rear of the great palace for light.

Seven Skull Shield swept the woman aside with a muscular arm, but collided full-on with three more who had the ill fortune to fill the doorway just as Seven Skull Shield was charging through like a bull buffalo at full gallop.

He had to admit—having smashed into all kinds of humans over his lifetime—piling full-bore into a bunch of women provided a much softer landing than smashing into a band of warriors. In fact, he'd come out of it without so much as a bruise. Amid the screams, howls, and shrieks, he was halfway to his feet when Farts came barreling through. With all four feet landing in Seven Skull Shield's back, he was knocked flat atop the shrieking women once more.

The squeals, screams, and howls were even louder the second time around.

Ten

Warriors! Warriors are burning everything!" an old woman screamed
from the darkness back by the warehouses. "I saw them. Four or five!
They set fire to a warehouse, going to burn all of River Mounds down!"

"Help!" another voice down the levee called. "Warriors are burning
anything they can!"

"How many?" Spotted Wrist knew that voice: Flying Squirrel.

"Just small bands!" came yet another call out of the dark and rain.
"Dressed in armor!"

Stamping back and forth by his firelit ramada, Spotted Wrist stared
out at the night, seeing no fewer than six fountains of flame in the closely
packed warehouses, temples, and workshops that crowded the levee.
Granted, it was raining, but if that got loose, caught the rest of the warehouse district on fire . . .

Spotted Wrist cupped his hands, bellowing, "Well, don't just stand
there while Columella burns down River City! Go drive them off! And
detail squads to put those pus-dripping fires out! Go!"

He watched as the shadowy forms of his warriors went filtering up the
sand, around the ramadas and Traders' stands, and into the buildings.

Was that the right call? But then, he'd seen how many canoes Columella
had left at her landing. No more than a handful when dusk had turned
to darkness. No way she could mount an assault. Nothing with any force
behind it, anyway.

"Leave guards on the camps!" he called. "Everyone else, go and save
the town!"

Spotted Wrist squinted as the rain picked up, hammering his head
in the darkness, trickling down his face and neck. Well, that, at least,

was good luck. It would keep the fires from spreading. The hot ashes, embers, and sparks wheeling up from the burning roofs would land on thatch and cane too wet to burn.

He turned on his heel to stare angrily at the line of bonfires across the inky Father Water. Up atop the bluff, Columella was no doubt watching the whole thing. Betting everything on her desperate measure to burn River City to the ground. Might have worked but for the storm.

"Bad plan, Matron." He wiped at the rain trickling down his face. "All this does is fix you as Cahokia's enemy. Turns the people against you. As you are going to find out when I hang each of your raiders in a square and burn little bits of their bodies before cutting them apart. And I will catch some. When I do, all of Cahokia will learn just how careless and coldhearted you are."

Screams erupted just up from his position, about halfway between the canoe landing and River Mounds plaza. The sound of combat, the clacking of shields, men bellowing taunts. Those would be Forest Squadron veterans. Didn't matter that they were fighting in the dark, in the close confines and narrow passages between the warehouses and workshops. No part-time warriors from Evening Star town would stand against them.

To his annoyance, another fire, on a rooftop barely visible, broke out behind the fighting. Had to be over by the plaza and chunkey courts. It sent a shiver through him.

Hunga Ahuito take him. Columella *had* tried to make an attack on River House.

"It's what I would have done," he told himself.

But how had she done it? He would have sworn that she couldn't land warriors in sufficient numbers to make anything but a token raid. Worse, in the darkness and rain, keeping command of the raiding parties would be impossible. Her raid leader and squadron firsts would find it impossible to organize an assault, let alone a retreat. It would descend into a chaos of every warrior on his own.

"That will cost you dearly," he told the distant Columella. "Oh, some of your people will escape, make their way back across the river, but most are going to die here. Tonight. Or when my squadrons hunt them down come daylight, I'll put the survivors in squares here, on the canoe landing. In plain sight where your people can watch as we torture them to death."

A sight that would sap the will of every Evening Star warrior.

For all Spotted Wrist knew, it might even incite an insurrection that would unseat Columella before his advancing squadrons could close on the town.

More screams could be heard from the fighting over by the plaza. Gods, if he could just see what was happening.

The fountain of fire over at the plaza leapt higher. The distant screams of "Fire! It's the palace! Retreat!" could barely be heard.

By Piasa's balls, what was happening over there? Surely even that soft and pudgy Broken Stone, backed by Three Fingers, could have defended his palace.

Up and down the canoe landing, the night was getting blacker as the desultory fires in the warriors' camps—with no one to tend them—burned out.

The inferno at the plaza, however, was a like a column of flame rising into the rainy night.

That's when, out of the darkness, one of the remaining warriors left to guard the canoes screamed, "Help! We're being attacked by . . ."

And nothing.

Then, down the bank, Spotted Wrist heard another shout. "Help me!" The brief sound of a scuffle, and a scream.

"What's going on?" he demanded, stepping out from the fire.

From the darkness, a figure came pounding his way across the sand. The dark form leaped over one of the dying fires, almost tripped over a pot, and charged closer, yelling, "War Leader, there are warriors on the beach! And they're not ours!"

And from there, all descended into chaos.

Eleven

Fire Cat would have run if he could. His heart beat faster than his pace
on the trail warranted. His muscles, which should have been fatigued
from the pace he'd forced, felt charged. He dared not hope but disre-
garded any better judgment that he should not disappoint himself. After
all, the tracks they had followed down the South Trail were definitely a
day old. Dried out. But perhaps, just perhaps, for whatever reason, Walking Smoke's party had spent the night in Willow Stem Village.

Perhaps the Mahica chief had wanted to feast them?

Maybe negotiations over Trade for canoes or transport had entailed a
complicated ritual? Something that had dragged on for more than a day?

Oh, he wanted to run, to sprint up to the palisade gate, calling out,
"Night Shadow Star? Lady? Are you here?"

But he couldn't run. Not with the heavy pack on his shoulder. Not
with Winder and Blood Talon laboring along under the burden of their
packs and Night Shadow Star's carved box. Not only that, but the turkey,
some nuts, berries, and roasted roots aside, they were running on empty
stomachs. Invigorated though Fire Cat might be, his companions were
exhausted and half-starved, on the verge of stumbling.

So Fire Cat forced himself to stride down the trail between the cornfields at a steady pace. He kept an air of decorum, the Trader's staff he'd
obtained in Cane Town held high with its white feathers dancing in the
breeze.

Fire Cat's Trader's staff was nowhere as gaudy as Winder's, which
made a full loop on the end all filled with white swan feathers from down
south. But then, Winder was a full-fledged Trader, not a sort of impostor

like Fire Cat. Blood Talon, despite his current appearance, would never be mistaken for anything but a footloose warrior down on his luck.

As they passed out of the fields and into the scattered houses, raised granaries, and workshops, the first of the dogs caught sight of them and charged, barking and milling, ears back, teeth flashing, hair standing on end.

People flocked out from the shade of the ramadas, some from the town gate.

In Trade pidgin, Winder bellowed, "Hello to the town! We are Traders from the south. We come under the Power of Trade. Is there anyone in Willow Stem Town to receive us?"

A tall man, maybe in his late twenties, wearing a simple tunic, came trotting out from inside the palisade, a long staff of office held before him. "Greetings! I am Red House, son of Born Jaw, the high chief of Willow Stem. You are bid welcome under the Power of Trade." He flung his arm out at some of the gawking locals. "You there, get those dogs under control."

Then, to Fire Cat's party, he asked, "You have come far?"

"From Joara."

"And how is the town?"

"Empty but for one old woman who gave us the news." Winder had stepped to the fore, where Fire Cat was happy to let him take the lead.

Red House pulled up, his staff held vertically before him. "We have heard but hoped it would not be this bad. Were you there when the witch was? Did you see what happened?"

"No," Winder told him. "We got there the morning after the witch left. As to what it means for Trade? That is hard to say. For the time being, there will be little. But people will move back. Maybe burn some of the buildings. Rebuild. The town is too important, sitting as it does on good soil and at the crossroads of so many trails."

"And what can Willow Stem Village do for you, good Traders?"

"We would like to hire a canoe. A fast one." Winder unhitched his pack and lowered it to the ground. "We have Trade. Good Trade. Enough to make our visit worth Willow Stem Village's time. And we will be thankful for your hospitality."

Red House cocked his head, rubbed his chin with his left hand. "The canoe might be a problem for the moment. The witch took our best, but Shell Hook should be coming in today or tomorrow. He is upriver. Went in search of any steatite or mica he could find. A Trader who was here, Six Toes, wanted those goods. But the miserable Cahokians and their witch took the canoes."

"I know Six Toes," Winder replied. "He's a good man. So, the witch got away with his canoe?"

Fire Cat closed his eyes. Pus-sucking luck. Night Shadow Star was already on the river. "How many canoes did they take?"

Red House shifted his attention to Fire Cat. "The big Trade canoe and three smaller craft that belonged to people here. All for a pile of Trade. So much so that it almost insults the Power of Trade, though we will make much from the largesse."

"The witch insisted on that?" Winder asked.

"No. It was the captive woman. She did the bargaining." Red House, despite holding his staff, made a gesture. "And I was happy to have her do so. That many stinking Cahokia warriors? And the wounded witch? We wanted them gone. It almost came to a fight as it was. Whatever it took, we wanted them as far away as we could get them."

"The woman was all right?" Fire Cat asked.

"She seemed to be." Red House hesitated. "Something about her . . ."

"Power," Winder supplied. "She was filled with Power."

"That's as good an explanation as any."

"What about the witch?" Fire Cat asked, trying to keep from sounding too impatient. "You said he was wounded?"

Red House's lips twitched, then he said, "He kept cupping his eggs and rod, and when he wasn't paying attention, his water dripped. He could barely stand upright. And that, when you think about it, is the best way to have a witch pass through. As I said, we wanted him gone."

Winder turned, met Fire Cat's eyes, and cocked an eyebrow in a way that said, *Well, it could have been a lot worse. At least she's alive.*

From behind, Blood Talon, who spoke only the simplest of Trade pidgin, asked, "So, what is happening?"

Fire Cat sighed, unhitched his pack, and shifted his Trader's staff. In Cahokian, he answered, "My lady is already on the river. There are no canoes, but one is coming in the next day or so."

Winder reached out, slapping Fire Cat on the shoulder. "That being the case, we have no recourse. For once, my friend, surrender yourself to the care of the River Fox, and let's make the best of this to rest and feast, for it may be a long time before we get such a chance again."

"Do I have any choice?"

"No. So bouncing up and down on your toes is not going to make things better. We will catch her. Just not today. You are very good at tackling the impossible. Therefore, hard as it will be, I suggest you embrace the opportunity to relax as a sort of ultimate challenge. See if you can do it."

"I'll bet against that," Blood Talon grumbled. "Bet he's up all night pacing in spite of any good sense you'd counsel."

But Fire Cat had ceased listening.

She's taking charge. That's my lady. And Walking Smoke is still wounded. This can go a lot of different ways.

Twelve

Behind his dark ramada, Spotted Wrist paced in anxious worry as he tried to come to grips with the night's chaos. None of it made sense. He could just see the first pale glow on the cloudy eastern horizon. His squadron firsts were finally sorting out the exhausted warriors as they filtered out of the predawn gloom.

Flying Squirrel appeared out of the darkness, gave him a salute and a humorless smile. "Orders, Keeper? Are we still launching on Evening Star Town?"

"We are." Fighting a shiver, Spotted Wrist rubbed his weary eyes. He was soaked to the bone from the night's rain, would have loved to have huddled over his fire. But in the chaos, the fire had gone out for lack of attention.

"Men are tired."

"So are those fools at Evening Star Town. I'm sure Columella and her people were up all night, standing on that bluff by those bonfires, watching the buildings burn. She'll think we're so exhausted and disorganized that we'll call it off for a day. And if she can disrupt us again tonight, that we'll call it off tomorrow, too."

"We'll need a couple of hands' time to get organized, pack our camps, and load the canoes." Flying Squirrel was staring out toward Evening Star Town, where the fires had finally begun to die down on the far bluff.

In the faint gray of dawn Spotted Wrist frowned. When it came to the night's raid, something didn't feel right.

He didn't have a single captive or dead raider to show for it. Didn't make sense. Like he'd been played.

But how?

His warriors had searched through the cluttered warrens and passages between the packed warehouses, workshops, temples, and clan houses. And, of course, in the storm-black and rainy darkness, they'd run full into the armed parties Broken Stone had sent out. Each, certain they were encountering enemy raiders, had attacked the other. And the sounds of combat had spread, so that other parties, certain that the enemy had been engaged, had attacked the first armed party they encountered in the maze of narrow passages and dead ends.

Of course, the River House warriors had sustained the worst of the combat. Not that such news was anything to crow about. It had taken precious time to sort out and disengage the parties while additional buildings burned. And, of course, the townspeople, hearing the commotion, had poured out into the cramped byways, only to run afoul of half-panicked warriors. Nothing good had come of those encounters but injured townspeople who'd been batted out of the way with war clubs or shields.

"What's the matter, Squadron First?" Spotted Wrist turned to follow the man's quizzical stare.

"Excuse me, Keeper, but did you have the canoes moved last night? Maybe to keep them away from any attack?"

"No, I . . ." Spotted Wrist stepped out from the ramada's shelter, squinted in the half light. Where the high prows of an entire line of Trade and war canoes should have been pulled up on the sand, the empty beach stretched down to the dark line of river that vanished into the dusky haze.

"No!" Spotted Wrist cried. Then he charged headlong down the beach. "I tell you, no! This can't be!"

As the light brightened, he could see the keel marks, the deeply incised footprints where straining men had dragged the heavy craft down to the river. A mere handful of canoes remained of the hundred-and-some that were supposed to ferry his squadrons across the river. But for an occasional canted canoe the sand leading down to the lapping water was empty.

"But how?" he wondered, stunned.

Flying Squirrel kicked at the drag mark where two lines of tracks marked the raiders' efforts. "They tricked us, Keeper. Got to tell you, it was masterfully done. River House is burned to the ground. We spent most of the night fighting each other. And half the local people hate us worse than spit in the eye as a result. And all the while, Columella's people were dragging our canoes out into the river."

But stare in disbelief, wish as he might, Spotted Wrist couldn't make his missing canoes reappear on the empty sand.

He turned his glare across the roiling water to the opposite bank, where only haphazard clusters of smaller canoes could be seen along the shore. "So, where are all the canoes?"

"Maybe they turned them loose on the current?"

"By pus and blood! We *paid* for those vessels! Traded for their use. We have to get them back! Detail warriors. Now! I want every one of them chased down and recovered! And if they have Evening Star Town warriors in them, I want the shit lickers brought back and hung in the squares."

Flying Squirrel's features puckered, as if he were experiencing something sour and foul. "Yes, Keeper."

As Spotted Wrist watched his squadron first turn on his heel and trot off, he slammed a knotted fist into his palm. "Someone is going to feel pain for this. Real pain."

Thirteen

The ashes that filled Blue Heron's hair itched. Some had run down the side of her face. Once, it would have been intolerable. Beyond countenance. A circumstance to be immediately dealt with even if she had to order her servants' legs and arms broken in order to make herself presentable.

On this partly sunny morning, with more puffs of white cumulus than blue sky visible overhead, she rather enjoyed the effect. Adding to the sight she must have been, she bent her mouth into an idiotic grin that displayed the gaps in her teeth. Sitting right there in plain sight, she was essentially invisible. For a woman who had been the center of attention all her life, this felt exhilarating.

The starburst and Four Winds Clan tattoos on her cheeks were covered with grime, and she wore a similarly filthy and singed basswood-fiber cloak over her shoulders. The skirt hanging on her hips might have been made of an old corn sack.

Beside her, dressed in a similarly shabby cloak, his hair pulled up in a bun and skewered with splinters, Seven Skull Shield sat with his knees pulled up. He appeared most pleased with himself as he stared at the people milling just beyond their blanket; and then a gleam of delight filled his dark eyes as he took in the charred remains of the River House palace atop its flat-topped earthen pyramid.

Blackened timbers stuck up from the smoldering rubble. Where the fire hadn't eaten through the plaster to the timbers beneath, sections of smoke-gray wall leaned precariously over the incinerated remains. People crowded around the wreckage, as close as they could get given the heat still radiating from the ruin.

The spot where Blue Heron had thrown out their blanket that morning was just back of the chunkey courts. A prime location for Trade—and given the chaos and confusion of the night before, they'd managed to claim it before any of their competition could.

The blanket they tended offered various simple shell necklaces made from freshwater mussel-shell beads, small brownware pots, and a couple of wooden bowls. Trade that was just good enough, but not too dazzling. Nothing so exotic as to make them suspicious given their appearance.

"Pus and blood. You had to burn it all down?" she asked as she pulled at the wattle under her chin. "It might have been taken over by Broken Stone, but both Round Pot and War Duck were inordinately proud of that palace. Built it themselves, they did, not more than a decade ago. Wherever they're hidden, bet they're stamping and stomping, fit to chew obsidian this morning."

"So, how about we don't tell them who might have burned their precious palace? Sometimes people are a lot happier not knowing what they don't know." Seven Skull Shield reached over to scratch Farts' ears.

The big dog uttered a sigh, rolled onto his side, and lifted his tail.

As Blue Heron made a face and waved the stink away, Seven Skull Shield cried, "Don't blame him! Had to be that stew. No telling what kind of concoction those usurping River City lunatics had in that pot. Might have been bat wings and snake meat for all we know."

"You're sure no one can recognize you? Or Farts? You really had to take him along?"

"He's got a stake in this, too. Remember when Spotted Wrist's warriors dragged me out of Night Shadow Star's palace? One of them warriors whacked poor old Farts a good one. Would have killed him if Farts hadn't run. As it was, that shit-sucking Robin Feather had him tied up. Was going to make a stew out of him and make me watch him eat it."

"How is the rope maker these days? He forgave you for running off with that poisonous and cunning wife of his? Actually, vile little sheath that she was, Robin Feather ought to hold a feast in your honor for saving him the misfortune of her continued presence in his bed."

"I think he's got his mind on other matters today."

"How's that? You really humiliated him over that woman."

"He had a fire last night. No telling how it happened."

"A lot of that going around." She gave him a sidelong glance. "Remind me not to get on your bad side."

"Actually, given that Spotted Wrist has already burned your palace, you're pretty free to treat me any way you want. Even if you were to get on my bad side—which you have to admit is highly unlikely given our unique association—you've got nothing left for me to set fire to."

"You have a twisted and malicious sense of humor, Thief." She gestured at the burned palace. "Do you know what a risk that was?"

"Not so much." He leaned forward, propped his chin on his knees as he studied the wreckage. "I shouted out that I was Spotted Wrist's messenger, and that the canoe landing was under attack. Told them that the Keeper ordered them to ambush the Evening Star Town raiders. Catch them from behind."

"And you thought they'd fall for that?"

Seven Skull Shield yawned. "Broken Stone's new at this whole high chief thing. If it had been War Duck, he'd have demanded that Spotted Wrist's messenger come up to the palace. Broken Stone might have had his pudgy butt in the coveted high chair—"

"Not anymore. I hear you burned it."

"Hope he doesn't take it too hard. Thing like that can have lasting effects: Bed-wetting, an inability to get one's shaft to harden when a voluptuous young thing strokes her fingers across a man's—"

"Why do I listen to you? Forget it. Broken Stone, he doesn't know enough to take such a catastrophe seriously. But Three Fingers does," she finished. "He's the brains behind deposing War Duck and Round Pot. He can't dispose of Broken Stone. Not yet. For the time being, he still needs him as a figurehead."

She paused, considered the wreckage and what it meant. "Needs him a heap less this morning than he did last night. After the fire? If I were Broken Stone? I'd be looking for a fast canoe to Pacaha and a long future as a downriver Trader. Bet he'll be a corpse by the end of the week."

"Um, you know that War Duck and Round Pot, well . . . they really don't like me."

"For a thief, you have a remarkable acuity when it comes to interpersonal relationships. They still suspect you were responsible for putting out the eternal fire that night."

"All the more reason why they should never learn just how this latest fire got set."

Blue Heron glanced sidelong at him again. "Any way that anyone up on that mound might recognize you?"

"Only if I sing. I have an unmistakable voice, sort of a miracle of harmony and catchy lyrics that—"

"You were singing while you set the place on fire?"

"Well, it was sort of a spirit-of-the-moment thing, you know? I had that welling sensation of doing something epic. It deserved a song."

Farts, asleep, voided more noxious gas. Shifted, and extended his huge paws.

Blue Heron pulled the soot-stained blanket across her nose, taking shallow breaths. "Outside of singing—a crime that anyone sane would consider as grounds for hanging you in a square—is there any way anyone could know it was you?"

"It was mostly dark. The central fire had gone out."

"Again?"

"They really shouldn't leave that much stew in a big round-bottomed pot like that—not to mention a great big teapot—next to a fire. Highly unstable when it's got a dog standing in it. But this woman, I think she was too distracted by what was burning to look at me. And then, on the way out, I was just a silhouette when I ran—"

"Quiet! Litter coming. Now, be a pus-dripping Trader for once, eh?"

Blue Heron watched the small cadre of North Star House warriors enter the plaza. Behind them came eight porters bearing an ornate litter complete with elevated chair and sunscreen. No way Blue Heron could mistake the occupant: Four Winds Clan Matron Rising Flame. The woman who had relieved her of the duties of Clan Keeper and replaced her with Spotted Wrist.

Rounding the chunkey courts, where boys were trying to smooth out some idiot miscreant's footprints in the sand, the bearers came to a stop and lowered their burden. Though they were not more than three paces from where Blue Heron's blanket lay, no one gave her or Seven Skull Shield a second glance. The Matron didn't even acknowledge Blue Heron's bowed head, or the way she touched her forehead in obeisance. One of the warriors offered Rising Flame a hand as she rose and stepped off the litter.

"Perfect," Blue Heron whispered, having had her own litter brought to that same spot before.

At Rising Flame's arrival, Broken Stone came trotting down the stairs, his belly jiggling. The man was in his late thirties, had a grim look on his face. A bloody gash on the left side of his forehead was bound up with fabric. The way he kept grinding his teeth, Blue Heron figured this wasn't his happiest moment ever.

"Clan Matron!" he called. "Greetings. I'm relieved that you are here. I only dispatched a runner to the Four Winds Clan House but a couple of hands before dawn. To see you here this quickly—"

"I was on the way. I was to watch Spotted Wrist launch the first of his squadrons against—"

"There will be no squadrons!" Broken Stone thundered.

If Rising Flame took offense at the tone, she ignored it. "What do you mean?"

"We were attacked last night!" Broken Stone thrust an arm in the direction of the smoking wreckage atop the palace mound. "Must have been a squadron at least. They burned buildings all along the levee. Then, when our warriors chased them, they vanished, just melted away into the night. For a while, we were fighting each other. That's how I got this!" He pointed to his head wound. "Can you imagine? One of those North Star warriors mistook me? I'm high chief. It's a miracle he didn't kill me! And then where would we be?"

From her expression, Rising Flame must have had a really good idea, but she didn't articulate it.

"Evening Star warriors burned your palace? How did they get past your defenses?"

"Spotted Wrist ordered us to attack the rear of the raiders who were advancing on the canoe landing." For the first time, Broken Stone looked abashed. "The palace was undefended."

Rising Flame's lips twitched. "So an entire war party just marched up your steps and set fire to the palace?"

"Well, the story is a little confused, the women who were here, two of my wives, some of the household slaves, they were—"

"Where were all the men?"

"I told you! We were acting in support of Spotted Wrist, who was—"

"Tits and blood, man!" Rising Flame exploded. "Before I find Spotted Wrist and get his report, do you know how many of the raiders were killed? How many captured?"

"I, uh . . ." Broken Stone winced, tried to turn away.

Rising Flame reached out, grabbed him by the arm, and jerked him back. "How many?"

"Reports are confused. You'll have to ask—"

"How many?"

Broken Stone swallowed hard. "We lost six. More are wounded."

"How many of the enemy? The raiders? Surely we have some idea."

The high chief of River House wouldn't meet her eyes when he said, "None. As far as I know, they all got away."

Rising Flame's hot glare would have melted a brownware pot.

"So Columella's raiders burned your palace and skipped away into the night while you were fighting each other?"

She turned, stamped off a couple of paces, knotted her fists. After taking deep breaths, she wheeled, stalked back, and thrust a finger into Broken Stone's face. "No one ever said Columella was a fool. But she'll pay for this. When we send our squadrons across the river—"

"I, uh, well, not today. No squadrons are going."

"Excuse me?"

Broken Stone flapped his arms up and down. "I haven't been down to the canoe landing yet. I was too busy here, trying to assess the damage."

Rising Flame went still, her face strained like a death mask. "And what seems to be the reason no squadrons are going?"

"All the canoes, Clan Matron. They were stolen last night. Well, all but a few that were pulled way up on shore and close to the—"

"The canoes are gone?"

Blue Heron thought the veins popping out of Rising Flame's forehead were about to burst.

"Where is Spotted Wrist? At the canoe landing?"

"You might want to wait," Broken Stone told her. "I hear that trying to have a meaningful conversation with the Keeper right now isn't the best—"

"Oh, he'll hear me all right. And he'll rotted well listen," Rising Flame hissed through clenched teeth.

Rising Flame didn't look back. Physically shaking, she paced to her litter and seated herself. The matron continued to glare balefully up at the smoking wreckage atop the flat-topped mound as her bearers silently lifted her. Expressions fixed, they trotted past Blue Heron and Seven Skull Shield's blanket and vanished between the Four Winds Clan charnel house and the Men's House, where the war medicine was kept.

Broken Stone was wearily climbing his steps, head down, as he returned to the incinerated remains of his palace.

Seven Skull Shield waved away another of Farts' odiferous emissions, then glanced at Blue Heron. "You think maybe we picked the wrong place for our blanket? Haven't made a single Trade all morning."

"Must be Farts," she told him dryly.

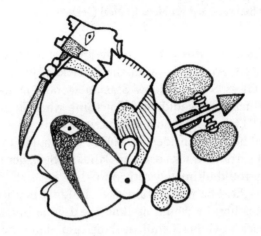

Fourteen

The headwaters of the Tenasee were split into a series of mostly parallel tributaries that ran down from the northeast and fed together as they wound their way south southwest along low floodplains. Behind the floodplains, timbered hogbacks rose in razor-like sandstone and shale ridges to either side, bounding the shallow valleys. The easternmost branch now carried Walking Smoke's party downstream toward the confluences that would create the main channel of the Tenasee.

Night Shadow Star had been placed between Bluefish and Made of Wood in the bow of Six Toes' canoe. Not only was she crowded between the paddling warriors but her feet were bound again. Chief Fire Light himself held the other end of the rope that had been tied around her ankles. The thought was that if she were to leap overboard and try to escape, he could reel her in and, together with his warriors, drag her back into the canoe.

As if escape were my plan.

Night Shadow Star turned, shooting a hard look back two seats to where Walking Smoke rode. Her brother looked worried for an instant, then in a seething rage the next. His lips were working, causing the pink mass of scar tissue on the left side of his face to flex. So smooth was the burned skin it seemed to gleam in the sunlight.

The space between them was packed with Fire Light's warriors, each bent to the paddles as they propelled the craft down the current's thread. Along the shores, the screening willows, cottonwoods, water oak, and brush raced past.

And in the stern Six Toes perched high, using his pointed paddle as a rudder to keep the big Trade canoe in the fastest water.

She had ceased to throw glances over her shoulder, looking ever in vain for Fire Cat. And how—after the debacle at Joara—was he ever to find her? As far as Night Shadow Star knew, no one had witnessed her abduction. What then would Fire Cat think when he finally arrived in Cofitachequi? That she had just up and vanished?

She chewed her lip, considering. If Fire Cat couldn't find her, eventually he would turn his tracks back to Cahokia. Seek her there. It was the one place she would ultimately return to.

That was right. She was certain of it. Finding neither the Lightning Shell witch nor her, he would assume she'd gone home. Searching for him, going back to Cofitachequi, seeking him along the river, would be futile.

Assuming he still lived. She had no proof that Fire Cat had survived after capsizing Blood Talon's canoe that long-ago day on the river. His corpse might be down there in the dark and moss, lying among the freshwater mussels, forgotten in Piasa's domain.

She had only Piasa's word that Fire Cat lived—not that she trusted the Spirit Beast. Power served its own interests, and it wouldn't have been beyond the Underwater Panther's spiteful nature to have drowned Fire Cat as punishment for her taking him into her bed.

Nor had Piasa been in her head, not even to torture her with his hissing threats. She'd barely had glimpses of the Spirit Beast ever since that night she'd been knocked on the head. Was that because of the blow? Or had the Underwater Panther been so disgusted with her failure, he'd abandoned her?

"Tell me, Lady," Chief Fire Light interrupted her reverie, "why did you give away all my Trade? Now we're destitute. How do we eat? How are we going to purchase our way down past the terrible rapids at the Suck and Rage? Or any of the other obstacles downriver?"

"We traded for nets, Chief. Your warriors carry bows and arrows. Mussels are plentiful on the shoals. With nets we can fish, with weapons we can hunt and shoot ducks and geese. Look along the bank. There, at the mouth of that creek. See the cattails? We can dig the roots to bake for bread. We're heading into late summer. Berries are ripening, fruits coming full and edible for the picking. Yellow lotus can be harvested from the backwaters and swamps. Every boulder and protruding log we pass is covered with turtles sunning themselves. How, in a land full of food, can we starve?"

He was watching her with a thoughtful expression. "Who do you expect to do this? You are a lady. I am a high chief of the Four Winds Clan's Morning Star House. My men are respected warriors. We do not do common labor, let alone scavenge for roots."

She held his eyes for a moment before turning back. Over her shoulder, she said, "Fine with me. You can starve. I will not."

Some communication passed between Bluefish and Made of Wood as they paddled on either side of her.

Apparently Fire Light wasn't going to let it rest, as he said, "You speak arrogantly for a captive, Cousin. But I promise you, I am a different kind than you are used to. You will not be escaping from my watch. And I owe you and your lineage. Blue Heron and Red Warrior Tenkiller ordered me exiled. That's your aunt and father. So I have no love for you."

"Escape is not my purpose," she told him. "I only need to kill my brother. Once that is done, I am free."

"You will not kill him. He is protected by the Thunderbirds. I saw. Back in Joara. Many tried to kill him. The Lightning Shell Witch cut their bodies apart and cooked them. He is too Powerful and protected."

"Then why is he cupping his balls and dribbling his water?"

From behind, Walking Smoke ordered, "She will not speak! At the next word, Chief, take your club and give her skull a rap or two."

Night Shadow Star chuckled. "Brother, Chief Fire Light has a problem. If he angers me, and you do not make it back to Cahokia, his exile will not be rescinded. If, on the other hand, I do make it back to Cahokia, and I am feeling grateful for his help on this journey, I will insist that the Morning Star lift his exile. So, how does Fire Light hedge his bets? What about his warriors?"

Again a look passed between Bluefish and Made of Wood.

"I told you to shut your mouth!" Walking Smoke snapped.

"How about it, Brother?" she asked. "These warriors have no wish to be caught between Sky and Underworld Power. What do they care if Piasa or the Thunderbirds win? You want to rape me, I want to kill you. It's a simple solution. Let us put in at the next beach. You and I each borrow a war club and go at each other."

When she looked back, Walking Smoke's gaze reminded her of smoldering embers. "I am no one's fool, Night Shadow Star. You are my prisoner, and until I am healed, and we are joined, you will remain that way. Chief Fire Light, take that cloth rag by your feet and gag her."

Fire Light lifted the rag. "It smells of fish guts and—"

"Gag her!"

"Bit by bit, you are losing yourself, Brother," she managed to say before the foul-tasting cloth was stuffed into her mouth and tied off at the back of her head. And to keep her from pulling it out of her mouth, the chief pulled her elbows back and bound them behind her.

In the process, however, Night Shadow Star got a good look at him. A deep and troubling hesitation lay behind her cousin's eyes, as if he were desperate to be anywhere rather than on the river, stuck between her and Walking Smoke.

From the half-panicked expressions of the paddling warriors, they were just plain terrified.

But what did that mean for her?

She stared out at the river. This was Piasa's domain. But where was the Water Panther? Normally he was a constant presence in her head, but since Joara?

Am I finally on my own?

Fifteen

When Matron Rising Flame issued her ultimatum that morning, Clan Keeper Spotted Wrist had no choice. The meeting on the canoe landing had begun poorly . . . and degenerated. Losing her temper, Rising Flame had ordered him—flat out—to return to central Cahokia. To be there that evening for a meeting in the Council House. Didn't matter that Spotted Wrist had warriors in the process of scouring their way down both banks of the Father Water in the few canoes they had left. The warriors' job was to hunt down and bring back each and every missing vessel. *Hunga Ahuito* alone knew how far the current had carried them. Or was still carrying them.

Then, in the midst of that confusion, Spotted Wrist was ordered back to the Council House?

As Spotted Wrist was carried past Night Shadow Star's vacant building, the baleful glare he gave the ornate palace should have charred the very thatch and plaster. He should have been irrevocably married to the woman before she journeyed off to the east. It should have been Clan Keeper Spotted Wrist who occupied that imposing residence, overlooking as it did the Great Plaza.

And where, by Piasa's swinging balls, was Blood Talon? The squadron first should have run the woman down and been back by now. Wasn't there anyone capable and competent that he could count on?

He pinched the bridge of his nose, as if it would kill the headache that had begun to build behind his eyes.

The sand-packed Avenue of the Sun was busy with people and dogs bearing loads. Didn't seem to matter that Spotted Wrist and his warriors had, for the most part, shut down imports from the canoe landing while they prepared for their attack on Evening Star Town. The great east-west artery that fed Cahokia remained crowded. Now, with the attack postponed, all the Traders who had been waiting up and down the river would be flocking to the canoe landing. Commerce would swell into a flood. Well, except for the howling Traders and Earth Clans who were missing their big canoes.

Cahokia, with its tens of thousands of people, was a voracious beast that consumed firewood, food, textiles, fibers, poles, clay, logs, thatch, oil, shell, sand, matting, tool stone, feathers, and luxury goods.

From the moment his litter had been carried past the huge Eagle guardian posts at the edge of River City, Spotted Wrist had passed an endless sprawl of temples, farmsteads, the occasional plaza, various society houses, charnel houses, burial mounds, workshops, warehouses, and granaries. The city never ceased to amaze him. In the span of his lifetime, he had seen Cahokia transformed from three large but separate villages to this single unified city. All these people, brought together by the miracle of the reincarnated god.

Why do I feel leadership slipping through my fingers?

On this day, he should have been watching his squadrons disappear up and down the river. He should have been pacing the beach with his remaining warriors, ready to leap into their canoes and paddle madly for the final assault on Evening Star Town. That last bastion of resistance had been all that stood between him and dominion over all of Cahokia.

Granted, he was forced to share authority with Rising Flame. She was, after all, the Clan Matron. Ultimately, he controlled the warriors, and he who controlled the military controlled the empire.

On those rare occasions when Morning Star made some proclamation, it would be a simple matter of acquiescing, showing his devout respect and obeisance to the living god. Engage in the rituals, ensure Morning Star was feted, feasted, and flattered, and all the while Spotted Wrist would be using the pageantry to ensure his own status and authority.

But for a few hiccups—like Night Shadow Star slipping through his fingers—it had all been falling into place.

Until this morning when his canoes had vanished.

Though he could admire the craft and skill by which it was done, Columella and all her House would have to pay. Though, to be sure, he rather enjoyed the sheer cheek of her having managed to burn the River House palace down right under Broken Stone's nose. Made him wonder how long the affable high chief would be breathing, given that Three Fingers was nearly apoplectic with rage.

And then there's my own problem.

Rising Flame. She'd been an ally—though not always an enthusiastic one. Lately, she'd been even less. As, for example, on that day when she'd stared down at Willow Blossom's body then given him that blank and emotionless stare.

The approach to the Great Stairway was crowded. Litters sat in a line, porters and messengers milling around. People squatting at—but not touching—the base of the great earthen pyramid. And across the avenue, what looked like a grudge match was being played on Morning Star's chunkey courts. A considerable crowd had gathered as a Bear Clan chief faced off against a Panther Clan rival. Hoots of either encouragement or derision, the cries of hawkers and Traders, and the shouts of those wagering on the outcome all created a chaos as the Bear Clan chief launched himself, rolled his stone, and cast just shy of the penalty line.

"Make way for Clan Keeper Spotted Wrist!" one his warriors called. "Make way!"

Because he was the Four Winds Clan Keeper, the crowd of nobles, messengers, and porters parted as if by magic, flowing back on all sides to allow Spotted Wrist's bearers to lower his litter immediately before the foot of the stairs.

Two guards, dressed in the impeccable armor of the Morning Star squadron, bowed their heads, touching their beaded forelocks respectfully. Their wood-and-leather armor had been polished to a sheen, their red war shirts spotless, wrist and arm guards decorated with feathers.

Spotted Wrist climbed to his feet, squinting against his headache as he gazed up the stairs. He could see the Council House roof rising above the palisade that surrounded the lower terrace of the Morning Star's great mound. Past it, the ramp and stairs led up to Morning Star's palace, with its soaring World Tree Pole and the hatchet-like roof with its carvings of *Hunga Ahuito*, Falcon, and Eagle.

Best to just get this over with.

Spotted Wrist forced himself to trot up the stairs. By the time he reached the top, he was winded, his heart thumping in his chest, his head throbbing. But, by pus and blood, with half of Cahokia watching from below, he'd be fried if he let them see the slightest weakness.

The two warriors at the Council Terrace's double gate—dressed in formal armor with feather splays on each shoulder—bowed, each touching his forehead in respect. Then Spotted Wrist stopped, glanced back at the sprawling Great Plaza, across the chunkey courts to the giant World Tree Pole, beyond the stickball field and Rides-the-Lightning's temple atop its earthen pyramid. Beside it stood the conical Earth Clans burial mound. From its side the Avenue of the Moon followed its causeway south to the eminence of the Rattlesnake Mound, then vanished to the southwest on its way to Horned Serpent town.

In all directions—except where water stood in the distant oxbows and barrow pits—lay the city. Temples and palaces atop their mounds were surrounded by thatch-roofed dwellings clustered around farmsteads and irregular plots of fields. Tens of thousands of humans. Smoke from their countless fires mixed with the haze to glow yellow-brown in the slanting sunlight.

I will own this, he promised himself. Then he stepped through the double gates and into the palisaded confines of the Council House Terrace plaza. The Council House itself stood against the western wall, a large ramada beside it. In the plaza's rear, the Morning Star's tall earthen pyramid slanted upward, its stairway rising to the high palisade. And beyond that, the Morning Star's World Tree jutted into the sky, soaring even higher than the Morning Star's steeply pitched thatch roof.

"Pus-dripping waste of time," Spotted Wrist muttered under his breath.

He should be back at the canoe landing, fixing the damage. His squadron firsts were good, but someone needed to be in overall command as the canoes were recovered. His squadrons needed to be kept busy, food and supply seen to, and his warriors motivated for the eventual attack on Evening Star Town. How was he supposed to do that while he was away in Cahokia attending a muck-and-rot "meeting" with a bunch of self-absorbed chiefs?

"This better be good, Clan Matron," he muttered as he stalked into the Council House. The place was hot, since it was midsummer, and to make matters worse, the fire was burning. Apparently for illumination of the Council House's dark interior.

Seated on the three clay daises behind the fire were Rising Flame, Lady Sun Wing, and—to Spotted Wrist's surprise—*Tonka'tzi* Wind. While Morning Star might be the living god and he whose word was law, the *Tonka'tzi*, or Great Sky, was the secular ruler of Cahokia. Or would have been were she not Spotted Wrist's hostage. *Tonka'tzi* Wind might be old, a direct descendant of Black Tail, aunt to Chunkey Boy and Night Shadow Star, and sister to the wretchedly dead lady Blue Heron, but these days she served only as a figurehead. *His* figurehead ever since he'd surrounded the *tonka'tzi*'s palace and marched a squad of his warriors in to take her prisoner.

The sixty-year-old woman studied him from across the fire and through slitted eyes. She reclined on her litter, her copper-clad staff of office in her veined, wrinkled hands. The starburst tattoos on her cheeks were faded, her broad mouth pinched. She wore her gray hair in a high bun that supported an eagle-plume headdress. A thin lace cape crafted from finely crocheted cottonwood down lay on her shoulders. Flat breasts hung down almost to the top of her high skirt, the latter woven of the finest dogbane and decorated with polished copper buttons.

From her lowest seat, crazy Lady Sun Wing watched him with eerily empty eyes. Her thin face had a half-vacant look. Her hair was up for once, combed, and with a swan-feather headdress. She wore a beautiful parakeet-feather cape, a skirt of intricately woven dogbane fiber, and high moccasins decorated with mica buttons. The woman's thin fingers kept stroking the Tortoise Bundle that she kept cradled in her lap.

The young woman's mind had been broken ever since Walking Smoke had held a knife to her throat to sacrifice her. Mostly she kept to herself, or spent time with the soul flier, Rides-the-Lightning. What was she doing here?

But, gods and pus, what was behind that weird stare she kept giving him? And he could barely hear the Song she murmured, something about the death of brothers. It sent a shiver down his souls.

Spotted Wrist shook off his apprehension, turning his attention to the other people in the room.

High Chief Green Chunkey, of the Horned Serpent House, stood to the left, his rotund belly jutting before him like the blunt end of a dugout canoe. He fingered a turkey-tail mace, one flaked from fine brown chert and then polished to a gleaming finish. His apron, the top obscured by his sagging belly, was white and dropped to a point between his knees. A fine repoussé copper headdress depicting a falcon adorned his high bun.

Three Fingers, looking half-apoplectic, had his muscular arms crossed. The man's hatchet of a face might have presaged thunder, his jaws clenched as if fit to chew obsidian. He wore his black hair in a simple bun, low at the back and pinned with a copper feather. A plain brown apron hung from the belt at his thin waist.

Finally, there was War Leader Five Fists, head of the Morning Star's personal security, nominal commander of the Morning Star squadrons, and—in Spotted Wrist's opinion—a perpetual irritant. The old warrior was leaning against the wall to one side. He watched Spotted Wrist with hard eyes, and rocked his crooked jaws.

Fixing on Rising Flame, Spotted Wrist took the offensive as he stopped just short of the fire. "I hope, Matron, that you have not called me here on some wild chase like boys after a skittering field mouse. You'd better have a stunningly good reason for dragging me away from my squadrons when I was in the—"

"Middle of a consummate disaster?" Rising Flame snapped, cutting him off. Behind her angry expression, firelight reflected from her black eyes. "You're supposed to be the Four Winds Clan Keeper. The person who hears in every corner, who knows the whisperings in the dark. The man with his fingers on Cahokia's very pulse. Despite that, on the eve of your attack on Columella, she manages to sneak who-knows-how-many warriors into River City, sets fire to a handful of warehouses, burns the River House palace to the ground, and sets all but a pitiful few of your canoes adrift in the Father Water. And you have no clue?"

"We'd have been better off with Blue Heron," Three Fingers muttered. "Even if she was an enemy. At least she knew what was going on in the city."

"Be glad I burned her alive," Spotted Wrist grumbled, and enjoyed the hardening of Wind's expression, reveled in the old woman's grinding of her teeth and the knotting of her fists.

"What matters," Green Chunkey declared, "is that as of today, it was supposed to be Evening Star House that was in ruins. Matron Columella's squadrons were supposed to have been broken, shattered, and fleeing, and the west side of the river pacified and brought back into the fold. Instead, she's stronger than ever."

"Not to mention," Three Fingers interjected, "that most of River City was already angry over the food levies we made to feed your warriors. And then there's the impact to Trade as you stopped up the canoe landing. Should I mention the general inconvenience to the artisans and craftspeople? Having half the warehouses—the palace itself!—burned has most of the population yelling for Round Pot and War Duck's return!"

"It wasn't *half* the warehouses. Just a handful. If you can't placate those few Traders and craftspeople, you're not going to be of much use to us when, and if, you take the high chair."

Three Fingers started to take a step forward, hesitated, fought to control his building anger.

Spotted Wrist raised his hands, trying to control the situation. "It will just be for as long as it takes my warriors to chase down those canoes," he insisted. "It's not as if the raiders sank them, or burned them. They just cast them loose into the current. It'll only be another few days."

"Another few days that I have to *feed* all your warriors!" Three Fingers rolled his eyes. "Are you as dense as a block of hickory, Keeper? This is already going to cost Broken Stone. I think we can salve the people's ill will by replacing him on the high chair."

Which was what you were seeking in the first place. Now you don't even need to drum up an excuse.

Three Fingers—looking heartbroken in a way he couldn't possibly feel—added, "Very well, let's say that we can buy some time by replacing Broken Stone. What does River City get in return?"

He looked around. "Do we receive additional food stocks like were given to Columella when the Cofitachequi stores were burned last spring?

We're taking the brunt of hosting all these warriors. They're eating our food. Do I hear Morning Star House, Horned Serpent House, or even the Keeper's own North Star House rushing to send us supplies?" He laughed bitterly. "No, all I hear is a deafening silence."

Spotted Wrist had enough, and thrust out his finger. "Stop your insipid whining!" And in a simpering falsetto voice, he mocked, "Too many warriors! My palace was burned! Somebody burned my warehouses! Ooh! They're eating my food!"

"That's gods-rotted enough," Rising Flame ordered, glaring first at Spotted Wrist and then at Three Fingers.

On her dais, *Tonka'tzi* Wind was struggling to keep a bitter smile from bending her lips.

Spotted Wrist gave a harsh laugh. "Three Fingers, you wouldn't *have* Morning Star House if it wasn't for me and my warriors. You'd still be a third cousin, marginalized, staring in from the outside as War Duck and Round Pot continued to skim wealth from the Trade coming through the canoe landing. Granted, now you can move on that moron, Broken Stone. But you wouldn't have even that opportunity without my squadrons having taken most of the city."

"I said, enough," Rising Flame insisted. "I won't say it again. This squabbling among us does no one any good. I called you all here so that we could put together a united front. With the debacle at River City and the loss of the canoes it's too easy for our enemies to move against us. Find cracks that they can lever into divides. All of Cahokia needs to be united."

"Horned Serpent House agrees." Green Chunkey stuck his thumbs into his belt. Then he glanced at Five Fists. "But where does Morning Star stand? Through all the changes and reorganization, the living god remains oddly quiet."

Five Fists shifted position. "The Morning Star has said nothing about the changes in leadership. I was only asked to observe. I offer you nothing beyond a warning, and it is my own, not Morning Star's: Do not let this burn out of control. If Columella and Evening Star Town have entrenched, find a way to bring her into the fold." He fixed his gaze on Spotted Wrist, one eye narrowing in emphasis. "Clan Keeper, you were a war leader before you were made Keeper, but you were never a fool. When it comes to war, you know just as well as I that once you have lost momentum, control of the ground, and advantage, it is time to withdraw, reassess, and re-form. As I see it, Columella now has the advantage. I don't think she will surrender it anytime soon." A pause. "I'd say the situation calls for diplomacy."

Spotted Wrist ground his teeth, felt the burn of bile in his gut. Crossing his arms, he struck a defiant pose. "With respect, War Leader, it has been years since you led squadrons. Sometimes, with advancing years, one's perspective becomes clouded. The raid on the canoes, while telling, is not permanent."

"You dream," Wind muttered, her stare hot enough to burn holes in Spotted Wrist's souls. "The current is in the process of scattering your precious canoes from here to down past the bluffs, maybe even to the Mother Water. Keep in mind that, as they come floating past, anyone on the river who encounters such a prize is going to lay claim to it. Hide it away. You think this is going to be solved quickly?"

Wind shifted to stare stone daggers at Rising Flame, and added, "And you thought *he* would be of more help to you than my sister?"

"This is all like the cackling of geese." Spotted Wrist almost spat the words. "I tell you, my warriors will have those canoes back within three days, four at the most. No one will stand against them when it comes to reclaiming them. I *Traded* for their use. That gives me priority over any silly fishermen who might stumble across one floating on the water."

"Four days, you say?" Rising Flame's expression had gone from doubtful to an infuriating and emotionless mask. "Let us hope you are correct."

"He won't be," Five Fists asserted. "But it will be amusing when I tell it to the Morning Star."

"I'd like to hear that myself," *Tonka'tzi* Wind mused.

"But you won't," Spotted Wrist snapped at her. "As soon as this council is over, my warriors are taking you right back to your palace, and you'll rotted stay there."

"Clan Matron," Wind said softly, a curiously mild expression behind her eyes, "you might want to consider what has been said here. What your options are. It is not too late."

"Open your mouth again," Spotted Wrist told her, "and you will *not* return to your palace. At least, not while your heart is still beating."

Rising Flame snapped, "Idiocy! Leave her alone. For the time being, we need every appearance we can get that we have the situation under control."

For the time being. Spotted Wrist let the words echo around the inside of his head. He gave Wind a mocking smile, full of promise.

That's when, for the first time, crazy Sun Wing's high voice broke out into laughter. She was staring fixedly at him, her slender fingers stroking the Tortoise Bundle. "Can you hear it, Lord Keeper?"

"Hear what, Lady?" Talking to her always sent quivers of unease up his spine.

"The Song? It's like a chime. It's the copper Singing to you. Caressing your Dreams. So close to your sleeping head. Do you Sing with it?"

He caught himself before he said something unkind. "I hear no copper Singing, Lady. I have other, more pressing concerns."

"Pity," she told him, her gaze going unfocused as if she were seeing through him to something beyond. "It's Singing your Death."

"What?" he cried. "Idiocy."

"Only for he who cannot find it," she replied in a distracted voice, then turned her attention to the Tortoise Bundle in her lap, Singing,

"Sun children . . . kill each other.
Long way south for the death of a brother.
Hot, dry, war is nigh.
Sing Sun God, blood rises . . . stingers in the Sky."

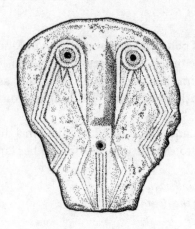

The Fasting in My Blood

I watch the flames leap up from the fire one of Chief Fire Light's warriors made with old driftwood. A lot of it has been piled up at the high-water mark by some long-forgotten flood.

Around me, the warriors are sullen, hungry. They sit crouched around the fire, some seated on the canoes where they are pulled up on the bank. They avoid my eyes. They always have. Back in Joara, they feared me. Now, I am not sure what they think. If I were not their only way back to Cahokia, back to family and friends, I think they would slip away into the darkness, one by one.

I know they hate even being close to me, and those who must paddle in my canoe are the worst. Constantly shrinking away, as if terrified they might brush against me.

The Trader Six Toes has separated himself, making his own fire at the end of the gravel bar. I am sure that given his choice in the matter, he would go back, refuse our Trade at Willow Stem Village, and maybe even wish he'd never landed there in the first place.

High Chief Fire Light is down at the Trader's fire, talking over some problem with Six Toes. I see the chief's hands gesturing, as if trying to smooth something over. The Trader shakes his head, glances uneasily my direction, and a sour expression crosses his face.

What are they plotting?

Doesn't matter. I have convinced Chief Fire Light that not only am I his only chance to be pardoned; he knows I have taken possession of pieces of his souls. If he betrays me in any way, I will shrivel his life soul, darken it, sicken it, and wind it out of his rotting body with a spindle whorl.

At the edge of the gravel bar, the dark waters of the river remind me of flow-

ing black oil, the surface faintly reflecting the waning moon. The shimmers of light on the inky water Dance and play, then vanish as if sucked away into the darkness. Devoured. Gone.

I stare up at the night sky where it is visible through the patchwork of branches. Cottonwoods and overcup oak line the bank here. Crickets sing in the forested slough behind our camp, barely audible through a cacophony of frogs.

Frogs. Vile things. Underworld creatures. And, even more to my dismay, when Chief Fire Light escorted my sister back into the swampy vegetation and out of sight of the others to attend to her toilet, the woman came back with no fewer than three bullfrogs that she had skewered with a sharp stick during her "sojourn."

Also, as she'd promised that day in the canoe, she'd kept them to herself. Pulled off the legs, extended them over the fire on sticks, and slowly roasted them.

While the warriors devoured watery and too-small portions of our last corn gruel, Night Shadow Star sank her teeth into the succulent frogs' legs. Then she tossed the stripped bones into the fire to sizzle and char.

The smell of it almost drove me insane.

Now she sits back on a half-buried log, gaze locked with mine across the fire. The flames leap and reflect in her dark eyes, as if she's staring at me from the Underworld itself.

If it wasn't for my wound, I would walk over and beat her half-senseless with one of the sticks of firewood.

I try to make sense of it. Ever since my brother exiled me from Cahokia all those long years ago, I have been in love with my sister. Deep love. Total love. The kind of love that exists as an ache within a man's bones. She is the other half of my soul, as if that part of me was left behind when I was born. That had to wait in mother's womb. As Night Shadow Star grew in our mother's belly, that part of me was absorbed. That has to be why I love her so.

I have lusted after other women, even sexually used them when I was in the process of sacrificing them during various ceremonies. Sometimes I just couldn't help myself, though doing so ruined the very Power and visions I was trying to conjure.

But I've only loved Night Shadow Star.

Once, to prove my worth to Power, I even tried to kill her as an offering. Why? Because killing her was the most pure and supreme sacrifice I could make. She was worth more to me than my life.

And still Power denied me and let her escape.

For whatever reason, nothing that I ever plan with regard to Night Shadow Star ever works the way it is supposed to. I need only try to stand up straight to be reminded of that ugly fact.

All of which gives me pause as I try and dominate her loathing stare across the flames. She doesn't even flinch. I see no give. She knows I must win. That I have no choice. In the end, if I am to become my destiny—be the Wild One, who finally defeats Morning Star and remakes the world—I have to mate my Power with hers. There is simply no other way.

As if in agreement, I hear the distant booming of thunder somewhere off to the west.

If any of the others hear it, they show no sign. Instead, all the warriors seem antsy, and one by one, they mutter something under their breaths and drift off to their blankets. I can feel their growing frustration.

I will no doubt have to deal with that. Perhaps cut someone's throat and eat his liver? But keeping the warriors in line will wait.

Tonight, it is only Night Shadow Star and I, staring at each other over the dying fire.

Sixteen

In the Spirit Dream, Night Shadow Star blinks her eyes and stares up at a clear and soot-black night sky. Myriads of stars, like a soft frost, make patterns in the vast black. The pale band of the Road of the Dead glows from one tree-thick horizon to the other; the southern constellation of Horned Serpent—who rises from the Underworld to guard the entrance to the Road of the Dead—gleams and twinkles. The bright red star that marks the Spirit Beast's head sparkles wickedly.

She lies on her back, her bedding laid out on soft sand beside the Upper Tenasee. She knows this place. It is the camp on a gravel bar beside the river.

Lifting her head, Night Shadow Star sees a blue glow down in the dark river where it laps against the gravel bar. The black waves lick at the shore like ink, caress the Trade canoe's stern where it touches the water.

Almost with relief she senses Piasa's presence. "Where have you been, Lord?"

And after so long an absence, why had he come now?

Crickets fill the night. In the distance, an owl hoots, and a whippoorwill answers with a *kureeee* call from somewhere back in the night-shadowed forest.

Around her, Chief Fire Light's warriors sleep deeply, souls lost in Dreams. They lay wrapped in their blankets, weapons close at hand. And behind them, next to the dying embers in the fire pit, her brother appears to be frozen where he's propped against a log cast high on the bank by a flood. His head is back, his mouth open. Both the mass of scar tissue marring his face and his wounded crotch reflect an eerie luminescence, like the dying embers in the fire.

Wounds made by Power. The words are whispered from the edge of the river.

Turning her head, she sees Piasa as the Spirit Beast slips from the depths, water slicking soundlessly from the panther hair on his sides. He fixes her with yellow eyes, the pupils like holes into an infinity of midnight. The three-fork-design of the Underworld surrounds the beast's eyes and extends down its cheeks. Red antlers rise from the cougar's head and contrast with the pink nose and stiff whiskers; when the beast bares its teeth, the fangs are white, long, and sharp.

As it emerges from the river, mighty raptor wings unfold from the beast's back, the feathers striped and barred. Instead of cougar paws, the monster walks on yellow eagle's feet. Long talons curl down into the sandy gravel with each step. Behind, a snake's tail whips back and forth, rattles, flicks water this way and that.

The beast's gaze flashes to Walking Smoke. "I thought you were going to kill him."

"I was. Would have." She inclined her head to the blanket-wrapped warriors on all sides. "He has allies."

The yellow eyes fix back on her, and the tail whips back and forth, the rattles shaking. "Perhaps Night Shadow Star has grown too arrogant and proud? Too full of her own sense of importance? You are not invincible, you poor frail woman, as your capture should have demonstrated. No, you are nothing more than a—"

"I *will* kill him! And then, master, you will give me Fire Cat. You can have your Power back, and I will no longer be yours. Fire Cat and I will go away. I will no longer be Lady Night Shadow Star. The balance between Sky and Underworld will be restored."

"Too late," Piasa says, the yellow eyes thinning to slits. "You had your chance. Power is changing. I can no longer gamble that you will somehow kill your brother. Other steps must be taken."

"What steps?" she demanded.

"Time to keep that balance you're so concerned with. A brother for a brother? If you had killed him at Joara, I might have been able to set you and Fire Cat free. A decision has been made. The balance will be kept. Events in Cahokia make it necessary that you return. You will find the Lightning Witch there."

"Return to Cahokia?" She knotted her fists and rose from her blanket, her binding thongs snapping as she did so. "He's right here! Where is Fire Cat? That was the deal. I kill my brother, and then Fire Cat and I are free to—"

"Do you think the Thunderbirds will allow you to just walk up behind the witch, pick up an oar, and brain their favorite gaming piece?"

Piasa thrusts his head forward, the pink nose not a hand's width from hers. His breath smells of death. "Power is at play, you putrid little woman. With Walking Smoke still alive, events in Cahokia now change the game. That which is Sky, must become Sky. That which is Underworld, must be Underworld."

"I don't understand."

"As long as you are in Walking Smoke's presence, the Thunderbirds will not allow you to kill him, and I cannot protect you. Power is stalemated. The only hope is to retreat, withdraw, and see how the gaming pieces are cast in Cahokia. We are not beaten yet, Night Shadow Star. But it will be a very closely run contest. There is one chance to save your city—and perhaps your beloved Fire Cat. The fate of the living god is now set. His decision is made. *Hunga Ahuito* and Old-Woman-Who-Never-Dies have made their will clear. What must be, must be."

"Wait! What do you mean? I don't understand what you're—"

"At that last moment, Night Shadow Star, you must face your brother. Alone. Fire Cat has to save the Morning Star, take him to the healer. Or all is lost. Do you understand?"

"What do you mean, Fire Cat has to save Morning Star? I don't—"

"Sleep, Night Shadow Star."

Piasa begins to fade, the river oily, dark, and rising like a black mist to . . .

Hard hands brought Night Shadow Star awake. She jerked, sucking a breath to scream, only to have a rag jammed into her mouth and a heavy body press down on hers. The sandy gravel beneath absorbed her struggles. Fear made her gasp against the gag being thrust deeper against her tongue.

"Shhh." Lips were pressed against her ear, and she blinked at the darkness. She was on the gravel bar, her legs and arms still tied. She could see the dark forms of sleeping warriors where they lay in their blankets. The man pressing her down was big, heavy, his body warm against hers.

"Not a sound," the voice warned in a barely audible hiss. "If you do, I swear, that whack I gave you at Joara will be like a love tap. Do you understand?"

Night Shadow Star nodded, her heart hammering at her ribs.

"Don't try to scream. Don't fight. This is for your own good, Lady."

With remarkable alacrity, Made of Wood shifted onto his knees. Strong arms encircled her, cradled her, and lifted. Two dark figures followed as she was carried stealthily down toward the water.

What in pus were they doing? Going to toss her into the midnight river to drown?

She was on the verge of screaming into the gag when the flickers of ghostly blue shimmered beneath the water's surface, and in their passing, outlined the shape of the five-man canoe where it floated, held by another dark figure. She could hear the hissing as Piasa whispered *Yes* behind her ear. She craned her head, trying to see the beast, but was blocked by Summer Ice's bulk.

Images from the Dream replayed in her mind's eye. Piasa had been here, stood right here beside the canoe.

"We've got her," Made of Wood whispered.

"Good," someone answered from the stern of the canoe. "Quietly, now. We can't make a sound."

Barely sloshing, the men waded out and carefully deposited Night Shadow Star amidships. Dark forms pushed the vessel out into the current before leaping on board. Not missing a beat, paddles were lifted and stroked to turn the craft toward the current.

"Can't see a pus-rotted thing out here," Bluefish whispered.

"Don't need to," Made of Wood told him. "We just need to follow the thread. And you can see the barest silhouette of the trees on either side. Use them for a reference. Trust me."

Against the gag, Night Shadow Star made a muffled, "Nufft nuh mfft."

"You going to scream?" Bluefish asked from behind her.

She shook her head with enough exaggeration that she hoped he could make it out in the darkness.

Even as the warrior leaned forward and removed the cloth, she could see the faint flicker of blue light down in the depths, keeping pace with the gliding canoe.

Piasa. Absent for so long, that presence of her master, once so dreaded, was almost like a balm to her souls. But the Spirit Beast's words confused her.

I have to get back to Cahokia? I can't kill Walking Smoke now?

She made a face, spat the taste left by the gag over the side. "What are we doing?"

"Getting you away from the witch," young Field Snake told her from up in front. "Saving ourselves. Now you belong to us. We're hoping that holding you keeps us alive. Gets us home."

"I didn't need saving. I was there to kill him. Would have if I hadn't been tied up all the time."

"Nice family you've got," Bluefish muttered.

The other warriors grunted in agreement.

Twisting around, Night Shadow Star tried to get a glimpse of their camp, only to find it hidden in the darkness. Given her brother's temper, her absence was going to make for a most unpleasant morning for those left behind.

"So, you want to go back?" Field Snake asked in amazement.

"No. For whatever reason, Piasa says I should go with you. That we have to get to Cahokia."

"Piasa?" Bluefish asked. "You mean, *the* Piasa?"

"She's joking," Summer Ice told them condescendingly. "No one talks to the Underwater Monster and lives."

"No, warrior, they don't," Night Shadow Star snapped back. "You don't know what you've gotten yourselves into, do you? You think the good High Chief Fire Light came to an accord with Walking Smoke to get you home? That you were just dealing with a soul-sick witch who happens to be a twisted Morning Star House noble?" She laughed bitterly. "You poor fools. You're in the middle of a war."

"What war?" Made of Wood now sounded unsure of himself.

"I had a husband, War Leader Makes Three. All of you would have been exiled by the time he led a battle walk up north against Red Wing Town. The Red Wing squadrons ambushed him, killed him, and threw his body into the river as an offering to Piasa. I was in mourning, couldn't stand the grief. I sent my souls to the Underworld to find him."

"You sent your souls where?" Bluefish sounded skeptical.

"Are you deaf? The Underworld. I was Dancing with Sister Datura," she told him. "Soul flying. I didn't care if I lived or died as long as I could find Makes Three's lost souls. I wanted to be with him. Feel his arms around me again. Stop the loneliness, the pain and grief."

"How did you escape?" Made of Wood sounded skeptical. "Even the best soul fliers, no matter how skilled, don't make it back every time. Some are caught, their souls trapped or eaten."

"Piasa was waiting. Used Makes Three as a lure. You get it? The last I remember was my skull crushing between Piasa's jaws. The beast devoured my souls. Consumed me. I *belong* to him. When he finally let my souls return to my body, I came back as *his* creature." She glared in the darkness. "He's *inside* me, High Chief. All the time. And tonight he's whispering in my ears."

"Really?" Summer Ice muttered. "Now I've heard everything."

"No. You haven't." Night Shadow Star shifted. "Cut these bindings loose. I'm a fair hand with a paddle."

"Do you think we're idiots?" Field Snake asked.

"Given that you made a deal with Walking Smoke to begin with, and after making off with me your fate is sealed should either Fire Light or my twisted brother ever catch you? I guess I'd have to say yes to that. Now, cut me loose."

"For all we know, you'll take the first chance to escape." Made of Wood was paddling in the rear.

"Not in the slightest," she told him. "Piasa tells me the game is changed. Something's happening in Cahokia."

"Piasa tells you this?"

"He does. Now, I give you my word as the Lady Night Shadow Star,

I will not bash your heads in with a paddle. You help me get to Cahokia, fastest, and I will make sure Morning Star revokes your banishment. On, my honor, I swear."

"I will probably live to regret this," Summer Ice muttered under his breath. "Go ahead, Bluefish, cut her free."

Night Shadow Star felt her bonds part under the warrior's sharp chert knife. She rubbed her wrists, then reached down to pull at the knots on her ankles. She could feel Bluefish's tension, knew he was ready to leap on her at a moment's notice. Then she felt around, found the paddle, and shifted to the side, where she began stroking, driving the canoe along in the darkness.

Fire Cat, my love, where are you?

He could be anywhere, futilely seeking her in Cofitachequi. Wandering aimlessly in the immensity that was the east. Would he know enough to return to Cahokia? And if or when he did, what would he find? That she was Spotted Wrist's wife? Forcefully taken, married off at the will and pleasure of the clan matron?

Before that happens, I will kill Spotted Wrist myself, she promised.

Piasa had hinted that things would be different after she dispatched her brother. But now, with the Spirit Beast's blessing, she'd been snatched away. The future was suddenly a confusing place, her role uncertain.

"What game are you playing at, master?" she muttered to herself.

The soft blue glow that paced them down in the depths didn't deign to answer.

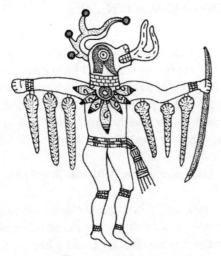

Seventeen

The canoe in which the Trader, Shell Hook, arrived at Willow Stem Village was a serviceable craft—if not a racy beauty like the bald-cypress canoes crafted by the master builders in the lower reaches of the Father Water. Whoever had found the hickory trunk from which it was made had lucked into a straight-grained specimen with only a few knot holes. The builder had also been as patient as Old-Woman-Who-Never-Dies, since it must have taken a couple of years to burn, chip, sand, and finish to shape the unforgiving wood.

As heavy as hickory was, the canoe-builder had compensated; the tough straight grain had allowed him to thin the canoe's sides to reduce weight without compromising integrity.

Four body-lengths long—and just shy of seating two people abreast—the craft was designed for shallow draft here on the upper river. Shell Hook—though not the most demanding of Traders—had driven a hard bargain. He would only carry Fire Cat and his party down as far as the mouth of the Wide Fast River and its confluence with the Tenasee.

From there, Fire Cat, Winder, and Blood Talon would have to find another vessel to continue their journey.

"It's better than nothing," Winder confided as they paddled headlong with the current. "Besides, now that we're on the river, the farther down-stream we go, the more chances there are of running into someone with a better, faster canoe. Someone who will take us all the way to Canyon Town above the Suck and Rage."

"And then?"

"Then all we have to do is get to Big Cane Village below the Mussel

Shallows. From there, I have a canoe that might not be as fast as the *Red Reed* was when it brought you upriver, but I have more people to paddle it."

"Assuming we haven't caught up with Night Shadow Star." Fire Cat drove his paddle deep, propelling them forward. The green wall of willows, brush, and cottonwoods lining the shore seemed to fly past. "Maybe she's killed him. Or she's driven him to kill her. Maybe they're both dead."

"Thought Piasa took care of her," Blood Talon called from where he paddled behind.

"That's what worries me," Fire Cat replied. "Belonging to the Spirit Beast is no blessing. Power almost got her killed when she tried to drown Walking Smoke in the Father Water. It gave her to the Itza to marry, drug, and abuse. It sent her souls down into the Underworld to rescue Morning Star's souls. Then it sent her here to kill Walking Smoke, and we all know how that is turning out. She has always won. Which is why Piasa keeps her. But one of these times she isn't going to be so lucky. As soon as she has no value, Power will discard her. When it does, I have to be there for her."

Winder's muscles flexed under tanned skin as he paddled, his movements those of a man long schooled in the practice. "Sometimes you confuse me, Red Wing. You're known as being a heretic, yet you abide by the ways of Power."

"It's not Power that I doubt. It's this whole nonsense that Morning Star exists in Chunkey Boy's body."

"Thought you rescued him that time when the Spirit moth carried him away to the Underworld. That you went to the Sacred Cave, saved his souls, and carried them back to his palace," Blood Talon reminded. "Coming home from the north, we all thought that story was a bit far-fetched."

"I was there," Fire Cat told him. "Down in the darkness with my lady in the depths of the Sacred Cave. I was surrounded by the souls of the Dead. Face to face with Horned Serpent and the Spirits of the Underworld. That was real."

He made a face. "As to the rest? Since then I have come to wonder. Consider this: If you were Chunkey Boy and selling yourself as the reincarnated god, every now and then you'd need to refresh the hoax. Keep the gullible fools believing. Enact another miracle to ensure the thriving masses in Cahokia remain awed by your supposed godhood."

"Then how do you think he pulled it off?" Winder asked. "I was in Cahokia while all that was going on. Wouldn't have got out of it alive if Seven Skull Shield hadn't saved me."

Fire Cat used his paddle to steer them away from a partially sunken log. "Chunkey Boy might have had one of those priests orchestrate the entire farce. Whisper the story into our ears as our souls were Dancing with Sister Datura."

Fire Cat turned, taking the moment to stare back at his friends. "Just because I believe that Power exists, that my lady is possessed by Piasa and Underworld Power, doesn't mean that Chunkey Boy can't perpetrate a fraud for his own purposes. He was a master manipulator as a boy. Why wouldn't he continue to be when people believe him to be a god?"

"So," Winder said wryly, "you're still a heretic?"

"Only when it comes to Chunkey Boy." Fire Cat leaned into his stroke as he drove the canoe forward.

"Does Morning Star know this?" Blood Talon asked warily.

"Chunkey Boy does. I have no clue about Morning Star, he's somewhere up in the Sky World."

"So, tell me, what does your lady say about this?" Winder asked.

"She is amused." Fire Cat smiled at the memory. "And before you ask, yes. She believes that Morning Star's Spirit has taken possession of Chunkey Boy. That her brother's souls are dead, consumed by the living god."

Fire Cat paused. "In a way, it makes sense. It starts with the defeat of Petaga and the Morning Star suddenly shining bright in the daytime sky. In a bid to solidify his leadership, Black Tail orchestrates the whole elaborate ritual, sacrifices Petaga and most of his lineage in a lavish ceremony. In one blow any chance for retaliation by Petaga's descendants is eliminated."

Fire Cat paused to drift them left into a faster current.

"There were what? A hundred and fifty of them? Not to mention the bundled skeletons of Petaga's ancestors from the charnel house. Petaga and his mother and sisters are laid on a shell blanket that tells the story of Morning Star's reincarnation. Meanwhile, he's in his own temple, fasting, sweating, praying. Then, as the Morning Star fades, Black Tail supposedly arises, possessed of the Morning Star's Spirit drawn down from the sky."

"That takes a lot of daring," Blood Talon muttered.

Winder told him, "But it plays right into the concept of soul quickening, of calling the ancestors to inhabit the bodies of our living."

Fire Cat added, "Through magicians' tricks Black Tail simulates a couple of miracles and poof! Suddenly he's the living god."

"But his family would know the difference," Winder replied with a dogged insistence.

"Maybe they did in the beginning. But after all these years, given the authority and privilege it has given them, it's easier to believe that Morning Star really is reincarnated in Chunkey Boy's body."

Blood Talon exhaled nervously. "I've been up there, in that palace. You ask me, that's the living god sitting there. I get nervous just being in the same room. I can feel the Power. Like a crackling when he enters the room."

"So," Fire Cat asked, "you really believe that's the mythical hero from the Beginning Times? The one born of First Man and First Woman who gambled his life against that of the giants? The same giants who murdered his father, First Man, after he bet his life against theirs in a chunkey game? The Morning Star who grew up, challenged those same giants to chunkey, and won? The Morning Star who cut off the giants' heads and used Power to bring his father back to life? Then, battling against his brother, the Wild One, that is the same Morning Star who helped form Creation before being elevated to the Sky World to sit just below *Hunga Ahuito*? Do you really think the mythical hero who did all that could come back and inhabit a frail human body? Hmm?"

"Well . . ." Blood Talon hesitated.

"Maybe Morning Star can be human," Winder insisted. "It's Power. Maybe spending that long just floating in the sky is boring. You, and a bunch of barbarian nations, can scoff all you want. Maybe Morning Star *does* live in Chunkey Boy's body."

Blood Talon added, "Thousands of thousands of people *believe*. Belief is Power, Red Wing. All you need to do is stand on the heights at Evening Star Town or up on the eastern bluffs and look across the sprawling extent of Cahokia."

Winder hastened to say, "I grew up in Cahokia. I've walked across it, from the Moon Mounds in the eastern prairie all the way down the Avenue of the Sun. Then I've been ferried to Evening Star Town and walked to the western forest. It took me two and a half days. Through constant city. And that's not counting from Serpent Woman Mounds in the north to Horned Serpent town in the south. I've seen the endless streams of the dirt farmers coming to share in the miracle. Hasn't stopped, either. People are still picking up entire villages and moving to Cahokia."

"And they all believe," Blood Talon agreed. "Can tens of tens of thousands of people be wrong? Or does that amount of belief make it true?"

"I don't have an answer for you," Fire Cat admitted. "I was raised a skeptic. Sometimes, even I start to believe. And then that part of me that questions begins to pick at the edges. I look at Chunkey Boy, sitting there on that raised dais in the palace; but when I peer past the face paint and gaudy jewelry, I see Chunkey Boy, smug, playing the part while women throw themselves at him, and feasts are laid before him. That's when I ask myself, if you were him, why wouldn't you play the role of a god?"

He was aware of the skeptical look that passed between Blood Talon and Winder, but neither deigned to answer.

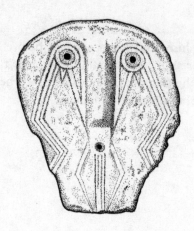

Inferno

I awakened to an almost empty beach. The five-man canoe, Night Shadow Star, and a couple of the dugouts are gone. I have only the Trade canoe left, my good cousin Fire Light, a handful of warriors, and that weasel-like Six Toes. Now the Trader watches me, sitting, arms crossed, on the gunwale of his canoe. Something like amusement lies behind his eyes. I'd murder him, flay his corpse, and scry the future as the blood pooled in his rib cage, but I need him and the few who are left to paddle the canoe.

High Chief Fire Light avoids my gaze, glowers at his remaining warriors. They look cowed in return, insisting they knew nothing of the plot by Made of Wood, Summer Ice, and that sniveling Field Snake.

The remaining warriors leaped awake at the sound of my first howl of rage. Gawking around, they took in the empty gravel bar, the missing canoes, and without a word, some grabbed up what they could and bolted for the willows.

Only my bellowing call: "I have pieces of your souls! Stop, or I'll turn your livers into pus! I'll curse your shafts and stones. I'll call maggots down from on high to eat holes in your hearts! You'll die just like those wretches in Joara!"

That stopped them cold. They returned crestfallen and afraid. So, I am left with the Trader, Fire Light, and his second, Flat Arrow—who is about as lazy as he is flabby around the middle. The man has all the smarts of a five-year-old and even less ambition. Then there is skinny old Four Braids with his bad left leg, and finally Twists His Hair. He's a small man with snake tattoos on his arms. And there are five others. Enough to drive the Trade canoe in rapid pursuit of Night Shadow Star and her errant warriors.

It is only a matter of time.

As my anger exhausts itself, I am left hollow, panting, my heart pounding dully in my chest.

Morning sunlight slants across the mountains to the east, sending bars of light through the river mist. The gods-accursed birds are singing cheerfully as they greet the sunrise. Happy idiots! I'd blast them to charred feathers and crisped flesh with a lightning bolt if I could.

Same with the chirring insects and the other creatures flitting about on diaphanous wings. All without a care while I stand there frustrated to my bones. Alone. Where but a few mere hands of time past, I was in my glory. Victorious in all but my joining with Night Shadow Star—and that was but a matter of time.

So, who was the instigator of the warriors' treason? Was it their idea to spirit Night Shadow Star away in the night? Or had that been her doing? Had she been eating away at their loyalty, hinting at rewards that would be theirs, or perhaps—and I find this notion totally enraging—even offering to warm their shafts?

If I discover it's the latter, I'll make their end an epic of pain and horror the likes of which I've never inflicted on human beings.

I can see the doubt building behind Fire Light's eyes. As if he is considering this to be my *failure.*

This is the trouble with people. They're weak, conniving, and have no respect for their betters. Who is my cousin to question me, of all people? Not only am I from a more exalted lineage, but I've overcome much more daunting obstacles on my path to greatness. He wasn't chosen by the Thunderbirds.

Unlike me, Fire Light would have let it all go to his head. He would never have accepted the burden with the same humility that I have.

I stomp around, shaking my fist and uttering curses as I look in vain for lightning from the clear morning sky. I shout and plead that it blast down from the heavens and strike Made of Wood, Night Shadow Star, and all those scurrilous and cowardly warriors.

But the golden morning remains frustratingly tranquil.

"Pus-eating maggots!" I spit. Then stalk over and kick through the belongings left behind. There are a couple of worn blankets, a sack of corn meal, and a cracked brownware pot.

Six Toes, of course, still has his Trade in the big canoe. He continues to watch me, his face impassive. Apparently the fool thinks that our deal—made under the Power of Trade—binds him to get me downriver.

I make a face, and use the brownware pot to scoop water out of the river, drop in a handful of corn meal, and drink it down.

"All right, let's be gone," I order, figuring the others have had their chance to eat when I did.

"You heard the man. Let's go hunt them down," Fire Light says.

Flat Arrow blinks stupidly, brow furrowing as he walks over. Then Six Toes and the others bend their backs as I throw the last of our possessions into the craft and wade out into the river.

My testicles ache, my groin stitched with pain, as I leap over the gunwale. Gasping, I find my seat. Picking up a paddle, I stroke it forward as Six Toes steers us into the current.

Eighteen

Night Shadow Star wondered if the difference was being free of Walking Smoke. Once on the river—her Sky Power–possessed brother left behind—Piasa seemed to be everywhere, whispering behind her ear, his blue gleam slipping along beneath their current-fast canoe.

They were making headway, and though the vessel might not have been as fast as *Red Reed*, or as quick handling, the current did most of the work.

"So, Lord, what does it mean?" she asked. "First I am told to race east to kill Walking Smoke, only to fail. But I leave him too crippled for him to consummate this incestuous rape that will give him access to Underworld Power. Then, I am whisked away and sent hurrying downriver?"

"*Power has changed.*" The Spirit Beast's hiss came from behind her ear.

"Changed how?"

"*The Morning Star has wearied of the game.*"

"This is no game, Lord. I have served you, done your bidding. If nothing else, I have kept Walking Smoke from winning from the very beginning. If you wanted him dead, why send me into Joara alone?"

"*Things unforeseen,*" the beast rasped hoarsely. "*Humans. Interfering, changing. What should be simple becomes muddled. Unpredictable. Even you, Night Shadow Star.*" A pause. "*Only the Red Wing remains a constant.*"

Mist drifted in a pale veil above the swirling and sucking water; slanting light shot through the treetops, sending golden bars through the dark haze as the sun rose inexorably above the distant mountains to the east. The moist odor of mud and vegetation hung in the air.

"Lady?" Bluefish asked cautiously. "Are you all right?"

"I have a Spirit Beast in my head, how can I be all right?"

"That was Piasa you were talking to?" Made of Wood asked from his seat in the rear. "We kept asking you, but you didn't seem to hear."

"It happens that way," she told him absently, Piasa's words echoing in her head. "Power's changed," she whispered.

Once again she was in a chase. With the realization, she smiled. Last time it was Blood Talon against Fire Cat, and now it would be her wits against Walking Smoke's. She knew the river, had been hunted before. Her brother had not.

She glanced back at the warriors. "You know that if they catch us, you will all die horribly."

Their heads bobbed, expressions grim.

She laughed bitterly. "Now, here I am, surrounded by desperate warriors. Let me guess. This 'rescue' you've orchestrated, it's not all about the nobility in your nature, is it? No, I'd guess that in your figuring, I've just changed one set of captors for another. Instead of Walking Smoke holding the lady Night Shadow Star captive for evil purposes, now the four of you believe you have a hostage that will make you wealthy."

"Lady," Made of Wood told her, "we just want to go home." A pause. "And, like we said, some of us didn't like the way the Lightning Shell witch was going to use you."

"Doesn't mean we don't have our own interests," Summer Ice added, his eyes refusing to meet hers.

Up front, Field Snake was giggling to himself as he paddled. Something about the sound of it set her teeth on edge.

"Now that we have you away from that hideous brother of yours," Bluefish added, "we might like something in the way of compensation."

"Really?" she asked dryly. "Wonder what that might be?"

"Lady like you," Bluefish shot back, "bet you'll think of something."

"Bet I will," Night Shadow Star agreed, a tightening in her gut. "But here is how it lines out: Walking Smoke, Fire Light, and the rest will be on the water by now. You know my brother. He's going to be in a rage. You've taken his prize from him, and he's going to want to pay you all back. Me? As long as his shaft hangs limp and his stones are aching, I'm going to be fine. I'll just be his prisoner again and wait for the moment he makes a slip. Then I'll kill him. I'll have fulfilled my duty to the Underwater Lord."

"Then what?" Bluefish asked. "You think Fire Light will just let it go? The witch was his only hope to get back to Cahokia."

"Only if Walking Smoke wins in the end," she countered. "To do that, he would have to kill the Morning Star. Take control of Cahokia. Or didn't he tell my good cousin the whole story? Walking Smoke murdered our father, *Tonka'tzi* Red Warrior, tried to murder Morning Star, and cut our sister Lace's throat before slicing her unborn baby from her womb. He'd be long dead, but for the Thunderbirds rescuing him from the depths of the Father Water. Didn't tell you that, did he?"

No one spoke.

Then Made of Wood asked, "Seriously?"

"Quite. What else would drag me—the *tonka'tzi*'s niece—halfway across the world to kill him? I told you last night, you're in the middle of a war. Knowing that, you have a decision to make: You can trust me to take charge. Follow my orders, and I will do my best to get you home to Cahokia. In addition, I will reward you handsomely."

"And what if we don't?" young Field Snake scoffed. "You're worth a fortune in ransom."

"I capsize the canoe when it will be the most disadvantageous for you. You will all drown."

"So will you," Bluefish growled.

She laughed in return. "Me? Oh, no. I'm protected by Piasa's Power. Are any of you?"

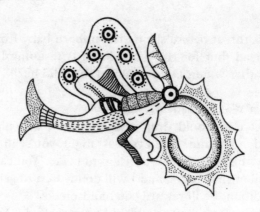

Nineteen

Evening Star Town dominated the high bluff on the western side of the river. Blue Heron was forever forgetting just how high the bluff was. As she and Seven Skull Shield—accompanied by Farts—climbed, she huffed and panted. The joint in her hip was aching. Her feet hurt. A slight wheeze could be heard in her lungs as she labored up the dirt swale from the west-bank canoe landing.

The two-headed *Hunga Ahuito* guardian posts marked the edge of town. As she passed between them, she touched her forehead reverently. Seven Skull Shield ignored them, of course. Nor did the thief notice when the big dog lifted his leg and peed on one.

Why hasn't Power struck that flea-infested creature dead? Blue Heron wondered.

They made their way between the clan houses, temples, and Deer Clan charnel house with its cloying odor of decomposing bodies.

"I always hate this climb," she declared.

"I could carry you." Seven Skull Shield shot her a sidelong look. "Or at best, tow you the rest of the way. Maybe hook up a harness and let Farts drag you all the way to Columella's palace."

"I'd rather be skinned alive and tanned into a parfleche," she growled between labored breaths.

Dragged by Farts? She gave the bearlike dog a disdainful glance from the corner of her eye. The beast was panting happily in the heat, tail swishing, his nose working. Farts turned his odd blue-and-brown eyes in her direction, and she'd swear the loathsome beast was grinning given the way his jaws hung open around the lolling tongue.

They passed the first of the warriors' camps, placed as they were between the buildings on either side of the path up from the landing. The atmosphere had decidedly changed—the camps more like a sporting outing instead of preparatory of invasion, combat, and death. The presence of children and spouses, the sounds of laughter, and the smell of cooking food carried on the wind made the camps feel like a holiday setting.

"There you are!" a voice called. Columella's son, young Panther Call, disengaged himself from a group of youngsters hanging around a squadron first and his officers.

"Hey, kid!" Seven Skull Shield greeted. "That really you? Got to have a talk with your mother. She keeps feeding you this way, you're going to grow so tall your head will be in the clouds."

Blue Heron studied the smiling boy. Growing indeed. Like goosefoot in a rainy year. Panther Call was already a head taller than she, and almost to the point of looking Seven Skull Shield eye-to-eye. Hard to believe he was sired by Flat Stone Pipe.

"How's your mother?" she asked.

"Wants to see you, Keeper. Sent me to peel an eye for you. She's over on the bluff. If you'll follow."

After ruffling Farts' head and ears, Panther Call turned on his heel and led the way across the corner of the plaza with its stickball fields and sacred World Tree pole, through the gap between the Evening Star House charnel mound and the surveyors' society house. Beyond them the way was packed with assorted workshops, Earth Clan council houses, a temple to Old-Woman-Who-Never-Dies and its contiguous sweat lodge, and finally wound around some tightly packed warehouses to the bluff's edge.

Columella had taken a stand atop a low mound, surrounded by her war leader, Falcon Sky, and a few of his squadron firsts and seconds. On the fringes, looking thoughtful, High Chief Burned Bone stood frowning down toward the river below.

Blue Heron stopped. The bluff gave her a wonderful view. The north wind had blown the brown haze of Cahokia's thousands of fires off to the south. From the heights she could not only see the roiling river below but the canoe landing on the opposite shore, the thick cluster of buildings on the levee, and the hook-shaped plaza of River City—though the River House palace, with its towering roof, was now missing. That left the World Tree pole in the plaza looking particularly lonely and out of place.

Beyond she could trace the urban sprawl as it stretched east northeast to Black Tail's tomb. All of it covered with farmsteads, chiefs' houses, temples, and domiciles. Well, all but the low marshes and old oxbow lakes where the water lay blue in the light.

There, across so much distance, Morning Star's great mound looked

like a pimple rising from the ground. And beyond that, she could barely
make out the eastern bluffs on the far-off horizon. Hard to think the city
stretched even beyond that for another half-day's walk.

"Keeper," Columella called, dismissing her warriors. The woman—
closing on her forties—wore a red skirt decorated with chevrons; a lace
cape hung from her shoulders, and several strands of beads draped over
her chest. Her hair bun supported a falcon-wing headdress emblematic
of war. The Matron cocked her head as Blue Heron labored up the slope
to the crest on which Columella stood.

Columella gave her quizzical appraisal. "You look like a dirt farmer's
worst nightmare. What's the matter? Not enough water in the river to
take a bath?"

"If I look like such a wreck, how'd you know it was me?"

"Seven Skull Shield may be many things, but the only ugly old woman
he'd ever travel with is you, Keeper." A pause. "Not to mention that disaster of a dog."

"I'm no longer the Keeper."

"You always will be to me and mine." She glanced up. "How are you
doing, Thief?"

"Tolerably well, Matron." Seven Skull Shield bent at the waist, touching his forehead in a gesture of respect. "Got to tell you, getting back to
Evening Star Town is a nice change. Other side of the river? You'd be
pus-rotted amazed at how tiring it can be for a man like me."

"Oh"—Columella arched an eyebrow—"did you linger too long in
some impressionable young woman's bed? Her husband chasing you
from one end of River City to the other?"

"Life hasn't been that good to me," the thief grumbled. "Too much
politics got in the way."

Columella pointed. "If that dog so much as sniffs at my stewpot, he's
going to be in it. In chunks. And last time he was here, the dais in my
palace reeked of urine for days."

In a weary voice, Blue Heron told her, "You think that's bad? If you
see the dog's tail lift, don't stand downwind." She made a face. "Some
things, old enemy, just . . . well, that's how they are. What's happening?"

Columella turned her attention to the river below. "By Piasa's swinging balls, we pulled it off. I've had runners coming and going. Spotted
Wrist's canoes are scattered almost to the confluence of the Mother Water
now, and still going." She pointed. "See that knot of men on the canoe
landing? The ones by that ramada?"

"Oh, yes," Blue Heron told her. "The thief and I were just over there.
Very loud. Lots of shouting. You might say that tempers are flaring.

Squadron First Cut Weasel is trying to keep all the Traders and Clans' representatives reassured that their canoes will be returned. People are demanding to speak to Spotted Wrist, but we're told he's been summoned to the Council House. After that, they want assurances from North Star House that their canoes will be returned, or that compensation will be offered."

"Confirms what my people tell me," Columella agreed, her chin cradled between thumb and forefinger, eyes slitted in thought. "Spotted Wrist will be lucky if he gets a third of them back, you know."

"I know." Blue Heron let her gaze travel over the canoe landing. The place was bustling again. Three rafts of logs had been floated in from the north, effectively tying up the upper third of the landing. The loggers were already swarming over their largesse, roping them one by one and dragging them ashore. Additional Trade canoes were unpacking bundled and baled goods. Trade had paused for long enough. Cahokia was reasserting its insatiable appetite for goods in a way Spotted Wrist couldn't deny.

"What's next?" Columella wondered. "It will take Spotted Wrist a half moon to reassemble any kind of military threat."

"If at all," Blue Heron agreed. "But think, old friend. He can't let this go."

Seven Skull Shield fingered one of the pink scars now decorating his skin. Mused: "No, he can't. Never met a more self-important man. Never forgives a slight. Figures it's a calling of honor to pay it back no matter the cost."

"And lately, he's had a lot of setbacks," Blue Heron said.

"The way Night Shadow Star slipped through his fingers humiliated him," Seven Skull Shield agreed. "Then there's me being rescued from his bear cage. He wasn't able to burn Blue Heron alive when he set fire to her palace. Now he's lost the chance to conquer Evening Star Town and looks the fool for having all those canoes stolen."

"He'll be desperate." Blue Heron pulled absently at her wattle. "Meanwhile, consider this: The River House palace is burned, his puppet, Broken Stone, made a fool of. And in addition to being on the hook for all these canoes, Rising Flame is out of patience. Especially since Evening Star House is stronger than ever."

"Think she'll dismiss him?" Seven Skull Shield wondered.

"She can't," Columella said thoughtfully. "No matter how much of an inconvenience he might be, or how incompetent he might look, the man commands too much military. His squadrons control most of the city and hold *Tonka'tzi* Wind hostage in her own palace. To his warriors, he's the Hero of the North. He brought them victory after victory, and they'll continue to back him."

Blue Heron added, "Not to mention that Green Chunkey and Horned Serpent House are feeling too frisky for their own good. With River House in disarray, Evening Star House essentially outlawed, and Morning Star quiet about all things political, they have more authority than they've had for years."

"North Star House might dispute that," Columella said dryly.

"High Chief Wolverine and that slippery sheath, Slender Fox, will dominate the other Houses as long as Spotted Wrist remains Keeper and in charge of his squadrons. Wish there was a way to play that against them."

"Well . . ." Seven Skull Shield began, "there is, given the way Slender Fox and Wolverine delight in each other's—"

Blue Heron blurted, "Their day will come, Thief. It's the Morning Star that I can't figure." Some secrets she wanted to keep to herself for the time being.

Seven Skull Shield—quick as always—gave a slight shrug, his face going neutral and mild.

"More to the point, where is the living god in all this? The Morning Star always plays a deep game." Columella rubbed her chin. "He did when Walking Smoke was creating havoc, and when the Itza arrived. And then there was that business about losing his souls to Sacred Moth and the Underworld. Somehow, it's like it was all building up to this."

"But to achieve what end?" Blue Heron flung a hand toward the canoe landing. "But for the lucky break of that storm, we'd have never managed to push all Spotted Wrist's canoes into the river. As we speak, he would be advancing on Evening Star Town, and you know he'd have taken it. All those festive warriors camped out and around your plaza would be dying, bleeding, or running for their lives. You'd be fighting a last-ditch defense with no way out."

Seven Skull Shield scratched behind his ear. "Maybe Morning Star sees the future?"

"Bah!" Blue Heron cried. "Then he'd never have allowed Night Shadow Star to go traipsing off in search of her brother. He'd have told Spotted Wrist to marry someone else and kept her here to use against Rising Flame."

"Unless Rising Flame serves his purpose," Seven Skull Shield noted.

"What purpose?" Columella wondered. "War between the Houses? As long as Blue Heron was the Four Winds Clan Keeper, she kept the Houses in balance. Not that we ever saw it, mind you. At least not until that fool Spotted Wrist was put in her place. I sure didn't." She turned her attention to Blue Heron. "And, while I still bristle over some of the things you did to me and my House, with hindsight, I can see the point of it."

"But why throw the city out of balance?" Blue Heron wondered. "It's not just us, not just the Houses, but the Earth Clans, and under them, the dirt farmers. It's like twirling a burning brand over a pile of dried leaves. One misstep and the whole thing goes up in a conflagration."

Blue Heron paused. "Something you should know, Matron. Morning Star has been in contact. Or someone from inside his palace has. Could be old Five Fists, but he rarely does anything that isn't with the Morning Star's blessing."

"In touch? How?"

"Beaded messages." Blue Heron arched an eyebrow. "Sent to me in Trade for kindling wood."

"Telling you what?" Columella demanded, her expression sharpening.

"The last message was: 'All is not lost. Work from the shadows.' I was told it was from Mallard's own hand."

"That's cryptic enough." Columella frowned. "Mallard's the Morning Star's personal recorder. He'd never act without the living god's approval."

"You're right, but there's more. A copper bead in the middle of the string. Something ambiguous about it. That either the southern copper will be our salvation, or, maybe, save the southern copper to the last. Master Lotus Leaf at the Recorders' Society House wasn't sure which."

"The southern copper?" Columella looked perplexed.

"Might be that missing Kora copper." Blue Heron shrugged, glancing sidelong to see Seven Skull Shield's face turn expressionless as a pool of wet clay. Confirmed what she'd always suspected: the thief knew something about the pus-sucking theft of that copper.

"Too bad we can't ask Morning Star what he's up to," Seven Skull Shield said innocently. Then he grinned when—even over the distance—they could hear someone shouting at poor Cut Weasel.

"Might be that's just what we ought to do." Blue Heron's eyes slitted as she watched the milling crowd around Cut Weasel's ramada.

"How are you going to do that?" Columella asked. "Spotted Wrist's warriors guard all access to the Great Mound and Morning Star's palace. They stand at the bottom of the stairs shoulder-to-shoulder with the Morning Star's guard."

Blue Heron glanced sidelong at Seven Skull Shield. "What do you think, Thief? You good enough to get us into the Morning Star's palace?

Or is it only the beds of impressionable and lonely young housewives where you shine?"

"I can get you in."

Columella looked down at Farts. "I think I'd leave the dog behind if I were you. His smell is a dead giveaway."

Twenty

The odor of mud and water filled Night Shadow Star's nose as she and the warriors crouched behind a thick screen of willows and cattails. Beyond their hiding place, the river ran smooth, its surface swirling. Some sort of hatch was underway, columns of thousands of gossamer-winged flies rising and corkscrewing up from the water; sunlight shone silver on their tiny wings.

Overhead, against a haze-blue sky, an osprey sailed and circled, hunting for fish.

They had their own problems with insects, the vegetation swarming with hoppers, caterpillars, and most of all, the bothersome flies that buzzed around them, drawn to their sweat as the heat of the day and muggy air almost steamed them.

Summer Ice plucked a tick from his calf, crushed it between thumb and fingernail, and pitched it off to the side. "This really necessary?"

Night Shadow Star tilted her head to study him. "You ever been hunted on the river? No? Let me guess, you've only been the hunters."

"And that's what we ought to be, woman," Field Snake told her arrogantly. "Paddle fast, get ahead. And here we sit? Waiting for the witch to catch us?"

Night Shadow Star twitched her lips as she shook her head. "You'd never survive your first battle walk, boy."

"I'm no boy! And I did survive my first battle walk. I was the *only* one who did. It was me who misled my enemies. Tricked them, I did, and escaped. I'm a full warrior. And High Chief Fire Light told me so, too."

"Oh, yes," Made of Wood agreed. "At least that was the story you told.

All those warriors killed, and you managed to elude an entire war party? Got back in time to warn us? Saved us in the nick of time?"

"What story is this?" Night Shadow Star asked as she shifted to keep the blood flowing in her right leg.

"Nothing," Summer Ice snapped, glaring at his companions. "Kid, shut up."

What was that look of warning all about, anyway? Some angry communication passed between the lot of them. And Field Snake, a triumphant gleam in his hot black eyes, was eyeing her as if she were a special prize.

Well, it beat the other gleam, the one he'd adopted more and more when he looked her way. When she found him studying her, his gaze fixing on her breasts, or her flat belly. The sharpening of his eyes as he followed the lines of her muscular thighs and calves. Oh, she knew that hungry look.

Nor was Field Snake the only one. She'd catch the others as they cast covetous looks her way. Made her wonder how much her "rescue" from Walking Smoke was motivated by keeping her out of his grasp so they could have her for themselves. Surely, being young and male, the fantasies had to have been at least a flicker down in their hearts, and perhaps even smoldering hot in their testicles.

I'll have to address that.

Most likely soon.

But first things first.

"The trick to surviving this journey," she told them, "is to have my brother ahead of us. Downriver."

"Why?" Made of Wood demanded. "He can lay a trap for us. Catch us unawares."

"How does he know we're behind him?" she asked. "Listen to me. This isn't my brother's kind of game. Oh, he's a predator all right. But think of him as a spider rather than a wolf. His cunning is in camouflage, subterfuge, misdirecting a victim, or luring them into his lair. He will take the offensive, as he did at Cahokia when he murdered my father and sister, but that's because he was on his home ground, working within an environment he understood."

Summer Ice told her, "But he could pick his place. Maybe Canyon Town? Set up his lair there. Be waiting for us when we land."

"I've heard the story you tell. How he appeared in Cofitachequi. Walked out of a burning temple. A miracle. And then he set himself up. Built his reputation. It took time to establish himself. To do the same in Canyon Town, he'd need another miracle. And then it would take time to establish himself again."

"But if he's ahead of us—"

"He's not stopping." She cut Field Snake's protest short. "His work is in Cahokia. The longer I am out of his grasp, the more he's going to fixate on that. In the end, being my brother, he's going to grow ever more impatient to get there. Like me, he knows the final confrontation is coming."

Made of Wood studied her thoughtfully. "What about his claim that he has to take you first? That he needs the Power he'd get from lying with you before confronting Morning Star?"

She pursed her lips, frowned. "Understand something: My brother has never been accountable for his actions. He's never had to pay for anything he's done, atone for any crime. When he was a boy he was *Tonka'tzi* Red Warrior's son; there were plenty of people to cover for his misdeeds. Nor was he punished the first time he raped me. Morning Star exiled him—an event my brother turned into a sort of fun adventure in the south. After he murdered my father and sister, tried to conjure Piasa's Spirit inside his own body, the Thunderbirds plucked him from the depths of the Father Water mere moments before Piasa could destroy him."

"The way you talk about these things . . ." Summer Ice made a face. "Like you toss one Spirit Power after another from hand to hand as if they were walnuts. These are like the stories women tell little children to make them gasp in awe. I believe in Power. I am humble in the presence of my ancestors, but these are living gods you talk of as if they were supper guests."

She fixed her gaze on his, felt Piasa swell within her. Summer Ice's image wavered, diminished in her sight as though she were seeing him at a distance. She heard Piasa speak through her, say, *"Then choose your side, human. Even a fly can pick which High Chief it wishes to pester."*

Then she snapped back to the willows beside the East Fork of the Upper Tenasee. She blinked. Long time since Piasa had filled her with such intensity. A cold shiver ran up her back.

Summer Ice—and Made of Wood behind him—were gaping at her, their eyes wide.

"How did you do that?" Summer Ice asked under his breath.

"She's playing with her voice, made it sound hollow," Field Snake growled from where he was peering out through the stems at the river. Then he lowered his voice, trying to boom, "And I can become a pesky fly, too!"

"You didn't see her eyes, boy." Made of Wood, looking shaken, nervously wiped a hand across his mouth.

"My Lord will feast on you one day, Field Snake," Night Shadow Star promised. "Curiously, I don't suspect that day is long in coming."

Made of Wood tried to shrug off a tremor of fear that ran through him. Summer Ice had gone a couple of shades paler.

"Shh!" Bluefish—who had his own hole in the willows—called. "They're coming!"

Night Shadow Star's lips bent into a knowing smile. She could feel it. The coming of blood and death. Perhaps Made of Wood and Summer Ice might be cowed for the moment, but Field Snake, the arrogant youth, hadn't a notion of the fate that lay in store for him. He kept shooting her those predatory glances, giving her that triumphant smile, as if he were already ripping her skirt from her hips.

A trout will always rise for a fly. And the Underwater Panther will rise for a corpse.

That was the moment her brother's party passed. Paddles flashing in the sunlight, the Trade canoe flew down the river. Steered by Six Toes in the rear, it ghosted silently past their hiding place. And, perched amidships, Walking Smoke stood erect, a knee braced on one of the canoe seats. He had his attention fixed downriver, as if certain he would see his prey appear around the next bend.

In the distance faint thunder could be heard; but for once, Night Shadow Star figured that her brother was too carried away with his own internal drama to heed the warning.

"What do we do now?" Summer Ice asked softly.

"Make camp," Bluefish told them. "It's late afternoon. If we're going to let them get ahead of us, now is as good a time as any. Wouldn't do to take off downriver and find ourselves running right into their camp."

"I'm all for that," Field Snake said with smug satisfaction. "Enjoy a little relaxation."

Bluefish shared a meaningful glance with the young warrior. He tried to hide the anticipatory smile on his lips as he and Field Snake each turned appreciative gazes Night Shadow Star's way.

A cold feeling slipped through her gut. *This is not going to end well.*

Twenty-one

Getting back to central Cahokia had been easy. All Blue Heron had had to do was wait for a couple hands of time outside, in the shade of Wooden Doll's ramada, as she shared company with Wooden Doll's servant, Whispering Dawn, and her new baby.

Seven Skull Shield had spent his time inside, enjoying Wooden Doll's company and talents as they cavorted in the paid woman's sumptuous bed.

Whispering Dawn had been a fount of information and a colossal gossip as she switched the child from one breast to the other and talked nonstop.

Even more rewarding than her enlightened conversation with Whispering Dawn was the litter that Wooden Doll offered to take Blue Heron back to central Cahokia. The wear and tear and pain it saved her hip made Blue Heron eternally grateful.

Even so, evening had fallen by the time they reached central Cahokia. Wooden Doll's porters deposited her at the edge of the Western Plaza, just shy of the Four Winds Clan House. This was about as far as Blue Heron considered it prudent to be carried. Too many people might question why an old woman dressed in rags was being borne into the Great Plaza atop an ornate litter like Wooden Doll's, not to mention being in the presence of a big ruffian like Seven Skull Shield. And then there was Farts with his odd eyes. Might as well shout out their identities to the whole pus-rotted plaza.

As she was helped to her feet by Wooden Doll's bearers, she told them, "Give your mistress my blessings. Tell her it won't be forgotten."

She watched them disappear into the growing gloom, headed back west down the Avenue of the Sun.

"We can finally talk," Seven Skull Shield told her. "According to Wooden Doll, Three Fingers expects to be sitting in the River House high chair within the next quarter moon. That is, he would if there was still a high chair to be sitting in. The Four Winds lineages that make up River House are pretty much figuring out that maybe they weren't so bad off when War Duck and Round Pot were in charge. A lot of uncertainty. As a result, the lineages aren't rushing to voice their support for either Broken Stone or Three Fingers as the new high chief."

"If Whispering Dawn can be trusted, the same's true for the rest of the city." Blue Heron pulled on her wattle as she turned her steps east toward Morning Star's Great Mound where it loomed against the darkening sky. She could just make out the high place, the roof shooting up at a steep angle.

What in the name of muck and blood is Morning Star doing up there?

"She told me that everyone's tired of the constant upheaval and inconvenience. Not to mention that the River House granaries are empty, and that the few people who have anything left have had to dip out of their personal stores to make up the difference to feed Spotted Wrist's squadrons. And, with the theft of the canoes, it all turns out to be for nothing. The good news is that Columella and Evening Star Town aren't getting the blame for the burned warehouses or the incineration of the palace. With the exception of some, like your friend Robin Wing, most think it was only fair given that Columella picked a rainy night so that the whole town didn't go up, and that she was, after all, pushed into it to keep it from being invaded."

Seven Skull Shield grunted. "Want to take any bets that Crazy Frog was spinning that story from the very beginning? Making sure that the right ears and mouths were hearing and saying that same thing?"

"No bets."

After a long pause she shot him a sidelong glance. "I know you love that woman. Why don't you settle down with her?"

Seven Skull Shield walked in silence, his fingers stroking the big dog's back as it matched his pace. "Tried. She knows me too well. Figures I'm going to end badly."

"Well, Thief, I guess I can't fault her for good sense."

As they passed Night Shadow Star's palace atop its earthen pyramid, they saw the high-roofed building dark, not a light to be seen. The Piasa and Horned Serpent guardian posts stared down the ramp stairway in shadowy menace.

And just down the avenue, the wreckage of her own torched palace littered the top of its flat-topped earthen mound. She assumed that no one would have begun clearing the charred timbers or started to pick through the wreckage of burned shell, cracked pottery, and powdery ash. Not that there would be much there. Perhaps some of the ceramic and stone statuary had survived, but the textiles, the wooden chests, the elaborate wooden carvings, all would be gone. Even the copper plate and repoussé reliefs would be scorched, warped, and discolored.

She shot another look up at the dark palace where Morning Star would be sitting down to his nightly feast.

Under her breath, she murmured, "All of Cahokia exists because of you, because of the miracle of your resurrection on earth. You could stop this with a word. Bring order out of chaos."

Seven Skull Shield chuckled as they turned south, away from the knot of warriors, porters, and nobles crowding the Avenue of the Sun, many waiting by the litters that had carried the various nobles to the foot of the Great Staircase.

"You laugh, Thief?"

"Keeper, were you ever a child?"

"Are you as dense as a knot of hickory? You think I was born looking like this?"

"Of course not. I know you were a most striking young woman. Dashing, dark-eyed, and voluptuous. They flocked around you like toms around a willing hen. You married enough of them."

Blue Heron stopped short, glaring up at him. "Thief, not that it isn't dangerous enough comparing me to a turkey, but you take chances. I could have you hung in a square so fast, you'd think you'd been kicked there."

His most placid smile mocked her in the night. "No, you couldn't. Not even if you walked right up to that warrior guarding the *tonka'tzi*'s stairs and told him to. He'd grab you up and tote you off to Spotted Wrist before you could turn, and by then I'd be nothing but flying feet pattering off into the distance." Another chuckle. "No, what I was getting at was the stories."

"Huh? What stories?"

Seven Skull Shield extended his arm, waving in a grand gesture to take in the Great Plaza with its World Tree Pole, the Morning Star's mound, the society and charnel houses, the stickball field and Earth Clans mounds to the south that stood along the Avenue of the Moon. "All of this. Your illustrious ancestors laid it out as a reflection of the Sky World on Earth, a celebration of the lunar minimum that happens every eighteen and a half years. A symbolic home for the reincarnated Morning Star. But it's all about the stories."

"There you go again. What stories?"

"The ones set in the Beginning Time." Seven Skull Shield paused, turning his attention back to where torches were being lit at the foot of the stairway leading up the Great Mound. "Morning Star and the Wild One. Don't you remember? How after they played chunkey with the giants and won, they cut off the giants' heads, and used Power conjured from them to bring their father back to life?"

"Of course I remember. Get to the point."

"Morning Star and the Wild One never agreed about anything, Keeper. And all around them was chaos, monsters; the world they created is the one we live in today. White against red, wisdom against creativity, death against rebirth, peace against war, wisdom versus passion, you name it. All in a perpetual need for balance. But the biggest balance is Sky World against Underworld."

She shifted the pack on her shoulder, uttered a snort of irritation. "Are you going to take all night to tell me what you're talking about?"

Seven Skull Shield had fixed his gaze on Morning Star's palace. "In the stories you heard when you were a little girl, it was all about making rules out of chaos. Do you remember how the stories all ended?"

"Of course. In the end, the Wild One, or Thrown-Away Boy, as he was sometimes called, was banished. And, having won, Morning Star was carried up into the Sky World where he became the actual star in the sky. And there he stayed until Black Tail—through an extended ritual—called Morning Star's Spiritual essence down from the Sky to inhabit Black Tail's body."

Farts had dropped on his butt to scratch behind his ear.

Blue Heron felt the slightest unease. "What are you hinting at, Thief?"

Seven Skull Shield was still fixed on the high palace. "It was seeing Whispering Dawn and her baby this morning. You know that baby is Morning Star's child from when she was in his bed. Remember how she poisoned him? Got his soul sent to the Underworld? Even when he was bedding her, he knew the risks. Had foreseen that she'd try to kill him."

"Gods don't always make sense."

"People say that. But why wouldn't they? You just have to think like a god."

"Well, I'm delighted that you can think like a god. Now, it's dark. I'm hungry. So why don't you turn your divine thoughts to getting us supper and a place—"

"He's tired," Seven Skull Shield said as if in revelation. "He's been here too long."

"Excuse me?"

"Morning Star's bored, Keeper. He doesn't care anymore. I wouldn't."

Not if I was hauled up to that palace, given anything I wanted. Day after day, play a little chunkey? Feast? Women lining up for my bed, desperate that I plant a child in them? Think that's worth waking up to the same roof overhead, the same fawning faces? Think having to listen to all the platitudes, the whining complaints, sitting in judgment over the petty jealousies is fun? After all this time, if you were Morning Star, would you want to be endlessly pestered by sycophants, bombarded by pleas for favor? What about all those conniving politicians? The ones desperate to manipulate you for their own gain? Knowing it was all about *them* and never about *you*?"

She pursed her lips, turning to stare up at the high palace, the faintest glow illuminating the soaring building behind the mound-top palisade. Someone had started the bonfire behind Morning Star's World Tree Pole. Its light was shining on the palace with a warm yellow glow.

She asked herself. "Gods know, there's been times I've had my fill of the self-gratifying weasels trying to worm some advantage out of my approval. But I always had Cahokia to fight for. Preservation of the Houses."

Seven Skull Shield gestured at the palace. "What's he got to fight for? He asks, it's given. He can't go for a walk without an escort, the dirt farmers would mob him, tear the very clothes off his back for a souvenir."

"Maybe even pull his hair out by the roots for a keepsake," she agreed. "They'd love him to death."

"That's why he sent Night Shadow Star off to the east. She's always saved him, one way or another."

"Her or the Red Wing," Blue Heron agreed. "Assuming she ever found Walking Smoke and managed to kill him."

"Puts a whole new meaning on the old turn of the tongue, doesn't it?"

She nodded, a coldness in her heart. "You mean the one that goes: 'Morning Star always plays a deep game'?"

"I do, indeed."

"What game this time, Thief?"

"I think he wants out. Wants out bad enough, he's ready to die if it means getting out of that palace."

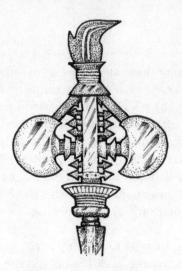

Twenty-two

Wind—once Matron of the Four Winds Clan and now the nominal *tonka'tzi*—had gone to bed late. Her slaves and servants had helped her to remove her copper headdress with its feathers and the forehead-mounted Spirit-Bundle box. She'd watched them place the piece on its rack, had allowed her slave to carefully wipe the red and blue face paint from her cheeks. Then White Rain had helped her to undress, had folded her cape and fine black dogbane-fabric skirt and placed them on one of the intricately carved storage chests against the wall.

Then White Rain had blown out the small hickory oil lamps as Wind crawled under her thin blanket. The wool was woven of the soft under hair curried from a winter bison hide. Not that she needed it in the warm summer night, but it kept the mosquitoes off.

In the darkness, she rubbed her brow, trying to think of a way, any way, that didn't lead to disaster. In the end, all she could come up with was assassination. Not that she had a chance of that. The pus-licking Clan Keeper had his warriors maintaining a constant guard and watch on Wind's every waking moment. No way she could summon anyone—not even Rides-the-Lightning—for a conference that wasn't overseen by one of her pus-dripping guards. Everything she said when she had visitors was promptly reported to Spotted Wrist.

Blue Heron would have known how to get around this constant surveillance.

Gods, but she missed her sister. Blue Heron had always been the practical one when it came to getting one's hands a bit bloody. As Keeper, she'd had the network of spies, informants, and, when necessary, assassins who could slip in under dark of night and empty a pouch full of water hemlock into some unsuspecting person's teapot.

Wind clamped her eyes shut against the grief. Spotted Wrist's warriors had made no secret about how it had been done. How they'd blocked Blue Heron's palace door, doused it with oil, and tossed burning coals onto the fuel.

So, she died. Her and Smooth Pebble.

Grief? Rage? They all roiled in Wind's tortured gut.

She stiffened, thought she heard sniffing, like some animal. Then came the sound of something like teeth grinding on bone just outside her door.

But the only thing with a bone in it was the deer haunch that had been brought in by her guards. According to plan, her people were supposed to set it to roast over the central hearth coals first thing in the morning. That way the meat would be slow-cooked and tender for the warriors to feast on by tomorrow night. The manner in which she and her people were treated, one would think they were Spotted Wrist's menials.

Oh, and if she were good, they might throw her a few scraps.

How long is this going to last?

Not long, she supposed. As Spotted Wrist was pushed further and further into a corner, she suspected the man was going to have to make some accommodation with High Chief Green Chunkey down in Horned Serpent House. Spotted Wrist had already promised Green Chunkey that he would be the next *tonka'tzi*. That had been the price of Horned Serpent House's loyalty to Rising Flame and Spotted Wrist. The offer that finally bridged the two Houses' rabid dislike of each other.

Because of it, Wind understood that her tenure as *tonka'tzi* was only supposed to be temporary, a figurehead of normality until Spotted Wrist could completely subdue the city.

But now that he had failed to take Evening Star Town? And with the coup at River House reeling, elements in the city openly calling for Round Pot and War Duck's return?

How long before Spotted Wrist and Rising Flame got around to realizing that good old Wind was no longer an asset?

She made a face, convinced that she heard the shearing of jaws, the slapping sounds of jowls as something was gulped. A thumping sounded just outside her door.

Here? In her palace?

Impossible.

And where were the guards? Surely they, along with her servants sleeping out in the great room, would have heard any intruder.

She was on the verge of throwing her blanket back when something stirred in the hallway. Her door was lifted, set quietly to one side. Just the faintest shift of shadow in darkness, and she could feel the stirring as someone stepped into her room.

Perhaps Spotted Wrist had made his decision?

"Who's there?" she demanded, hand searching around for the long-bladed chert knife she kept hidden where her bedding met the wall. If this was Spotted Wrist's assassin, she wasn't going to go without a fight.

"Shhh!" a low voice hissed.

Another, barely audible, called, "Farts! Here. Over here. That's a good dog."

More movement, then the faint tang of fresh venison came to her nose. Something heavy flopped onto the matting beside her bed, and any doubt about a beast chewing, ripping, and gnawing was removed.

"By pus-dripping Piasa's balls!" she gritted. "Who are you? What in all that's . . . ?"

"Shhh! Quiet, sister," a familiar voice whispered as another shadow moved by her door.

"Blue Heron?" she almost squeaked. "They told me you were dead!"

"Will you stop making such a racket? I can't be dead. No way I'd be this pus-dripping hungry and tired . . . and my hip wouldn't hurt this bad."

Wind had pulled herself up in bed, was staring as her heart beat desperately. "What? How? I mean . . ."

Blue Heron's shadowy form picked her way around whatever creature was happily thumping, gnawing, and licking the deer haunch on her floor. "The thief got me and Smooth Pebble out. She's staying with kin down in Horned Serpent Town until this is all settled."

Wind placed a hand to her heart. "Pus and rot, I can't tell you what a relief this is. It's like I had a hole ripped in my heart. But how did you get in here? There's warriors all around—"

"They got sloppy," the thief's voice informed from the door. "Figured the threat was over, that Morning Star House had gone soggy as acorn bread in water, and there wasn't much use watching the back. When this is all over, you really should see to fixing that thatch over the storeroom."

"You got in through the roof?" Wind tried to keep the incredulity out of her voice.

"Not me," Blue Heron answered. "I'm not that young and limber. Thief did that. Me and Farts, we walked in the front door after they'd all nodded off . . . along with the help of a jar of nightshade juice the thief added to the warriors' tea. The only worry was crossing the great room with all the servants sleeping along the walls." A pause. "What idiot left a deer haunch by the fire? Try being quiet with a deer haunch just lying there in front of a mongrel mutt as big as a—"

"He's a Spirit dog," the thief corrected. "Hush. You'll hurt his feelings."

On the floor, a snapping long bone sounded like a loud clap of the hands, only to be followed by spine-grating crunching.

"We're here to rescue you," the thief added. "Grab what things you need, and we'll have you safe and out of sight by—"

"No!" Wind snapped, struggling to keep her voice down. As if that was needed when it sounded like a grizzly was rendering a buffalo carcass on her floor. "If I'm gone missing, Green Chunkey will be the *tonka'tzi* by nightfall. I don't know if you're aware, but there's a mess down at River Mounds City. Someone—"

"And an accursed splendid mess it is, too. Glad to have had a hand in cooking it up. Fine entertainment watching our new Clan Keeper getting a finger poked in his eye for once." Blue Heron had that smug tone in her voice, the one that used to drive Wind half-insane. "We'd love to have known what was said when Spotted Wrist was called back to the Council House yesterday."

"I was there. A figurehead to be sure, and mostly I kept my mouth shut. Mostly. Rising Flame is enraged, worried, and not a little frightened. My suspicion? She's regretting a lot of things these days. Including Spotted Wrist's appointment as the Clan Keeper. Unfortunately, she's stuck with him for the duration."

"Where's Morning Star in all this?"

"No clue. Five Fists was at the Council House for the meeting. Not sure how he fits in. Claims he was just there to observe at the Morning Star's insistence. But he said nothing in the name of the Morning Star, only offered his own advice. Old bent face made it pus-rotted clear that he was only talking for himself."

"What did he say?"

"Told Spotted Wrist that he'd lost the advantage, that the time had come to make amends with Columella. That pursuing any kind of military solution would lead to disaster. I think it had an impact on Rising Flame. But I'd say the import of it flew past Green Chunkey's and Three Fingers' ears like a lark on the wing."

Blue Heron said, "The last we heard was through a beaded message. Came from Mallard. Said we didn't fight alone, and that we needed to keep to the shadows."

"But you're sure it was from Morning Star?"

"Mallard wouldn't send a message like that on his own."

"Work from the shadows?" Wind rubbed her brow. "That's cryptic."

"Morning Star never tells you the rules when you play his games, let alone what the end goal is." Blue Heron sighed. "But, sister, I'm getting tired of it."

"So, what are you going to do?"

A pause. "You sure you don't want to come? Help me fight from the shadows?"

"No." But, spit and piss, she was tempted. "Ultimately my fight is here. And, Spirits know, I might hear something, be in a position to act when the time comes."

Wind reveled in the old familiar sight of Blue Heron pulling at the sagging wattle under her chin. Having thought her sister dead, it brought tears to her eyes.

Blue Heron said, "Might be that you will. All right. You hang on here. Me and the thief, we've got nothing to lose. If Spotted Wrist or Rising Flame catch either one of us, we're going to die a lingering death, so what's the point of waiting for them to find us? Better to hit them before they know I'm alive."

"You be curse-rotted careful."

"You, too, sister. But be ready. If it looks like Spotted Wrist is going to replace you, the roof is loose over the back corner of the storeroom. Just don't break your leg when you jump down."

"They're going to know something's wrong when this deer leg is missing in the morning."

It was the thief who said, "Well, tell them that you were hungry. Everyone likes a middle-of-the-night snack on occasion."

She thought of sticking him with her long chert knife, but the man's howl might have awakened half of Cahokia.

Twenty-three

In the bow of the canoe, Fire Cat used his paddle to steer them into the fast water. He perched high, partially braced by his pack, filled as it was with his armor, weapons, and chunkey gear. Behind him, Winder paddled, then Night Shadow Star's box of Trade rested neatly between the gunwales, followed by Blood Talon and Shell Hook, who steered in the rear.

Three days on the river, and from the villages they'd passed, the people he'd called to on shore, he knew she was ahead of him. Now, it was only a matter of time.

If he closed his eyes, he could see her. The image, almost ghostly, hovered above the dark water. The late-afternoon beams of light shooting through her spectral form as she floated above the roiling and sucking current.

An instant later, the golden beams vanished, the sun cut off behind the high ridge to the west.

"We've only got a couple of hands of daylight," Winder observed from where he paddled behind Fire Cat. "Not much between here and Willow Swamp Village, as I remember. While there's daylight we might want to pick a place where we can make camp. Get a fire going."

On the verge of agreeing, Fire Cat hesitated. Long shadows reached out from the willows and cottonwoods lining the bank. And, in that moment, he would have sworn he saw a faint blue gleam. Something shining down in the depths, almost like a reflection, that matched their pace.

Reflexively Fire Cat shot a look at the darkening sky above them, would have sworn he heard the faint rumble of thunder in the cloudless sky.

And when he glanced back at the shadows, he could still see it: the weird blue glow slipping along beneath the surface. Cocking his head, he studied it, shifted his gaze. No, this wasn't a curious reflection cast by their hull. From the angles of the shadows, the way the cerulean light shifted slightly from side to side, this was no refracted light from above.

"Piasa is here," he whispered to himself.

"What?" Apparently Winder had overheard.

"The Underworld Lord is pacing us." Fire Cat indicated the glow with a tilt of his head. "Can you see him down there? The faint blue gleam?"

Winder craned his neck, peering over the side. "I see water, War Leader. Shadowed as the depths are, I can't see past the surface."

"He's there," Fire Cat said flatly. "He wouldn't be pacing us unless there's a reason."

In the seat behind Winder, Blood Talon, too, was staring over the side. "I see nothing, Fire Cat. Just murky dark water."

"We're going on," Fire Cat decided.

"Got fast water ahead of us," Shell Hook called from where he perched in the rear. "Nothing to worry about in daylight, but I don't want to chance it in the dark. Can't see the boulders. We hit one of them, we're going over. Getting dumped in fast water, in the dark, is a good way to drown."

"I'll let you off at the next sand bar," Fire Cat told him.

"It's my canoe!"

"You can pick it up at the mouth of the Wide Fast, or maybe Canyon Town if we can't find another Trader to carry us downriver."

"Now wait a moment! I didn't sign on for—"

"You heard the war leader," Blood Talon told the Trader stiffly. "If he says we're paddling all night, we're paddling."

"Squadron First, you're as crazy as Fire Cat," Winder muttered. "Tackling that water in the darkness? Insane."

"You want to be left onshore, too?" Fire Cat asked.

"Not me, Red Wing," Winder told him. "Since I hired on at Big Cane Town, I've seen enough to know that Power guides you and Lady Night Shadow Star. You say Piasa's down there? That he wants us to keep to the river? I put my faith in you and your visions."

"Red Wing, if we were meant to drown," Blood Talon added, "it would have happened back when you capsized my war canoe. Lead on. I'm with you."

"You are all idiots," Shell Hook growled. "Fortunately, I can swim. Hope you can. You're going to need it."

Fire Cat would have smiled at the dispirited tone in the Trader's voice, but when it came to the presence of that weird blue glow that now moved out ahead of them? It set every nerve in his body on edge.

If Piasa is here, he wants us to hurry. And that means Night Shadow Star must be . . .

He couldn't finish the thought, his heart beginning to pound as he drove his paddle deep, sending the bulky Trade canoe flying after the blue glow that led the canoe into the night.

Twenty-four

Distant thunder shook Night Shadow Star out of the Dream. Brought her awake in the predawn. Her bladder was pressing for relief. Her stomach growled and gurgled. Supper last night had been freshwater mussels they'd collected from the gravel bar that extended out into the river below their camp. For the first night since leaving Standing Willow Village, they'd eaten to satiety. The pile of shells back of the fire stood testimony to the bounty. Not to mention three nice pearls they'd recovered.

She rubbed the sleep from her eyes, pulled the blanket back, and listened to the morning. Frogs were raising a racket on the riverbanks, and predawn birdsong filled the air. The sky above reflected a dull gray, clouds sucking up the coming light. Even through the scent of smoke permeating her blanket, clothing, and hair, she could smell the damp mud, the sweetness of the willows and midsummer blossoms.

Sitting up, she glanced around the camp. The men remained motionless, blankets rising and falling as they slept. Dew had settled on the canoe, leaving the gunwales and stacked paddles gleaming.

Somewhere off to the west, the staccato of an ivory-billed woodpecker, as the war bird hammered on a hardwood.

In her heart, the longing ache for Fire Cat filled her with a physical pain.

She threw the blanket aside, clawed her unruly thick hair back over her shoulder, and pulled her high moccasins onto her feet. Then she quietly made her way past the smoldering remains of the fire and into the willows.

Finding an opening in the brush, she squatted to relieve herself. High water in the not-so-distant past had piled rounded cobbles and gravel in a lenticular bar. Vegetation was just now starting to reclaim the deposit, green shoots spearing up between the river-rounded stones.

The scrape of a branch was her only warning. She rose and turned, finding herself face-to-face with Field Snake. The young warrior had a crooked smile on his lips as he made a shushing gesture with his finger, then said, "Not a word, woman."

To emphasize his point, he smacked his war club into a hard palm. "You scream? I'll clip you hard, do you hear? Have to really make you hurt so that when I tell the others you were running, going to try and escape, they'll believe me."

"What do you want?"

"What does any man want with a woman?"

His grin turned crafty again, and he gestured toward her with his war club. "It's been moons, ever since before your brother came to Joara. Had a couple of slave girls that didn't mind spreading their legs for a handful of shell beads. But the Lightning Witch came, and the old woman who owned them left and took them with her. All the women a man would be interested in left."

"Too bad. It would take a great deal more than a handful of shell beads to interest me."

"A lot less, actually. You see, I've got the war club, and you've got a simple choice: Do I beat you half to death? Or do you lie back, pull up your skirt, and let me do what a man does with a woman? As I hear it, it's nothing more than what you were doing with Fire Cat. Surely, if you'd stoop to letting your bound man slick your sheath, a warrior's hard shaft will be an improvement."

"What would you know of Fire Cat?"

Again that knowing grin, almost insolent as his eyes narrowed. "Oh, all he could do was brag about what he did with you under the covers. You never heard about that, did you? How close he was? It was me who kept him, Winder, and Blood Talon from reaching you that night."

"What are you talking about?" Her heart skipped. Fire Cat? This young idiot had seen Fire Cat?

"They didn't want you to know. The Lightning Shell Witch and High Chief Fire Light, they ordered me to keep quiet. That night before you got to Joara, I was sent with a party to find you. And we did. Well, we found your camp up by the rock spring. Had Winder and those Traders captive. That's when Fire Cat and Blood Talon appeared. Killed all the others. All but me. But I got even. Told them I'd lead them to you. Then I tricked them into following a trail up into the mountains and slipped away in the dark. Left them lost and confused."

"What?" Her heart continued to hammer away. "He was that close?"

Field Snake shrugged. "People underestimate me. You underestimate me. But not now. Not this morning." Again he wiggled the war club suggestively. "Lie down. Right over there. On that grass."

"It's rocky."

"What do I care? I'll have plenty of cushion with you between me and the rocks. Now do it, or I'm breaking your arm. And if you still refuse, I'll crack some ribs. Or I might just knock you half-silly. I don't need you conscious for what I'm going to do to you."

"The others are going to—"

"Take their own turns," he snapped. "But that's for later. Piss and spit, woman, do you think we did this for your benefit? Bluefish is still trying to get up the courage, given that you're Four Winds and all. But me? I'm a long way away from any Four Winds Clan, let alone their authority."

"I think you'd better—"

"*Enough* talk. Now. Down on your back and spread, and don't get any ideas." He waggled the war club. "I'm keeping this in my hand, laying the handle across your throat. You try anything, and I'll choke you."

She nodded, feeling that old familiar revulsion in the pit of her stomach. Step by step she backed to the grassy spot, glanced down at the rock-studded surface. She settled herself onto the lumpy stones, lay back, and tugged her skirt up.

Above her, Field Snake let out a long sigh. "Yes. Never had me a so-called lady before." With one hand he pulled his breechcloth down over his hips, let it fall. His erection bobbed as he stepped between her legs and dropped to his knees in anticipation.

She ground her teeth as he laid the handle of his war club across her throat. But told him, "You're right. Nothing I haven't done before. You won't need that war club."

He was leering into her face as he crawled onto her. "I'll keep the war club. Some women lose all sense when it comes to coupling."

She pulled her knees up. When he reached down to insert himself, she clutched the nearest fist-sized cobble. Tightening her grip, she smashed it hard into his temple. Even as he jerked at the impact, she hit him again, and again, pounding the stone into the side of his head with all her strength.

He rolled off her and she followed, used the stone to crush his nose.

Field Snake let out a dazed scream, flailed, and shrieked. Batted halfheartedly at her with his war club. She ducked it, paused only long enough to lay her hands on a larger rock, and with both hands, pulled it loose and drove it into his face.

Whimpering, he tried to scramble away. She tripped him, got the advantage, and from above hammered the heavy cobble into his head.

Then again and again. She was still raising and slamming her bloody stone into his pulped remains as Made of Wood and Bluefish came tearing through the willows.

They stopped short, gaping, as Night Shadow Star drove the stone down one last time onto the flattened and leaking wreckage of Field Snake's broken head.

Panting, she stood, resettling her skirt as she stared with distaste at the blood on her hands.

Shooting a sidelong glance at the two warriors, she said, "He thought all he needed was a war club to force me. You know how it is, some men lose all sense when it comes to coupling."

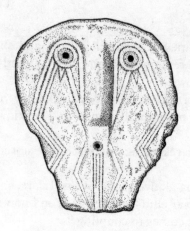

Invincible

Six Toes tells me the people who live here are called Catawba. This is an out-lier village, but I know from my time in Cofitachequi that most of their people live in communities up in the mountains and across the divide.

We put in here to rest, to try and dicker for something to eat besides fish, cattail roots, and bladderwort that we have been surviving on since leaving Willow Stem Village.

Not that we have much to Trade—or that we would even have been welcomed here but for Six Toes; he Trades here often.

It is apparent that the Catawba have no real use for Cahokians, more so since apparently a generation ago it was Moon Blade who attacked their old village, defeated their warriors, and caused them to flee to this side of the mountain.

Through Six Toes' supposed good graces, we were able to barter for a meal of cooked corn, boiled venison stew rich in onions, coontie root, and chunks of yellow lotus.

It cost my warriors some of their jewelry and other small personal items. They were not happy, even less so when I ordered Fire Light to make them hand their things over.

The entire evening reminds me of hawks and ravens. You know how they are over a kill? The hawks sit atop the carcass, stripping off meat and glaring at the ravens hopping around the periphery, hoping for enough of an opening to snatch a bite.

In the end, though the hawks could rip the ravens to pieces, it is always the canny ravens who finally trick the hawks into surrendering the carcass.

And that leads me right back to Six Toes, the supposedly neutral Trader who orchestrated a deal whereby my Cahokian warriors had to hand over precious *carvings, beadwork, and shell for a rather mundane meal. Hardly the Power of Trade.*

Doesn't matter that all through that meal, Six Toes kept his expression emotionless as he sat in the back of the rude ramada and conversed with the Catawba chief, his headmen, and clan matrons. I could tell he was among friends. Nor did I need to speak Catawba to understand what he was saying. Though Six Toes was feigning indifference—his voice in a monotone—the Catawba would shoot knowing glances, in unison, at me or High Chief Fire Light. Flickers of amusement or enjoyment would cross their faces.

My warriors, however, suspected nothing, just pursued their meal in surly silence.

Six Toes keeps telling them about how Night Shadow Star eludes me. I understand that, both from Six Toes' unwitting hand signs and the amused chuckles breaking from the Catawba as they shoot derisive glances my way.

In return, I narrow my eyes, give them the slit-eyed stare that, in the past, has sent anyone who knows me into a quaking fear.

The Catawba just grin.

Very well, Six Toes. I think you have served your purpose.

I return my attention to the wooden trencher and use a bit of acorn bread to soak up some of the last of the soup. A sensation of joyous anticipation is born in my chest.

The Catawba have given us a hut to sleep in for the night. It is a rude bent-pole structure covered with thatch, but it has a central fire and a couple of beds built into the walls. In our original inspection that afternoon, most of the warriors had seen enough vermin crawling around that they'd decided to sleep down on the landing beside the canoe.

Which well serves my plans.

After the meal, as my Cahokians rise to retire, I tell Fire Light, "I need you to sleep with the men. Whatever excuse you need, make it."

"And leave you alone with Six Toes?" he asks. "Are you sure that's wise?"

"Oh, yes," I tell him. "The Trader is going to help me discover some things. Somehow I think he's going to be more helpful to me tonight than he has ever been."

Not more than a hand of time after I retire to the hut and build up the fire, Six Toes ducks through the door. He glances around, asking, "Just you?"

"Just me," I tell him. "The others are down at the canoe landing. But you are going to help me tonight. I need to see."

"See what?" he asks, turning toward his pack where it lies atop one of the beds.

"I need to know where Night Shadow Star is. I need to discover a way of healing this pain in my shaft and stones. I need to look past the horizons, and discover what Power has in store for me."

He is still bent over, pulling at his pack strings when I slam my war club into the back of his head. Accompanied by the hollow sound of his snapping skull, he drops like a pile of meat.

"To do that," I tell his twitching and dying body, "I have to remove your organs and see what is reflected in the blood pooling in your rib cage." I pause. "Or did you think that traveling with a witch didn't have its downsides?"

I have plenty of time.

We will be gone long before the Catawba find the body. And on the way, I will take enough Trade with me to compensate the warriors for the trinkets they've lost.

I do hesitate long enough to wonder how Cahokians will be greeted the next time they come to the Catawba.

But that, I tell myself as I pull out my sharp chert knife, is not my problem.

I hear the distant rumble of thunder as I make my first cut.

Twenty-five

Night Shadow Star took immediate advantage of her companions' stunned reaction. As they stood over the young man's body, she plucked up the naive fool's war club, tested it, and found the weight a bit more than she would have preferred. Fanning it before her, she turned on Bluefish, declaring, "That bit of twitching and dying garbage said you wanted to be next. That as soon as he finished with me, and you could get up the nerve, it was going to be your turn."

She stalked up to the wide-eyed warrior, took a slashing cut through the air not a hand's width short of his face. The man backheeled, recovered, and put his hands out in surrender as he cried, "No, Lady, no!"

She pressed forward, chasing him back through the willows into the camp, where he almost collided with Summer Ice.

"Right now," she thundered, "we end this. I am Lady Night Shadow Star. Not anyone's bed toy. Come on, Bluefish. You want me? Stand still you pus-gutted worm! Unless you've got a good reason, you're dying like that simpering maggot Field Snake."

"Wait! Stop! On my honor! I'll never touch you. I swear!" Bluefish staggered back, slipped on some of the loose mussel shells, and almost fell into the fire. His hands were still up, a pleading desperation matching the terror in his eyes.

"On your knees," she snapped. "Touch your head when you're talking to a Cahokian noble. Now! Or I crush your skull like an eggshell. You *serve* me! Night Shadow Star of the Morning Star House of the Four Winds Clan. From this moment on, I am your lady."

"Yes!" Bluefish dropped to his knees, bowed his head, and touched his forehead in a gesture of obeisance.

Night Shadow Star shot a sidelong glance at the confused Summer Ice, who was gaping at the scene like an idiot. "And you, warrior? Do you serve me, or do you serve yourself? Choose."

Summer Ice, still clueless about what was going on, asked, "Serve you?"

At that moment Made of Wood stepped out of the willows, a grim look on his face. "We serve you, Lady." To Summer Ice he added, "That fool Field Snake tried to force the lady. She left him with his head flattened into mush."

Then Made of Wood respectfully touched his forehead. "At your service, my lady."

Nor had they said a word as she dragged Field Snake's body to the river, shoved it out into the current, and called, "As I promised, my Lord! An offering for our safe passage. Take this two-footed fool for your own."

Field Snake's corpse, floating low, was seized by the current, whirled around, and carried to the center of the river. As they watched from shore, a great ripple formed around the body. She swore a clawed foot dragged the dead youth down into the depths.

"Did you see that?" Summer Ice whispered. "Something seized him. Pulled him down."

"I serve my Lord," she told them, "and you serve me. Don't forget it."

That day she clambered into the rear of the canoe and took up the steering paddle. Then they set out, riding the fastest current downriver. She could hear Piasa, whispering, his voice muffled but filled with satisfaction.

"Yes, Lord. Now speed us along. And do not forget that I am trying to keep our bargain." A pause. "And that includes Fire Cat."

As they paddled, she got the whole story about how close Fire Cat had come to finding her and learned Field Snake's part in thwarting Fire Cat's arrival in Joara.

Bluefish finished it. "So Field Snake came trotting into Joara in the middle of the night. Claimed that an entire Cahokian war party was hot and close behind him. That he'd managed to misdirect them onto a supposed shortcut."

"And you believed him?" she asked, stroking and then steering them into the current's thread where it ran wide rounding a bend. "You ask me, I'd have called him a loud-mouthed braggart even before he tried to rape me. Makes me want to go back and kill him all over again."

"Some things didn't make sense," Made of Wood agreed as he paddled. "But that was later. Things he talked about. That he couldn't help himself, had to brag about hitting the Trader in the head with a branch. According to Field Snake, he dashed the man's brains out."

"That would have been Winder," she said thoughtfully. "So, he and Fire Cat were together again. But Blood Talon? I wonder if Field Snake was sure about the name. Blood Talon is working for Lord Spotted Wrist. He was sent to bring me back to Cahokia. He was responsible for Fire Cat's defeat at Red Wing Town. Tried to kill Fire Cat more than once. It makes no sense that he would be traveling with the Red Wing."

She paused, considering, as her gaze took in the thick forest that ran down to the river's banks, the oaks, maples, and sweet gum towering so high that she could barely catch glimpses of the mountains rising beyond. A blue heron took flight as they rounded the bend, the great bird flapping its wings across the flat surface of the water.

"I don't think there was any war party," Summer Ice added from where he paddled at the bow. "The way Field Snake bragged, he never mentioned any more than three men. Nothing about ranks of warriors on the trail. No descriptions of their armor, or how many there were. Nothing about their clans, or who gave the orders. Believe me, we all tried to pry what we could out of him. Might have had to fight them, right? So we wanted to know what, and how many, we were up against. He could never quite answer that. And over the course of our travel, the story kept changing. Little details that were inconsistent."

"Squadron First Blood Talon was in charge of a party of twenty-some warriors. I just can't imagine how Fire Cat could ally with them. It makes no sense."

Bluefish said, "Lady, Field Snake always insisted that Fire Cat was in charge. Bragged about how easily he fooled the war leader."

"War leader?" she echoed. "The Blood Talon I know would never bestow such an honorific on a man he'd made a slave. Perhaps this is another Blood Talon? Someone with the same name?"

"You know as much as we do, Lady," Made of Wood told her. "We always thought it was Field Snake trying to be more than he was."

"Why didn't you tell me?"

"Orders from the High Chief. 'Make no mention of a Cahokian war party in Lady Night Shadow Star's presence. Don't let her have any hope of rescue.'"

"Explains why he and my brother were so intent on hiding our trail, on making time from Joara to the river." She couldn't help it. She had to look back over her shoulder, wondering if, by chance, she was going to see Fire Cat paddling vigorously in pursuit.

Instead, all she saw was the narrow ribbon of water, the surface gleaming silver in a shaft of sunlight that pierced the clouds.

"What now, Lady?" Made of Wood asked. "We're on our own. Just the four of us. And we're far from anywhere that recognizes your authority."

"First thing?" she told them. "You're going to have to stop looking like warriors. Nothing we can do about the war shirts, but the beaded forelocks? The warrior's hair styles, they have to go. We can't look like Cahokians. We have to become Traders."

"What have we got to Trade?" Summer Ice asked.

"Have to pick that up as we travel," she told him. "If I'd been thinking, we'd have kept those mussel shells from supper last night."

"That would have barely been a sack of shells," Bluefish muttered. "Almost worthless."

"Almost," she agreed. "But worth something. And we've got three pearls. Got to start somewhere."

"Wishing you hadn't given all that Trade away at Willow Stem Town?" Made of Wood asked.

She shrugged, steered them wide of a submerged snag where the sheen on the surface betrayed its location. "At the time, my only goal was to kill Walking Smoke. Figured your high chief would order my death when I did. Long-term planning wasn't in the cast of the gaming pieces."

"Guess we changed that." Made of Wood stroked deeply with his paddle. "What about these villages we keep passing? If there's any way to find Trade, it's going to have to be with the local people."

"No." She glanced warily at the thick vegetation back from the riverbank. "These are mostly Mahica, others are related to the Chalakee, some Catawba. All are either suspicious of Cahokians or have bad history with them. With your tattoos and weapons, you don't look like Traders. I think we're best served by avoiding the locals until we get south of the Wide Fast."

As the river curled into a tight bend, a fish weir appeared as nothing more than sticks protruding from the surface and angling into a funnel along the right bank. To miss it, Night Shadow Star steered them closer to the left bank, seeking to pass wide of it.

As they rounded the bend they came upon a series of three canoes, all holding position around the circular fish trap at the bottom of the weir. The half-naked men and a single woman were in the final process of pulling up a net from the bottom of the trap. Fish could be seen straining and flopping, light streaking from their sides as they were hoisted over the gunwale and into the largest of the canoes. When the catch filled the hull, the canoe settled lower in the water.

At that point, the woman looked up, her eyes fixing with Night Shadow Star's across the roiling water. She pointed, a sharp cry escaping her lips, to be followed by an order in some language Night Shadow Star could only guess at.

The fishermen wheeled, craning their heads. They were dressed only in breechcloths, hair up in a barbarian's piled curls. One looked to be in his teens, the rest in their twenties and thirties. They didn't hesitate as they clambered about their canoes, pulling up bows, slinging quivers around their shoulders.

The woman shouted something that sounded like *"Achaeeia!"* and the two smaller canoes were pushed back from the weir. While some men reached for paddles, others were madly stringing their bows.

The two men in the big canoe also pushed free, bending to their paddles, sending their craft with its cargo of still-flopping fish into rapid flight.

"Greetings!" Night Shadow Star called in Trade pidgin, rising in the rear. "We come under the Power of Trade. We're just passing through."

The woman, her face reflecting fear and anger, kept shouting, pointing as her two canoes shot out to intercept Night Shadow Star's vessel as it rushed down toward them.

"Stop!" Night Shadow Star cried. "We come under the Power of Trade. You hear? Trade!" She dropped her paddle, using her hands to overemphasize the sign-language gesture for Trade.

Even as she did, the man in the first canoe rose high enough to clear the lower stave of his bow and released an arrow that hissed within a hand's distance of Night Shadow Star's head.

"That cuts it!" Bluefish cried, dropping his paddle to grab for his own weapons where they lay amidships.

The canoe rocked wildly as the Cahokian warriors scrambled for their bows and quivers; Night Shadow Star fought for balance and kept repeating, "Trade! We Trade!" and signing furiously.

"Pus and rot!" Bluefish cried. He was pulling his bow from its case when an arrow drove deeply into his side. The warrior jerked, his expression stunned, eyes popping wide. Desperately he whirled, mouth opening in disbelief at the sight of the shaft sticking out of his gut.

In the rear, Made of Wood had managed to free his bow, was struggling in the confines of the canoe to string it, almost capsizing the craft in the process.

Up front, another arrow thumped into Bluefish's body, the warrior now stiffening, a whimper deep in his throat.

"Stop!" Night Shadow Star screamed. "Trade, pus take you! We are *Traders!*"

In the second canoe, the woman kept shrieking, pointing, her features twisted in rage. The men were bent to the paddles, all but the one in front who, like the man in the first canoe, rose to his knees to loose an arrow. This one cut the air between Bluefish's and Summer Ice's heads.

As it did, Made of Wood managed to string his bow, rip an arrow from his quiver, and rise. Taking his time, he ignored the third arrow that drove itself into Bluefish's cowering body. Made of Wood's release took the lead archer, driving full into the man's breast. Perched high as he was, the fisherman slipped sideways, dropped his bow, and clutched the arrow with both hands. Then he collapsed, dragging the canoe and its paddlers into the water.

"Summer Ice!" Made of Wood snapped. "Hold Bluefish! Keep him upright! Use his body for a shield. Lady, point us straight at that last canoe!"

She glimpsed the arrow as it sailed from the oncoming canoe, watched the shaft gleam in the sunlight as it arched and drove into Bluefish's body. Felt the impact through the hull as Bluefish kicked in response. But Summer Ice had him now, had wrapped his arms around Bluefish's shoulders, was holding him upright, the body bristling with arrows.

Made of Wood drew, muscles knotting, and released. Like a sun-streaked dart, his shaft flew true; the fletching imparted a spin as the razor-sharp chert war point drove into the archer's stomach.

The man looked down, dropped his bow to clutch the arrow, and slumped backward. The paddler behind him fumbled to retrieve the man's bow, wrenched an arrow from beneath the body, and rose to shoot.

Made of Wood had his rhythm now, whipping another arrow from his quiver. He nocked, drew, aimed, and released. The arrow took the second man high and left. Drove through his shoulder so that a hand's length of point and the fore shaft were visible as the man spun under the impact.

Night Shadow Star, jaws clenched, propelled the canoe toward the fishermen, glaring her disbelief as the furious local woman continued to exhort her men to attack. But with two dying, the last two men in her craft refused, and broke off. The woman was still screaming as the two paddlers struck out for the wooded shoreline.

In the water just ahead, the capsized canoe bobbed, three men kicking and swimming away for all they were worth. As they thrashed toward shore, they cast frightened glances over their shoulders, eyes panicked.

Made of Wood drew, took a bead, picking his target.

"Let them go," Night Shadow Star told him. "We've won."

"Lady?"

"It is all right, Warrior." To Summer Ice, "How is Bluefish?"

"Barely breathing, Lady. His gut has gone hard. Bleeding out internally if I'm any judge. He's got to be seeing the ancestors, knows they're close."

"What in seven shades of shit possessed them?" Made of Wood demanded as the local woman's canoe hit the bank and the living grabbed their dying friends. Together they dragged them up the bank, into the screen of vegetation.

The woman, un-chastened, continued to stand on the shore, water lapping at her feet, her fist raised and shaking as she screamed curses and imprecations their way.

Night Shadow Star considered their situation. "We're in range of the bank if they decide to shoot from cover. Paddle. Hurry. We need to leave this place behind us. Now!"

Made of Wood dropped his bow for his paddle.

"What of Bluefish?" Summer Ice asked softly. "I can't feel his heartbeat. He's no longer breathing."

"Put him over the side," Made of Wood said.

Summer Ice jerked his head around. "Are you out of your mind? He's a Hawk Clan warrior. His ancestors are in the Sky World."

"Let him go," Night Shadow Star added in a soothing voice. "My Lord will take care of his soul. I give you my word."

Night Shadow Star clenched her jaws in response to the horrified look on Summer Ice's face as he wrestled Bluefish's dead weight, balanced it on the gunwale, and let his friend slide into the water.

"Paddle now!" Night Shadow Star told them. "We need to be . . ." She lost the words as they rounded the next bend.

The village was there, perhaps two bowshots back from the bank. She could see the canoe landing, the big canoe with its load of fish hastily pulled up. The fishermen were running full up from the landing, calling out. More shouting came from the forest upriver. The survivors from the woman's canoe, running to raise the alarm.

"I said, *paddle*!" Night Shadow Star cried as she raised herself, bending to the task as she drove her paddle deep and sent the canoe shooting forward.

Behind them, Bluefish's arrow-riddled corpse bobbed low in the current, then vanished amid the swirling eddies.

Twenty-six

They had to rest. No way could Fire Cat escape that single haunting reality. For two days now, he had driven them. Winder was blinking like some day-blind owl. Blood Talon had fallen asleep, his paddle in hand, and was slumped low in the canoe's hull, Night Shadow Star's box of Trade supporting the squadron first's back. Shell Hook's chin had fallen onto his chest where he sat in the back, and this time the hard nod of his head hadn't awakened him.

They were passing a fish weir when a canoe broke from the weeds, a warrior rising in the front, a bow held at the ready, an arrow nocked but not drawn.

The man called in a language Fire Cat had never heard. In pidgin he called back, "Traders." And set his paddle aside to reach for his Trader's staff.

Behind him, Winder said, "Catawba, given the cut of their hair and tattoos." Then he, too, lifted his Trader's staff and called, "What news?"

"Then, you are indeed Traders?" the man asked uncertainly.

"We are," Shell Hook, having blinked himself awake, called back and added something in what had to be Catawba.

"What's the news?" Winder asked. "I don't speak their tongue."

"Witchery," Shell Hook translated. "Two nights ago, Six Toes brought a witch and a party of Cahokians to their village. The next morning they found Six Toes dead, his body cut apart, his heart and liver cooked and partially eaten. Most of his skin was flayed. The Cahokians were gone."

"Walking Smoke," Fire Cat growled under his breath. In pidgin he asked, "Was there a woman with the witch?"

"No," the man called back. "But a woman and three Cahokians

passed this morning. Being Cahokian, and after what happened to us, we tried to take them. We needed to sacrifice them as appeasement to the ancestors and Power, to cleanse our village of the Cahokian witch's pollution."

"Where is she?" Fire Cat demanded, starting to rise.

Winder put a firm hand on his shoulder, forcing him back down and whispering, "Don't give us away, Red Wing."

"She is downriver, being pursued," the man called.

"Hope you catch her," Winder called back. "We want no part of your troubles. We'll just paddle on past."

"Go!" the man called. "But be warned the witch is somewhere downriver."

"We'll be careful," Shell Hook called back. "Thank you for the warning."

Fire Cat had already replaced his Trader's staff, was driving his paddle deep, sending them racing ahead.

"How do you want to play this?" Winder asked.

"Let's just hope she's still alive," Fire Cat told him, and gritted his teeth as he poured new strength into his paddle.

Come on, Piasa. You're not going to let her down now, are you?

They rounded two more bends, the current running wide and close to the bank. The chorus of insects, the birdsong, all grated on Fire Cat's nerves. As they cleared the second bend, they saw a tree that had fallen in the shallows, its branches and trunk, shorn of leaves, poking down into the murky water. Vs of ripples trailed out like wakes from each of the branches.

The thing bobbing in the tree's backwater got Fire Cat's attention. There's something about a floating body, the way the shoulders and back of the head barely break the surface. The limpid way the corpse bobs in the current. How the arms and legs, unseen and submerged, dangle into the depths. Facedown, the body seemed to waffle in the current, as though one of the feet was caught up in one of the tree's submerged branches. The man's hair was up. Looked like a warrior's bun.

Adding to the unsettling sight was the fletching and shaft that protruded from the corpse's right shoulder; most of the length had been driven into the dead man's chest, which indicated the shot had come from close range.

"Do we want to take a look?" Winder asked. "Maybe hope that it's Walking Smoke?"

"That's a warrior's hair bun," Blood Talon noted. "I'd call it Cahokian."

Fire Cat hesitated for half a stroke. Then he drove their canoe forward. "Doesn't matter who it is. Nothing we can do for him now. My Lady is up ahead somewhere."

The pounding of Fire Cat's heart felt like a hammer against his breastbone. Fear began to rise, bitter and acidic in his stomach.

Where is Night Shadow Star? Where?

But when he looked down, no weird blue glow paced them down in the depths.

As they rounded the next bend, Fire Cat's heart skipped. The Catawba onshore had just dragged yet another corpse from the water. Two of them held the dead warrior by the arms, pulling him up the muddy bank. The dead warrior's head lolled over the man's breast, a water-logged war shirt draining in streams. The man's heels made shallow furrows in the black mud, the feet canted to the right. Even as the Catawba paused in their labor, the red stain could be seen spreading on the dead man's chest as blood drained from a puncture.

"Traders!" Winder called, lifting his staff. "We're just passing through!"

"Paddle," Blood Talon gritted out.

As the Catawba continued to wrestle with their grisly prize, the dead warrior's head rolled. Fire Cat's jaws hardened as the bare skull was exposed, the wound washed pink from immersion in the river. Whatever else they were going to inflict on the dead warrior, they'd already taken his scalp.

"Cahokian," Blood Talon growled as he reflexively stroked his paddle. "I don't know what to tell you, War Leader."

Which is when they saw yet another body wedged under the bank, where the current had dragged it beneath some willows. Catawba this time, from the hairstyle and dress.

"Please, Piasa," Fire Cat prayed. "Lead me to her."

Don't let me be too late!

Twenty-seven

An arrow thunked into the shagbark hickory that Night Shadow Star was using for cover. She peeked out past the bole; the attacking canoe was heading straight for the tip of the island. If they landed, she was dead. Since she'd taken refuge here, one other canoe had already slipped past. Not a doubt but that it had landed the two men and single woman somewhere in the trees behind her.

She nocked an arrow, struggled against Summer Ice's bow. The heavy pull was almost more than she could draw. Trembling, she braced herself against the shagbark, willed her straining arm to be still. Sighted down the arrow and released. The shaft leapt out in a blur. It took the lead warrior low and left, cut through his side, and stopped in the second man's thigh.

At the screams of pain and rage, the two men behind dipped their paddles and steered them back, then off to the side, seeking to slip past the head of the island. Get behind her.

"Pus and blood," Night Shadow Star hissed under her breath.

She peered out past the shagbark, discovered the river upstream to be wondrously empty of additional pursuit.

She reached behind her. Three arrows left from Summer Ice's quiver. Not that he'd need them anymore. She'd lost Made of Wood's quiver when she dove from the canoe, letting it and her dead warriors drift off downriver in hopes they would lead pursuit away from her as she swam to the island.

And it almost worked; two of the Catawba canoes had gone chasing after it. But the third had slowed; that same accursed woman who'd sent her men to the attack back at the fish weir ordered the two men in her canoe to land to search the island.

Night Shadow Star had waited until they were close enough that she couldn't miss and killed them both. Would have killed that gods-cursed woman, too, if she hadn't bailed off the backside of the canoe, striking off downstream and screaming her bloody head off.

But the damage was done. Night Shadow Star's hiding place was discovered.

Nothing to do but fight it out.

Against how many Catawba?

What in the name of pus sent them after us in the first place?

Didn't the triple-dyed fools understand what "Trader" meant?

Night Shadow Star filled her lungs, a bitter smile playing on her lips. Well, this was as fine a place to die as any. Nice little island, rocky center covered with gravel and silt. Enough to support the trees, give them sufficient root to withstand the occasional floods that had piled driftwood in tangles between the trunks.

The good news was that the interlaced trunks of driftwood and flood debris created natural fortifications. Places she could hide, allow her pursuers to close, and shoot them from cover. A perfect warren she could crawl through, perhaps slip away. Maybe even allow her to duck into the river, dive, and swim clear. Or get around the hunters, kill whoever was guarding the canoes, and make an escape.

Shouts came from beyond the trees.

"That's it," she whispered. "Keep calling to each other. Let me know just where you are."

Gods, she wished for her own bow. Drawing Summer Ice's was like trying to bend an oak. Strong as she was from her months on the river, it took all her might. Not the sort of thing she could shoot reliably. Or fast.

Three arrows left.

None of it made sense. Why were they hunting her? It was bad enough that they'd killed Bluefish, Summer Ice, and Made of Wood, but in turn they had lost six men, with an additional three or four badly wounded. And for no reason.

Another shout from beyond the trees.

Night Shadow Star eased her way through a pile of logs that reminded her of interlaced fingers, each step placed carefully on the crackling leaf mat.

Bending and weaving, she clambered through the gray-bleached trunks and found a shadowed hollow. There she leaned against the thick bole of a bark-scarred sweet gum and waited.

Movement. There.

Her hunter had a problem: She could wait in ambush. Silent. Motionless in the shadows. Carefully, braced against the gum, she nocked her arrow. Ever patient.

The hunter, a man in his twenties, stepped out into Night Shadow Star's line of sight. His eyes darting this way and that, he carefully took another step. Bow held at the ready, an arrow nocked. He stopped short, and Night Shadow Star threw all her effort into drawing the bow; a faint rustle of the leaves came from her left.

Don't look. Finish it!

Arms quaking, she squinted down the arrow, past the sharp chert head, and let the hunter step into her shot as she released. Even as the arrow drove home, she dropped, scrambling away as an arrow from off to her left hissed and smacked into the gum where she had been but half a heartbeat before.

Leaping up, Night Shadow Star grabbed the shaft, pulled. Only to have the stone head snap off clean in the bark. So much for adding to her count.

Two arrows left.

"Piss and spit!" She tossed the useless arrow aside, ducked and scrambled back into the tangle. Wondered where that second archer was. Somewhere she couldn't see. There, off to the left!

She cocked her head, listening for all she was worth for that faint crackle of a foot on the leaf mat or the brush of a dried branch against skin or leather.

Meanwhile, the warrior she'd shot was staggering away, thrashing through the tangled mess of driftwood and debris in his desperate flight.

She wasn't sure how badly he'd been wounded. Hoped she'd hit him center and hard.

That accursed woman called in accented pidgin from the other side of the trees: "Cahokian! Power has deserted you. You cannot escape. You are beaten."

Night Shadow Star, like a snake, wiggled her way between two of the flood-tossed trunks, working the long bow through the tangle.

If she could get closer to that unseen hunter, be someplace he didn't expect her, she might have a chance.

"You are dead, Cahokian!" the woman's voice called again from the eastern shore. "Your Power is broken. The ancestors have abandoned you."

Night Shadow Star reached down, pulled a piece of splintered branch from the leaf mat at her feet. Picking a hole, she tossed it. Heard it thump back by the gum where she'd taken her last shot.

Please. Let her hunter have heard that.

Did her imagination fool her? Or did she hear a crunching of a carefully placed foot on the leaf mat?

Barely daring to breathe, she slowly craned her neck, eyes searching each gap in the tangle of driftwood. Piss and rot, if she could just stop her heart from beating. How could he not hear its hammering as it tried to slam its way through her breastbone?

There, the faintest of movements. Staring through a narrow slit between the logs, she could made out the angle of an elbow.

Close.

Not more than four paces away on the other side of the logs. And no way she could shoot, cramped and contorted as she was.

What to do?

This hunt would be decided by whoever turned out to be the cleverest. The loser would be the one who moved first.

But the longer it took, the greater the probability of even more hunters arriving on the island. And when they did, the net would be drawn tight around her.

She still had a chance. If she could ease away from this man, ghost her way to the river, perhaps she could still wiggle into the water. Ducking and diving, she'd let the current carry her past the canoes on the lower end of the island.

The elbow vanished.

Night Shadow Star listened. Thought she heard a muffled crackle headed in the direction of the gum tree.

The hunter? Or a distraction?

Gods, what a game of wits.

Night Shadow Star lifted a leg, slid it over a half-rotten maple trunk. Eased over the log and remained crouched. Again she carefully peered through each of the cracks and gaps, saw nothing.

Then she ducked low, shinnied under a thigh-thick birch branch, and congratulated herself on making another step toward freedom.

A chattering of jays erupted in the direction the woman's voice had come from. A squirrel called from up in the leaves.

This close to her hunter, it could have been either of them who had set the squirrel off, but the hunter would be more irritated at the rodent.

She stepped over the last of the logs, taking a long and careful look at the surrounding vegetation. Sumac grew between her and the river, and then tall riparian grasses. All to the better, if she could make it that far, she could belly crawl all the way to the water's edge.

Alert as she was, she almost missed it. Just a fleeting glimpse of something from the corner of her eye.

She didn't jerk her head around; instead she eased her eyes to the left.

The hunter. A man in his thirties, bow up, but not drawn. His eyes were fixed on the tangle she'd just emerged from, intense gaze searching as he slowly craned his head this way and that and studied each gap.

At any moment he would see her standing out in the open. Then survival went to whoever drew first and shot straightest.

And that would be him, with his familiar bow.

Piasa take me. Only one chance left.

Night Shadow Star filled her lungs, fear running bright and powering her muscles as she raised Summer Ice's heavy bow, struggled against the pull.

The moment she did, he was moving, reacting, spinning as he drew to his cheek.

Her arrow flashed in the dappled forest light, caught him just under the left arm. Even as her point punctured the warrior's chest, his arrow came at her in a blur. Whisked along her cheek, tugging her hair and slapping her ear as it hissed past like a sour breeze.

The hunter seemed to waver, tried to lower his bow, stopped short when his arm came up against the fletched shaft. The man gasped at the pain. His eyes, dark and shining, had gone wide to expose the whites.

One arrow left.

"Sorry," she told him. Swallowed hard and was lowering her bow. She felt the trickle: warm liquid beginning to run down her cheek and neck. A questing finger found the sting in her cheek and ear to be cuts left as the stone-tipped arrow had passed.

The river. Need to get to the river.

She turned. Saw the boy step out from the sumac, a bow in his hands. He was grinning wide, exposing large white teeth. His Catawba tattoos looked fresh, barely healed, the way they'd appear if he'd just made his passage from a boy to manhood.

He said something in his own language that she thought might be "I got you!"

No way she was going to be able to pull her last arrow. Nock it, let alone draw and release, before his shaft took her full in the chest.

"Guess you'll have to find another fool to possess, Piasa," she muttered with resignation.

Couldn't believe it.

Out of nowhere an arrow made that unforgettable hollow thumping sound as it struck the boy's chest. Seemed to magically appear. Fletching and a finger's length of shaft stuck out just below the young man's right nipple. Another finger's length of bloody point and hafting protruded from his left scapula.

Even as the boy staggered and his arrow drove into the leaf mat at her feet, a voice softly said, "If you'll come, Lady, we really should be getting away from here."

Twenty-eight

As Night Shadow Star wheeled, gaping, the bow she held at the ready, Fire Cat had another arrow already nocked. In that glimpse, he saw the blood coursing down her cheek, the startled wonder in her magnificent eyes. Yes, it was her. His Lady. As beautiful and Powerful as he imagined.

He rose from the riparian grass, his heart beating like a thing gone wild. Desperate to run to her, he nevertheless kept his gaze fixed on the youth, watched the boy drop to his knees and fold into a seated position.

"You're a hard woman to catch," Winder added, stepping out from the sumac.

"What do you expect?" she asked, her knees seeming to go weak. "I'm not done here."

"Keep an eye out," Fire Cat told Winder. Then he ran those last few paces, swept her up in his arms, and whirled her around. "I thought I was too late."

"I've missed you like my heart was tearing in two." She was hugging him with such force it drove the bow into his back. Forced the wind from his lungs.

"I came," he whispered, burying his face in her hair, inhaling her scent. Then he pushed her back, lifted a finger to the bleeding cut on her cheek. Tried not to wince at the split in her ear. "You're hurt."

"Just a scratch." Her eyes were swimming with tears, and she clasped him to her again. "Pus and rot, but I've missed you. Prayed for you. I've never been so thankful. You're a miracle. Never leave me again."

Winder cleared his throat, muttered, "Um, escape now? Hug later?" He paused when Night Shadow Star wouldn't let go of Fire Cat. "Excuse me. Angry Catawba are still at large."

"I've still got one arrow left." Night Shadow Star finally pushed Fire Cat back, reached up with her free hand, and ran her fingers down his cheek. "Gods, yes. You're real. And you're here."

Again Winder made that suggestive clearing of the throat, his worried eyes searching the island's tangled trees and brush.

The dying youth had ceased to cough up blood, his eyes gone vacant, his right heel kicking out one last time to groove the leaf mat.

"Let's go." Fire Cat took her hand and led her down through the grass to the river where a high-prowed Trade canoe was held against shore by—impossibly—Blood Talon and some Trader.

"Let me take a look at that wound," Fire Cat told her, his souls still so joyous he could barely stand it.

"Later," Blood Talon told him as he picked up a paddle.

Winder was pushing them out into the current, before grabbing up his Trader's staff. "And get Night Shadow Star out of sight, War Leader. These Catawba catch sight of her, there's going to be a whole lot more bodies floating. And most of them will be ours."

"But she's bleeding," Fire Cat cried.

"It will heal," Night Shadow Star told him with a smile that must have stung like cactus, because she winced and reached instinctively for her cheek.

"Use that heavy Trade tarp," Blood Talon suggested. "Lady, if you'd climb down beside the Trade box, we can make you look just like the rest of the load."

"What's he doing here?" Night Shadow Star asked as she pulled the folded tarp loose.

"Long story, Lady," Fire Cat told her. "Now, duck. I see some woman making her way through the brush."

Night Shadow Star had dropped to the bottom, hunched, and pulled the tarp down tight by the time the old woman stormed her way to the edge of the island. "You seen a woman?" she called.

"Back up at the head of the island!" Shell Hook called. "The silly camp bitch shot an arrow at us! Us, can you believe? Traders! What's happened to the Power of Trade?"

"She's a foul witch!" the woman screamed. "Attacked us for no good reason. Cahokians. All of them. Scum like ticks and chiggers that need to die."

"Well, kill her for us!" Winder called back, waving his Trader's staff. "We just want to get as far as we can from you, her, and the rest of this madness!"

"Go on," the woman called, waving them ahead. "We've no quarrel with honest Traders. Just Cahokians."

Fire Cat heard Night Shadow Star's muffled "Liar" from under the tarp. "Wish I could have killed her, too."

As the last of the island passed behind them, Fire Cat sighed and glanced back at Winder. "Now you know why I pushed so hard. How could a man help but love a lady like mine with all his heart?"

Winder chuckled. "You ever get tired of her, Red Wing, I'll make you an offer you can't refuse."

"You take chances, River Fox," Night Shadow Star's muffled voice warned. "I've still got that one arrow left."

Fire Cat smiled, driving his paddle into the Tenasee's silty current. "I think I'm the happiest man alive."

His heart just wouldn't stop Dancing in his chest. He'd done it. He'd found her!

No matter what, everything would be all right now.

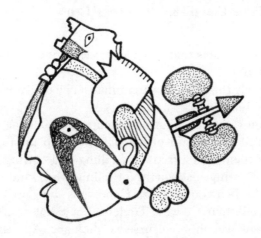

Twenty-nine

I don't know how you found me," Night Shadow Star whispered again as they lay side by side beneath the blanket.

Fire Cat gave her his best grin. "Easy. I went looking for the worst trouble I could find. And there you were right in the middle of it."

In the flickering firelight, a thousand stars overhead, Fire Cat let his fingers trace through Night Shadow Star's hair. They had tended to the slice that ran along her smooth cheek as best they could and sewn up the two halves of her ear where the Catawba arrow had severed the cartilage.

Across the fire from where they had made their bed, Winder, Blood Talon, and Shell Hook slept. The men might have been logs; only Blood Talon's soft snoring penetrated the night song of crickets, a distant owl, and a thousand frogs. Clouds had darkened the heavens, and far-off lightning flashing over the mountains to the east.

For Fire Cat, nothing else mattered. He could stay thus. Forever. Holding the woman he loved.

She shifted. "Do you know how cramped it was, having to spend the entire day curled into a ball on the bottom of Shell Button's canoe? I could barely breathe under that tarp. Thought my joints would never stop aching."

"Have to tell you, you made the best-looking Trader's pack I've ever seen. But it was a whole lot better than having one of the Catawba see you. I've seen angry people before, but those Catawba reminded me of a kicked anthill. They were swarming up and down both sides of the river.

I think caution dictates that you stay hidden under that tarp for another day or two at least."

"You probably think it's easy to imitate a pile of Trade goods. My back was about to break."

"Would you rather be fighting a long retreat all the way to the Fast Wide?" He rolled a strand of her hair between his fingers. "Walking Smoke drove them into a frenzy by killing and cutting up that Trader, Six Toes, and eating his heart. Not telling what kind of witchcraft he practiced. And then you and your Cahokians show up."

"I tried to tell them we were Traders. They shot first."

"All they saw was more accursed Cahokians. And things went from bad to worse."

"We need to tell anyone we meet who is headed upriver that they are hostile." She shifted, the long bloody wound in her cheek black in the night. "Speaking of hostile. What is Blood Talon doing in your canoe? Last I heard, he wanted you dead and me safely returned to Spotted Wrist's bed. What happened when you turned his canoe over?"

"I drowned all his men," Fire Cat told her softly. "Almost drowned myself, but I made it to that island we'd just passed. I was headed upriver when I found him. He'd been taken by locals who'd lost kin when a tree toppled onto a house in a storm. They'd tied him to their version of a square and were going to cut him apart as a sacrifice to their ancestors."

"So you saved him?" she asked incredulously.

"Call it a moment of madness."

"Ah, that's what all those healing scars are about. They tortured him." She paused. "You trust him?"

"As much as I can trust any man. But yes. The man who came out the other side of that trial is very different from the one I tried to drown that day."

"What about Winder?" she asked.

"In the end, I don't know. Never forget that he is in this for whatever he can get out of it. For the time being, he thinks being in the service of Night Shadow Star of the Morning Star House will bring him fortune." He paused. "But you traveled with him. You know him better than I."

"He's right. Serving me will bring him fortune. And yes, he's as much a scoundrel as Seven Skull Shield, but without that odd streak of honor deep down in his bones." She smiled, which made her wince from the stinging cut. "And he's every bit as much of a lecherous dog."

"Do I need to . . ."

"Shhh." She placed fingers to his lips. "Nothing I couldn't handle. Besides, you can't blame a man for being a man."

He chuckled at that. "Gods, I have missed you. I came so close back at Joara. When we finally catch up to that pus-dripping Field Snake, it will be a close-run thing to see if I can get to him before Winder does."

"Field Snake?" she mused. "Young man in his late teens? Had a smile as slippery as pond scum? Claimed to have saved Walking Smoke from a Cahokian war party?"

"You know him?"

She shifted in his arms, her eyes like dark holes in her night-pale face. "I beat his head in with a rock."

"What?"

"Hammered it into a flattened pulp of blood, bones, and brains. He thought he might warm his shaft in my sheath. It was necessary to disabuse my warriors of entertaining any such fantasies. Fed Field Snake's corpse to Piasa as an offering. Maybe that's why he let you catch up and appear at just the right moment." A pause. "Fed each of those warriors to Piasa. Made of Wood and Summer Ice? Both were good men. Bluefish, perhaps not so, but in the end, he saved us."

Fire Cat drew a deep breath. "And what now, Lady?"

"We chase down Walking Smoke. I still have a duty and a promise to keep. After that, my husband, you and I can be free."

"Husband?"

"Is that not what you wish?"

In the dim flicker of the firelight, he saw the lines of doubt deepen in her forehead, and told her, "With all my heart. But until this entire mess is brought to a conclusion I can only—"

"While we were separated I had a lot of time to think," she interrupted. "Even if we are forced to return to Cahokia, I will marry no other man. Not on the matron's order or even the Morning Star's. *You* are my husband. From here on, that cannot be denied. Nor will I allow it to be."

Her words kindled a warmth in his breast. "It would be my honor, Lady."

"Then you must call me wife."

"Not sure I can do that."

She gave off a soft sigh of annoyance. "Well, Red Wing, you've always been more than a little thickheaded. I will just have to show you what it means to be a husband. Make sure you understand your new duties."

And so saying, she reached down under the blankets until her questing fingers encircled his shaft. With a gentle insistence, she pulled him along as she rolled onto her back.

"Who says I'm thickheaded?" he whispered into her unwounded ear. "Wife."

Thirty

Never had Spotted Wrist felt so impotent or enraged. Not even the night when that foul thief, Seven Skull Shield, was stolen out from under him. He mused on that as his litter was carried down the Avenue of the Sun toward Morning Star's high temple mound. The day was hot, brassy, and sweltering. He wished he had a sunshade for his litter, but somehow it had been left behind in the morning rush to get on the road.

On top of it all, the pus-rotted gods alone knew what he'd been summoned to discuss. Anything having to do with Morning Star was dyspeptic. No doubt the living god wanted another update on that gods-accursed Koroa copper or some such. Just, please, by Piasa's balls, don't let it be about the pus-dripping canoes.

As the days had passed, a quarter moon stretched into a half. And now they were past that. In all that time his warriors had only managed to recover a pitiful fraction of the canoes he had been responsible for. A fact for which he was still being assailed. Seemed like complaints were coming from every quarter. The Traders he could ignore. Especially the foreign ones. What could they do? But the ones from the Earth Clans? That got a bit more tricky.

The whole situation was intolerable.

In response to the endless heckling, he traveled with an armed escort of twenty warriors, Squadron First Cut Weasel at their head. It might have been a nuisance, but while surrounded by an armed box of warriors, the closest his hounding creditors could get was mere shouting distance as they bellowed, "Where is my gods-rotted canoe, Keeper? You owe me! You owe my clan." Or some such.

The worst was that the various Traders and Earth Clans claimants had taken to camping out at Serpent Woman Town, pressing their claims to his nephew, High Chief Wolverine. When they couldn't get to him, they'd plague his niece, Matron Slender Fox. And—married to Cut Weasel as she was—that *always* got back to Spotted Wrist.

Both the high chief and matron had made it clear to the owners of the missing boats that North Star House was *not* liable for the loss of the canoes. That, they insisted, was the Keeper's responsibility. When it came to communicating their displeasure concerning the situation, they didn't mince words.

All of which fed a constant and increasing anger and frustration, which necessitated the never-ending redeployment of his scattered squadrons ever farther downriver. But the farther they got, the fewer canoes they recovered. So, how did a rank-and-file warrior tell a lost canoe from a passing Trader's? Sure, if they found one empty and lodged against the shore, but they couldn't seize every thrice-blasted canoe they encountered on the river.

"How in a piss-pot did that many canoes just disappear?" he groused as his litter was carried past Night Shadow Star's palace. The building looked grand atop its grassy earthen pyramid where it overlooked the Great Plaza. He gave the tall palace a slit-eyed scowl. In the front, at the top of the stairs, Piasa and Horned Serpent might have been glaring balefully down at him alone.

His troubles had started with Night Shadow Star and her refusal to marry him. Until that moment, he had been triumphant. Everything had been falling into place.

Pus and spit! He should have been *living* in that most opulent of palaces instead of the almost invisible dwelling he'd built atop Lady Lace's vacant mound. Didn't matter that he'd had a layer of earth laid atop the charred surface where Lace's palace had stood. The tall and imposing trench-wall building he'd had constructed seemed to carry a taint. One he'd barely begun to understand when, somehow, the thief had been rescued from the bear cage he'd been locked in.

Only to vanish.

Completely.

As if he'd never been.

"Headed downriver if he has a brain in his head." Spotted Wrist suffered the first hints of that acid-in-the-gut feeling that promised only to get worse.

He need but look up the avenue running north along the base of the Morning Star's Great Mound to see Lady Blue Heron's mound just past the society houses. Atop its flat summit, he could make out the charred posts. Left untouched for so many moons now. *Tonka'tzi* Wind, for whatever reason, had ordered it left as it was. To his surprise, Clan Matron Rising Flame had not objected.

What did that mean? Didn't matter that he'd heard rumors. That Blue Heron was seen here, or spotted there, or that she'd been dressed as this, or sometimes disguised as that. When he sent his warriors searching, they found nothing.

And they'd done their duty, watching the Four Winds Clan House, the *Tonka'tzi*'s palace, the stairway to the Council House, and even Evening Star's palace.

Fact was, Blue Heron would have been noticed. After Wind, she was the highest-ranked noble in the Morning Star's direct lineage. Like Wind, she'd been born to privilege. The woman had her standards when it came to the environs in which she'd allow herself to live. Yet not a single sighting of her had panned out.

She's dead. No other explanation.

But why, then, did he have that uneasy sensation of something out of place as Cut Weasel bellowed, "Make way! Make way for the Clan Keeper, the Hero of the North!"

From his high position on his litter, Spotted Wrist watched the milling crowd before the Morning Star's mound slowly part. Here, at the foot of the Great Mound, the knot of pilgrims, porters, petitioners, and servants to foreign embassies blocked the entire Avenue of the Sun, and it was only midday. Traders, craftspeople, and travelers trying to pass were forced out into the Great Plaza, but only as far as Morning Star's chunkey courts, where—with Morning Star's warriors on guard—they had to press into a moving mass lest they blunder onto the groomed sand where two Earth Clans nobles now played, followed by their audiences and those who were betting on the sidelines.

"Make way!" Cut Weasel thundered.

Spotted Wrist's warriors were reaching out past their shields, using war clubs to move the less motivated of the gawkers, hawkers, and porters who crowded just back from the stacked litters awaiting those who were already involved in business either on the Council Terrace level or up at Morning Star's palace.

"Hey!" someone screamed after being on the receiving end of a club. "I'm a chief in the Deer Clan, I'll have your hind end skinned, warrior."

"Tell that to the Keeper," the warrior replied. "Now move your chapped butt."

Spotted Wrist bit off a smile, let his warriors clear a space at the foot of the stairs. Then they carefully lowered his litter.

"Oh, yeah?" the Deer Clan chief declared in a loud voice. "Where's the missing canoes your great Keeper took and let get stolen? How's the

Hero of the North expect to run Cahokia if he can't even get a squadron across the river?"

From all sides, a cackle of laughter rolled through the crowd, accompanied by whistles and jeers.

Stunned by the insolence, all Spotted Wrist could do was stare in murderous hatred; his heart began to thud in his chest. In a dazed sort of way, he blinked, taking in the faces on all sides. These were riffraff. Mere commoners. Earth Clans folk, and even dirt farmers, and they dared to laugh at him?

"After that man!" Cut Weasel ordered, his face contorting as he pointed with his staff of office. "Get him! Bring him to the Keeper!"

The Deer Clan chief—a man in his early forties—artfully sidestepped, dodged, and slipped away in the now riotous crowd.

Someone started shouting, *"Canoes! Canoes! Canoes! They're all missing, but whose?"*

"Canoes! Canoes! Canoes!" The crowd took up the chant. *"They're all missing, but whose?"*

The two warriors who'd charged off into the crowd, having lost the Deer Clan chief, slowly worked their way back, glowering and red-faced as they shoved their way through the throng.

"Come on," Cut Weasel said as he stepped back and gave Spotted Wrist a hand up.

Climbing to his feet, Spotted Wrist heard someone yell, "Got a special on canoes this quarter moon. A dozen for a copper plate. Fresh from the attack against Evening Star Town. Only one previous owner!"

Another thunderous roar of laughter went up from the mob.

At the foot of the stairs, Spotted Wrist—a violent rage burning free in his breast—said, "Squadron First?"

"Keeper?"

"Turn the warriors loose. I want those vermin beaten to within a hair's breadth of dead."

"Keeper?" Cut Weasel, face pale, his tattoos twitching in time to his nervous lips, raised a cautionary hand. "There's but twenty of us. Maybe a couple hundred in that crowd. We'd have to kill some of them, Keeper. Maybe a lot of them before we could disperse them. Earth Clans chiefs? Might be some foreign lords in the mix. You really want that kind of complication?"

Spotted Wrist made himself climb. One foot ahead of the other. Under his feet the squared-log steps were polished so fine the grain looked like it had been waxed. "No. Not that those vile human rodents don't deserve it, but . . . but . . ."

"It would make more problems than it would solve," Cut Weasel finished for him.

Not exactly the words he'd had in mind, but he'd go with them.

At the top—one on either side of the gaping Council Terrace Gates—the two Morning Star House warriors stood their posts. Resplendent in their shiny wood-and-leather uniforms, feather splays on their shoulders and waxed hardwood shields catching the sunlight, they bowed, touching their foreheads in respect.

Spotted Wrist caught the barely smothered smiles, the carefully averted eyes.

Stalking through the gates, he kept his eyes ahead as he crossed the Council House Plaza, was again saluted by the guards at the bottom of the steps. But this time, ignorant of what had transpired below, they were a model of decorum.

Spotted Wrist pounded his way up the long stairway, used the climb to burn the adrenaline surging in his veins.

Blood and spit, he was about to be face-to-face with Morning Star. Rising Flame would be there along with who-knew-what others.

He made himself stop, take a deep breath, and look out over the city. To the east, he could see the clutter of temples, dwellings, and society mounds lining the Avenue of the Sun. Farmsteads crowded every inch of arable land, their fields green. Interspersed among them were the various ponds, the curving lakes left by old meanders, and the borrow pits, all sparkling and blue under the afternoon sun. Beyond these lay the bluffs, complete with the ramped cut where the Avenue of the Sun climbed up the steep incline to the uplands beyond. There the sprawling city continued. The whole of the uplands was a polyglot of dirt farmers, their temples, rude chunkey courts, world tree poles, and plazas surrounded by crowded farmsteads with their fields of corn, beans, and squash, bobbing sunflowers, and stands of goosefoot, maygrass, and berry bushes. And in the center of each, a palace, charnel house, and temple where one of the Earth Clans maintained a chief and a matron, a priest, and enough kin to act as a sort of governance for the dirt farmers.

And that was just to the east.

Look to the south, across the Great Plaza to the raised causeway and the Avenue of the Moon, or west toward River City Mounds, or north across the Cahokia Creek bottoms to the old oxbow lakes, the associated mounds, and finally Serpent Woman Town in the distant north, and he'd see the same thing.

This is what I have to gain. But to claim it, I must keep my anger under control.

He passed through the high palisade gate into the small plaza. In the center stood the mighty World Tree Pole, with its relief carvings depicting Morning Star's history in the Beginning Times. Lightning strikes had traced patterns down the sculpted length, adding to the tall pole's Power.

A group of nobles—most of them high chiefs from various Earth Clans, their matrons, along with a smattering of lesser Four Winds nobility and their servants—waited before Morning Star's soaring palace or walked along the bastioned walls. At Spotted Wrist's arrival, they seemed to pause, taking a moment before either bowing or touching their foreheads.

Was it just him, or did he detect an unusual reserve in their gazes? Did he see ridicule, suspicion, or unease reflected in their pursed lips, in the narrowing of their eyes?

Ignore it. You're the Keeper.

He kept his head high, Cut Weasel—in his armor—striding along just behind his right shoulder.

At the great double doors with their carvings depicting Morning Star borne aloft by eagle wings, Spotted Wrist took the salute of two of Morning Star's guards and waited while they opened the heavy portals.

Inside, Spotted Wrist paused to let his eyes adjust to the gloom.

The great central fire had been allowed to burn low, no doubt in compensation for the heat of the day. The place was already warm enough to make him wish he'd worn a lighter cape—and that was after having been out in the blazing sun.

He strode forward across the intricately woven floor mat, glancing from side to side and taking in the ornately carved wall beds, the hanging textiles, carvings, and statuary.

Along the west wall, Morning Star's recorders, messengers, several guards, and various servants waited. There, too, was the old Earth Clans soul flier, Rides-the-Lightning, his white-blind eyes elevated as if he could see past the high thatch roof and into the Sky World beyond.

At his feet an old humpbacked woman in a coarsely woven smock, her face painted white, squatted on the floor. She seemed to fix on Spotted Wrist with uncommon interest. Must have been the old priest's servant or who-knew-what? Though what purpose she served wasn't immediately apparent. Maybe it had something to do with the worn fabric bag that lay under her right hand.

Clan Matron Rising Flame was seated with her knees together off to the right of the eternal fire. Seeing his entry, she now rose, giving him a slight nod. So, too, did Five Fists, the old lopper-jawed warrior and commander of both Morning Star's personal guard and the Morning Star squadron.

In the back, behind the fire, perched on his panther hide–covered litter atop its dais, the lounging Morning Star fixed his black gaze on Spotted Wrist.

The living god's face was painted white with black forked-eye designs running down each cheek. He wore an eagle-feather cloak thrown back over his shoulders. On his head a copper headdress in the form of *Hunga Ahuito* had been polished to a dazzling shine. A Spirit-bundle was affixed to his hair bun and rested just above the beaded forelock that dangled before his nose.

A white apron clad the living god's hips—scalp locks sewn on the front—and dropped to a long tail that extended to between his knees. Thick necklaces of white shell beads draped his throat.

And there, on the bottom step of the living god's dais, sat spooky Lady Sun Wing, her oversized and vacant gaze fixed on Spotted Wrist. The expression on her thin face gave the impression that she was watching him with some sort of anticipation. Meeting her gaze sent a spiral of worry down his back. She grinned vacuously, as if reading his discomfort. The way she kept running her fingers over the Tortoise Bundle in her lap reminded him of spiders skittering over a skull.

A shadow of a smile—almost mocking—seemed to play at Morning Star's lips, and in that instant, Spotted Wrist saw not a celestial deity, but an arrogant young man carried away with his sense of superiority.

Which, of course, couldn't be.

Stopping shy of the smoldering fire, Spotted Wrist bowed low and touched his forehead. Straightening, he asked, "You asked to see me, Lord?"

"I'm sure you are aware that the Green Corn ceremony is coming up, Clan Keeper. We are less than a quarter moon away from the first day of fasting. For the most part, *Tonka'tzi* Wind is handling the details. However, I have received a messenger sent from Evening Star House. Matron Columella has promised a substantial donation of food for the concluding feast. She would like assurances that it can be delivered without interference or delay. She has further expressed the desire that not only her House but the Earth Clans within her territory be allowed to participate in the ceremonies and celebration. As willing as she is to support the holiday, the matron has reservations concerning the safety of herself and her people, not to mention her House, during the holy days."

"I see."

"Do you, Clan Keeper?" Morning Star's gaze didn't waver. "The matron wonders how she and her people can participate in our most sacred annual ceremony, in the lighting of the eternal fire, in the games, and ultimately in the feast and Dancing that initiates a new year when you are technically at war with Evening Star House."

Is Morning Star all right? He wondered. Something about the living god looked as if he weren't quite right. Was it the posture? How he sat? As if his stomach were bothering him?

Spotted Wrist narrowed an eye, considered. "Every action I have taken has been to promote unity throughout your empire, Great Lord. When I was appointed Keeper, the Houses were on the verge of tearing this city apart. I have restored order."

"If you have indeed restored order, Keeper, why is Lady Columella afraid to send food, gifts, and her people to the city's most cherished ceremony and celebration? She tells me she cannot leave her House undefended."

"Lord, you must understand. Evening Star Town is a festering hive of resistance. A threat to the continued peace and—"

"Clan Matron?" Morning Star interrupted. "Are you aware of this threat?"

Rising Flame, her expression back in that irritating and emotionless mask, said, "I have suggested to the Keeper that he might want to open negotiations with Evening Star House. As it is, we have enough trouble along the river. Nothing that's hindering Trade, mind you, but I was just informed this morning that High Chief Broken Stone was found dead in his bed."

"What?" Spotted Wrist turned. "Why wasn't I told about this?"

Rising Flame arched a challenging eyebrow. "I would have thought, *Clan Keeper*, that you would have known before I did. But then I guess the constant search for your missing canoes must have kept you from receiving your daily reports."

Snickers sounded from along the walls.

Sun Wing, talking to the Tortoise Bundle, said, "He can't hear the Song of the southern copper, and it's just beneath his ear."

That cut it. Figures the accursed Koroa copper would come up. Spotted Wrist thrust a hard finger in Rising Flame's direction. "Don't you dare. And let's not make Broken Stone into something more than he was. I can pretty much assure you that River House, by this evening, will be sorted out. If Broken Stone died in his sleep, it would surprise me if Three Fingers isn't already declared High Chief and sitting in the high chair."

The gods alone knew the man had been trying to solidify his support among the various lineages in River House. Not that many were happy. They'd provided the lion's share of the missing canoes. Should there be any real opposition to Three Fingers ascending the high chair, Flying Squirrel—with what remained of North Star Squadron's warriors—would back him up.

That was the thing about being the Hero of the North. Ultimately, it came down to his warriors. And not all were scattered up and down the river.

No, the time for that was over. Call the loss of the canoes what it was: a military setback.

And the owners of those missing craft?

A crooked smile bent his lips. Let them try to collect. After all, he had the protection of his squadrons.

Rising Flame, after a long pause said, "As to that latter part? I doubt he's sitting in the high chair. According to my recollection, it burned along with the River House palace the night that someone stole all your canoes."

Before he could think better of it, he asked, "Are you purposely trying to bait me, Matron?"

Her eyes had narrowed. "No, Clan Keeper, just trying to determine where your priorities are."

"With Cahokia!" he barked.

"Admirable, Clan Keeper," Morning Star interjected. "I would hope that your concern would extend to the Busk ceremonies?"

He turned back to Morning Star, "Lord. I shall send word to Lady Columella that she need fear no threat against her House during the Busk celebration. Nor will her shipments of food or gifts be interfered with."

"And her personal safety?" Five Fists asked from the side. "And that of her people?"

Spotted Wrist shot the old fool a withering glance. "They may pass in peace during the holy days. My warriors will pick no quarrel with them . . . assuming they reciprocate in kind."

Now that he thought about it, that actually might work for the best. Give him time to recall his scattered warriors, but rather than have them return to Cahokia, he could slowly assemble them downstream, on the river's west bank. Perhaps in the uplands around the Chains. Supplying them would be an issue, but they'd only be three or four days' hard march below Evening Star Town.

Sun Wing, seeming to hear something the rest didn't, nodded thoughtfully. Said, "He really hasn't a clue about what's important, does he?"

"I hope you can work it all out," Morning Star told him, eyes half-lidded. "Matron Columella has indicated her willingness to keep the peace during the Green Corn Ceremony. It would be to everyone's interest to see that nothing interfered."

Spotted Wrist bowed low, his mind already racing. Touching his forehead, he added, "Of course, Lord. I shall begin making the arrangements immediately."

Who knew? If he played it correctly, Columella may have handed him Evening Star House on a carved wooden platter.

Thirty-one

Taking Rides-the-Lightning's frail hand in her own, her bag over her shoulder, Blue Heron led the Earth Clans' soul flier out through the great double doors of Morning Star's palace and into the slanting afternoon sunlight. There, in the plaza, she directed the old shaman to the shade cast by the western palisade wall.

Fascinating. Dressed as she was, her face painted white, her hair completely grayed with ash, no one gave her or her bag a second glance. To the nobles scattered about the yard, she was as good as invisible. Just some accoutrement of Rides-the-Lightning's. Perhaps another healer for all they knew. Not worth so much as a second glance, let alone a thought.

The shade might not have been cool, but at least it provided some respite from the burning sun.

And there Five Fists found them, stalking up, his war club in hand, and asking, "Well, what do you think?"

Blue Heron told him, "The miracle is that it's taken Three Fingers this long to eliminate that clod Broken Stone."

"And where do the River House lineages come down on Three Fingers?" Five Fists asked.

"Though they don't speak openly of it, the lineage elders are firmly in support of War Duck and Round Pot. Since the two of them have been deposed, the lineages have seen Trade disrupted, their palace and too many warehouses burned. No one is skimming a share from what Trade is passing through River City, not to mention that the chunkey games are disrupted and the hawkers and vendors are barely scraping by."

Five Fists asked, "Why do they not speak openly if they have so many grievances?"

"It's not worth irritating Three Fingers while he has Spotted Wrist's warriors at his beck and call. Keep in mind, Spotted Wrist has a vested interest in helping Three Fingers. Those missing canoes? Most of them belonged to different folks in River Mounds. With Spotted Wrist's warriors to back him, Three Fingers won't be causing the Keeper any trouble over the canoes."

Rides-the-Lightning said, "Seems like the warriors are Spotted Wrist's only strength."

"But not without their own cost," Blue Heron told him. "They've eaten the city's warehouses empty. First Broken Stone, and now Three Fingers is ordering people to contribute a basket of corn here, a sack of squash there. The fact that larders are bare just before the Busk? The symbolism is telling. Especially when Three Fingers was already demanding tribute to rebuild the palace before Broken Stone was murdered. But for those selfsame warriors occupying the city, War Duck and Round Pot would already be back in charge."

Five Fists rubbed his off-kilter jaw; dislocated years ago, it had never healed. "Sounds like the Keeper has worn out his welcome."

Blue Heron smiled. "The only way Spotted Wrist is attacking Evening Star House is if he transports his squadrons in bits and drabs, by tens and twenties, assembles them on the west bank, and marches them cross-country. In doing it that way, Columella will have more than enough advance warning to deal him a crushing blow long before he can accumulate sufficient strength."

"He will try something during the Busk," Rides-the-Lightning said in his reedy voice. "One does not need to talk to the Spirits to know that Spotted Wrist will not let this go."

"No, he won't." Five Fists stared thoughtfully at the white-blind elder. "He will try something. It's in his nature."

"And it will be clumsy. Seems that's also in his nature," Blue Heron added. "But what about Rising Flame? I don't have the insight I used to when it comes to Four Winds Clan politics."

"She is unhappy," Five Fists told her. "She wanted a stable Cahokia with all the Houses brought to heel. Now she has a split city. Horned Serpent House and North Star House continue to keep an uneasy alliance, though High Chief Green Chunkey chafes to become the *tonka'tzi*. All that keeps your sister Wind alive is Rising Flame's caution. She will not allow Spotted Wrist to replace Wind as *tonka'tzi*. Especially not while Wind is preparing for a Busk celebration as important as this one will be."

"She has a great deal riding on this," Rides-the-Lightning mused thoughtfully. "Anything going wrong with the Green Corn celebration this year will be taken as a sign from Power. Keeping Wind as *tonka'tzi* suggests continuity. Replacing her with Green Chunkey at the last minute would send a destabilizing message."

Five Fists rubbed his scarred jaw. "Rising Flame doesn't want to give Green Chunkey that much Power until she has ways of curbing his excesses."

"But Green Chunkey will not wait forever," Rides-the-Lightning said. "I hear that he is out of patience, sending daily messages to Spotted Wrist and Serpent Woman Town for North Star House to honor their agreement."

"Wind understands." Blue Heron pulled at the wattle under her chin. "She's being very careful to keep from giving Spotted Wrist any reason to act against her. She knows that at any moment, armed warriors could slip into her quarters and she, too, would be 'found dead in her bed.'" She paused. "My question is, where is Morning Star in all this?"

"Remote," Five Fists told her. "How should I know what goes on in the mind of the living god? After all these years, I have no clue. All I can tell you is that he acts as if he's waiting for something. But what? I can't tell you. When I ask, he just says, 'Opposites crossed, Warrior. Only he who doubts with all his heart can become the truest of all believers.'"

"Blood and spit," Blue Heron groused. "What is that supposed to mean?"

"Just what it says, Keeper," Rides-the-Lightning replied, his blind face bending into a weary smile. "Sky and Underworld. Heresy and faith. Male and female." Then the smile morphed into a slight frown. "Doubt to belief? But belief in what?"

"The man talks in riddles these days." Five Fists shook his head in irritation as he let his gaze rove over the assorted people crowding in front of the palace doors. "The other day he was going on about how his death and salvation came from the same womb. That his deliverance was borne ever closer by the relentless currents. That the Sky could 'Only be set free by the Underworld.' And that 'Only when the high chair was finally occupied by heresy, would the Houses know true faith.'"

"Sounds typically cryptic." Blue Heron shot him a wary glance. "Doesn't give us a clue as to what his game is. Let alone how he wants us to play it. I don't have to remind you, *old friend*, that Morning Star has rewarded people who thought they were serving his best interests by having them rounded up and hung in squares."

"Thinking about how close you came after that mess with Walking Smoke?"

"Among other times, yes."

"I don't think you were in danger," Five Fists told her. "I think that was more for show. Particularly for Columella. That, and he knew that Night Shadow Star would come to your defense. Morning Star does like his theater."

"Glad he does," she said with a snort. "Scares the spit right out of the rest of us."

Rides-the-Lightning chuckled, then sobered. Raising his hand, he spread his fingers as if to grasp something. "I can feel the Spirits. Power has shifted. United one way, sundered another. A new casting of the gaming pieces. Something with Morning Star. A change. Blackness spinning."

"Good or bad, Elder?" Five Fists asked.

The old man shook his head, frown lines etching the mass of wrinkles in his age-withered face. "Don't know, War Leader. Different." He cocked his head as though listening. Nodded. "I see."

"See what?" Blue Heron gave him a sour look. "Piss and spit, don't you get all mysterious and spooky, too."

"I finally understand," the blind soul flier whispered as if to himself. "Morning Star knew from the beginning that his time was limited. He didn't send Night Shadow Star to Cofitachequi to kill Walking Smoke."

"Excuse me?" Five Fists asked. "Now you're making less sense than Morning Star."

But Rides-the-Lightning, his expression echoing confusion, softly said, "He sent her there to bring him back."

"And the Spirits just told you this?" Blue Heron continued to give the old shaman a thin-lidded glare.

"Oh yes," Rides-the-Lightning said with a slight nod. "And suddenly everything Morning Star said makes perfect sense."

"Do you want to explain that?" Five Fists couldn't hide his expression of distaste.

"Of course." Rides-the-Lightning turned his white-blind eyes on Five Fists. "Doesn't matter if it's by Walking Smoke or by some other means, Morning Star doesn't expect to come out of this alive."

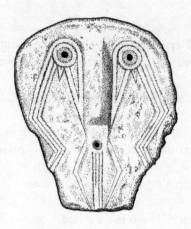

The Fingerless Fist

E *ver wonder what a fingerless fist would look like? Or perhaps a lipless smile? A legless Dance? A lidless blink?*

These things obsess me. Once, when I was a boy, the Sky priests would have told me that the contemplation of such inanities would lead me to illumination. Teach me to understand the contradictions and reconciliation of opposites. All that white versus red, order versus chaos, peace versus war, crap over which the mystics like to wind their thoughts into circles and knots.

I have become much more pragmatic: Power isn't about achieving balances or finding some harmonic cosmic understanding. The proper use of Power is to get what you want. Pretty simple, actually. Anything else is self-delusion propagated by the priests, shamans, and soul fliers to keep competition to a minimum.

Of course, they've done it so often most of them have come to believe it themselves. Mass self-delusion.

But if we were meant to sit around thinking all these profound thoughts about the nature of Power, enlightenment, and illumination, why were we created with a sense of taste that marvels over a sweet bread? Why does that magical moment when my semen jets hot into a woman's willing sheath send such pulsing delight through my hips? Why does a soft blanket and a warm crackling fire fill me with contentment on a cold and snowy night? What makes taking revenge on someone who slighted me so fulfilling? Why do I experience that rush of enjoyment when I stand over a cowering victim? Why do I crave to hear thousands call my name in worship?

Hey! Hello! Come awake! Think it through.

We are created with these appetites, needs, and drives for a reason. Creation gave them to us so that we would strive and struggle to enjoy them. If Creation wanted us to sit in caves and contemplate the darkness it would have made us to resemble bats. And given us much larger eyes.

Instead, we are born squalling, hungry, and demanding. Most of growing up is the process of having those qualities beaten out of us. Do you remember those long and tedious lectures on why throwing tantrums, sating our appetites, and having our way was bad? Do you remember being told that catering to others' demands, serving their needs, and fulfilling their wants was supposedly good?

It's all lies!

When I make a fist, figuratively or literally, I use all my fingers. I want it to make an impression when I strike someone.

And my figurative fist works well. We made extraordinary progress down the river, past the confluences of the Upper Tenasee and beyond the mouth of the Wide Fast. The day after that, we passed the last major confluence and headed down the wide valley toward Hiawasee Island. Spent the night there outside the palisaded town with its famous mounds, and first learned of the coming of the Cahokians.

A large expedition, it was said. One headed all the way to Cofitachequi. Night Shadow Star must have known. Maybe even kept it in reserve—the cunning sheath. An omission I'll use my clenched fist to repay her for . . . along with that knock she gave my still-unhealed shaft and stones.

An army of Cahokians? This amuses me. As far as I am concerned, they can have Cofitachequi. All of it. My destiny lies in Cahokia.

Still, it gives me pause. If Night Shadow Star is ahead of me, she could order whatever squadron first is in charge to detain me. But then, if what I saw in Six Toes' blood was true, she's somehow behind me, and in pursuit.

What do I believe?

As I sit here by the fire tonight, ensuring that all my warriors remain in their beds, I consider it. So far, none of these two-footed weasels has dared to try and abandon me. Above Hiawasee, a lone Cahokian was just as likely to end up scalped, tied in a square, and alternately cooked and cut to pieces.

But below? The Cahokians are supposed to be encamped at Canyon Town. And we will be there by late tomorrow.

So, what should I do?

Sacrifice Fire Light in search of the answer?

Not that the thought of peering into the future as the blood pools inside Fire Light's empty rib cage doesn't have a certain appeal, but for the time being, I really need the good chief alive. I can always cut him open, strip out his guts, and scry his blood later.

For the moment, I need a plan. A way to bypass the Cahokians.

So, what if we don't stop? Don't offer any of these crawling and terrified warriors the chance to make their escape? Or take the chance that Night Shadow Star has reached the Cahokians first and has ordered my seizure?

One by one I tuck my fingers into a fist.

"We bypass Canyon Town," I say softly to the crackling fire.

I will take my chances in the rapids of the Suck and Rage.

Even as I think it, lightning flashes across the night-black sky.

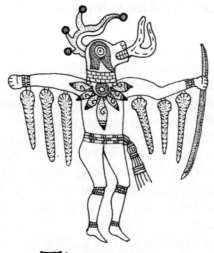

Thirty-two

Things could have been much better: High Chief Green Chunkey, of the Horned Serpent House of the Four Winds Clan, could already have been proclaimed *tonka'tzi* by Clan Matron Rising Flame and Spotted Wrist.

Green Chunkey—steeped as he was in politics—understood the delay. He'd been up to his serpent-tattooed cheeks in Cahokian intrigue his entire life. He fully understood how the game was played. That he had remained high chief for three of the five decades he had been alive was proof of his mastery of Cahokian politics.

But, by pus and spit, that didn't make him ache any less for the day when he'd be carried into the *tonka'tzi*'s palace and have his litter placed atop the dais as was his right.

Now he sat on that selfsame litter in the Four Winds Clan House across the fire from Clan Matron Rising Flame. He had ordered his bearers to carry him up from Horned Serpent Town that afternoon, leaving his second wife, Feather Worn, and his oldest son, Lance, in charge of the palace.

The rest of his household, including his first wife, Red Shawl Woman, and his sister, Matron Robin Wing, were following in an entourage that was currently wending its way up the Avenue of the Moon. As they proceeded, they made offerings at the various tombs, burial mounds, and shrines. Everything leading up to this most important Busk of all was being done to assure that Green Chunkey and Horned Serpent House appeared reverent, blessed, and pious.

He needed everything to be perfect.

If he played it right, he would be called *tonka'tzi* by the time this Green Corn Ceremony was finished.

For that reason, he had scheduled this interview with Rising Flame.

When he was ushered into the great room in the Four Winds Clan House, with its opulent carvings and rich furnishings, Rising Flame was reposed on her litter atop the dais behind the eternal fire.

As he approached and seated himself on the matting, she watched him through half-lidded eyes. At his request, she had dismissed most of her household staff and sent away the other Four Winds nobles. Only a broken-down old woman—looked to be a slave—huddled in the back corner. The crone had stayed to serve food, drop the occasional length of firewood into the smoldering hearth, and keep his shell cup full of black drink. Now the withered hag sat in the back, her hands spiderlike as she mended an old blanket.

"For this meeting, you have my thanks," Green Chunkey told Rising Flame. "And I appreciate the fine feast of buffalo backstrap, and that you have brewed black drink."

He lifted the large shell cup that the old woman had dipped from the steaming pot beside the fire. He drank deeply of the tea, enjoying the taste of the charred leaves, how its Power sent a charge through his muscles and nerves.

"Now that the rituals have been attended to, Lord Green Chunkey, what specifically did you have in mind?" For as young as Rising Flame was, only a fool underestimated her cunning or acumen.

"Quite honestly, Matron, I am becoming concerned. There is no secret that Horned Serpent House and North Star House have had our conflicts over the years. Last winter, however, at the request of the Clan Keeper, we set aside our differences. In return, certain agreements were made."

"I know. You expect to become the next *tonka'tzi* when Wind is no longer able to discharge her duties. I am familiar with the terms."

"Clan Matron, I have fulfilled each and every one of my obligations. Kept every promise. Yet Wind is still the *tonka'tzi*, and I am curious as to why." He accursed well knew why. But better to have Rising Flame state it clearly.

"The political situation, High Chief, is currently better served with Wind remaining exactly where she is."

"I thought we were going to talk without dissembling." He leaned forward, cradling the big shell cup in his lap. "The reason old Wind is still *tonka'tzi* is because that incompetent fool, Spotted Wrist, has made a disaster out of his attempt to bring Columella and the west side of the river to heel."

"Precisely." Nothing changed behind Rising Flame's dark eyes. She might have been discussing the heat and humidity outside.

"Not that I mind if Spotted Wrist makes a fool out of himself. His bumbling actions have increased the amount of Trade flowing through

Horned Serpent Town. And that's despite the difficulty in transporting it from our canoe landing, across the marsh, and then up the causeway to Cahokia proper. But that doesn't serve the city."

"And, in your mind, what does? Declaring your agreement with me and the Clan Keeper to be over? You no longer wish to be *tonka'tzi*?"

"Oh, come," Green Chunkey gestured with his tea. "We're not going to play silly little games, are we? You know exactly why I'm here. I can think of no better time to declare a new *tonka'tzi* than at the conclusion of the Busk. I would think that just after Morning Star delivers his traditional prayers, you can make the declaration as a final announcement, a culmination of the celebration. We will be side by side at the top of the Council Terrace gates, Morning Star having just given away his cloak. A grand gesture of the sort that would proclaim my appointment to the entire city."

"And Wind?"

"She might abdicate due to reasons of health. Perhaps she's tired? Maybe she'd like to spend more time with family? Would like to pursue other interests? Died in her sleep? Collapsed after a meal? Was blasted by a freak bolt of lightning? For all I care, you can claim she sprouted wings and flew up to the starry Road of the Dead in the Sky World to join her ancestors. Call it a miracle. I'll leave it up to you and the Keeper. Whatever you think would best suit the narrative."

"I see."

"For my part," he continued, "I will be most solicitous, proclaim my deepest appreciation for Wind's service in the days since the untimely death of her brother. Hope that I can live up to the legacy she leaves behind. Dedicate myself to being as competent, wise, and caring."

"Got it all planned, have you?"

He gave her a half-lidded gaze over the top of his cup. "Indeed I have. For the occasion, I've had everything remaining in our granaries packed up—little as it is after that idiocy last winter stripped us bare. I have half of Horned Serpent Town packing food by the basketload for the feast. I have had our men and women practicing twice as hard at stickball. I want them to win, and most particularly, to decisively beat any team Columella might field."

"That, it is said, is up to Power, High Chief."

"And our Dancers. On the final night, they will be dressed in costumes the likes of which Cahokia has rarely seen. Matron Robin Wing and I are going to make sure that no one forgets Horned Serpent Town after this is over." He paused. "You might want to mention that fact to Morning Star before he judges the final Dance competition. Last year it went to that Natchez. I suppose you remember how that turned out?

Better if it were bestowed on someone from my lineage; yet another reminder of how Horned Serpent House serves the city."

"One would think I was giving Horned Serpent House preference, High Chief. Is there a reason I should? Some special service that you are doing for the Four Winds Clan? For the people?"

Green Chunkey narrowed his eyes, glanced suggestively at the old woman in the corner.

"She can barely hear," Rising Flame told him. "She shows up on days when Clay Fine isn't feeling well. I don't think she has the wits in her head to understand anything but the simplest of instructions. That's why I allowed her to stay."

"With all that paint, I can't see her tattoos."

"Want to get to the point? Why should I show Horned Serpent House preference over any of the others?"

"Ah, we're back to the silly games, I see." He took another swig of the black drink, felt it charging his muscles, sharpening his brain. "North Star House is a military powerhouse, but they're stalemated against Columella. Without War Duck in the high chair and Round Pot as matron, River House is a rudderless joke. Since the extinguishing of their eternal fire, they've been thought of as a 'bad luck' House. Morning Star House, given the living god's lack of interest, is little more than Spotted Wrist's puppet. Unless you, too, are nothing more than the Clan Keeper's tool to use as he will, you need me and my House as a counterweight against Spotted Wrist and Wolverine's aspirations."

As she considered, he took another sip of tea and added, "Where else are you going to go, Matron? You certainly can't turn to Columella."

In precise tones she said, "We all exist in the shadow of the living god. We're here because of the miracle of his descent to earth and reincarnation. Had you asked anyone alive when Black Tail surrendered his body to Morning Star's re-quickened Spirit, they would never have believed that tens of thousands of people would come flooding into Cahokia. When the Houses were established to help control the Earth Clans that were in turn needed to govern the dirt farmers, no one could have predicted the size and complexity of the city."

"No, that's why—"

"Let me finish!" She glared at him. "I thought, in my arrogance, that being Clan Matron, I could bring an end to the constant bickering between the Houses. Nevertheless, within days of my appointment, we were at each other's throats. I thought Spotted Wrist could discover threats and enforce the peace in a way that Blue Heron never could. That might have been a mistake. But, High Chief, you must understand: The one thing this city cannot afford is an outbreak of war between the Houses."

"I agree." He gave her a conspiratorial smile. "But accomplices also need to be rewarded for their support."

"And you would have me replace Wind? For the moment she's the only reassurance Morning Star House lineages have that they will not be eclipsed and rendered meaningless. By placing you on the *tonka'tzi*'s chair, I might have violence in the streets, and this time Morning Star might decide to involve himself."

Green Chunkey nodded. "Yes, but I can add succulent meat to the feast, so to speak. I can bring my squadrons in to help keep the peace." He paused. "Especially since, if my sources are correct, Matron Columella might suffer an inconvenient accident during her stay in central Cahokia during the Busk."

"The Keeper has given Morning Star his word that she can pass in peace."

"I'm sure he has." Green Chunkey glanced suspiciously at the old crone fiddling with her holey blanket. Then he added softly, "Were something to happen to Columella on the final day of the Busk, I've assured the Keeper that nothing will ever be traced back to him." He smiled. "I need not remind the Clan Matron that with Columella suddenly and so unfortunately removed from the game, that ultimate goal of a unified Cahokia will be so much closer."

"And when might this 'unfortunate accident' occur?"

"The Keeper thinks on the third day. It would look suspicious on the fourth just before the feast, don't you think?"

"What would this 'accident' be?"

"Much like with Broken Stone. She goes to sleep and just doesn't wake up. Her people find her dead that morning. These things happen. No one's fault." He paused. "As the new *tonka'tzi*, I will of course make a full investigation, even as a new Matron more, um, responsive to Cahokia's needs, takes the high chair in Evening Star House. Consider it a gift from Horned Serpent House."

She was still giving him that slit-eyed scrutiny, as if trying to see past his bland expression into his very soul. "My goal, my only goal, is to save this city. To see it unified and peaceful. So help me, if you fail . . ."

Holding the drinking shell in one hand, he gestured with his other. "Then leave it up to a sign from Power. See how the people react to our offerings of food, and as our Dancers, chunkey players, and stickball teams take the field. I give you my word, Horned Serpent House is on the rise, and there's nothing that can stop us."

Thirty-three

Cleaning up the dishes, the old woman tottered her way around the Four Winds Clan Council House great room. She kept grunting, walking with a limp. The others—called back after High Chief Green Chunkey's litter had been ceremoniously carried from the room—were astute enough not to openly speculate on what might have been said. From the curious and speculative glances passed between them, however, it was foremost in their thoughts.

Clan Matron Rising Flame remained on her litter atop the dais, one leg drawn up, her chin propped on a slender palm. The expression on her young face was anything but placid. Her niece, White Frond, had taken a seat by her side, saying softly, "You look worried, Aunt. A private meeting? Had to be something Green Chunkey didn't want anyone else to hear."

Rising Flame grunted, shot a sidelong glance at her niece, and kept her voice low enough the others couldn't hear. "He's right about several things. North Star House, with its squadrons under Spotted Wrist's command, is like having a grizzly amid a family of black bears. Only Columella is keeping him from ripping the rest of us apart. But in the doing, she's been so marginalized I'm not sure how to ever bring Evening Star House back into the fold. If there were a way, I'd do it. Spotted Wrist and Green Chunkey are plotting her death. I don't know what I can do to stop it, or if I should."

The old woman tottered back from the wall benches where the plates were stored to pick up the shell cup. She walked with her back bowed, her spine having curved with old age. Grunting again, she fumbled for the drinking shell. Hesitated, and seemed to be struggling for balance.

White Frond asked, "So, do you think giving the *tonka'tzi*'s chair to Green Chunkey will make things better?"

"Just the opposite," Rising Flame said as the old woman got her fingers on the cup at last. "He said I should look for a sign from Power. Right now, I'd give just about anything to see Horned Serpent House knocked off its high litter. I need something, anything, to keep Wind as *tonka'tzi*. She's a voice of reason, even muffled as she is by Spotted Wrist's guards."

"Only four days until the final day of the Busk," White Frond told her. "Not much time for a sign from Power when it comes to Horned Serpent House, and everyone's going to be busy fasting and praying."

The old woman tucked the drinking shell to her chest, hobbled back to the box, and carefully placed it atop the others before lowering the intricately carved lid.

Then, turning, she made her wobbly way to the door and out into the bright daylight. Passing the Eagle and Falcon guardian posts, she somehow tottered down the wooden stairway to the avenue below the mound. There, at the edge of the thoroughfare, people passing in a constant stream, she stopped at the side of the Trader's blanket. The man had picked a spot, his butt not quite touching the forbidden edge of the Four Winds Clan mound. The big dog by his side looked up, recognized the old woman, and thumped his tail.

"Have a delightful time?" the Trader asked.

The old woman straightened, gave a gasp of relief, and arched her back. "Pus and blood, Thief. It feels like my backbone's on fire. If that's what it's like to get old, hang me in a square now."

"I take it no one noticed you?"

She grunted. "I was invisible to them. People I've known all my life. They don't even look twice, not sure they would even if I didn't paint over the tattoos. I tell you, Thief, it's a hard lesson, but one I'm never going to forget. Never going to mistake someone for being less than they are."

Seven Skull Shield waved his fingers at a little girl who was being dragged past by her mother. The girl had given him a big-eyed stare, a thumb in her mouth. As the oblivious mother tugged her along by the other hand, she smiled in return.

"Looks to be a busy Busk coming," Seven Skull Shield noted. "While you were in there, I Traded for a whole three sacks of corn, a bag of dried squash, and this entire sack of mussel shells."

"So, we're rich? Huh!" She reached behind to press her lower back into an arch. "Pus and vomit, that feels better."

"Glad to hear. I've got a hole where my stomach used to be. Now, I know where this rather nasty old woman sets up a booth to trade roasted turkey and baked squash. She always gets in early to claim the space right next to the southwest corner of the stickball field on the Great Plaza. With the crowds coming through it's easy to distract her, and while you do that, I could grab us a half a bird and a—"

"Pack up! You've got work to do."

"Best news I've heard all day! In less than a finger of time from now, we'll be stuffing ourselves with the finest smoked turkey you've ever eaten."

Seven Skull Shield started collecting their Trade, cramming it in one of the packs as he said, "You know, those Four Wind matrons are a sorry lot. There you are, doing all those menial chores, and you'd think they'd at least let you eat a bite. See what I mean about the nobility, they—"

"Food's not the issue." She gave him a gap-toothed grin. "We need a sign from Power."

"How's that?" Seven Skull Shield finished packing and stood, swinging the packs over his muscle-thick shoulder. "Did you miss the part about me being hungry?"

Farts climbed to his feet, stretched his front end, then his back, before dropping to scratch his belly, foot thumping the ground.

"How soon can you make it to Horned Serpent Town?" she asked. "I've got something that's right in line with your abilities. A specialty, if you will."

Seven Skull Shield cocked a scarred eyebrow. "Ah, good. It's been too long since I've had the pleasure of parting some young woman's—"

"Not *that* specialty. Your other one."

"I have another specialty?" He gave her a perplexed look.

"Oh, yes. You're going to Horned Serpent Town. And to see you off, I'll even help you steal that turkey." She paused. "But you don't have much time so eat it along the way."

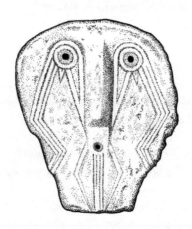

Lightning and Water

I perch in the high bow of the canoe and raise my arms to the storm clouds. Black, turbulent, and angry, they cling low against the mountain walls on either side of the river. I have never seen the like. These clouds seethe, twist upon themselves, and churn in a blue-black vortex that spawns the first bolts of lightning.

Storm gusts race down the valley of the Tenasee, tossing the trees as the wind roars, drowning the shishing of wind-battered leaves. It blows from behind in bursts that drive us forward with such speed that water curls from the bow, splashing out as we buck through the turbulent waves.

The effect is that we are flying forward—a sort of cresting arrow that shoots down the river. Onshore, the forested banks with their cottonwood, poplar, oak, and maple pass with such speed they are a blur.

Even so, my warriors are paddling for all they are worth, thinking that Canyon Town lies just ahead at the mouth of the sheer-walled canyon that marks the start of the Suck and Rage.

They think in terms of reaching the canoe landing, of the huge encampment of Cahokians we have heard are finishing the portage up the gorge above the treacherous white water. Not only do they think they are racing the storm in hopes of finding a dry shelter, a fire, food and drink, but they fully expect a sanctuary. That they will be able to sneak away, lose themselves in the packed ranks of Cahokians who are traveling upriver.

The fools figure that they are finally going to escape.

I lean my head back as a ragged bolt of lightning splits into a three-forked pattern that arcs from one mountain wall, across the valley, to the other. As the hot white light flashes, laughter bursts from my tight throat.

"Yes, my Lords! I am here! Unleash your Power! Blast your rage around me like a web! I am yours!"

In answer, another bolt blinds me, sears my vision, and the deafening crack almost blows me out of the bow. My ears are ringing as I blink in the afterimages, black-on-white behind my eyes.

The canoe seems to pitch sideways, and I look back to see my warriors, frozen in terror, their paddles motionless in their hands.

"Paddle!" I shriek. "Paddle, or I'll call the next one down to cook you all! We ride the lightning!"

One by one they return to their senses, dipping their paddles, driven by a new fear. Again we shoot forward, lancing across the water.

The first drops of rain patter down. Hard. Cold. Like small stones that smack into the wood, explode on my head, and pock the storm-driven waves with rings that vanish in the wind-blasted ripples.

From my vantage, I can just see the canoe landing through the wall of falling rain. It sits on the left bank, a dark collection of rain-wet vessels packed hull to hull. So many that a man could step from canoe to canoe and cross the entire landing without having to set foot on sand. And above them, masked by the gray streamers, are a clutter of ramadas and shelters. But I can see no more; the rain obscures the town up on the terrace.

"Stay to the current," I order Chief Fire Light in the rear. "Keep to the thread."

I am lucky. As the torrent increases, the warriors bow their heads, paddling in misery as the downpour unleashes its fury.

We are even with the Canyon Town canoe landing when Twists His Hair squints across the water at the beached canoes, asking, "What's that?"

"Paddle, you fool!" I scream at him. "Do you want to die out here?"

He bends to the effort, still glancing uncertainly at the landing as we shoot past.

And by then, it is too late for them. We pass into the mouth of the gorge. The current picks up, shooting us forward between the looming canyon walls.

I keep my perch, bellowing against the storm as bolt after bolt of lightning illuminates the gorge into which we are now committed.

"By the ancestors!" Fire Light screams where he's steering in the rear. "Where are we?"

"In the lair of Piasa and the Tie Snakes!" I scream back, jerking a knotted fist at the heavens. "Come and get us, Piasa! You gutless creature! Come to the surface! Face the lightning, you spit-licking beast!"

The instant the words pass my lips, we drop a body length, splashing deep, bobbing up as we pass wide of a boulder. White water boils around us. I look back, see Fire Light, his eyes terror-wide despite the rain pounding on his head and running down his face. A man gripped with dread, he steers with a quaking desperation, seeking the swiftest current away from the rocks.

"Paddle!" I scream as the warriors hesitate. "The lightning will keep you safe. Paddle!"

As if proof, a searing-white bolt blasts the river to our right. Blinding. The bang in this narrow canyon like the sky being blown apart.

I raise my face to the storm and howl in delight.

As the canoe is tossed from foaming rapid to thundering roar, the storm hammers at us. Runoff is pouring down the canyon walls, streams of it. It sluices from the leaves, arches off the rocky outcrops in ephemeral waterfalls, and rushes in torrents down steep cuts.

"Paddle!" I bellow. "You are in the hands of the Thunderbirds! Paddle!"

Lightning splits the heavens, the bolt so close I wonder if I could but reach up and touch it.

And, for the first time, I realize that I am not stooped. That the pain in my testicles has gone. I can stand straight again, healed by the lightning.

I am cured!

"Take that, Piasa! And a curse on the Tie Snakes as well! Cower, you twisted Spirit beasts of the Underworld! I am coming for you!"

As I rail at the raging river, we round a bend. I stare in awe. Carried by the surging current we are propelled out over emptiness. As we plummet, I glimpse the thundering, churning spray. Hear the booming roar. See the raging white turbulence and boiling clouds of mist.

Then we hit bottom, the canoe driving deep, down, into the maelstrom. The canoe slams up and down, water cascading. I scream as I am thrown against the hull.

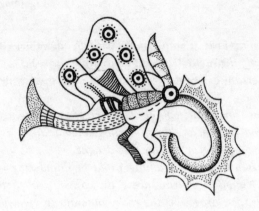

Thirty-four

That first night of the Green Corn ceremony, Lady Feather Worn, of the Panther Clan, second wife of High Chief Green Chunkey, saw to the eternal fire by adding another two knots of firewood. The last one left awake, she took a final look around the Horned Serpent House palace great room. Bare dirt remained—the year-old matting having been torn up and hauled out.

She had supervised the removal, seen it transported down to the plaza and piled with similar matting pulled out of the Four Winds Clan House, the Men's House, the Women's House, and the major society houses. She would also oversee its ritual burning at dawn on the morning of the fourth day before the new matting was installed in the palace and the sacred flame was carried to Horned Serpent Town from Morning Star's rekindled fire. That event would mark the final ritual purification, the beginning of a new year.

Most of the beds were empty, the rest of the household having made the daylong journey up to the Great Plaza. But someone had to attend to these ritual acts. Especially now, with so much at stake. Everything had to be perfect, a demonstration of Horned Serpent House's worthiness and piety. That responsibility had fallen to her and a couple of the old slaves who were too feeble to travel. Even her son, Lance, was gone. He had left to spend the night with the warriors at the Men's House where it overlooked the plaza. There, he was the high chief's representative as the Men's Society undertook the somber rituals of renewing the sacred War Medicine Bundle.

She considered the stew pot. A meat-rich broth covered the bottom third of the big corrugated cooking vessel. Come the morning, she would pour the broth, bit by bit, into the fire as an offering of thanks to the Sky World for the House's prosperity during the last year.

On the morning of the last day she would symbolically extinguish the eternal fire and await the torch carried down from Morning Star's palace.

And then, and only then, would the first of the green corn be boiled, and the great feast would begin.

A huge responsibility.

She rubbed the back of her neck, feeling the weight of the day. And, to tell the truth, a little lonely.

Not that she missed Green Chunkey. She had been married to him for thirty years now. Green Chunkey's first wife, Red Shawl, attended to any ceremonial duties, and the two women tolerated each other well enough. Something about the shared burden of being married to the same man for all these years. And Green Chunkey was Green Chunkey.

She allowed herself a small rueful smile. The silence, lack of drama, and chance to simply sit and rest would turn out to be too fleeting.

Unless, of course, her husband managed to force Rising Flame and Spotted Wrist to appoint him *tonka'tzi*. No telling how that was going to change her life. Hopefully Lance, as Green Chunkey's oldest surviving son, would take over the day-to-day operations while the high chief spent his time in the *tonka'tzi*'s palace.

She considered the implications of that as she made her way back to Green Chunkey's personal quarters behind the great room. Tonight she'd enjoy the High Chief's better-cushioned bed, with its furs and soft buffalo-wool blankets.

She felt her way in the darkness, located the bed, and didn't land on her face when she tripped over the storage box Green Chunkey had left in the middle of the floor.

She kicked off her sandals, slipped off her skirt, and lowered herself onto the plush bedding. Literally and figuratively, it beat the stuffing out of her thin grass-filled pad.

With a sigh, she drifted off.

Sometime in the middle of the night, she came awake. Bothered. But by what? The silence and darkness were complete. Feather Worn turned over onto her side. Yawned. Fragmented Dreams like fluffy clouds in her head.

She frowned. Dream? Or real? She thought she heard the distant lapping of water. Like waves slapping against a canoe's hull.

No, it was more like a dog drinking. A slurp-slurp-slurp sound.

Had to be her imagination. There were no dogs in the palace since Lance had taken his hunting dog to the Men's House.

She heard the unmistakable hollow clatter of two ceramic pots clunking together.

Ah! Old Chigger must be up. He had problems with his bladder during the night. It had gotten worse as he aged. The man kept a chipped brownware jug under his bed instead of stumbling out into the night.

Any concerns slipped away as sleep reclaimed her. So many things to do in the morning . . .

She floated off to a Dream of her youth, the recurring one where she and White Oak were Dancing at the Busk. She'd been fifteen, madly in love. And he'd been seventeen, just made a man. His white teeth flashed in the firelight as his feet shuffled to the beat of the drums; hands clapped in time to the music, and she and White Oak moved in perfect unison.

He took her hand, warm in his, that gleaming anticipation in his firelit eyes as they Danced their way out of the circle. Her pulse began to race as they reached the darkness and he pulled her close. Her breath went short as she ran her hands over his smooth, muscular chest. And then she followed him to the ground where she stripped off her skirt and . . .

"Matron!" The voice brought her out of the Dream, and for a moment Feather Worn couldn't recognize where she was. Then it came back. Not on the Dance ground. Not reliving the happiest moment of her life.

She was in her husband's personal quarters. The Green Corn Ceremony. Matron Robin Wing was gone. Up in Cahokia, for the Busk.

"Matron? Anyone?" The voice carried a note of desperation. "Help!"

Feather Worn fought her way free of the blankets, yanked her skirt on, and felt around for her sandals. She barked her shin on the gods-rotted box in the middle of the floor, then stumbled her way through the door and into the great room.

The first thing that registered was Old Chigger's voice growling, "Who is it? What's wrong?" from his bed at the front of the room.

The second thing was the pitch black. But, what . . . ?

"Fire!" A frantic voice yelled from the palace door. "Matron! Someone! The plaza is on fire!"

"The Matron is in Cahokia with the High Chief!" Feather Worn bellowed with all the irritation she could force into her voice. Feeling her way out into the dark room, she made herself ask in a kinder tone, "What's on fire? Speak!"

"The matting," a shadowy form by the door called. "It's all burning!"

She stopped short, bumping into the clay dais that normally supported Green Chunkey's litter.

That's when it hit her: She should be able to orient herself by the eternal fire. Even this late at night, it should be a large glowing red eye of coals. Instead, the great room's interior was dark as soot.

Her heart skipped, a sick feeling in her gut as she felt her way forward, located the hearth, and felt around.

Wet! Sticky! Cold.

"By the gods!" she screamed. "Bring me a torch! Now."

"But Matron! the voice from the door cried. "The fire is outside!"

"I said, bring me a torch," she insisted.

She could make out the palace doorway, outlined by the flickering of a great fire somewhere beyond. Rushing to the double doors, she stared in disbelief at the plaza, at the fountain of flame leaping into the night sky. It illuminated the chunkey courts, the World Tree pole, and all the clan and society houses lining the plaza.

The piled matting, the offerings for the last day of the Green Corn Ceremony, were spouting yellow tongues of flame as high as the World Tree Pole. The whole offering was consumed in a roaring inferno that spat sparks to twirl on high and flicker out. People were flooding into the plaza, pointing, calling to each other in horror.

She sank to the ground, heart pounding, her stomach tight as a knotted rope. One hand rose to her mouth as she shook her head in disbelief.

How could this have happened?

And then it got worse.

When a torch was finally brought, and she staggered back to the great hearth where the eternal fire was supposed to burn, it was to find that indeed it lay cold and dead. She had checked. Made sure the fire had enough fuel to last until morning.

Feather Worn bent down, fingering the damp ashes, and noticed the stew pot, canted on its side and knocked against one of the empty water jars. She tried to understand. There had been no water jar. Just the stew-pot with the remains for the morning offering.

"We are ruined," she whispered, looking up at the growing number of Earth Clan chiefs and matrons who'd come at word of the catastrophe. People were crowding into the dark great room, whispering, their staring eyes reflecting in the single torch's light.

On the first night of the Busk?

It couldn't be worse.

"Look!" One of the chiefs pointed at the edge of the hearth.

There, in the wet ash, she could make out a single track. Looked like it had been made by a huge dog.

"Spirit wolf!" the chief breathed. "Power has been here this night. Power is witness to this affront to the Spirit world."

"Spirit wolf," another agreed. "This is bad. Really, really bad. Power has abandoned Horned Serpent House. Quick! Back to your own palaces and dwellings. Barricade your doors, sacrifice, and offer your apologies in prayer."

Tears were streaking down Feather Worn's face as she fingered the wet ash. Stared at the *wolf* track. Here? In the soaked charcoal?

When she blinked and looked up, the room was empty. Not only had the chiefs left quickly but they hadn't made a sound.

Thirty-five

The second day of the Busk dawned hot and humid, a searing sun burning down through the smoky haze that hung low over Cahokia. Sitting by her Trade blanket, her bottom against the Healers' Society House mound, Blue Heron watched the celebratory crowd lining the southern half of the Great Plaza. While the raging stickball game being waged out on the grass had the masses engrossed, a steady flow of people pressed their way through the narrow space left between the stickball crowd and the vendors who lined the avenue that separated the Great Plaza from the society houses and temples.

Blue Heron was, for the most part, ignored. The only notice she received was from occasional prospective customers. And even then their interest hinged on what she'd take in Trade for one of the trinkets on her blanket.

A roar went up from the crowd: shouts of dismay from the Fish Clan fans, bellows of joy from those backing the Deer Clan's men's team as they scored a point. This was a grudge match. One that had been building for five months now. Silly how these things started, but the anger and vitriol had begun over a squabble in the uplands east of the bluffs. It started between two dirt farmers over a field boundary. By chance, the line between Fish Clan's jurisdiction and Deer Clan's fell right in the middle of the field. The dirt farmers went to their respective council houses, one petitioning a Deer Clan subchief to do something about the situation, the other appealing to his local Fish Clan subchief. The subchiefs had gotten into a name-calling match and called in their local chiefs, who called in the high chiefs. No Four Winds Great House had jurisdiction up on the bluff, so it was referred to the *tonka'tzi*. Wind had decreed that it would be settled here, during the Busk. So, whoever won this knockdown blood-for-blood match would finally determine which of the two dirt farmers could lay claim to a plot of farmland no bigger than a council-house floor.

Both clans had hired shamans, priests, and soul fliers to "doctor" the playing grounds in favor of their teams. Sacrifices had been made, even to the point of strangling a couple of young slave women and burying their corpses under newly erected World Tree Poles in an effort to curry favor from Old-Woman-Who-Never-Dies. Curses had been invoked, claims of witchery traded back and forth. Not to mention that a fortune was being wagered on the outcome.

Currently Fish Clan was ahead sixteen to thirteen, and at the rate the game was progressing, Fish Clan making four points seemed a great deal more likely than Deer Clan making seven.

Lifting her water jar, Blue Heron took a drink. She waved a feather fan to cool herself, then glared up at the sun blazing down hot enough to cook the sweat right out of her. Even the usual pestilence of flies had taken a break, though they'd be back as the day cooled. Either that, or because of the mobs crowding into central Cahokia, the myriads of buzzing beasts had so many tens of thousands to pester that they were spread too thin to bother one impostor of an old lady Trader.

And between her and the stickball fans, the crowd continued to flow past. Even the dirt farmers—their flocks of children in tow—had dressed in their very best. The women wore simple skirts dyed in greens and yellows they'd processed from leaves, grass, and flowers. The red designs had been drawn with clay, the black with charcoal. The same for the breechcloths and light fabric capes the men wore. Depending upon the ethnic identity of the parents, their swarms of children ranged in attire—anywhere from naked for the littlest, up to minimal skirts or tunics. If anything set the dirt farmers apart, it was the way they'd fixed their hair. High poms for some, buns for others, crests, some shaved, cut short on one side, or braided and clipped.

She pulled at her wattle as a group with origins on the other side of the Wabash passed by in a herd. Some offshoot of Shawnee. The Red Buck? Blue Buck? Something like that. She recognized the hairstyle, the tattoos, but couldn't remember the actual name.

She used to know. It lay on the tip of her tongue.

"I'm slipping in my old age," she murmured. Then cried, "Hey! Mind your feet!" as a Pacaha Trader stumbled past and clipped the corner of her blanket. She'd never known being a Trader was such an undertaking.

As she swatted at a lone fly that had managed somehow to locate her in the press, she saw the Horned Serpent House runner pound his way past. Recognized the staff of office first, then she placed his strained and sweaty face, the distinctive tattoos. Lance, Green Chunkey's oldest son. And the man didn't look happy in the least.

Ignoring the ache in her hips, Blue Heron climbed to her feet, traced his path as Lance trotted through the crowd and vanished in the sea of bobbing heads. She didn't see him climb the steps to the *tonka'tzi*'s palace, so he was headed somewhere beyond.

She gave him adequate time, then—taking a chance with her Trade— she climbed up on the earthen apron of the Healers' Society house's low mound. It gave her just enough elevation to look across the sea of humanity to the Great Staircase. And yes, how right was she? She made out Lance as he trudged wearily up the stairs and was passed by the Council Terrace Gate guards.

A slow smile bent her lips.

She eased down the slope, found her blanket undisturbed, and was on the verge of resuming her seat when the big brindle dog shoved through the press of passersby.

The beast pricked its floppy ears, the panting jowls drawn back in what could have been a happy grin but for the incongruity of the lolling pink tongue. The odd eyes, one blue, the other brown, fixed on her while the tail swished back and forth like a deadly weapon.

"Don't even think it," she warned, putting out her hands.

Farts came at a lope, leaped up to plant oversized paws on her shoulders—knocked her back three steps as he licked a sloppy wet tongue up the side of her cheek.

"Get away from me, you disgusting beast! I swear, you ruin my disguise, I'll stew your kidneys for supper!" Staggered as she was by the beast's weight, the dog's foul breath had her on the verge of passing out.

"Farts! Down!" Seven Skull Shield bellowed as he bulled his way through a throng of Panther Clan farmers.

Blue Heron coughed and gasped for fresh air when the unruly beast finally dropped to all fours. As quickly, she was forgotten as Farts' nose started twitching as it sniffed. Catching the odor from the catfish vendor's stand down the way, the big dog was gone, slipping through the crowd with all the grace of a battering ram.

Wiping her cheek as carefully as she could to keep from smearing her face paint, she glared at Seven Skull Shield. "Upon Piasa's stones, Thief, the day will come when I brain that wretched beast with a hickory knot and leave his carcass for the crows."

"How's Trade?" Seven Skull Shield asked mildly, his wide mouth curved in a satisfied grin. She could see the triumphant gleam animating his dark eyes. Perspiration was beading, trickling down the side of his face, and the underarms on his simple hunting shirt were dark with sweat. He'd obviously come far and fast.

With a gesture to the blanket with its familiar Trade, she told him, "Slow. I just saw Lord Lance trot past. Looked a bit put out, if you ask me. You involved in anything interesting down in Horned Serpent Town?"

The thief dropped onto his rear with a sigh; sitting cross-legged, he grabbed her water jar. Lifting it, he drained it dry. "Long hard run to get here. And pus and spit, it's a hot one today."

"That was the last of my water."

"Hard place to find a meal, that Horned Serpent Town. Farts and me, we sort of looked around. Watched all the muck-and-clucks pulling the matting out of their palaces, temples, and society houses. Worked like a bunch of frantic ants they did. Made Farts real hungry. And you know how the first day of the Busk is. Everyone was offering fixings, corn mush, lotus-root bread, maygrass stew, all in anticipation of the fasting. But nothing for poor old Farts."

She crossed her arms, glaring down at him. "Do you want to get to the point, or, as usual, is this all buildup for one of your wild tales?"

Seven Skull Shield gave her a hurt look. "It's not like I was wasting time down there. After all we've been through together, you being a master of a spy web and all, I've been learning. So I spent my time doing what your spies do. I went looking around. Listened to people. Hardly shared so much as a smile with that lonely young Hawk Clan woman I struck up a conversation with."

"Gods and rot, don't tell me. Her husband was out of town?"

"Trading down to the mouth of the Tenasee, but I want you to know that I didn't linger, sweet as she was. Had to hurry before everyone had to be celibate. We weren't under the robes for more than a hand of time, and it near broke her heart when I insisted I had to—"

"Pus, blood, and spit, Thief! Did you or did you not get into—"

"Easy, Keeper!" Seven Skull Shield gave her a mystified look as he tugged on one ear. He glanced as the stickball crowd exploded in shouts and jeers. "By the time she and I were finished exploring the depths and delights of her . . . um, well, never mind that part. As I was saying, by then it was dark. I could hardly see to make my way across the plaza. So I lit a fire to see by. Would have been dangerous to just go plodding out there, blind as a bat. No telling what I might have stumbled over. Might have barked my shin or something."

"Really?" She rolled her eyes. "How remarkably practical."

"By this time Farts was getting pretty hungry. That Hawk Clan gal, she'd already emptied her larder for the fast. And all the food had vanished, as it does at sundown on the first day. And, having a fire to light

my way I was able to locate the stairway that led up to the Horned Serpent Palace."

"And?" She was almost bouncing on her toes.

A sort of moan could be heard. Different from the howls of disap-
pointment of the stickball crowd when their team lost a point. This came
from down south, on the other side of the stickball game. Down by where
the Avenue of the Moon had its terminus on the east side of Rides-the-
Lightning's mound.

"Oh, my," Seven Skull Shield mumbled and climbed to his feet, peering off across the crowd past Rides-the-Lightning's temple mound. "I
wonder if that's the news?"

"Will you get to the point? I swear, there's times I want to break a
hickory branch over that thick skull of yours."

Seven Skull Shield then turned, staring off to the north. Taller than
she was, he said, "Looks like a bunch of nobles flooding down the Great
Staircase. Given how long it's been since Lord Lance must have climbed
up, it's about right for them to come rushing back down."

"You did it?" Blue Heron asked hopefully. "You did as I asked?"

"Well, I just wanted to get something for Farts to eat. And there was a
stew pot. But it was awfully close to the fire. And I didn't want Farts to
burn his paws."

She reached out, slapped him on his meaty shoulder. "Let's just hope
that knowledge isn't confined to the inner circle of Horned Serpent
House. That they can't just restart the fire and pretend it never happened."

"Oh, you needn't worry about that, Keeper." Seven Skull Shield was
picking his teeth with a thumbnail. "Didn't matter that it was the middle
of the night. Half the town was up."

"Why's that?"

He made a face. "Hmm. Did I forget to mention that I made a fire?
One to see by? That it was dark?"

"And you were able to find the palace, yes. You said that."

"There was all this old matting, old clothing and stuff, all those sacred
offerings. Who would have thought they'd burn that brightly?"

She took a deep breath, dryly asked, "You didn't?"

"You said make mischief. Now, being the simple and devout fellow
that I am, I'd never act out of—"

"Pus rot you! Did you *or didn't you?*"

"You take the fun out of everything. Short version: Eternal fire's out
in the palace. Offerings got burned in the plaza. The whole town down
there's gone crazy as head-struck geese. And Farts did get a full meal."
He gestured toward the Great Mound. "I'd say that's Green Chunkey's

entourage that just charged headlong down the stairs. Bet they're headed home to try and get a handle on the damage. Might even make it before sunset."

"That means Wind is safe for the time being." She sidled close, laid an arm over his muscle-thick shoulder. "Thief, there are times when I worship the ground you walk on."

"Why, Keeper, given some of the horrible things you've called me, I'll keep that close to my . . ."

"*Somebody! Stop that foul dog!*" The cry came from the catfish vendor's booth half a stone's throw up the line. "*Grab that beast! Quick! It just stole my fish!*"

A jostling broke out, people scrambling. And then Farts burst through the press. Knocked a Quiz Quiz Trader flat onto his rear in the process.

Blue Heron watched the brindle dog race past, ears flopping with each stride, big feet pounding the avenue as he darted around pedestrians, a cooked catfish hanging out of either side of Farts' oversized jaws.

The catfish vendor appeared half a heartbeat later, his fist up, howling his rage as he raced in pursuit. Not a chance that he'd ever catch the dog, let alone wreak his vengeance on the beast.

"And then I have to rethink my relationship with you," Blue Heron said in a melancholy voice. "And wonder what I ever did to Power to deserve this."

Thirty-six

Thick clouds hung low and threatening, filling the narrow Tenasee River valley. Gray, dull, and misty, they swept along the thickly forested slopes, tearing off in cottony wisps that threaded through the branches, packing around the outcrops of hard stone. Night Shadow Star thought it one of the most beautiful sights she'd ever seen. Mystical and magical.

And through it all, the light rain fell, stippling the surface of the river, pooling in the bottom of the canoe, soaking everything. She wore an improvised bark rain hat, her cloak and blanket sodden and dripping. She gripped the paddle with hands pruned and stiff from cold. She lived on the edge of shivers; only the endless labor of paddling warmed her blood.

Seated in the canoe behind her, Fire Cat stroked deeply with his paddle. Didn't matter how dreary the day, or endless the rain, a smile lit his face. Not a single word of complaint passed his lips. He might have glowed with a happy warmth, buoyant and joyful.

"How do you do it?" she'd asked him as she took another stroke with the paddle.

"I am the happiest man alive," he told her. "I'm with you."

"We're cold, hungry, aching from the effort, and . . ."

He reached forward just long enough to place his fingers against her unwounded cheek. "Cold, wet, and tired, I am with you. Nothing else matters. This is all I prayed for."

"You are a lunatic," she told him, bending her head down to trap his fingers against her shoulder. "I thank the moon and stars that you are my lunatic."

The weather had made things difficult.

Neither Blood Talon nor Winder had voiced the slightest complaint.

Only the Trader, Shell Hook, had muttered, groused, and moaned about the forced pace, about the cold food, the half-raw fish they cooked over smoking and heatless fires made with drenched wood. However, he had carried them farther than originally agreed, past the confluence of the Wide Fast, past Hiawasee Island, and all the way to Canyon Town.

But today they would be rid of him.

As it appeared out of the drizzle, she barely recognized the landing at Canyon Town, or *Ikansofke*, as it was known in the native Muskogee tongue. The memory of what it looked like had been burned into her soul as she and Winder had paddled away that seemingly long-ago morning in the wake of the Casqui's attack. What she saw now amazed her; the packed ranks of canoes extended halfway up the landing.

Even as they turned for shore, Shell Hook muttered, "There's hardly a place to set foot, let alone drag the canoe out of the water."

"Cahokia's grand expedition," Fire Cat told him. "Behold the crowning effort of Clan Matron Rising Flame and Keeper Spotted Wrist's conniving. You see all the malcontents, the politically disenfranchised, and the poor pitiful few without connections or patrons to speak for them. All sent out for the greater glory of Cahokia and the living god."

"More canoes than I've ever seen anyplace but the Cahokia canoe landing at Busk," Winder agreed.

"And this is only half of them," Night Shadow Star told him. "The others have already reached their destinations, reinforcing colonies, building new towns in places where Cahokia wants to expand its influence."

"All these canoes?" Shell Hook wondered. "They were all portaged? Carried up that narrow canyon trail past the Suck and Rage from White Chief Town?"

"Amazing what you can do with an army, isn't it?" Blood Talon chuckled faintly to himself. "Once, I would have been in charge of the expedition's squadrons. That portage would have been my responsibility to organize."

"And that brings us to a problem," Winder reminded. "We don't want to be recognized. Lady Night Shadow Star and I had a bit of trouble here. We broke the peace. If the locals recognize her, there will be . . . well, it will be unpleasant."

Blood Talon added, "Which won't be nearly the trouble if any of the Cahokians recognize her, or me. We'll be ensnared for days explaining things to chiefs and squadron firsts." A pause. "War Leader, how do you want to handle this?"

Fire Cat shipped his paddle, thoughtful. "We're dressed as Traders. It's raining. I say we slather mud on our faces at the canoe landing. Night Shadow Star's box should be covered with a blanket. Even a pie-eyed half-blind fool would recognize those carvings as being Four Winds Clan. Not the sort of thing Upper River Traders would have in their possession. Maybe pile that old netting and some of the fabric bags on it?"

"Just walk right through them?" Winder considered it, shrugged. "Might work." He glanced up. "It's raining. Night will be coming soon."

"We do have the two Trader's staffs," Blood Talon said. "It's worked before when we didn't want to be recognized. This is Canyon Town. Trade is everything here."

"And it's filled with Cahokians," Night Shadow Star agreed. "Lots of strangers. All we have to do is climb the trail, cross the plaza, then pass through the houses to reach the canyon trail."

"And hope none of the chunkey players are out," Blood Talon reminded. "Lady, you should know, your Red Wing made quite a name for himself playing chunkey last time we were here."

"You didn't tell me that," she said over her shoulder to Fire Cat.

"Didn't seem important. We needed Trade."

"What is it with you people?" Shell Hook asked. "Do you disrupt things everywhere you go?"

"Pretty much," Blood Talon replied. "And it's not like we're trying to. Things just seem to happen."

When Shell Hook's canoe slid onto the sand at the mucky edge of the landing, Night Shadow Star was first over the side. She held the hull as Fire Cat, Winder, and Blood Talon climbed out.

"*Careful here*," Piasa whispered from just behind her ear.

She shot another glance up at the town, remembering the last time she'd been here, when Walking Smoke's agents had tried to abduct her.

Were there others? Waiting?

And how are you going to avoid them if there are?

In Trade pidgin, she told the Trader, "Tell no one what you know. You are being well paid, and by the Power of Trade, hold your tongue. At least until we are long gone."

He nodded, said something in Mahica, and told her, "That's my solemn oath, Lady. I wish you luck." He glanced up at the lines of canoes. "I should be able to find Trade here, perhaps offer my services."

"I would hope so," Blood Talon said. "Find the squadron first, it's probably a man named Tall Dancer. Tell him you have worked for Clan Keeper Spotted Wrist. Tell him you have served with, and I quote, 'strength and honor.' He will know what that means."

"Thank you." Shell Hook bowed at the waist.

Meanwhile, Night Shadow Star smeared some of the charcoal-stained mud on her good cheek, figuring the long scab on her right pretty much obscured the tattoo on that side. Fire Cat was doing the same, and Blood Talon followed suit. As to Winder?

He grunted. "There's not much I can do. Mud or not, they know me well here. If any of my old friends notice, maybe they'll just think I'm working for the Cahokians."

"Take the back of the Trade box," Fire Cat told him. "Blood Talon, you take the front. I'd say try to look like less than you are, but that's a hope beyond hope. The lady and I shall take the Trader's staffs and walk in front. Wet and bedraggled as we are, maybe they'll let us pass for the half-drowned dogs we appear to be."

How do I look less than a lady?

And it came to her.

"Let us be about it, husband," Night Shadow Star told him, taking up Winder's staff. As she did, she heard Piasa hiss his displeasure behind her ear. Could feel the beast seething, just there, on the other side of the thin fabric of reality. Could almost see him slash out with his taloned feet.

"And if someone important recognizes you, overhears you calling your slave husband?" Fire Cat slung his pack with its armor, weapons, and chunkey gear over his shoulder.

Neither Winder nor Blood Talon so much as blinked, each betraying but the slightest smile as if it had been too long in coming as it was.

She said, "The whole world knows that Lady Night Shadow Star would never marry a mere slave, and a Red Wing at that. Therefore, there's no way this woman would ever be mistaken for Night Shadow Star." She arched a challenging eyebrow. "Or do you object?"

Fire Cat's lips quirked as he stared up at the town. "Never in a thousand years, Lady."

Piasa screamed in rage, almost making her wince.

"That's wife. The term is *wife*. Or do you want to get us caught?"

"Never that, wife." He drew a deep breath, raised his staff on high, and started forward.

In the corner of her eye, she saw the flicker of movement, the shifting shadow as Piasa darted between the packed ranks of canoes.

"*You mock me,*" Piasa's words echoed in the drizzle-filled air.

"Oh, go drown a crawfish," she growled back and followed in the footsteps of her husband.

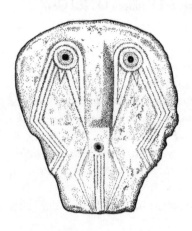

Floating

I stare up at the canyon walls, parting now as the valley widens. Roiling clouds remain overhead; the rumble of thunder booms and echoes down from the high peaks.

I am Sky Born. Of the Four Winds Clan. My Spirit guardian is the lightning, the deadly weapon of the Thunderbirds in their eternal war against the Spirit Creatures of the Underworld.

For the moment I float in between, half-submerged in the wreckage of our smashed canoe. Sometimes one of the gunwales is exposed in the troughs between wave crests. But swamped and cracked as it is, it is still keeping us afloat.

Barely.

We are cold, so very cold. Shivers rack my body. I wonder if I will ever be warm again.

In the rear, High Chief Fire Light holds tight to the wave-washed gunwale, his face reflecting shock and disbelief. Somewhere in the passage, his head hit a rock. The water has left wet blood coagulated on the side of his head and matted in his hair. I wonder if the man's souls are still firmly anchored to his bones. He seems, well, lost, his eyes vacant in his head and unable to focus.

Twists His Hair looks equally traumatized where he clings, teeth chattering, to the outside of the canoe. But Flat Arrow and Four Braids are lost. Tossed out of the canoe in the violently churning waters of the Suck and Rage.

Remembering, I nearly break into tears. In my entire life, nothing terrified me like that passage down the canyon through that tortured and pounding chaos of rapids and falls. I would never have believed that water, let alone a moving mass of water, could be goaded into such titanic fury.

I remain stunned by what I've just survived. Realize that no words exist to *describe that maelstrom of current, rock, and rapids. A river violently tearing itself apart, only to spit us out at the bottom of the canyon and finally set us adrift in a placid and quiet flow.*

We have our lives and the battered canoe. All that's left to me are the clothes on my back and the pouch with the lightning shell mask tied to my waist. That's it. The paddles, the packs, blankets, netting, all gone. Lost in the thrashing tumult. The only reason we remain is somehow we clung to our flooded canoe. Half-drowned. Somehow able to keep hold of one of the gunwales as we were dashed back and forth.

A sucking of current whips us around in a slow circle, and I can only gape in dazed stupor.

I attribute our survival to the lightning. It's the only explanation. Piasa and his servants, the Tie Snakes, paid the price last time they tried to take me. Enough so that the underwater panther didn't dare try and take me in the canyon. Let me pass rather than give the Thunderbirds another chance to kill him.

I can feel Twists His Hair's shivers as he shakes the canoe. Fire Light's teeth are chattering so hard they clack together like rocks. I am so cold I can barely feel my body through the misery.

Would have loved to have made shore at the town on the south bank as the torrent spat us out, but without paddles, exhausted as we were, we could only float past.

Whirling and twirling this way and that with the current, watching the verdant canyon spin around us, we are like flotsam. Our fatigued bodies are teetering on the verge of despair.

I didn't see when Twists His Hair's body floated free. I was so cold it didn't register that he was floating facedown. Just the back of his head and his shoulders visible as we drifted ever farther apart.

Somewhere in the merging of time and suffering, he disappeared.

Not that I ever would have cared, but it just didn't matter.

I saw it first. Thought it a vision. Something conjured by my too-cold brain. Just the flash of paddles stroking in unison.

An eddy whips us around, and I lose sight of it.

Only to see it again as we slowly drift in a circle. Yes. A canoe.

I raise a hand, hoping they will see.

From my throat, I manage a hoarse cry.

They are almost even with us, water curling at the canoe's high bow as they fly down the river.

A fast canoe, paddled by two ranks of warriors. I see a man perched in the rear, a high headdress, his cloak that of a leader.

"Here!" I finally manage to squeak, and the warrior glances my way. I can

see him staring, realize that all he sees are heads, hands, perhaps part of the canoe's hull above the water.

"Help!" My voice breaks.

For a terrifying moment, I fear they will continue past. But in the end, the warrior utters a command.

I see the fast canoe turn, backing water. I almost drift off, feeling my souls coming loose from my body.

And then hands reach down. Grip me under the armpits, and I am pulled up and over a gunwale.

My thoughts swimming, I see a distant bolt of lightning forking through the clouds.

"Who are you?" a voice asks. Cahokian.

"Four Winds Clan," I whisper. "Morning Star House."

"Piss in a pot," the warrior in charge swears. "How did you get here?"

"Rode . . . the lightning . . ." and then I fade away.

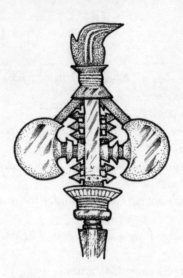

Thirty-seven

On the second night of the Busk, the way Spotted Wrist saw it, the very fates were working against him. The disaster at Horned Serpent House was going to hang like a pall over the remainder of the Green Corn Festival.

He stood at the Council Terrace gate as sunset glowed yellow and orange across the northwestern horizon and shaded the sky into lavender above and deep purple where it met the bluffs in the east. The usual haze floated over the city: smoke from a thousand fires contributing to the low-hanging pall. These, however, weren't cooking fires—given that the entire city was fasting—but blazes that heated stones for countless sweat lodges, or for bonfire light as different lineages gathered for the telling of the traditional stories, for Dancing, and for socializing with visiting kin.

Thankfully, despite Cahokia's ravenous appetite for firewood, the city was surrounded by forests in all directions. And though supplies had been tight while his warriors crowded the canoe landing at River Mounds and slowed Trade, with its usual resilience the city had compensated from other sources.

In the plaza below, the last of the chunkey games and stickball had been called at sunset. Now the Dancers were taking possession of the southern half of the plaza, gathering at the base of the World Tree Pole. The thumping of drums, whoops of delight, and calls could be heard as clan elders tried to organize the teeming throngs into a Dance line.

All those people. And this was without the multitudes from Horned Serpent town. Or many of them, anyway. A lot of people had defied clan decisions to withdraw from the festivities while Green Chunkey presided over emergency rituals to purify Horned Serpent Town, his House, and subordinate Earth Clans. The disaster perpetrated by the extinguishing of the sacred fire was too demoralizing. The miracle would be if Green Chunkey and Matron Round Pot survived the next quarter moon. Their House was shaken to the roots.

"From the pinnacle of success," Spotted Wrist whispered under his breath, "just as he reached out to grasp it all and climb onto the *tonka'tzi*'s high chair, blind fate strikes and pulls him . . ."

He smelled the smoke-heavy breeze, laden with the pungent odors of so much humanity packed into such a small space. He narrowed his eyes, staring out across the crowds, listening to the pulse of the city.

Adding to his unease, he'd just been face-to-face with that accursed Lady Sun Wing. She'd treated him as if he wasn't even there. Watching her carry on a conversation with a leather bag full of who knew what was eerie enough, but between humming lines of some ancient Song about death, she'd told the Bundle, "His salvation lies just beneath his sleep. All that enchanted copper, Singing to him in his Dreams, while the women he wants to control just keep slipping through his fingers."

For a second, she'd seemed lucid. Looked up at him, awareness in her large-eyed gaze. "The copper will get you killed, you know."

And then she'd wandered back into Morning Star's palace.

"It's all idiocy."

Nothing was working right. Horned Serpent House's calamity couldn't have come at a worse time.

Well, for Green Chunkey, at least. That thought brought a smile to Spotted Wrist's lips. The need to place a potential rival to North Star House on the *tonka'tzi*'s high chair had just been eliminated. For the immediate future, Spotted Wrist had no need to accommodate an old enemy's demands.

While the thought was still rolling around in his mind, the two Morning Star House guards at either side of the gate—decked out as they were—dipped their heads and saluted as Lady Columella, followed by six of her warriors, stepped out from inside the Council Terrace palisade.

She took in the fading light as it illuminated the crowd, then started as she recognized Spotted Wrist.

"Oh, it's you." Her voice dripped with loathing.

"Lady," he told her shortly, not even bothering to flip an insolent greeting with his fingers.

Indeed, had the timing of Green Chunkey's humiliation been too perfect? And this nonsense of a Spirit wolf having been witness to the event? Its track left in the sodden ashes of a drowned fire? Seriously? Suddenly it all made sense.

"Put out any fires lately, Matron?" he asked casually.

"Haven't needed to," she told him airily. "Seems they've dampened themselves without any action on my part." Then her gaze quickened. "Oh, I see. Perhaps you don't refer to mismanaged attacks on my House. No, indeed. Sorry, but I'm afraid I had no hand in the unfortunate events suffered by Round Pot and Green Chunkey."

She hesitated a beat. "Though, now that you mention it, I wish I'd thought of it myself. Might have been worth it, even if the act was an affront to Power."

"Why don't I believe you?"

"I couldn't give a mold-covered acorn when it comes to what you choose to believe, Keeper. From what I hear, it was Power that extinguished Green Chunkey's sacred fire. Something about a Spirit wolf."

"You and your agents are behind every bit of misfortune in Cahokia. I'm to believe you had no knowledge of this?"

"None."

"The timing is too—"

"Keeper, isn't it *your* job to uncover any such nefarious plots?" She raised an eyebrow. "But I'll give you this: None of my sources or agents are privy to any knowledge that Horned Serpent House's misfortune was anything but an accident."

"It was too well planned!"

"By whom? My people were *not* involved, and despite my earlier flippant remark, even if we'd thought of it, we wouldn't risk the offense to Power or Morning Star. Only a lunatic would dare such an affront."

Spotted Wrist ground his teeth, the sneaking suspicion that she was telling the truth adding to his anger. But then, Green Chunkey would have already dispatched his agents. Would have been too distraught over the disaster back home to have called them off. Even if he'd thought of it.

One way or another, Green Chunkey's agents would see to it that come tomorrow morning, Evening Star House would have to choose another matron.

Before he could fashion a clever reply, she added, "I do, however, appear to have a surplus of canoes these days. Seems that I'm better at keeping track of them than some. Should you be in need, come see me."

He turned, knotting a fist. "Beware, Matron."

The warriors behind her shifted, some pulling their war clubs from the thongs at their belts.

"Just making conversation, Keeper." She lifted a cautionary hand to stop her bristling warriors. "Canoes, you know. Seems they are a subject on everyone's lips these days."

The acid in Spotted Wrist's stomach churned, his every muscle going tense. "I gave my word you'd have free passage. But, be warned, woman, your mouth could lead you to—"

Careful! Don't let her goad you into making a foolish statement.

She cocked her head, eyes narrowing as she studied him. "I just had an audience with Clan Matron Rising Flame. Curious thing. She most candidly offered the White Arrow, as the Muskogee would say. She wondered if there was any way that our current, um, she called them 'tensions,' might be alleviated." A wary smile. "Am I to understand that was mistaken on her part? That you are still intending to do me and my House harm? You and Matron Rising Flame remain in agreement when it comes to the Houses, do you not?"

He bit off the stinging riposte before it passed his lips. Smiled. No, all he needed was to wait. Come morning, he could offer his deepest sympathy. Could truthfully say that whatever terrible fate had befallen the matron, neither he nor any of his people had acted contrary to their oaths.

Her half-mocking inquiring brow lifted while she awaited his answer. All he said was, "Enjoy the Busk, Matron. It's a delightful evening."

It will be your last.

Without a backward glance, he started down the stairs, leaving her to fume at the top. As he skipped down the squared logs, he imagined himself in Evening Star Town, his squadrons formed up in the plaza. Standing atop her palace landing, he'd glance down, off to the side, where Columella's stinking little dwarf and her surviving kin hung in squares. Witness to the end of her house and her lineage, he would revel in every moment of it. Too bad she wouldn't be around to know the extent and depth of her defeat.

And just maybe, Matron, I'll burn your palace in retaliation for your burning of River House's.

At the bottom of the stairs, the crowd was thick along the Avenue of the Sun. Held back by the Morning Star guards, the wall of humanity was packed shoulder-to-shoulder and spilling out onto the plaza. This was the second evening of the Busk, after all. That seething ocean of people—porters, litters, servants, and runners belonging to the nobles on the Council Terrace and those up at Morning Star's palace. And then there were the entourages from the foreign embassies, the pilgrims, the Traders, and the crush of dirt farmers all come to central Cahokia in hopes of seeing Morning Star, or just to share in the celebration.

As Spotted Wrist stepped onto the Avenue of the Sun, Cut Weasel, at the head of Spotted Wrist's escort, bellowed an order. The warriors, having more or less held a position at the edge of the stairs, shoved and butted a hollow out of the masses so that Spotted Wrist could mount his litter.

Then, calling, "Make way! Make way for Clan Keeper Spotted Wrist!" they battered their way through the press.

Somehow, they pushed through the sea of bodies, eliciting the occasional scream from some individual who didn't move fast enough. From his high seat atop the litter, the sight reminded Spotted Wrist of a log propelled through thick flood debris.

And then they were free of the massed humanity, able to make progress on the still-crowded avenue as people had room to at least get out of the way.

Rounding the southeastern corner of Morning Star's great mound, Spotted Wrist's warriors carried him north past the various palaces, dwellings, temples, and society houses to his relatively modest abode atop its low mound on the margins of the eastern plaza. This had traditionally been Morning Star House territory; his own palace mound had once belonged to Lady Lace. But then, this was only supposed to have been a temporary dwelling. By now he should have been living in Night Shadow Star's opulent dwelling, with its commanding view of the Great Plaza.

When Spotted Wrist's litter was lowered before his short flight of stairs, he noticed that a glow was coming from inside, that a fire had been lit for the night. A group of warriors on his veranda rose to their feet.

Pounding up his steps, Spotted Wrist took the warriors' salutes, and called, "Who comes?"

A dark form stepped out. "Squadron Second Sharp Twig, Keeper. I come with a message from Squadron First Heart Warrior."

"Well, praise to Morning Star," Spotted Wrist growled. "At least something has gone right. Come, enter, Squadron Second. Can I get you anything to drink? Tea perhaps?"

"No, Keeper." Sharp Twig bowed respectfully before following Spotted Wrist into the palace great room, such as it was. The matting had, of course, been stripped out to leave the floor bare dirt. Each of the wall benches was piled with his personal guard's blankets, their possessions shoved beneath. With all the war trophies on his walls, the place looked more like a Men's House than a palace.

Which gave his stomach another sour twist.

Marching to the dais behind the fire, Spotted Wrist seated himself, asking, "Very well. What news?"

Sharp Twig pulled himself up, his armor looking grimy, sweat-stained, and unkempt. "I have just returned with another five canoes from downriver, Clan Keeper. Squadron First Heart Warrior wishes you to know that he continues to pursue canoes down past the confluence with the Mother Water. He wants you to know—"

"The Mother Water?" Spotted Wrist cried. "What's he doing down there?"

"Why, retrieving the stolen canoes, Lord Keeper." Sharp Twig looked confused. "Following the Keeper's orders. That he was not to return until he had recovered every single—"

"He's *supposed* to be forming ranks of warriors three-days' march south of Evening Star town! Ready to occupy it while the Evening Star House clans are squabbling over who should replace Columella!"

"Keeper, sir?" Sharp Twig looked totally mystified.

Spotted Wrist clamped his eyes shut, pinched his nose. "I sent two messengers by canoe. Dispatched them but a half moon past. You're telling me that my commander remains unaware that he is supposed to be assembling Forest Squadron three-days' march downriver of Evening Star Town? That instead of preparing to attack Evening Star Town, he is blithely chasing down the Father Water collecting ever fewer canoes? Let's see, with your five, I now have recovered twenty-eight of the eighty-some missing canoes. *Twenty-eight!*"

Sharp Twig winced.

"And how far is Heart Warrior taking his squadron in this mad quest? *All the way to the Gulf?*" Spotted Wrist thundered.

"I don't know, Lord Keeper. The Squadron First's last orders were not to return until every single canoe—"

"I *gods-rotted* know the orders, Second. I *gave* them." Spotted Wrist gulped for air, tried to slow his pounding heart. "But what you're telling me is that no squadron of warriors is being quietly assembled? That we have no ability to take the disorganized Evening Star forces by surprise? That any hope of that possibility is paddling gaily down the Father Water until who knows when?"

Sharp Twig pulled himself upright, finding some remnant of a spine that might have turned to water. "After all these years, the Lord Keeper knows that if Squadron First Heart Warrior had received orders to give up the hunt for the canoes and assemble a squadron three days' march south of Evening Star Town, he would have done so."

Spotted Wrist clamped his eyes shut, making himself breathe. Just breathe. That's it. Breathe in, breathe out. Breathe in, breathe out. *Yes, my heart. Slow. Steady. Get control. Think rationally.*

But what did this mean?

He could almost believe that Power was making a mockery of him. This was the perfect time to strike at Evening Star Town. Columella would be dead by morning. Her people would have no clue until it was too late.

Gone. The chance has vanished like morning mist on a hot day.

"Squadron Second," Spotted Wrist snapped.

"Lord Keeper," Sharp Twig cried, slapping a hand to his chest.

"You will turn right around, collect your warriors, and fly your canoe downriver until you find Heart Warrior. You will order the squadron first to *immediately* collect all his warriors and whatever canoes he has. That he will . . . he will . . ."

"Assemble the squadron three days' march south of—"

"*No!* Rot you! We're too late for that!" Spotted Wrist struggled for control. "Pus and blood, let me think."

So, what was the move? Given the time it would take for Sharp Twig to find the squadron and then to paddle back upriver, Heart Warrior couldn't make his return to Cahokia in less than a half moon. Maybe longer than that. Indeed, figure longer.

Meanwhile, Evening Star Town will be in chaos.

Didn't matter that Columella would be dead, Rising Flame was willing to make peace with Evening Star House. Spotted Wrist could no longer consider the clan matron a solid ally. At this stage, it was every man and woman for his or herself.

A full moon. That's how long he'd have to hold Cahokia with what was left of North Star and Wolverine Squadrons. Though he could, if necessary, call up the Earth Clans squadrons that were subordinated to North Star House. But only as a last resort. Doing so would trigger a call-up from every other House in the city.

I play a most dangerous game.

But ultimately he had to hold central Cahokia, and with it, Morning Star. He could accomplish that with just his two remaining squadrons and North Star House to back him. If he had Horned Serpent House—or what was left of it—he'd still control enough warriors to prevail. But he'd have to have a guarantee that Horned Serpent House would back him.

"Squadron Second," he said at last, "you will find Squadron First Heart Warrior and order him to assemble his squadron and proceed as rapidly as he can. He is to land at the Horned Serpent Town's canoe landing. The squadron will assemble and proceed at fast march to Horned Serpent Town. There it will be supported by High Chief Green Chunkey. And, if the high chief has been replaced, Forest Squadron will find additional orders awaiting its arrival. But tell Heart Warrior to prepare for the fact that he might have to seize the House on my orders."

Sharp Twig blinked. "Seize Horned Serpent—"

"Did I stutter, Squadron Second?"

"No, Lord Keeper!"

"Well? Why are you still standing here? Get your sorry chafed carcass out of my palace and back on the river. The sooner you find Heart Warrior, the sooner my pus-dripping squadron is in Horned Serpent Town. Do you understand?"

"Yes, Clan Keeper!" Sharp Twig hammered off a salute, turned on his heel, and ran from the palace.

For a moment the room hung in stunned silence, then Cut Weasel asked, "Horned Serpent Town?" He raised an inquiring brow. "In a moon or so?"

In the eye of his soul, Spotted Wrist thought he saw how the parts could come together. "My friend, the only thing that will save us in the long run is ourselves. We just need to buy ourselves enough time for Heart Warrior to get back. Assuming the worst, that Green Chunkey is deposed, we'll need Heart Warrior to secure Horned Serpent Town in the south. After that, I think we're going to have to take sterner measures."

"And if Clan Matron Rising Flame objects?" Cut Weasel asked uncertainly.

"At first sign of that, the good Matron might have an unlucky fire."

"Sort of like Blue Heron had?"

"That's right, Squadron Second. Seems like that happens a lot to the women who stand against me."

Thirty-eight

To Fire Cat's amazement, it worked. Partly because of the gray day, the drizzle, the late hour, and half-light, they marched right through the middle of Canyon Town, their heads down, features half-hidden in the soggy blankets draped over their heads and shoulders.

He and Night Shadow Star held the Trader's staffs at half mast, the feathers dripping. Plodding between the Cahokian shelters, they skirted smoldering fires surrounded by knots of warriors, Earth Clans farmers, tradesmen and their families. All looking miserable. None casting more than a dismissive glance their way.

The nobles, of course, had commandeered all the bent-pole dwellings, displacing the locals, and to no one's surprise the Trade House at the edge of the plaza was packed.

Fire Cat caught Night Shadow Star's sidelong glance at the building, knew that lining of her brow, the mocking twist to her lips. "Wife?"

"They can have it," she told him. "Not a place where a decent female Trader can sleep in peace. Power of Trade or no."

"Could have been worse," Winder called from behind. "I might have stumbled upon some gorgeous young woman willing to share her blankets for the night in return for a string of shell beads. Wouldn't have known you were missing until the next morning."

"You and Seven Skull Shield." Night Shadow Star made a wry face, then winced as it pulled at the scab on her cut cheek. "Is that all you think about?"

Winder—burdened by the disguised box of Trade—kept a straight face. "Well, there's also food."

"And making a nuisance of yourselves," Fire Cat added.

"Ah, yes, there's that." Winder grinned in a most satisfied way.

They passed along the side of the plaza; the low-humped shape of the *Tchkofa* resembled a wet turtle's back—though a thread of blue rose from the smoke hole, vanishing into the drizzle.

"Would you look at that?" Blood Talon said in awe. "War Leader, would you recognize those as the same chunkey courts you played on?"

Fire Cat allowed a faint shake of the head, told Night Shadow Star, "They were just strips of dirt. Now look, graded flat with packed sand, and someone spent a lot of labor leveling them. Even Crazy Frog would approve."

Night Shadow Star shifted her pack on her back. "I'd say that Squadron First Tall Dancer is planning on leaving a garrison here. Maybe a detachment of warriors and a bunch of priests. They wouldn't put that much effort into the courts otherwise. I think, whether the locals like it or not, Canyon Town just became a Cahokian colony."

"Makes sense," Blood Talon agreed. "My bet is that Cahokia might have come here under the Power of Trade, but it's going to stay under the power of might. Same with White Chief Town on the other side of the Suck and Rage. Both towns are strategically important when it comes to controlling the river Trade. From here on out, Cahokia can use the portage as a chokepoint."

Winder vented a wistful sigh, plodding along at the back of the Trade box.

"That bothers you, Trader?" Fire Cat asked.

"Aye, Red Wing. The Power of Trade gives way before the might of Cahokia." A pause. "Nothing will be the same. Some of the river's charm dies with each new colony. We can say that we were among the last to travel the old river, who knew it as it was. By the time this grand expedition of Spotted Wrist's has run its course, the Tenasee will be nothing more than a Cahokian creek from its confluence with the Mother Water to the Wide Fast. And maybe all the way to Cofitachequi."

"And that saddens you?" Night Shadow Star asked. "You're Cahokian."

"Doesn't mean I don't have a fondness for the variety, Lady. An appreciation for all these different peoples with their varied ways, languages, and quaint customs."

"So much for their quaint customs," Blood Talon muttered. "A bunch of them just down from here were going to hack me into roasted pieces because a tree fell on a house." He made a growling noise. "I'm not sympathetic. Let the Cahokians come. Civilize the whole lot of them."

"After my brush with the Catawba, Squadron First, the idea has a certain appeal," Night Shadow Star agreed. "What's the Power of Trade worth if just anyone can ambush a canoe, murder its occupants, and use them for sacrificial revenge? Not that Walking Smoke didn't commit an atrocity in their village, but why take it out on the innocent? So much for the Power of Trade among the barbarians. Say what you will about Cahokia, where it goes, peace follows."

Fire Cat bit his lip, let his eyes linger on the chunkey grounds as he and the rest continued past.

The Cahokians would build a palace dedicated to the worship of Morning Star next, priests expounding upon the miracle of the living god. Religion, Trade, and conquest—all with the military strength to back them up—marching hand-in-hand up the Tenasee. Tying together the colonies all the way to Cofitachequi.

Winder, however, wasn't about to give it a rest. "What about you, Red Wing? You're not Cahokian. Do you see it the same way?"

Fire Cat bit his lip harder, but to his surprise it was Blood Talon who said, "Leave it be, Trader. The War Leader has more than enough reason to hate Cahokia and all that it stands for. I was there, I was responsible. I know what it cost him at Red Wing Town, and what it costs him every day of his life."

"And yet he saved the city, even saved the living god, if the stories can be believed." Winder continued to worry it as they marched past the far end of the court.

The mountain wall was just visible under the low-hanging curtain of drizzling clouds. As they passed the last of the bent-pole dwellings, they saw a small cluster of warriors standing under a ramada at the trail head.

Night Shadow Star took a deep breath. "What Fire Cat did, he did in service to me," she told them. "First with Walking Smoke, then with the Itza, and finally in the Underworld. That was honor. Not a love for Cahokia."

"Quiet now. Finish this conversation later," Fire Cat said as they followed the sloppy path to the trailhead. "We're just Traders. If they ask, we're headed to White Chief Town. Just traveling under the Power of Trade."

One of the warriors stepped out, called in horribly accented Trade pidgin, "Who comes?"

"Traders," Fire Cat called back. "Headed downriver to White Chief Town. Hope to hire a canoe. Been over Cofitachequi way. We have Trade that will fetch us a profit downriver."

The warrior squinted at them. "It's getting dark. A bit late to leave town, isn't it?"

Night Shadow Star, in pidgin, asked, "You been to the Trade House? Not a bed to be had."

"Unless you want to sleep three-deep on the ground," Winder added.

"We know where there's a shelter a hand's journey down the path. Off the trail and half a stone's throw up the slope. Bark-sided. Hunters from town built it. It'll keep us dry for the night."

"Not anymore." The warrior was peering intently at Blood Talon. "Don't I know you?"

"Maybe. Been Trading up by Joara, have you?" Blood Talon shrugged.

The warrior turned, "Jay Tail. Come over here. Something about this one—"

"Oh, come," Fire Cat offered in a jovial voice. "We're just Traders. It's getting dark. That shelter—"

"Is gone." The warrior slicked the water from his hair, his beaded forelock swinging. "They used it for material when they upgraded the portage. You think the War Leader wanted to carry all those canoes over that original rut you people call a trail?"

Jay Tail—who by the cut of the single feather stuck in his hair must have been a squadron third—emerged from the ramada's shelter to ask, "What's this about?"

"Something not right. These Traders—"

"Want to get on about our business," Night Shadow Star snapped. "It's going to be dark soon, and we need to find someplace to stay out of the weather."

"What's wrong with Canyon Town?" The squadron third bristled at the authoritative tone that had crept into Night Shadow Star's voice.

"No room," Winder said easily. "Even fewer beds if we stay the night. For all we know, we'd have to sneak into the *Tchkofa* to find a dry place, and you know they take a really dim view of that sort of thing here."

Jay Tail, seeming not to buy it, stepped close, reached out with his war club, and used the hafted stone head to lift the corner of the netting that covered Night Shadow Star's box. He seemed puzzled at first, blinked as he took in the intricate carving, the shell-and-pearl inlays and the damning Four Winds Clan designs.

"Upriver Traders, huh?" Jay Tail beckoned his other warriors with his free hand. "Maybe you'd better start talking, and you'd best hope to high *Hunga Ahuito* that it makes more sense than this dung you've been spouting."

Fire Cat took a deep breath, considered trying to take the five warriors, and gave it up as a bad option.

"Well, wife?" he asked Night Shadow Star. "When has anything we've said ever made sense?"

He tried to smile at the surrounding warriors and failed.

Thirty-nine

Having passed midnight, this was now officially the third day of the Busk, though sunrise wouldn't come for another five hands of time.

Creeping Panther paused just before the veranda, looked back over his shoulder at Seven Sticks' shadowy form as he eased his way along the flattened top of the mound. The dwelling was generally kept for foreign embassies to occupy. For the duration of the Busk it had been designated for Evening Star House's sole use. Seemed the good Matron Columella had reservations about staying at the Four Winds Clan House, where Rising Flame kept her residence.

Who would have thought that Columella might not be safe in the city?

The notion brought a twist of amusement to Creeping Panther's lips.

From the elevated step, he and Seven Sticks could hear the drums, the chanting, and the clapping of hands. Even the shuffle of thousands of moccasins on the beaten grass of the Great Plaza. Flickers of light from the bonfires cast the palaces, society houses, temples, and charnel houses in black silhouette where they fronted the plaza.

This late in the night, the orange glow had faded from the smoke and haze that cloaked the rest of the city.

The odors of Cahokia carried on the night breeze, damp, acrid, filled with the pungency of packed humanity. He caught the cloying scent of rotting corpses as the breeze shifted from the Fish Clan charnel house to the west. Somewhere to the north, across the Avenue of the Sun, a lone dog barked.

Creeping Panther slipped his war club from where it hung at his leather strap of a belt. In the faint light, he could see Seven Sticks do the same.

With a careful step, he eased onto the veranda, feeling the split-plank floor under his bare feet. Have to be most careful now. Columella's warriors were laid out in a line, their blanket-wrapped forms barely visible in the night's orange glow. Step by easy step, Creeping Panther lived up to his name. But then Green Chunkey hadn't chosen him and Seven Sticks randomly.

At the plank door, the two shifted their weapons, each grabbing the portal. In unison they eased it up, shifted it, and leaned the door against the plastered wall to one side. Then, noiseless as smoke on the water, they felt their way into the great room. Here the eternal fire in its puddled-clay hearth cast enough glow that Creeping Panther could make out the wall benches where Columella's entourage slept. These were Evening Star House nobles, Columella's kin, and high-ranking Earth Clans chiefs and matrons under her command. Their servants and lackeys slept rolled in blankets on the white-clay floor, exposed as it was with the matting ripped out.

On feet of air, Creeping Panther led the way down the narrow path left open beside the fire. Not that he worried so much now. Room full of people like this? No one would remark on two shadows walking across the floor. Could have been any of them up to empty night water, attend to some personal chore. With this many allies, and this much protection around, no one would entertain the notion of an assassin.

At the rear, a second door had been pulled back and left half open. This, too, from long practice, Creeping Panther and Seven Sticks carefully lifted aside, working in unison like the well-functioning team they were.

And then they were inside the sleeping quarters.

Here it got a little tricky. The room was dark as pitch. The problem would be locating Columella without alerting anyone else who might be sleeping in the stygian room. Reaching out, he laid a light finger on Seven Sticks' shoulder, their signal to stop, wait, and study.

Cocking his head, Creeping Panther listened carefully. And yes, there. He could hear the soft rasping of breath, the gentle exhalation of a sleeping human.

Wait, and another on a second bench farther back.

Sniffing, he sought to smell out the difference. Columella, being a matron who, according to their surveillance, had spent the day at the Four Winds Clan House, at the Council Terrace, and maybe even Morning Star's palace, should have a slightly perfumed odor. A servant or guard would have been outside, waiting, sweating in the hot sun and humid air.

This one. In the nearer bed. She might even have had that faint feminine musk.

He tapped his finger on Seven Sticks' shoulder and eased his foot forward. Felt the string with his toes, and before he could understand, heard something clatter at the far end of the room.

"I guess they're here," a voice said in a most reasonable tone.

"Lift the basket," another voice declared.

Frozen in a half step, Creeping Panther gaped as a basket was lifted at the far end of the room. With that, soft yellow light from an oil lamp cast its glow across the confines of the sleeping quarters.

The woman who rose from the bed was young, in her early thirties, with a Turtle Clan tattoo on her cheeks. Wiry, muscular, she carried a light wicker shield, a stone-bitted war club in her right hand. In the dim light, her thin-lipped mouth bent into a smile.

Creeping Panther back-stepped, felt more than heard Seven Sticks turn on his heel, and winced as voices from the great room called, "They're not going anywhere. We've got the exit blocked."

On the second bed, a dwarf threw back the blanket and stood, the added elevation placing him at head height with Creeping Panther. Had to be Flat Stone Pipe, Columella's famous consort.

A burly warrior, a squadron first's feathers on his shoulders, full armor encasing his torso and forearms, set the basket to one side before nocking and pulling a war arrow to full draw. He said, "First one of you moves, I'll skewer you. Second one moves, White Iris here will smack your brains out. And just because she's a woman, don't even think you can beat her. She trains with me."

"Oh, Uncle," the woman said as she narrowed a disappointed eye, "you take the fun out of everything." Then her tone hardened. "Drop the war clubs. Then raise your hands where we can see them."

"This is all a mistake," Creeping Panther cried as he dropped his war club, which landed on the bare clay with a thump. "We just got lost. Apologies. In the dark we walked into the wrong building. We'll just—"

"Indeed you did," Matron Columella interrupted from the door. She was studying them with thoughtful eyes. "Squadron First? Think you and White Iris can manage to get them back to our side of the river before sunrise?"

"Plenty of time, Matron," the grinning warrior said. "Have them in the squares by sunup."

"And I'll be happy to make them talk," White Iris added, leaning close, a dancing excitement in her eyes as she asked Creeping Panther, "You ever been tortured by a woman with a vivid imagination?"

He swallowed hard, half wheezed, "This is a mistake."

From the door Columella added, "White Iris is quite good at her job and does have a most ingenious imagination when it comes to naked men hanging in squares. I think it has something to do with a woman's curiosity about the male body. But I give you my word: The pain stops and you'll be taken down as soon as you tell us everything Green Chunkey ordered you to do here."

When Creeping Panther shot a glance at Seven Sticks, the man was already shivering, tears leaking down his cheeks.

Forty

Leave it be, Squadron Third Jay Tail," Blood Talon said in Cahokian as he lowered his end of the box and stepped forward. "Yes, I know you. Served under Slim Arrow during the Shawnee campaign, as I recall. Didn't fare too well, if memory serves." Blood Talon glanced around at the low clouds, the stringers of drizzle. "Doesn't look like your prospects have picked up any either, now does it?"

"You take chances, Trader." Jay Tail stiffened. "You talk to me in that tone of voice? I'm a squadron third under Tall Dancer's command, and you're about to—"

"Feed you that war club if you don't shut your empty hole of a mouth and let us pass!" Blood Talon barked. "You didn't serve War Leader Spotted Wrist well when he took on the Shawnee, and now you're about to make a worse mess out of a simple sentry detail."

Jay Tail had puffed up like a freezing robin, his face darkening. He wagged his war club in Blood Talon's face, saying, "I'll have your hide, you worthless—"

"You address me as Squadron Leader Blood Talon! First in command under War Leader and Clan Keeper Spotted Wrist."

Jay Tail gaped, jerked as if slapped when Blood Talon ripped the war club from the squadron third's grip.

"I thought I knew you!" the first warrior crowed. "Yes, that's you! The mud on your face, the way you're dressed—"

"Is for a gods-rotted reason," Blood Talon hissed as he advanced on the hapless Jay Tail. "Now, you do one of two things. You let us pass and be on about our mission, or you take us right to Tall Dancer. After I have to explain why War Leader and Clan Keeper Spotted Wrist's plans are being fouled up by some pus-licking maggot of a lowly squadron third, I'm going to see you hung in a square for the locals. Let them take out any upset and frustrations they might be feeling about Cahokians. And more than that, I'll light the first torch!"

Jay Tail looked like he was trying to swallow past a stuck plum pit.

Not finished, Blood Talon added, "Now, we're headed down that blood-rotted trail. And not another word, you hear?" He spun. "All of you! Not a pus-dripping word! None of you saw me. I don't exist. Neither do these Traders, and especially that spit-licking box! It's not real. Not even a high fancy in your mud-clotted imaginations. This meeting never happened! You get that?"

"Yes, Squadron First!" Jay Tail banged out a salute, knocking a fist to his wet chest so hard that water spattered out from his soaked tunic.

Blood Talon muttered, "Good," and handed the squadron third's war club to the first warrior. The cowed man took it as if it were a live snake instead of wood and stone.

Blood Talon growled, "Not a fetid word," as he picked up his end of the box and jerked a hard nod for the Red Wing to proceed.

It wasn't until they were well out of earshot and entering the canyon that Blood Talon muttered, "No wonder he was exiled to the colonies. Idiot couldn't find his balls with two hands on a bright and sunny day."

Forty-one

As she was carried into the *tonka'tzi*'s council room, Clan Matron Rising Flame ordered, "Place my litter before the eternal fire. Then leave us."

She was lowered carefully. Then her porters bowed and left. *Tonka'tzi* Wind's floor now sported striking new cattail matting, all woven with remarkable finesse. It was said to be a product of a group of women from a settlement just outside the Moon Mounds, where the Avenue of the Sun reached its eastern terminus out in the Grand Prairie.

Rising Flame glanced around, seeing the new white-clay plaster, how the wall benches were polished. Despite the traditional hangings, the Four Winds Clan relief carving that dominated the rear of the room, and the collections of textiles, copper repoussé, and various masks, the room had a refreshed, new look.

Turning her head, Rising Flame told the four warriors standing in the rear, "You are dismissed."

The leader, an older man in armor decorated with North Star House designs, touched his head respectfully and said, "Clan Matron, I mean no disrespect, but my orders—"

"Warrior, while I'm sure you are Keeper Spotted Wrist's good and loyal servant, the Keeper serves at *my* will and pleasure. Now, you will take yourself and your warriors, and along with everyone else, you will leave the *tonka'tzi* and me to converse in peace. Is that understood?"

All the recorders, the messengers and runners, along with the servants, knowing the routine, promptly picked up their belongings and began filing out of the room.

The warrior, his face reflecting frustration, glanced uneasily at his comrades before saying, "Clan Matron, I'm afraid I—"

"It's been a while since I've hung anyone in the squares. It's about time that I did so again to reinforce my authority. I can't think of a better way than letting the crowd cut apart four of Spotted Wrist's trusted warriors. Nothing would send a clearer signal about who is in control of the Four Winds Clan, or do you disagree?" She ended by giving him a deadly smile.

"No, Clan Matron!" The warrior slammed a fist to his chest in a military salute, turned on his heel, and with a jerk of the head, led the other warriors out.

Across the fire, Great Sky Wind perched on her panther hide–covered litter, chin propped on a palm. She had her gray hair pulled up in a severe bun; an immaculately rendered *Hunga Ahuito* copper headpiece with a Spirit Bundle topped her head. The woman's shoulders were covered with a rainbow-colored cloak crafted of painted bunting feathers. Her skirt, of a finely woven dogbane fabric, draped down over her knees. She studied Rising Flame through half-lidded eyes.

As an opener, Rising Flame said, "Looks like you've had a great deal of work done. New plaster and all. I had heard that you used the Busk as an opportunity to make some changes. Tore out part of the back wall."

"All new buildings need some remodeling. Plaster was flaking off. Especially in the back rooms, and some thatch had been poorly installed. Had to tear out a section of wall back there and replace it. Needed to fix some problems with drainage in the southeast corner, too. Would have led to mound slumping. That why you're here? Wanted to see the repairs?"

"No." Rising Flame took a deep breath. "We need to talk. Seriously and honestly."

"About putting Spotted Wrist's enforcers in place? Or admitting that you misjudged the Hero of the North's abilities when it came to solving the problem of Cahokia's constantly bickering Houses?"

"My concern is Cahokia."

Wind, chin still propped, said, "I take it that new realities are causing you to rethink all those idealistic assumptions you once made about Cahokian politics."

"Oh, I don't know. So far the city seems to be—"

"Stop it," Wind snapped. "The reasons behind Morning Star's efforts to place you in the Matron's chair still defy my abilities to comprehend. And believe me, I can comprehend a lot. Why you? A woman with no experience given the deep currents through which you would have to swim."

"Obviously, Morning Star thought I would be the best choice to bring new leadership to the Four Winds Clan. Change the way in which the city was governed. Someone younger, who could see past those deep currents you refer to, who wasn't indoctrinated to do things the way they had always been done. A fresh wind blows old smoke from the room, *Tonka'tzi*."

"And how's that working out for you, Matron?"

Rising Flame chuckled softly to herself. "I made a severe miscalculation about someone whose support I depended upon."

"I'm sure that grates. However, you appointed him, you can remove him."

"Ah, you mean Spotted Wrist? That's a different problem. But yes, I expected the Hero of the North to be a great deal more competent at his job. Your sister called him . . . I believe her words were, 'A blunt instrument.' Unfortunately, after working with him, I'm not sure how he managed all those military triumphs."

"Marching an army cross-country and fighting pitched battles is a different kind of fish from Cahokian politics," Wind told her. "But, as those warriors you just dismissed prove, a blunt instrument carries its own dangers."

Rising Flame's lips twitched. "I needed him, *Tonka'tzi*. Horned Serpent House, River House, and North Star House were on the verge of tearing Cahokia apart after that last stunt Morning Star pulled. The city was on the verge of civil war, and without Spotted Wrist's massed squadrons, we'd never have cowed Green Chunkey back into submission."

"Had to pay Spotted Wrist off with something? So you appointed him Clan Keeper?"

"Surely a man who could accomplish all that he had could . . . Well, as you say, it's a different kind of fish."

Wind's right eye narrowed to a slit. "What do you want to get out of all this?"

Rising Flame jabbed a hard finger Wind's way. "I want the city unified, *Tonka'tzi*. I know how the nations downriver think. And I've been to some of the colonies on the lower Tenasee. With each major expedition and colony, Cahokia is becoming something greater. But then, you receive the embassies, take the reports from the colonies. If anyone in Morning Star House knows this, it's you."

"And yet you would have replaced me with Green Chunkey, of all people?"

Rising Flame let a fleeting smile cross her lips. "At the time, I didn't have much choice. You've been in my seat; you were Clan Matron before your brother's murder. You know that sometimes decisions are thrust upon you. In this case that blunt instrument was insistent." She made a face. "And it's not like I could turn back time."

"And if you could?"

"I'd have kept your sister, with her network of spies, as Keeper." Rising Flame leaned forward, squinted an eye. "What I came to tell you today is that I will do everything I can to keep you as *tonka'tzi*. I think the city needs your wisdom and experience."

"I see."

"What I cannot do, however, is protect you from a squad of Spotted Wrist's warriors if they come for you. Ultimately the man's authority is backed by his fawning and loyal squadrons."

"That is indeed the case," Wind agreed, fingering her chin.

"I had a conversation with Matron Columella during the Busk. We made a Trade. I gave her information that saved her life. In return she promised to avoid inciting any further confrontation with Spotted Wrist. Now, if I can restrain the Hero of the North from any additional idiocy while both Horned Serpent and River Houses recover, maybe tempers can cool enough that I can broker a peaceful resolution."

"You know, don't you, that the only way Spotted Wrist can be contained is by his removal, his defeat, or his death."

Rising Flame nodded. "As long as he remains in command of his squadrons, and they obey his orders, the only way to remove him is through civil war. That would take the combined resources of Evening Star House's squadrons and the Morning Star squadrons, not to mention that civil war would destroy the city."

"Why don't you ask Morning Star to simply order Spotted Wrist to stand down?"

Rising Flame studied her fingers as she rubbed them together, as if an answer was hidden in their fragile movement. "Yes, well, remember when I said I had miscalculated about the support I would be given? You thought it was Spotted Wrist. On the contrary, my problem is with Morning Star."

"How so? I'm rarely allowed access to the hallowed chambers of Morning Star's palace these days. My guards won't let me past the gates."

Rising Flame spread her hands. "You're not alone in that. Few get up to see him these days. But to the point: Morning Star made the decision to stand down when Spotted Wrist sent his squadrons into central Cahokia and moved on River House. It was his order that the Morning Star squadrons *not* be called up when Five Fists wanted to take counteraction. *Tonka'tzi*, if we can stop squabbling among ourselves, Cahokia is poised on the verge of its greatest days, a shining miracle that will remake the world. Despite that, Morning Star has no more interest than he might have over a basket of unshelled corn."

"It's always said that he plays a deep game." Wind shifted on her litter. "Are you sure?"

"He refuses to listen to anything I try to tell him. Won't let me within ten paces. He just smiles like he's bored. Dismisses me with a wave of the hand. It's been how many moons since he's played a game of chunkey? It's like he's waiting for something."

"Might be at that," Wind mused emotionlessly. "What, exactly, did you come here for?"

"I plan to save this city, and I have come to realize that you provide one of my best chances for success. When Spotted Wrist is finally removed, I will need you, and your authority with Morning Star House, to put the pieces back together."

"I see."

"To do that, I must have some way of communicating with you that isn't constantly being monitored by Spotted Wrist's spies."

Wind chuckled dryly. "Just that quick, huh? Let bygones be bygones?"

Rising Flame arched an eyebrow. "I don't need to lecture you on the realities of politics, *Tonka'tzi*."

"No." A pause. "You don't."

"If you need to get a message to me, perhaps you could send a slave out. Maybe with a token, something like an article of clothing that she could display—"

"Oh, gods rot it, that's much too cumbersome." Wind had an amused look. "When I need to get a message to you, you'll get it."

"Just like that?"

"Don't play the fool, Matron. If you're serious about this, and Spotted Wrist finds out, you and I will both disappear in the night. And if, as you say, Morning Star doesn't care, no one will be the wiser."

Forty-two

Miserable and bedraggled but with her sodden Trader's staff held high, Night Shadow Star led the way into White Chief Town. Called *Haktimikko* in the local Muskogean dialect, the settlement—situated on a bluff overlooking the river—lay at the western terminus of the trail. This time the two Cahokian warriors standing guard at the trailhead just watched them through narrowed, hostile eyes. But when she bowed low and touched her forehead in respect, they seemed to relax, even gave a slight nod in return.

"Guess things aren't as rigid on this end of the portage when War Leader Tall Dancer is on the other," Fire Cat said as he plodded along behind her. Blood Talon and Winder followed with the Trade box, each looking as weary as Night Shadow Star felt.

Part of their lukewarm welcome might have been the way they looked. No need this time to go out of their way to mask their appearance. The two-day portage had left them caked with mud and their hair matted and filthy, their skin smudged. Half staggering, hungry and exhausted, they looked more like refugees than Traders. Fire Cat added to the effect as he carried Winder's staff propped over his shoulder, the feathers dangling limply.

The upgraded trail—almost an avenue, actually—had been widened, roots chopped out, shoring added to the sides where the path threaded along sheer drop-offs. All the steep inclines and descents on the trail had been graded, filled, and leveled as much as the terrain allowed. The only problem had been the fill meant to smooth the way. Barely compacted as it had been, the rain had turned the loose dirt into muck that sucked the moccasins off their feet with each step.

As they walked into town, past the outlying bent-pole dwellings with their bark sidings, Night Shadow Star and her companions were watched with wary suspicion. The locals kept their children close, looked eerily on edge. The *talwa* had an entirely different feel to it as Night Shadow Star led the way past the tightly packed farmsteads to the Trade House that stood on the east side of the town's plaza. The site of the plaza came as a shock, so different than when she and Winder had passed this way but a couple of moons past. Only the *Tchkofa* in the plaza's center remained.

Buildings were going up on the plaza's margins—large buildings in Cahokian style, with their trademark design. Even as she watched, a collection of local Muskogean men labored, digging, raising a wall, lashing it with rope. As they struggled, the overseeing Cahokians called directions—apparently backed up by a small squad of weapon-toting warriors who loitered off to the side. The locals looked none too happy as they carried out the hard work. Slipping and slogging in the mud, they shot resentful glances toward their new masters.

"I'd call that a forced labor detail," Blood Talon declared as he heaved his end of the Trade box.

"The old Muskogee clan and moiety houses, the charnel temples, even the burial mounds, have been torn down," Winder noted. "Being replaced by Cahokian society houses. Look yonder. See the new mound? Used to be the chief's house. My bet? All those posts piled beside it? That's for a new palace to be built atop the mound."

"Think it will be an Earth Clan chief or a Four Winds Clan chief who will live in it?" Fire Cat asked, the crow's feet at the sides of his eyes tightening.

"Bet we'll know by the time we leave," Winder murmured. He gestured toward the far end of the plaza. "But I'd say not everyone is overjoyed with the arrangement."

Night Shadow Star squinted, making out the line of squares to the side of the new mound construction and beside the log-sided Muskogean summer house. Even from here she could tell that people hung in the wooden frames. "So much for the Power of Trade keeping the peace. Something tells me it's Cahokian military might that rules here these days."

"Wish they'd been here last time we came through. It sure would have simplified my life," Blood Talon muttered.

"Oh, I don't know, Squadron First." Fire Cat had an airy and carefree tone in his voice. "Back then, you'd have handed me over to the nearest batch of Cahokian warriors, which means that before we got here, I'd have had to break your neck and sink your corpse in the river for Piasa.

Real shame that, after all the effort I spent to rescue you and tend to your wounds."

"Not to mention that being dead and drowned, I'd have never seen the upper river or crossed the mountains," Blood Talon agreed. "And today, instead of being a broke Trader without so much as a ceramic cup to piss in, I'd be condemned to suffer as Tall Dancer's second. And a terrible fate that would be. Too much food to eat, all those soft beds filled with willing women, the endless pomp and pageantry. Such a fate might have led me to despair. Enough that I'd have had to slit my throat with a dull quartzite blade."

Night Shadow Star's lips quirked as she led the way to the Trade House, surprised to see old Seven Root still sitting on his stump before the entrance. She lowered the looped Trader's staff and gave the old man a smile. In pidgin she said, "Greetings, Elder. My apology, but we didn't have time to find your mushrooms. If you would allow me—"

"Ah, Cahokians." Seven Root glanced up, his old eyes dark and shrunken in his wrinkled face. "I hear it in your accent. No Trade. Not for Cahokians." He raised an age-freckled hand, the back of it thick with wormlike veins. "That's by order of the chief. Any others, though, Muskogeans, Yuchi, Chicaza and the like, they come second. Have to offer Trade for a bed."

Winder stepped forward, lowering the box. "Greetings, old friend." He gestured toward the new construction. "Looks like changes. What happened to the people? Don't see but a handful of dogs and children."

"Dogs?" The old man smiled, exposing toothless gums. "The Cahokians, they emptied the granaries first thing. Ate the dogs second. Even took most of the green corn . . ." Seven Root's expression darkened. "Before the ceremony, could you believe?"

Night Shadow Star reached in her pouch, took out a shell gorget depicting Mother Spider carrying souls across the night sky. "This is for you, Elder. Winder and I, we pay our debts. According to the Power of Trade we'd like—"

"The Power of Trade is dead here, good lady." Seven Root took the gorget, running his fingers over the carving. "Here it is the Power of the living god that rules."

"Pick any bed?" Winder asked, glancing back at where Blood Talon and Fire Cat watched.

"Yes, most are open now that the Cahokians have left. The Cahokians who stayed have taken people's houses for their own. But you, good Traders, listen: Don't do anything that would antagonize the Cahokians. At best they'll beat you over the slightest offense. Assuming they don't kill you without so much as a sidelong glance. At worst, hang you in a square to die in misery."

"We'll be careful, Elder," Winder told him. Then asked, "Can we still get a meal from Old Woman White Egret?"

Seven Root's gaze went distant. "The first night the Cahokians came, she demanded Trade. Some war chief took offense. Clubbed her in the head. Just like that." He made a clubbing motion with his withered arm. "She wasn't the same after that. No. Just wasn't the same." He frowned. "I think her family took her to the forest. Went and hid. Like so many."

"Sorry to hear that," Night Shadow Star said. "She cooked the most delicious fish."

"She did, didn't she?" Seven Root waved them toward the door. "Go on in. No charge for Cahokians. Only for the rest of us."

Ducking inside, she and Winder led the way. Compared to the last time she'd been here, the place looked empty. She chose the same cane-walled cubicle where she and Winder had bunked last time, tossed her pack onto the same lower bunk. With a finger, she indicated where Blood Talon and Winder should set the box of Trade.

Fire Cat glanced around, saying to Blood Talon, "Would have been a better place to stay than camping on the trail like we did last time."

"Oh, I remember really well, War Leader, you were in a terrible kind of a hurry. Some excitement about a woman and a witch." Blood Talon took a lower bunk opposite them.

Winder sighed, scratched the back of his head where his hair was mussed with bits of forest detritus. "Red Wing? Why don't you and I go see what there is to eat here. Lady, unlike last time, I don't think we can leave the packs untended. As the old man said, the Power of Trade no longer holds."

She turned, placed her hands on Fire Cat's chest, looked into his eyes. "You be careful. Piasa has been suspiciously out of my mind, hasn't been whispering in my ear today. That always makes me nervous."

He gave her a warm smile, ran a gentle finger down her cheek where the arrow wound was healing. "We'll be all right. Winder knows this place."

She watched her husband and the burly Trader step out and into the fading afternoon light. Anxiously, she rubbed at the mud on her high-topped moccasins, wished for a bath, and spared Blood Talon a sidelong look where he'd found a bunk in the mat-walled cubicle across from her.

He, too, had taken to knocking the dried mud free from his gear. Caught her looking at him. "Yes, Lady?"

"That was quick work with the sentries back at Canyon Town. You could have just . . . well, let's say, chosen an easier path. Ordered us taken captive and gone home to Cahokia with an escort. Tall Dancer would have given you a canoe and the warriors to paddle it. You would have become Spotted Wrist's darling. Why didn't you?"

Blood Talon sighed, laid his pack on the bed frame, and unfolded his still-damp blanket. He hung it out to dry. Turned. Gave her a long stare. "Do you think so little of me?"

"You helped destroy my husband's world in Red Wing Town. I watched you try to kill him that day outside my palace. You chased us halfway across the country. I *heard* you at Rainbow Town. You called me a 'southern swamp slut.' Laughed when your second, Nutcracker, slapped his hand on my butt like I was a paid woman. Told me you'd Trade a war canoe for a tumble in my robes. So now I'm to believe that man, that Squadron First Blood Talon, is gone? Miraculously turned into this new man?"

"You *heard* me at Rainbow Town?" He looked perplexed.

"Fire Cat didn't tell you? I walked up to your canoe when you landed, offered Trade. I was—"

"That was *you*, that Trader? I . . . how could . . . ?"

"I used your prejudices against you. Why, by *Hunga Ahuito*'s claws, should I trust you now?"

His eyes shifted to the floor matting as if he'd found something fascinating there. "Fire Cat saved my life."

"After he *drowned* all your warriors, including your good friend Nutcracker. You expect me to believe that knowing he capsized your canoe, killed your warriors, doesn't sit and fester down between your souls?"

"It had to be done, Lady." His smile had grown wistful. "They were good men, friends with whom I'd shared fires, blood, and suffering. But I didn't understand the Power. How it played me for a fool."

"So, what happens if we all make it back to Cahokia? What do you do when I march in to face your lord, the Keeper Spotted Wrist? I thought you swore to bring me back to his bed. You going to just stand by? Is that what your word is worth?"

"I didn't give him my word, Lady. He gave me an order. One that, at great cost to myself, I am not going to obey." He raised his gaze, met her eyes. "I will stand with you and War Leader Fire Cat."

"War Leader? Curious words from the man who dragged him out of his bed in Red Wing Town, murdered his children, and turned him into a slave."

Blood Talon gave her a somber nod of the head. "Yes, I call him War Leader. The man defeated three Cahokian armies, might have defeated us, too, had we given him a fighting chance. I have heard the stories of how many times he has saved Cahokia, saved you, and even Morning

Star himself. He saved me, Lady, when he had every justification to leave me to die; the man tended to my wounds as if I were not his mortal enemy."

He smiled wistfully at the skepticism behind her gaze, said, "I could ask the same of you, Lady. You cut him down from the square, that cold and shivering man you had vowed to torture to death. You made him swear to serve you, bound him to you, and now, here, all these moons later, you call him husband. You tell me that Fire Cat doesn't change people's lives. That he isn't worth serving."

She chuckled at that. "You are going to find yourself in a very uncomfortable position. When we make it back to Cahokia I will kill my brother, and then I will destroy Spotted Wrist."

He pursed his lips, his forehead lining. "I know. And I will help you. Anything you or the war leader ask."

"Really, Squadron First? It's that easy for you?"

He settled himself on the bed, cocked his head as he studied her. "I think we're a lot alike, Lady. Before Makes Three's death, I know what kind of woman you were. I heard the stories about Red Warrior's spoiled and pampered daughter. How you raged that Spotted Wrist was supposed to murder every man, woman, and child for you when he took Red Wing Town."

Blood Talon made his point with a callused finger. "I don't know everything that's happened to you since then, the murder of your father, the fight with your brother, losing yourself to Piasa, or that marriage to the Itza. But you survived, unbroken, to become the woman you are today. You are not the spoiled Night Shadow Star you used to be, and I am not that same obedient squadron first."

"No, I suppose not," she said. "But what do you expect to get out of this? A chieftainship? Some appointment that makes you nobility?"

The ghost of a smile was back. "I will be happy to discover that I am worthy and proud."

"Worthy of what?"

"Self-respect, Lady. And proud of who I am as a human being. Beyond that, there really isn't anything else a person can strive for."

Forty-three

When White Frond entered the Clan Matron's great room, Rising Flame was seated on her litter atop the dais. She'd propped her chin on her knee, back supported by a rolled hair-on buffalo hide.

Most of the servants and slaves had retired, the Clan House going quiet enough she could hear the light patter of rain on the thatch roof.

"Aunt?" White Frond asked. "Are you all right?"

Rising Flame chuckled humorlessly. "The Busk has been a disaster."

White Frond stepped around the eternal fire. As she did, the flames hit a pitch pocket in the piece of pine; it crackled and spat sparks. White Frond seated herself, rearranging her bright red skirt. "Not from the perspective of the common people, or even the Earth Clans. The ceremonies reinforced their responsibilities to keep the dirt farmers and immigrants in line. The visiting embassies, the Pacaha, Quigualtam, Chitimacha, Caddo, Chicaza, and others, they came to see the splendor, to share in the sacred fasting and relighting of the eternal fire. From what I saw, they rejoiced in the final feasting and Dancing as a celebration of the renewal of the very world around them."

Rising Flame shot her niece a sidelong glance. "And, of course, they got to see the physical miracle of Morning Star in his human reincarnation." She waved a hand. "So far as they are concerned, Cahokia lives for another year."

"You're worried about Horned Serpent House?" White Frond saw right through Rising Flame's turmoil.

"The premature burning of the offerings and the extinction of the Sacred Fire on the first night of the Busk is like a cactus thorn driven into Green Chunkey's heart. But what does it mean for me?"

White Frond rubbed her tanned shin. "It affected Horned Serpent's entire ceremony. Their stickball team lost miserably. Their chunkey players didn't even take to the courts, and their Dancers barely put on a show, mostly going through the motions. Hard to win when you think Power has deserted you."

Rising Flame had to agree.

In the end, when Morning Star made his traditional gift of the cloak to a Dancer, it was to a Fish Clan chief in an ivory billed woodpecker costume that looked real. Nor had the chief stinted on the performance but he had mimicked the war bird so well that from her vantage on the head of the Great Staircase outside the Council Terrace gates, Rising Flame would have sworn she was seeing the actual bird pirouetting through the other Dancers. Yes, rot it, the Dancer was best, and Morning Star had awarded his cloak to the Fish Clan chief, only to discover that he was one of Columella's. That he served Evening Star House, and even had commanded one of her squadrons.

Rising Flame told her niece, "Not that I had any great love for Green Chunkey, but the last thing I needed was the collapse of Horned Serpent House. Do you understand? Cahokia may have looked strong and reeking of Power during the ceremonies, but it's falling apart. As if the bones that hold it up are breaking down deep in the flesh."

White Frond watched her warily. "When Morning Star gifted that cloak, Spotted Wrist was enraged. I thought he was going to do something stupid."

"I barely kept the idiot from stomping down the Great Staircase and ripping the cloak away. Had he done so, it would have set the entire city on fire. Do you see how close to disaster we are?"

And there was no telling how Morning Star would have reacted.

No, no telling at all. Each day the living god became more of an enigma. Inscrutable, reserved. Call him reclusive, for he rarely saw anyone. Even his servants were now kept at a distance. Only Sun Wing was allowed close to him.

As if Rising Flame didn't have enough to worry about, word was spreading that Morning Star was fasting, praying, preparing himself for some impending and terrible Spirit battle.

"I know," White Frond told her as she rose. "Go get some rest, Matron. Maybe Power will send you a Spirit Dream, some sort of sign that will give you direction."

Rising Flame watched her niece walk from the room. She rubbed the back of her neck as she climbed down from her litter and walked to her private quarters in the rear.

She could hear faint calls from the Avenue of the Sun where it passed just below the edge of the Four Winds Clan mound. In the two days since the end of the Busk, people were still clogging the city. Cahokia was back to normal as far as they were concerned, well, all but for the phenomenon of Horned Serpent House having let their fire go out. Especially that a Spirit Wolf had been involved. Lots of speculation about that. What it meant for Green Chunkey and Robin Wing, even more for their subordinates. Surely some terrible thing was going to befall the House.

"And you're certainly *not* going to be *tonka'tzi* anytime soon," she whispered as she crossed her small room with its storage boxes, the large ceramic jars, her clothing and ritual wear, the headdresses and statuary. She had the finest of blankets and furs on her bed where it was built into the back wall. Rising Flame slipped out of her skirt, delighted that her slaves had lit a lamp that cast a faint light from its floating wick.

She tossed her cape onto one of the boxes and pried the moccasins from her feet. Unpinning her high copper headdress, she placed it on its stand and unfolded a fine hemp-weave blanket, laid it out on the bedding. Then she blew out the lamp.

In hot darkness, she slipped under the thin blanket, and enjoyed the scent of the hickory smoke that remained from her lamp.

She was further from taking control of Cahokia now than she had been six moons back. Columella had played her hand perfectly. And more to the point, she remained alive. The extent of Green Chunkey's assassins' failure was never to be known outside of a small circle.

If anyone came out of the Green Corn Ceremony a winner, it had been Columella. Her ostentatious donation of food for the feasts had bought her the people's goodwill. The Evening Star Town stickball teams had placed well; her Dancer had even taken the cloak. More to Matron Columella's credit, every time Spotted Wrist's agents had incited trouble, she'd quashed it. Didn't matter that Columella's people were fuming, as far as the Four Winds nobility were concerned, she came off the better for it.

Rising Flame was just on the verge of drifting into Dreams when a soft voice whispered, "We need to talk."

Rising Flame blinked awake, asked, "Who's there?"

"Just a shadow. Don't raise your voice. Don't call out. I'm not here to do you any harm. Only to have a frank conversation."

"Who are you?"

"Like I said, a shadow. Yes, you can call me that. What's in a name anyhow?"

She fought the sudden beating of her heart. Did she dare scream? "What do you want?"

"*Tonka'tzi* Wind sends her regards," the hoarse whisper said. A man's voice. Strain as she might, she couldn't place it. "But, to answer your question, as much as it hurts to say, I guess the same thing you do."

"And what do I want?" she countered, buying time.

"Your problem is that you can't win. Every time you think you have a victory, like putting Green Chunkey on the *tonka'tzi*'s chair, or the Keeper invading Evening Star Town, something unforeseen goes wrong."

She sat up in bed, anger stirring to replace fear. "What do you want?"

"It's a lot more complicated than you thought back in the beginning, isn't it? All those things you promised Morning Star, they're not working out like you had planned. Figured you could do better than Blue Heron and Wind, that you could beat, charm, and finagle the Houses into working together. Unify the high chiefs and matrons under your control. Be the greatest clan matron the city had ever known."

"I still will."

"Not with that fool Spotted Wrist as Keeper. Shhh! Don't bother to deny it. We all know the Hero of the North is a mistake going somewhere to happen. And don't place your bets on North Star House either. They might come across as a towering cottonwood, but like the tree, they're hollow and rotten at the core."

"How do you know this?"

"Been around." A pause, and the hoarse voice asked, "You scared? Down deep? You know, soul-scared when you wake up in the middle of the night and are drowning in the knowledge that you're facing disaster in all directions?"

"Never!" she lied.

"Nice try, but we know better."

"Who are you? How did you get in here?"

"I'm a messenger. A sort of go-between. I'm here to get the answer to one question: Are you willing to deal?"

For a long moment, she hesitated, desperate for a way out.

"Tell the *tonka'tzi* . . ." Did she dare do this? ". . . the answer is yes."

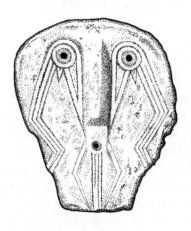

Canebrake

*I*t is almost a half moon since we were pulled from the water, and we are making remarkably rapid progress down the Tenasee, but much of that is due to Canebrake, the squadron second. He is in charge of carrying a sack full of beaded messages and numerous verbal reports of the expedition's progress up the Tenasee. The man is relentless, his picked warriors—all men of endurance and strength—claim to be hewn of hickory and bound with oak.

This night, we are camped beside the river. I sit beside the fire, wondering if I will ever be warm again. Doesn't matter how hot the day gets, the chill remains. Even when I bake in the hot late-summer sun, and sweat trickles down my skin, I can feel the cold hovering down below my heart, in the center of my core. Ice in my stomach.

I study the warriors from my seat at the back of the ramada; a blanket wraps my shoulders despite the warm night. Crickets and insects fill the evening with Song, and I can hear people drumming and Singing in the village just back from us near the trees. In Trade for a couple of packets of yaupon, the local Yuchi have fed us a meal of baked turtle, boiled fish seasoned with sassafras, knotweed bread, and baked cattail pods.

We also get to sleep under the protection of the ramadas down by their canoe landing. Not that Canebrake's warriors want anything to do with me. They are smarter than that. Most come from a mixture of Earth Clans and are leery of anything to do with either me or Fire Light.

Despite Fire Light's fumbling attempts to strike up any kind of camaraderie with the warriors, he is tainted. First, he's Four Winds Clan, and second, he is traveling in my company. Not only that, but since the Suck and Rage, he's not been quite right in the head.

Smart warriors, these. They know instinctively that a vast gulf separates us. That we are nobles in Morning Star's lineage, which places us at the pinnacle of the Four Winds Clan. Knowing that—even more than my scarred features or brooding disposition—causes them to keep their distance. I couldn't be happier.

Like I said, High Chief Fire Light has changed. I watch him, studying him with narrowed eyes. He sits atop a wooden box of Trade that Canebrake uses to broker accommodations such as we enjoy tonight. The high chief's gaze is distant, his expression what I'd call hollow. I think he had shivered so hard in the Suck and Rage that small parts of his souls broke loose and slipped away from his body. Maybe they mixed with the river water he sucked into his lungs, only to be coughed out and vanish during the several times he'd almost drowned.

And yes, he also smashed his head against a rock sometime in that melee of wild water. A blow like that can knock the life soul loose.

I look past the High Chief's vacant eyes to what is inside. Not only are pieces of his souls missing, but what is left is dying. A suppurating rot is festering there, eating away at Fire Light's life soul, splotches of it corroding his breath soul, darkening his very bones.

This, too, Canebrake and his warriors can sense. So much so that they have changed the seating in their fast war canoe, leaving Fire Light the right-hand middle row seat, and me the left. They switch off when it comes to who has to sit immediately ahead and behind us. As if sharing the onus of proximity.

I frighten them, but I also know that they are my best and fastest way to get to Cahokia. They understand that the quickest way to be rid of Chief Fire Light and me is to get us to the canoe landing below River City Mounds. That once they hit the beach, we will be gone from their lives for good.

Motivating people has never been a problem.

Fortunately, Squadron Second Canebrake comes from Raccoon Clan; they have always had a loyalty to Morning Star House. The history of that goes back to Black Tail when he was consumed by Morning Star's Spirit. Obviously, Raccoon is the Spirit totem of the clan, and Raccoon ever since the Beginning Times is the messenger of the Dead. He also has been known to carry souls from charnel houses to the portals of the Underworld. Spirit Beings with those attributes, for some reason, make people nervous.

As a result, Raccoon Clan has never been particularly popular, let alone prominent.

But after the reincarnation of the living god, Morning Star gave their high chief and matron special recognition. Raccoon Clan has taken their duties seriously ever since.

Looking down past the fire, I can make out the canoe, a high-bowed, thin-walled craft some six body lengths long, with a beam wide enough that, stretching, I can barely reach from gunwale to gunwale. It's a fast vessel to start with and fairly slips through the water. It is called, appropriately, Trout.

"*Does it bother you?*" Fire Light asks out of nowhere, his gaze now fixed on the leaping flames in the fire pit.

"*Does what bother me?*"

"*Being such a monster?*"

I narrow an eye. "*I'm not sure I understand.*"

"*You're so . . . distasteful. Disgusting in so many ways.*"

"*If you are trying to goad me into something you will regret, you are succeeding.*" I feel anger begin to stir.

Fire Light flexes his fingers open and closed, over and over, but it's a nervous reaction of his. "*I'm trying to understand is all. To figure out what it must be like to be you.*"

"*You shouldn't. I am the only way I can be. Power saw to that. I have a destiny that I was born to.*"

He stirs, glances at me with a perplexed frown. "*I understand duty, clan, and responsibility. I'm Morning Star House, like you. My sister Rising Flame is Clan Matron. But . . . I watch you . . .*"

"*I suppose it beats watching the river. Not much there. Just swirling, rising, and sucking water. After this trip, I never need to see a river again. It's just endless flowing water, the banks choked with overpacked trees, brush, and mud. Travel one river, you've pretty much traveled them all.*" I raise a finger. "*Though the lower reaches of the Father Water are different. Wider. More like a huge moving lake. And even then, I've never been all the way down to the Gulf. I can only imagine.*"

"*Like that,*" he says. "*You can't talk about yourself. But tell me, doesn't it make you feel lonely? No one wants to be around you. You're diseased, contagious. Don't you ever miss the company?*"

I give him a disdainful look. "*Do you ever miss the company of crawfish?*"

"*I don't understand.*"

"*Now there's a revelation. Let me make it simple for you: If you had a large ceramic jar full of crawfish, would you enjoy spending time with them?*"

"*No. People don't socialize with crawfish.*"

"*Exactly.*"

"*But there has to be something human inside you that . . .*" Then he seemed to lose the words, turning his eyes away and whispering, "*Maybe there isn't. And that's the most frightening thing of all.*"

When he glances back my way, I meet his eyes and grin.

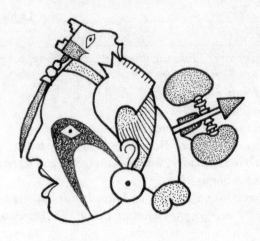

Forty-four

From the elevated bastion on the Council Terrace palisade, Spotted Wrist let his gaze drift across the familiar city landscape and into the setting sun. Hanging low over the western horizon, the orb burned a dull yellow-brown in Cahokia's smoke-filled skies. Searing silver reflected from the old oxbow lakes and water-filled borrow pits. The elevated temples, palaces, and warehouses were cast as silhouettes that stippled the land as they faded into the distance. Even the high ridge mound that marked Black Tail's tomb at the bend of the Avenue of the Sun appeared as a low outline. From this height, Spotted Wrist could see the long shadows cast by the poles in the Great Observatory, where the Sky Priests went about their ceaseless observations of the heavens.

And there, way off in the distance, Spotted Wrist could just barely distinguish the thin line of the river's west bank. The haze hid any details of Evening Star Town.

"The day will come, Columella, you pus-dripping sheath," he muttered as he leaned both elbows on the plastered top of the palisade. But how long would it take? And how did he play the game until then? How did he choreograph his steps in this whole awkward Dance of a city divided? A city that went about its business heedless of his and Columella's impending violence. The Earth Clans, Traders, and dirt farmers simply ignored his warriors and hers, shuttled back and forth across the river as they passed beneath the glaring eyes of stalemated combatants. The city, it seemed, couldn't care less.

The latest festering irritation was the failure and capture of Green Chunkey's two assassins. Not that Spotted Wrist couldn't revel in the Horned Serpent House's various agonies and embarrassments. They'd been adversaries for too many generations to have earned any genuine sympathy. What mattered, though, was that all of Cahokia was talking about how Green Chunkey had sent two nefarious assassins after Columella during the Busk! Outrageous! No wonder Power had used a Spirit Wolf to strike down Horned Serpent House. They had profaned the most sacred ceremony in the Cahokian annual cycle.

Calls were circulating for Green Chunkey to respond to the sacrilegious affront.

For Horned Serpent House's part, the high palace might have been a deep-water mussel, clamped tight and silent. The doors remained closed; warriors stood guard on the stairs. All a spokesman would say was that the entire House was involved in fasting, sweats, prayers, and sacrifices as they struggled to atone for the terrible calamity that had befallen them when some evil force sent a mysterious Spirit wolf to put out their eternal fire. If you could believe the spokesman—a Deer Clan priest—Green Chunkey and Matron Robin Wing spent their days in a sacred sweat lodge seeking visions from the Spirit World.

"You ask me," Spotted Wrist growled to himself, "that wily snake is living behind locked doors so that none of his relatives can slip up behind him and smash his skull in with a war club."

Which still left the problem of the two assassins Columella had caught in the act and now had in her custody. Both rather notorious bullies Green Chunkey had employed because of their lack of scruples when it came to the darkest of deeds.

Spotted Wrist squinted into the sinking sun, feeling its warmth on his face; the pungency of smoke, city, and humanity cloyed in his nose. So, what was the smart next move?

He barely noticed when Cut Weasel climbed up to the bastion platform and called, "Lord Keeper, if you have a moment."

"Come, Squadron First. I was just pondering my options. Do I declare Green Chunkey's assassins to be liars and their statements to be an Evening Star House deceit? Or do I respond with outrage, demanding the immediate dismissal of the foul and profane Green Chunkey? One way, it will cast doubt on Columella. The other, well, if Green Chunkey and Robin Wing go down it's no great loss. The problem is the timing and how their replacement would affect the situation when Heart Warrior finally comes trooping into Horned Serpent Town with his squadron."

"I don't understand, Lord Keeper."

"We want the town in ferment so that Forest Squadron can march in and restore order, stabilize it, be welcomed as the solution instead of be seen as a threat. If Green Chunkey and Robin Wing are taken out too quickly, their replacements might be capable enough to have the situation well in hand by the time Squadron First Heart Warrior finally arrives."

Cut Weasel asked, "Could we take the assassins ourselves? Steal them away from Columella? If we had them, we could use them against Green Chunkey whenever we wanted."

"Not so easy." Spotted Wrist gave the western horizon a dismissive slit-eyed glare. "Columella keeps a lot of protection around them. It would almost take a surprise raid with a full squadron to pull them out of her sticky-fingered grasp."

"Doesn't mean that when the time is right we couldn't slip someone in close, Keeper. Maybe close enough to slip a deer-bone stiletto between the ribs and into the heart? Or perhaps give them each a quick knock to the head? Killed like that, it can be played against Horned Serpent House. We can howl in outrage about Green Chunkey covering his tracks through murder most foul, and at the same time denying Columella valuable assets."

"You don't have a knack for this, Squadron First. We'd lose control of the situation. Columella would have their dead bodies dragged down the Avenue of the Sun so that everyone could see, crying all the time, 'Look what the Keeper and High Chief Green Chunkey have done! Tried to cover their cowardly tracks!'"

Cut Weasel made a face. "I suppose."

With a knotted fist, Spotted Wrist pounded the fire-hardened clay plaster, irritated to see a big chunk spall off to fall down the wall, bounce, and tumble down the slanting side of the high earthen mound. When it slammed into the avenue at the bottom, it exploded into clods and dust. Worse, it did so under the feet of a procession of dirt farmers come down from the north with burden baskets on their backs. Spooked and startled, they jumped and shrieked, and several dropped their loads to spill onto the hard-packed avenue. Wide-eyed, they looked up, shaking their fists and screaming insults.

"Rot in Piasa's jaws, you two-footed vermin!" Spotted Wrist bellowed in return. As he uttered the name of the Underworld Spirit Beast, he gave Night Shadow Star's tall palace a glance. The thing stood to his left, across the avenue, its roof weather-grayed, grass growing on the flat behind the guardian posts. Night Shadow Star's slaves and servants still lived there and mostly kept it in repair.

But when it came to Night Shadow Star? The woman seemed to have vanished. Blood Talon should have run the Keeper's errant bride to ground. Should have had her captured, tightly bound, and paddled back upriver and right into Spotted Wrist's bed.

"What's that look?" Cut Weasel asked.

"Night Shadow Star." Spotted Wrist gave his second an inquisitive glance. "Blood Talon isn't one to fail at carrying out an order. Just track Night Shadow Star down and bring her and her slave back to Cahokia. But it's what? Almost six moons?"

"What have you heard from the Tenasee expedition?" Cut Weasel asked. "They should have sent word about either Blood Talon or Lady Night Shadow Star. You gave War Leader Tall Dancer specific instructions in that regard. That's a lot of eyes and ears. They should have come across something."

"I've had reports from the various messengers regarding the expedition's progress. The last word was from Big Cane Village. No one has seen her. Not in any of the colonies, not even in any of the riverside towns. To hear them tell it, no Cahokian lady passed up the Tenasee ahead of the expedition."

"So . . . maybe she went south? Down the Father Water?" Cut Weasel spread his hands wide.

"Why?" Spotted Wrist countered. "Her agreement with Morning Star was that she was supposed to go kill Walking Smoke in Cofitachequi. But I thought Walking Smoke was supposed to have died in the river the day Columella's first palace was burned. I tell you, none of this business makes sense."

"Blood Talon had an entire squad with him. Twenty warriors. Not the sort of party to travel unnoticed. What do you hear about that?"

"At Red Bluff Town, Blood Talon asked for help. Mobilized the entire chiefdom, and then paddled upriver." Spotted Wrist continued to glare at Night Shadow Star's palace where it overlooked the Great Plaza.

I should be living there.

"Doesn't make sense," Cut Weasel agreed.

"The last anyone can tell, they made it as far as Big Cane Village. That was the final word to reach here. And by that time, Blood Talon still hadn't run the woman down."

"It shouldn't be that hard, Keeper. She's a Four Winds lady, from Black Tail's lineage. That kind of woman is hard to miss."

"You'd think, wouldn't you?"

"Or . . . not." Cut Weasel straightened, obviously onto something.

"Squadron First?"

Cut Weasel squinted down at the city as he rubbed the back of his neck. "The reason I came to find you, Keeper, is that I've had word of old Blue Heron. A Panther Clan chief came to see me. Said he had information to sell. Said that Blue Heron once used him and his kin badly. He claims she's alive, Lord. Not only that, but she's traveling freely about the city."

"Impossible! How?"

"According to the Panther Clan chief, she's dressed as an old lady. Wearing rags. Passing as a dirt farmer. Or a Trader, or some such."

"Lady Blue Heron?" Spotted Wrist raised a mocking eyebrow. "Posing like some clanless old wretch?"

"Maybe she learned it from the thief, Lord?"

"This Panther Clan chief would have me believe that one of the most important and feared women in Cahokia willingly disguises herself as a bit of human flotsam and is slipping around the city with impunity?"

"That's what the Panther Clan chief says."

Spotted Wrist turned, fixing his troubled gaze on Cut Weasel. "Do you think this is true?"

The Squadron First raised his muscular shoulders in a shrug. "We didn't find her body in the remains of her palace."

Spotted Wrist craned his neck, looking north along the base of the Great Mound to where the charred wreckage of Blue Heron's palace blackened the top of her mound.

Looking like a homeless old woman? It would be the perfect disguise. He frowned. *But surely, she couldn't pose any kind of threat.*

He came to a decision. "If she's out there, I want her run down, Squadron First. Even if you have to interrogate every little old lady you run across."

Forty-five

It didn't matter that he knew he was Dreaming, Fire Cat heard the voice as clearly as if he were standing in the Morning Star palace great room. He could feel the heat from the eternal fire on his back, was staring into Chunkey Boy's dark, gleaming eyes as the young man reclined on his panther hide–covered litter atop its dais.

"Perhaps I am preparing you—by the most cunning means—for the day that I will need you to do me some terrible service. Molding you so that when the time comes you won't hesitate to strike."

That same cold rush, so familiar and haunting, crept up Fire Cat's spine. Chunkey Boy's eyes expanded, grew empty and yawning until Fire Cat felt himself falling into the void, weightless, plummeting into the stygian . . .

He jerked awake. His heart hammering fear. Every muscle in his body pulsed, electric.

"Fire Cat?" Night Shadow Star shifted beside him as he bolted up-right in the blankets.

As the Dream shattered, Chunkey Boy's hollow voice vanished under the onslaught of birdsong, the chirring of insects in the ash, hickory, and gum trees around their camp. The smoky pungency of Morning Star's palace surrendered to the scents of the forest and river.

"You were having a bad Dream," Night Shadow Star told him, her slender brown hand resting on his shoulder. Her gaze—in some ways so like her brother's—was filled with concern.

Fire Cat rubbed his face, winced, and took a deep breath. Yes, he was on the river. Camped just up from the low bank on a grassy flat that Winder had pointed out the night before. Around them, the Traders they were traveling with had laid out their bedrolls. Occasional traces of the foul-smelling puccoon-and-sassafras-root rub they used to discourage chiggers and mosquitoes carried on the faint breeze. The fire was a gray bed of ash, fingers of smoke rising from the hardwood embers.

"I was back in Chunkey Boy's palace. Standing there before his dais. Those words he spoke that day. So clear, like he was right here, speaking them into my ears."

"Which time was this?" She shifted, and he could see the long scab peeling from her cheek. The scar it would leave, along with her slightly misshapen ear, would only make her beauty even more exotic. But it did make a mess of her Four Winds Clan tattoo on that side.

"Remember that time after we returned from the Sacred Cave? When he had the copper spike from my war club? The one Chunkey Boy couldn't have had because I left it in the Underworld?"

"I remember that day perfectly." She pulled herself up to sit beside him, her shoulder against his as she stared up into the sweet gum tree where a mockingbird raucously greeted the morning, flitting from branch to branch in pursuit of a darting butterfly.

"His words," Fire Cat said softly as he arched his neck, eyes slitted to the silvering dawn. "That it was all an elaborate hoax to prepare me for some future task."

"Doesn't make sense. He knows you think he is a fraud."

Fire Cat stared at the lavender sky. "He went to such lengths to tell me how he could have orchestrated the fraud in the cave. How he could have had a priest steal my war club so that he could give me back the copper spike."

"Give me one reason why Morning Star would put that kind of effort into deceiving you?"

He shook his head. "I can't. And, I have to tell you, Lady, I've thought it through up and down, back and forth. What were his words? Something about my skepticism served his purposes? That maybe it kept your ambitions in check? What ambitions? You had no designs on Cahokia, let alone challenging his authority in any way."

"I remember. But he also said that using you might be a reminder to skeptics that they'd end up as slaves, that your situation provided an object lesson to the heretics."

Fire Cat chuckled. "If sharing my life with you is punishment for heresy, I'll . . ."

He knew the moment that Piasa possessed her, felt it in the sudden rigidity where her shoulder pressed against his. Could see the vacancy grow behind her eyes, the slackness in her face. It was Piasa's voice, guttural and deep, that parroted Chunkey Boy's words that day in the palace: *"Having Danced in the merging of light and dark, I now understand his Power. And yours. I finally know who you are. What you might become."*

Fire Cat turned, grabbed Night Shadow Star by the shoulders, and shook her. "Leave my Lady alone! Get out of her. Let her be. It's enough that she serves you, Lord. How much more do you want from us?"

When Night Shadow Star's dark eyes fastened on his, it was Piasa who peered into his very soul. *"All that you have to give, Red Wing. And then more. So go on. Live. Now that you know the price."*

"Price? What price?" He was shouting, shaking her with such intensity that her hair was bouncing.

And in an instant, Night Shadow Star was back, eyes panicked by the vigor of his assault. A look of terror gave way to a hard swallow as he let go of her.

"Did you hear?" Fire Cat demanded.

She nodded, seemed to collect herself as she fumbled with her thick locks. "They're in it together. Piasa, Morning Star. Some grand game. And you and I, and Walking Smoke. Like it's all been arranged from the very beginning. And we're just . . . just . . ."

"Gaming pieces cast out on the blanket? To see which way the carved bones fall? Win or lose?"

She gave a defeated shrug, wouldn't meet his eyes.

Around them, the entire camp was awake. The Traders they'd hired to carry them down to Big Cane Town were half out of their blankets, watching with wide and somber eyes.

Winder and Blood Talon—also sitting up in their beds—shot each other knowing glances, then rose.

Fire Cat rubbed his face. "All you have to give. And then more."

But that could mean anything. And none of it was good.

Forty-six

Seven Skull Shield was sitting in his usual place with Blue Heron just off the avenue on the southeastern side of the Great Plaza. Their blanket of Trade lay spread before them. The sun was playing hide-and-seek with a series of towering thunderheads moving in from the northwest. Considering what they'd started with, Blue Heron had proven a most successful Trader. Her acumen had increased the value of their goods by at least tenfold. Some of the statuary, carvings, and copper pieces alone could have been Traded for a year's worth of corn, beans, and squash, or bought them passage clear down to the Koroa lands at the mouth of the Father Water.

As it was a slow day—with only a scratch stickball game out on the grass—Seven Skull Shield had plenty of time to enjoy gazing at the women passing by. Looking at women was one of his favorite pastimes. He would wink and grin at the children, and periodically pet Farts.

He had cast his gaze on a particularly voluptuous young woman, who'd shot him a smile in return. As she made her way north on the avenue, she'd added a bit more swish to the skirt that hung down to her knees. Seven Skull Shield, scratching Farts' ears, watched her vanish as she made the turn west on the Avenue of the Sun.

Which is how he saw the warriors start out from the base of Morning Star's Great Mound. Must have been twenty of them, all wearing armor and moving with a definite plan. From the foot of the Great Stairs, they fanned out in groups of five along the northern edge of the Great Plaza, avoiding the chunkey courts.

Mostly they just passed people, nodding, but each time they encountered an older woman, they stopped, inspected her closely, scrubbed at her cheeks. Asked her harsh questions and searched her possessions. If she was accompanied by her husband or others—and they objected—the warriors ensured that protective friends or family didn't interfere. Even if it meant a whack or two with a war club to make the point.

Giving Farts the command to stay by the Trade blanket with Blue Heron, Seven Skull Shield rose, sauntered up the avenue, and eased close, pretending to be inspecting some brownware jugs at a dirt farmer's Trade stall.

He could just hear as the closest band of warriors surrounded a gray-haired woman with Hawk Clan tattoos on her cheeks. She had a blanket of Trade laid out just up the line. The top of the woman's head was barely even with Seven Skull Shield's navel, and her back looked painfully curved. But she greeted the warriors with a smile, gesturing at the coils of vines her son had carried in to stack atop her blanket. "Can I interest you in fresh green vine? Strong and supple. Just cut yesterday. Perfect for lashing roofing poles, house staves, or tying sections of wall together. Finest grape, I tell you."

The leader—might have been a squadron third—reached out, grabbed the woman by the jaw, and yanked her forward. Almost toppled her over the coils of vines as she squawked.

"You Blue Heron?" the warrior demanded as he used a thumb to scrub at the squealing woman's age-wrinkled cheeks. "That you hiding under those fake tattoos?"

Seven Skull Shield's heart skipped a beat. He turned, ambled slowly back to the blanket of Trade where Blue Heron was sitting and smiling at the passersby. Farts wagged his tail, each thump raising dust as it slapped the packed clay.

"Warriors are coming," Seven Skull Shield warned. "They know you're alive and disguised as a Trader. Run! Now."

Blue Heron's eyes narrowed. "How do you know?"

"Look for yourself." He jerked his head as the warriors abandoned the vine Trader and grabbed a hapless old female dirt farmer with a sack of unshelled corn over one shoulder. They were twisting the howling woman's head this way and that, searching for tattoos.

"Rides-the-Lightning's palace," Seven Skull Shield told her. "They won't search there."

She artfully scrambled to grab up the corners of their Trade blanket.

"What are you doing?" he demanded.

"Hey! I worked too hard to build up this Trade. Think I'm leaving it behind?"

"It's your life we're talking about!"

"It's my pus-dripping dignity, Thief." She lifted the corners, which tumbled the bits and pieces of Trade into the middle for carrying. This she extended to Seven Skull Shield. "Come on. Let's go."

He glanced back. Saw another group of warriors cutting across the stickball field after questioning an old woman who'd been watching the scratch game.

"There's no time. You take the Trade. Farts and me, we're going to create a little distraction." Seven Skull Shield gave her a grin. "Just get to Rides-the-Lightning."

And then he turned on his heel. They were closer now, not a stone's throw away. If they looked up, saw Blue Heron hobbling away under her load of Trade . . . Well, that couldn't be allowed to happen.

Seven Skull Shield stepped over to the pot Trader, picked up one of the jugs. The thing was spherical, with a vertical neck, and as wide across as his forearm measured from elbow to fingertips. Looked like it would hold a week's worth of water. The sides had been burnished to a fine gleam. The workmanship—if Seven Skull Shield was any judge—was superb.

"You come back!" the dirt farmer cried. "Make you Trade, yes?"

"Depends," Seven Skull Shield replied, balancing the jar on his hand, hefting the weight. "Quality pot, yes?"

"Wife make. She make good. Fired hot. Thin wall. Shell temper for strength. You know shell temper?"

"I do."

The warriors were done with the vine Trader, coming on with a vengeance. Looking back, Blue Heron was pretty much alone, obviously making haste on her bad hip, the sack of Trade bouncing on her shoulders. Blood and piss, the load was too heavy for her to make good time. And worse, she kept throwing worried glances back over her shoulder.

"Woman doesn't know the first thing about how to run away," Seven Skull Shield muttered to Farts. To the Trader he asked, "You sure this is a sturdy pot?"

"Oh, yes, yes. Two strings salt-water shell beads, you take. Yes?" From the dirt farmer's accent, he was from somewhere down in the White River Mountains southwest of Evening Star Town.

"Hey! Look!" The cry came from one of the closest warriors. "See that old woman? She's running. Let's get her!"

The warriors lined out, and the squadron third in the lead called, "Bet we got her."

"Two strings?" Seven Skull Shield mused.

The second band of warriors, cueing on the first, were angling in from the stickball field, also fixed on the fleeing Blue Heron.

Whipping his arm back, Seven Skull Shield cupped the ceramic jug in the hollow of his hand and tested its balance. He narrowed an eye—and heaved it with all his strength.

The squadron third was totally fixed on Blue Heron. At the last second, catching movement from the corner of his eye, he twisted his head. The pot caught him full in the face. Shattered with a loud *pop*. The impact knocked the man back, his feet flying, his arms akimbo.

As the burst vessel showered the squadron third and his warriors with flying sherds, the man fell back, landed with a hollow thump on the flat of his back. His head bounced hard on the packed avenue, and then he lay still.

For a startled moment, the rest of the warriors clattered to a stop, stared incredulously at the fallen squadron third. He lay unmoving on the clay, covered with fragments of broken pot. Blood began to leak from the man's nose. His eyes were dull and half-lidded.

The dirt farmer's mouth dropped open in disbelief, his eyes wide.

"Guess your jugs aren't as sturdy as you said they were," Seven Skull Shield told him. "But definitely worth the two strings of shell beads."

To Farts, he added, "Run!"

Behind him, he heard someone shout, "Get him! Get that man! Now!"

Seven Skull Shield sprinted around the side of the Weavers' Society House, pounding for the cluttered mess of temples, council houses, and dwellings that crammed in close to the southwest. He knew this part of the city from when Whispering Dawn's Chicaza embassy had been living here. The place was packed with large houses, granaries, workshops, and smaller Earth Clans temple mounds dedicated to Old-Woman-Who-Never-Dies.

At Seven Skull Shield's side, Farts was bounding happily, his tongue lolling out the side of his mouth.

Breaking the cardinal sin when running for one's life, Seven Skull Shield threw a glance over his shoulder.

To his delight, elements of both groups of warriors were hammering their way after him.

Blue Heron was forgotten.

Seven Skull Shield always said he was built for strength, not for speed. That didn't mean that panic couldn't elicit a remarkable alacrity when needed. The knowledge of imminent death provided exactly that kind of electric energy as he ran around the clutter of tightly packed farmsteads, council houses, sweat lodges, and ramadas.

This part of Cahokia, just off the southwestern corner of the Great Plaza, was where the *tonka'tzi* liked to house foreign embassies when they came to visit, conduct Trade, or have political dealings. Lots of buildings, set close. Plenty of good places to hide if he could just get the chance.

Where storm clouds built in the west, Seven Skull Shield was delighted to have the cooler temperatures; especially so because he was sweating like a turkey carcass on a roasting spit. Not to mention that his breath was coming in hoarse gasps, and that his muscles were in burning agony and on the verge of failure.

He pounded across a yard filled with squash, tripped on the vines, and slipped as his feet crushed a couple of large gourds. Wind-milling for balance, he almost stepped full on a woman who was crouched over the clay hearth before the house door. She screamed, he caught his balance, and avoided the log pestle and mortar. Then he careened through the attached ramada. In the process he knocked over several ceramic pots and toppled a loom with a half-finished weaving.

As Seven Skull Shield half staggered and caught his balance, a look over his shoulder added to his panic. The first of the pursuing warriors rounded the woman's house, pointed, yelling, "There he is! Get him!"

Seven Skull Shield had already ducked behind an earth-covered council house, and was sprinting headlong.

Then the thought hit him: *All right, now what am I going to do?*

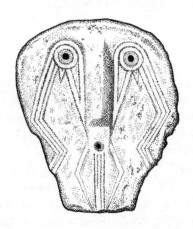

The Black Shadow Worm

T rout *has made excellent time in its journey, the warriors—seemingly built of endless muscle—have propelled us downriver to Rainbow Town. Along the way we stopped just long enough at various villages and riverside towns to pick up reports from colonies and Cahokian garrisons. Sometimes these are shell-beaded mats woven by the recorders, other times verbal assessments and various progress reports from the new or reinforced colonies along the way.*

I approved of Squadron Second Canebrake in the beginning. What he lacks in imagination, humor, and gregariousness is compensated for by his narrow focus on duty and responsibility. If I were to describe the squadron second in a nutshell, it would be single-minded.

But I couldn't figure out for the longest time why I didn't trust him. Maybe it was because he kept to himself. Was always respectful but distant. More than once, I heard him tell one of the other warriors, "Your personal feelings are not at issue. They're Four Winds Clan nobles. Our job is to get them to Cahokia, not to become best friends."

And why would he take that attitude? In all my dealings with people, they either feared or wanted something from me. And all of a sudden, just because he'd pulled us out of a river, Canebrake will just ignore us?

It doesn't make sense. I'm Walking Smoke, brother to Chunkey Boy. By the booming thunder, I'm the Lightning Shell Witch! Those who aren't awed to be in my presence are smart enough to fear me to the depths of their very souls. And the smartest of them understand I can give them something. Do them some service or grant a wish.

Canebrake treats Fire Light and me like we are nothing more than . . . business!

For the longest time, I couldn't figure it out. Until Rainbow Town. Canebrake wanted to Trade for sacks of goosefoot meal, knotweed flour, and lotus roots for baking. Fish, turtles, waterfowl, and mussels we obtain on our own.

At the landing—where the creek empties out below the bluff-top town—I keep watching Canebrake. It had bothered me all that morning as we rode the current toward the town. The question, like a persistent and irritating bur, has been tumbling around in my head.

What is it about him?

The squadron second filled my dreams last night, kept bobbing up like a half-sunken log. He'd just be there, peeking out from around corners, watching me while I climbed the Great Staircase, or stood over the body of a sacrificial victim.

I remember one Dream image: I was reaching down into a little girl's gut cavity, removing her intestines. They kept squirming around in my fingers like muscular snakes. If you know how to look, have the Power of "True Sight," you can see the future in the patterns of a victim's intestines. But the way this little girl's kept winding around, the image was changing, like a picture of a mountain that becomes a lake, or a warrior's image that merges into that of a deer. Who then shifts and flows into that of an old oak. And just when you can really make out the patterns of leaves, it all blurs, fades, and turns into an eagle rising from a pond's surface, its wings spread, the yellow beak gaping wide to display the pointed tongue.

Through that entire Dream, I kept looking over my shoulder to see Canebrake; his passionless eyes watch my every move.

Every time during that long day, when I'd turn around in the canoe, it was to find him watching me from his high seat in the stern. And his eyes would be level, unconcerned. Watching with that same face he'd worn in my Dream.

I keep chewing on that. No one ever takes me, of all people, for granted. Never, in my entire life, have I been dismissed as just another duty. And Canebrake treats me exactly that way. He will carry Fire Light and me to Cahokia because we are Four Winds Clan. What he will not do is make a production of it.

As we stretch our legs at the Rainbow Town canoe landing, I watch Canebrake as he and the warrior Ten Man Trade for the staples we desire. The landing is busy, people coming and going, loading canoes with goods before paddling away to their homes, or unloading goods to carry up to the palisaded town atop the bluff.

High Chief Fire Light—with that now-familiar emptiness to his eyes—walks listlessly past the ramadas up the slope. He acts like he doesn't see the Trade on display. His actions are those of a man whose souls are incomplete. No matter what the circumstances or situation, Fire Light goes through the motions. Heedless, passionless, he moves, eats, defecates, and sleeps as though only following directions.

Him I can ignore until I need him. He takes no effort, causes me no concern. But Canebrake?

He's . . . not right. The Dreams prove that. Like Power is telling me something. But what?

The squadron second and his warrior have finished their Trade, handing over strings of shell beads for the woven sacks of seeds and flour.

It is only when Canebrake comes walking down the slope that I see it.

He passes in front of a Trader's ramada, where, laid out on a red, white, and black–banded blanket, a large sheet of mica is displayed. About as big around as a man's head. The mica is propped up at an angle by two thin-necked brownware jars so that it can be seen in its entirety.

The instant Canebrake walks between the sheet of mica and me, the sun hits at just the right angle. As the squadron second breaks the glaring beam of light, the image is burned into my brain. Reflected light shines through Canebrake's head. In that burning image I see the black shadow hiding inside the man's skull. From the shape, I can tell it's a worm.

Suddenly, everything makes sense.

Yes, of course.

I narrow my eyes. Canebrake has a black shadow worm living in his head. Worms are Underworld creatures, living down in the soil, consuming dead things.

I laugh softly to myself. The curious thing is that I'm actually delighted that Piasa is this clever. And it all makes sense. During our passage of the Suck and Rage, when I was most vulnerable to Piasa, exposed in the crashing water, I was protected by the Thunderbirds and their deadly lightning. Any attempt Piasa or the Tie Snakes might have made to grab me, suck me under, and devour me, would have been met by the Thunderbirds' searing bolts of lightning.

Oh, how that must have enraged the Powers of the Underworld. To have me bobbing, at their mercy, and so tempting. All Piasa needed to do was rise from the depths, snag me with a clawed foot, and drag me down. But all the time, the Thunderbirds were circling above, ready to blast their ancient adversary into ash.

Piasa is nothing if not cunning. How he inserted a black shadow worm into Canebrake's head will probably remain a mystery, some secret Underworld magic. If I remember when the time comes, maybe I can torture Night Shadow Star to divulge the manner of it. Surely she would know.

A cold shiver runs down my spine as I consider Canebrake. Since he is Piasa's creature, I must plan accordingly, take the necessary steps to protect myself.

How will I deal with Canebrake? Ah, that will be determined by time and the unfolding of events. For the moment, I will let him live. Use him. See, the thing about a weapon is that it can always be turned against its owner. All you have to do is get your hands on it.

As I consider this, two little Yuchi girls run up. They are maybe four or five. Twins? They look alike, with sparkling black eyes, wide grins missing baby teeth and growing new ones. They are wearing only smudged girdles. They giggle up at me and then pause when they see my face.

I pull my lips back to expose my teeth. This turns my burn-scarred face into a hideous rictus.

They run screaming.

I am delighted by the knowledge that they will have nightmares about me tonight.

Then I glance at Canebrake, who is carrying sacks of grain and flour down to Trout. There will be nightmares aplenty to go around.

Forty-seven

Threaded Leather let the rage burn through him as he ran after the culprit. That vile bit of human flotsam, that worm, that two-footed pus-licking *maggot* had smashed Squadron Third Burnt Web's face with a thrown pot!

Intolerable.

Worse, the bit of bloody vomit looked like a dirt farmer with his frayed and worn hunting shirt belted at the waist by nothing more than a rope. Had to be a dirt farmer. The tattoos on that big and homely face didn't look like any clan design Threaded Leather had ever seen. Not to mention the big dog. Might have been a pack animal, given its thick-boned frame, oversized paws, and bear-blunt head.

Feet pounding the ground, Threaded Leather ran for all he was worth. Let the rage drive his fevered muscles as he wove around the trench-wall and thatch-roofed dwellings, trampled his way across gardens, and leaped over pots, baskets, fire pits, and storage pits.

The only saving grace came from the high thunderheads now blocking the blazing afternoon sun. Not that they helped much. In the hot and muggy air, sweat beaded and trickled from under his helmet. The same with his chest and sides; sweat soaked his war shirt beneath the wood-and-leather cuirass.

A woman was screaming hysterically as he rounded the corner of a house and saw the villain careening off-balance through a ramada, almost falling over his own feet.

For a half heartbeat, their eyes locked across the distance, and the fugitive caught his stride, the dog already disappearing around the curve of a council house.

As Threaded Leather's feet hammered across the woman's garden, trampling vines, smashing squash and bean plants, she rose to her feet. Her wild eyes fixed on where his sandaled feet churned through her crops. He could hear his warriors, Woven Rope and Hanging Duck, panting behind him as they followed.

"Beasts!" she screamed, falling back to the pestle sticking up out of a log mortar beside her open door.

Threaded Leather was almost even with her when she lifted the long wooden pestle from the mortar's hollow and swung it with all her might. His years in the north saved him. Instinct kicked in and he caught the blow as he raised his shield and sent the heavy pestle ricocheting upward. Carried away with the vigor of her swing, the woman was spun around, toppled backward into her doorway, and fell butt-first into the depths of her subterranean pit floor.

She was still screaming from down below as Threaded Leather wobbled to the side, caught himself, and got his balance.

"You all right?" Woven Rope asked between ragged breaths as he pulled up beside Threaded Leather. The warrior's face was red from exertion, the sweat trickling down in beads from under his helmet leaving tracks on his hollow cheeks and around his shining nose.

"Yes. Let's get him!" Threaded Leather resettled his armor and charge ahead, trampling a toppled loom and taking time to swing his war club down to smash a couple of the large ceramic jars as he hit his stride.

Payback for the old woman and practice for what he was going to do to the dirt farmer's head when he caught him.

Following his prey wasn't all that hard. He could hear the occasional shout, the crashing of breaking wood.

Spit and piss, he wished he wasn't wearing his armor. The weight of the wood and leather slowed him, seemed fit to drag him down with each dogged stride as he willed himself forward.

Keeping the image of Burnt Web lying there, knocked cold, bits and shards of broken jug littering the squadron third's body and gleaming on the hard avenue, gave Threaded Leather strength.

Through hoarse breaths, he swore, "When I catch you, you two-footed maggot, I'm going to make you wish you'd been squirted out of your mother's sheath upside-down and already dead!"

The others were lined out, feet thumping on the ground, following as Threaded Leather wound through the buildings, seeing overturned pots, dodging the locals shouting and waving fists in the direction of the fleeing fugitive.

It wouldn't be long now. Just up ahead, the thick press of buildings, temples, and farmsteads would give way to a low marsh and a series of flooded borrow pits. There would be no place to hide. Nowhere to run.

"Only one way this is going to end," Threaded Leather swore as he raced full-bore into a narrow passage between the back of a high granary and a low-ranking Duck Clan chief's palace. With plastered wall on one side and wattle-and-daub on the other, the narrow way was blocked by a pile of matting obviously torn down by the fleeing malefactor.

"Got you now!" Threaded Leather gloated as he vaulted the woven-cattail matting.

He realized his mistake in midair.

Glanced down where his extended foot would land. Already disturbed by the destruction of the matting, a swirling cloud of flies parted as Threaded Leather's foot splashed through the scummy green-brown surface. The stench hit his nose the barest instant before Threaded Leather sank thigh-deep in the latrine. His foot went out from under him, and he fell into the latrine's liquid goo.

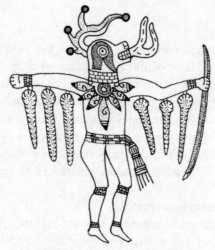

Forty-eight

Earlier that day, thick clouds had rolled in across the hilly uplands to the south, dark against the green forest that cloaked the ridges and uplifts rising behind Big Cane Village. Now a gentle rain fell. Through the open door of White Mat's bent-pole and thatch-covered house, Night Shadow Star had a partial view of the settlement. The squat dwellings, the raised charnel house on its mound, and one of the moiety chiefs' palaces—such as it was—were just visible.

The beaten soil, patched here and there with scrubby, trampled grass, reflected a wet sheen, while puddles stippled with raindrops. Runoff from the ramada roof outside trickled in a musical staccato where it pattered behind the house.

From this angle, the river with its canoe landing was hidden from sight below the edge of the terrace.

Inside, a small fire crackled, fingers of flame adding but little illumination. Night Shadow Star sat to the right of the doorway in the guest's position, Fire Cat beside her. In the rear, the Trader, White Mat, sat shoulder-to-shoulder with Shedding Bird. She could tell with a glance they were brothers, the only glaring difference being Shedding Bird's larger nose. Both were in their early thirties, broad shouldered, with the muscle-thick arms common to river Traders.

"The Cahokians were here for a quarter moon," Shedding Bird said warily. "Most of us, we just packed up and left the town to them. That many people? Trying to pack into Big Cane Town? We made a Trade with some Hawk Clan chief. Let him have the house for a shank of poor beads. Handled the same kind of transactions for most of our friends and neighbors. Figured we'd take bad bargains rather than no bargains at all.

Then we took to the forest until they left. Figured that being Yuchi, and allies and everything, we got a better deal than folks like the Muskogee upriver were going to get."

"At least they didn't leave a garrison here." Night Shadow Star rubbed her smooth shins with callused hands.

"We're Yuchi." Shedding Bird yawned. "Good friends to Cahokia."

"That doesn't always mean anything. How did they treat people here?" Fire Cat asked. "You can talk freely. You know I have my own issues with Cahokians."

That brought a laugh. "When you come with that many warriors, chiefs, and matrons, you can do whatever you want. From the word on the river, they were much better by the time they got here, and especially at Rainbow Town. Given the parity in strength, they treated the *Tsoyaha*"—he used the Yuchi name for themselves—"with respect. Lots of feasting and Dancing. Some Cahokian warriors even joined a Yuchi war party for a punitive raid on the Chicaza down south. I think they'd worn the sharp edges off by the time they reached here," Shedding Bird said. "The word downriver is that they just landed and took whatever they needed, that they were mostly fighting with each other."

"I can tell you for a fact, they were back to just taking whatever they wanted as they moved on upriver," Night Shadow Star told them. "When we went through Canyon Town and White Chief Town, they reminded us of conquered communities."

"And they're being garrisoned," Fire Cat added. "I think from here on, they're part of the Cahokian empire."

The brothers glanced at each other, sharing some subtle communication. "Nothing will be the same."

"Winder agrees," Night Shadow Star told them.

Hardly waiting for the canoe to lance the beach at the town's canoe landing, the big Trader had headed for his house at a dogtrot. Night Shadow Star could well imagine what he and his cute young wife were occupying themselves with that afternoon. Blood Talon had insisted he'd be fine keeping an eye on their possessions where they were placed in the shelter of a ramada above the landing. He'd found the company of a couple of Traders who spoke Cahokian and was pumping them for any news on events downriver.

Fire Cat glanced at Night Shadow Star, then said, "We heard that a Cahokian canoe is a couple of days ahead of us. Some sort of official messengers carrying a report from the expedition. That it's on its way back to Cahokia. That there's a Cahokian Lord on board. You know anything about that?"

"They overnighted here." Shedding Bird rubbed his callused hands together. "And they're traveling fast. Traded for a cooked meal and were back on the water before dawn. Just a thought, but no one on that boat looked happy. Least of all the squadron second. And there's two nobles. The scar-faced Cahokian lord, and some Four Winds high chief. I didn't get the particulars."

White Mat added, "And they're a full quarter moon ahead of you."

"Walking Smoke and Fire Light," Night Shadow Star mused. "And they're that far ahead of us?"

"Seven whole days." Fire Cat chewed his lips, frowning. "He's going to make it to Cahokia long before we can. I don't know what kind of canoe Winder has, or how fast he can get people to paddle it, but we've got to make up the time."

White Mat squinted a skeptical eye. "In the telling of your adventures so far, you've told us how you got that wound on your face, about being separated, and finding each other. You haven't said if you killed this man you went to Cofitachequi to find."

"He's the man with the scarred face," Night Shadow Star told them. "I didn't quite get the job done. Whacked him a good one in the shaft and eggs, though. Last I saw, he was bent double holding his tenders and dribbling his water. Said the pain was terrible."

"That man was walking fine," White Mat confided. "Strutting around giving orders. Arrogant pus bucket, if you ask me."

"He's healed," Fire Cat murmured.

"So, that's Walking Smoke?" Shedding Bird put the pieces together. "How did he get away?"

"Power still plays us, old friend." Night Shadow Star's gaze strayed to the rain beyond the door. "He had allies of his own." She held up thumb and forefinger. "I came that close to killing him."

"And then Power intervened," Fire Cat finished. "And something between Sky and Underworld shifted. Now we are led to believe that it will all be decided back in Cahokia."

"All that way, just to go back to Cahokia?" White Mat asked incredulously.

Night Shadow Star told him, "Walking Smoke is on his way to try and kill Morning Star. Some insane notion that by doing so, he will become Thrown Away Boy, and unleash unholy chaos."

The two brothers glanced at each other, even more uneasy.

It was White Mat who said, "Were it anyone but you, Lady, we'd nod. Think it was a wonderful and scary story. But just a story."

Shedding Bird added, "Unfortunately, it's you. So it's real. I *saw* him when he was here." He shook his head. "It isn't often that just seeing a man sends a shiver down one's spine. But he did. And *that's* the man you're sworn to kill?"

"If I can catch him in time."

Again the brothers looked at each other.

"We're rich," White Mat told Shedding Bird.

"And famous," Shedding Bird replied.

"We could be richer."

"And more famous."

"What are you talking about?" Fire Cat asked.

White Mat gave him a saucy wink, his lips bending into a smile. "Winder's canoe is for carrying big packs, chunky and wide, complete with a woven-cattail mat covering."

"You know," Shedding Bird told him, "so you can paddle in the shade on hot sunny days."

"And stay pleasantly dry when it's raining." White Mat gestured to the weather outside. "All built for comfort and bulk."

"Not for speed." Shedding Bird nodded his head authoritatively.

"So, you're saying . . . ?" Night Shadow Star asked.

"Half Root is pregnant," White Mat told her. "Made Man will want to be with her. See his child born."

"And Mixed Shell is off with his family in the forest. Nuts are starting to fall, you know." Shedding Bark narrowed an eye. "Leaves us three short. But with Winder and this other man . . . ?" He made a face. "Blood Talon? Seriously?"

Fire Cat spread his hands, his heart quickening. "Seriously."

Shedding Bark said, "That would be enough, assuming we can get any work out of Winder. The River Fox likes to sit in the back and steer while he's drinking blackberry juice."

"He'll paddle," Night Shadow Star told them. "But are you seriously offering *Red Reed*?"

"How rich and famous can you make us?" Shedding Bird asked mildly.

"Really rich and famous," Fire Cat told them.

White Mat curled his lips in a broad smile.

Forty-nine

Holding a cup of steaming black drink, Spotted Wrist glared across the fire at Cut Weasel. The Squadron Leader stood with his chin high, his hands clasped behind him, gaze elevated, as if he'd found something fascinating on the rear wall of the Keeper's palace. In the flickering of the flames, Cut Weasel's face had a reddish sheen, as if the cheeks, firm nose, brow, and chin were molded of formed copper burnished to a fine glisten. The man's tattoos were barely visible in the leaping, Dancing light.

"So, is Blue Heron alive, or isn't she?" Spotted Wrist demanded.

"I don't know, Lord Keeper." Cut Weasel kept his gaze fixed on the rear wall. "All I can tell you is that since I was given the tip by that Panther Clan chief, we've questioned half the old women in Cahokia."

"Irritated, enraged, and inflamed them, you mean," Spotted Wrist growled. "Though I doubt you've come close to even a tenth of the old women in Cahokia."

"Do you know how *many* old women there are?" Cut Weasel cried.

"By blood and spit, I do!" Spotted Wrist thundered back. "And every one of their pious, obsequious, and sniveling families have stomped their way into my presence demanding an apology. And the ones who haven't are telling me, *me!* that if I dare harass their dear sweet mothers, they'll have my balls!" He waved it away. "Or some such."

"Lord Keeper, I—"

"You'll gods-rotted pay attention, Squadron First." Spotted Wrist rubbed his forehead. Tried to keep his temper from exploding.

Just that afternoon he'd run into Lady Sun Wing. She'd given him that half-vacant look, cuddled the Tortoise Bundle to her chest, and said, "I hear you've lost yet another woman, Keeper. Must be frustrating when even a dead one eludes your grasp."

No, Spotted Wrist wasn't in any kind of good mood.

He thrust a finger into Cut Weasel's face. "Listen, I need you to understand. Some of these people, especially the Earth Clans matrons and chiefs, we can't treat them like conquered barbarians. We have to have a certain sensitivity when dealing with them."

"It's the Earth Clans who are the problem," Cut Weasel insisted. "The dirt farmers just smile at us, answer questions, and let us look through their things. It's the pus-dripping Earth Clans who demand to know what right we have to . . ." He swallowed hard, waving it away. "Never mind, Keeper. You've heard it all before."

"That will change," Spotted Wrist promised. "When the squadrons are reassembled, and we have Horned Serpent House for our own, we'll control everything on this side of the river."

Cut Weasel finally shifted his gaze, the question unasked as he met Spotted Wrist's eyes.

"Yes, it's only a matter of time." Spotted Wrist nodded, as if to assure himself as well. "In the end, Squadron Leader, the ultimate authority rests with he who controls the greatest number of warriors." And that was North Star House. At least on this side of the river.

Cut Weasel said nothing, raised his gaze to the back wall again.

"And there's no other word about Blue Heron?" Spotted Wrist returned to his greatest vexation. The woman was supposed to be dead.

"Just that one incident. Maybe it was her. Squadron third Burnt Web couldn't be sure. Neither could his warriors. But the story has gone all over the city. How some dirt farmer, if that's what he was, smashed a pot into a North Star Squadron third's face, then somehow eluded them. About how Threaded Leather ended up face-first and dripping shit in the latrine. Oh, the jokes they made. But after the squadron third nearly beat a Fish Clan man to death, they've learned to hold their tongues. The story has taken on almost epic proportions. Like it was some remarkable tale from the Beginning Times."

"And?"

"I've had to reassign the squads involved. They wanted to tear that part of the city into little pieces searching for the assailant. As it was, they took it out on some poor Duck Clan woman. Went after her with willow switches for taking a swing at Threaded Leather with a pestle."

"Before or after he ended up in the latrine?" Spotted Wrist didn't so much as crack a smile. The whole accursed thing was humiliating. Be a lesson to the dolts if he relented and let the squadron take its frustration out on that entire section of the city.

"After. No one in North Star Squadron has much sympathy for anyone in that part of town."

"But the culprit who threw the pot just disappeared?"

"We figure it has to be someone local, Lord. Someone who knew the layout of that part of the city intimately. So we've had our people keeping watch. We know he had a dog with him, so we've questioned everyone in that area who has a dog. And we've kept watch on every dog owner there. We have five on our list, but we can't prove they did it." Cut Weasel paused. "Unless we take more severe measures."

"Such as?"

"Hang all five in the squares until one confesses?"

Spotted Wrist considered it, then waved it away. "If we were anywhere but Cahokia, I'd say do it. As a demonstration of our authority if nothing else. As much as I'd like to put these people in their place, we can't afford to alienate anyone else. Not at the moment. After we have Horned Serpent Town under Heart Warrior's control . . . well, things will be different."

"Hope so, Keeper."

"What about Wind? I heard that she was escorted up to Morning Star's palace." Escorted? That was a sham if ever there was one. He fought the urge to grind his teeth. The *tonka'tzi* was *his* prisoner, not Rising Flame's to order about at her whim and pleasure.

"Blue Stone is with her. He'll report whatever was said up there." Cut Weasel kept his eyes fixed on the wall. "Since he hasn't, she's probably still up at the palace."

"I want you to . . ."

He lost the thought as one of his warriors stepped into the room, knocking out a salute with a fist. "Lord Keeper, the Matron Rising Flame's litter has just arrived. She is being lowered right now and is asking to see you."

"Send her in." Spotted Wrist shot an irritated look at Cut Weasel. "Oh, joy. My heart leaps. This late at night? What do you want to bet the good Clan Matron isn't here looking for romance?"

Cut Weasel's lips bent in amusement, but his gaze remained wary.

"Clan Matron Rising Flame!" the warrior at the door announced, followed immediately by Rising Flame's entrance.

The woman had her hair up in a tight parietal bun, a splay of white egret feathers fixed behind it. Her face was formally painted in white, symbolic of wisdom and peace. But was that for his benefit? Or—given that she'd just come from Morning Star's palace—had it been part of whatever function that was?

A colorful parakeet-feather cloak was draped around her shoulders, shell necklaces hanging down between her breasts. The clinging knee-length skirt belted at her narrow waist was finely woven hemp, dyed black, with shining bits of mica in chevron patterns. Shell tinklers dangled from fringe at the hem.

Rising Flame carried her copper-clad staff of office at an angle as she strode into the room, stopped before the fire, and let her gaze take in the trophies and the empty bear cage that had once held Seven Skull Shield.

I really ought to find someone to put in that cage, Spotted Wrist thought. Too bad it wasn't Blue Heron.

If she was really alive.

If that hadn't just been smoke blown by that Panther Clan chief.

"Clan Matron," Spotted Wrist greeted. "To what do I owe the pleasure? Come for black drink? Maybe you're hungry? Sorry, we've eaten for the night, but I could have my warriors fetch something. Shouldn't be too hard to run some victual down."

"No, I've just come from Morning Star's palace. Ate there. I had an interesting discussion with Wind. I'm sure that your warriors informed you that I had asked that she be brought up to the palace?"

"They did. We were just discussing whether Blue Stone had escorted . . . wasn't that the word you used? Anyway, I will assume the warrior is even now *escorting* the *tonka'tzi* back to her quarters."

Rising Flame didn't rise to the bait. Her face had gone back to that insufferable emotionless stare. "Actually, that's what I came here to discuss. I want your warriors out of her palace. I have no objection to them standing guard outside, ensuring that she doesn't traipse off to, oh, organize rebellion against the Four Winds Clan Keeper, or engage in some such nefarious doings. But I want your warriors out of her palace."

Spotted Wrist laughed. "Matron, perhaps you'd like to take a stroll around the Great Plaza, take note of exactly whose warriors are patrolling the area. Oh, and there's the problem of River House, and whose warriors are ensuring that Three Fingers is still high chief. In case you hadn't noticed while you've been lounging around Morning Star's palace feasting with the Pacaha, the Chicaza, or whatever Oneota chief happens to be in the city, but River City Mounds is anything but secure. Without my warriors to back him, Three Fingers' control of his local Earth Clans' squadrons could switch to that pus-sucking War Duck in an instant. And don't think Columella wouldn't back him."

"I couldn't care less which side you back in River City, Keeper. And Morning Star has shown no interest in having your squadrons stand down. Actually, Morning Star has shown no interest in much of anything."

"What are you after, Matron?"

She crossed her arms, no give in her expression. "The same thing I've been after from the beginning, Keeper. I want Cahokia unified. I'm happy to achieve that end with your squadrons. But because of recent events, *Tonka'tzi* Wind remains an asset. To elaborate on that, she's the *only* viable asset I have at my disposal now that Green Chunkey has fallen into such Spiritual disregard. She's willing to work with us."

"Us?"

"She didn't get to where she is now by being anyone's fool. Nor did I. The original plan didn't work, Keeper. You weren't able to subdue Columella. Things deteriorated. Fell apart. In case you hadn't noticed, we're stalemated. For a time, Horned Serpent House tipped the balance in our favor, but that advantage is gone."

"For the time being." He gave her a bland smile.

If she read anything else into it, she gave no hint, saying, "Surely your warriors are capable of guarding an old woman's palace. If you think they can't keep track of her, I can call on an entire squadron of—"

"My people can keep track of her," Spotted Wrist snapped. Pus and blood! She hadn't been talking to that thrice-accursed mentally addled Sun Wing, had she?

"Assuming you can keep them out of latrines," she shot back. "Squadron Third Burnt Web's little fiasco didn't do us any favors. And that's another reason to back off the *tonka'tzi*. It's a way to relieve some of the festering resentment your warriors incited with that merry little hunt for a . . . what? A dirt farmer and a dog? From the moment you started searching for Blue Heron, you've looked like bumbling incompetents."

"Don't. You. Dare." He jammed a trembling finger in her direction.

"Thought Blue Heron was dead," she told him in an inflectionless voice. "You swore on it, and now you're searching for her? Checking tattoos? Manhandling every elderly female you run across? So, what is it? Is Blue Heron alive or dead?"

He clamped his jaws, the smoldering anger brewing in his gut.

Cut Weasel stood to the side, hard at attention, his eyes still fixed on the back wall.

"Get out," Spotted Wrist told her. "Now, Clan Matron. The last thing you want to do is pursue this conversation any further."

She gave him a slight nod, touching her forehead in the process. Turning on her heel, she strode for the door and out into the night.

The only sound in his palace was the crackling of the fire as it burned into a pitch pocket in the wood.

After a time, Cut Weasel asked softly, "Keeper?"

"Not a word. Not one single pus-rotted word, First."

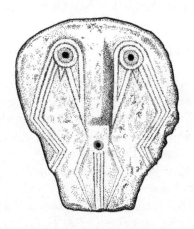

Counter Moves

*R*ed Bluff Town is our last scheduled stop. This is a Cahokian colony built atop a high terrace above the confluence of the River of Ducks and the Tenasee.

One of the first Cahokian colonies, it was established back when Morning Star's Spirit inhabited my grandfather's body. A war leader by the name of Red Tooth had quarreled with the then tonka'tzi and in his pique had asked Morning Star's blessing to take a band of warriors and farmers to find a place of their own. Said that in doing so, they would pay homage to the living god and spread his worship among the barbarians.

They had ended up here. And nothing about the settlement, in those early days, had been easy. Red Bluff was not named in honor of Red Tooth, but because of all the blood spilled in the establishment of the place and the subsequent conquest of the entire River of Ducks up to its headwaters.

Canebrake, while not daring to forbid me from accompanying him up the steep climb to the town, said we would be here no longer than it took to pick up the record mats, take High Chief Tanned Wolf's report, and then hotfoot it back to Trout.

In this instance, I can agree with him. I no more want to be here, stared at by the locals, than I want to be questioned by every passing Trader, farmer, and fisherman. "What happened to your face?" Over and over again is a curdling bore. As if I owed these colonial dirt farmers any more recognition than I would have given a beetle toddling across moldy leaf mat.

Ever since I discovered that Piasa's black shadow worm was slithering through Canebrake's brain and souls, our relationship—never what you'd call amiable—has been tense.

I suspect the good squadron second has been reevaluating his dedication to *duty in the days since he plucked me and Fire Light from the water below the Suck and Rage.*

The warriors paddling the canoe are fully aware; their own distaste at sharing our company is more than ample.

"Second?" Split Shaft had asked once when they didn't know I was relieving myself on the other side of a willow patch. "Why are you doing this? Couldn't you just leave them at the next town?"

"Warrior, they are Four Winds Clan. You can see it yourself from their tattoos." A pause. "I have a duty. One I am sworn to."

"You know we'd all follow you anywhere, Second. But since we picked those two up, we've been having nightmares. Two Gills dreamed of gutted corpses lying on their backs, chests slit wide. And when he leaned over, he could see images in the blood that pooled inside."

That had made me wonder if my own Dreams had strayed into the hapless Two Gills' souls, or if he had divining Power of his own.

"Why do you think I'm pushing so hard?" Canebrake had told Split Shaft. "The only honorable way I can be rid of them is to get to Cahokia with as much speed as possible."

"They don't worry you?" Split Shaft had wondered.

To which Canebrake had replied, "When I look at High Chief Fire Light, I think I see half a human being. As if he's hollow inside. But when I look into Lord Walking Smoke's eyes?" He had paused, and by this time I could see him through the willow stems. The squadron second shivered as he added, "All I can tell you, warrior, is that something in my blood freezes."

That brought a satisfied smile to my face. Knowing the black shadow worm had riddled the second's souls with holes made it ever more satisfying. It meant that Piasa's creature was worried.

As I wait, I sit atop a use-polished log that someone had dragged up for a seat at the edge of the landing. Behind me, sweet gum, overcap oak, and bald cypress stand tall where the marshy floodplain meets the River of Ducks. A great white heron wades in the pool and seems to ignore the racket made by the chirring insects and the endless birdsong. In the distance the tat-tat-tat-ta-tat of an ivory-billed woodpecker adds its own cadence.

I watch the brown waters of the River of Ducks, irritated by the roiling, sucking, swirling patterns that form and shift continuously on the surface. That's the thing about rivers. They're always so active. Moving, churning. Never still. It's exhausting.

And that's when a large twenty-man war canoe rounds the bend downriver and just above the confluence. I watch the lines of paddlers as they push the V-bowed craft up along the south bank, where the current is weakest. The River of Ducks is slow here in the confluence. They make good time.

One of the locals strolls down, meets the craft, and pulls it ashore as the paddlers in the bow leap out to slosh their way to shore. "Where from?" he asks.

"Cahokia!" the man in the rear calls cheerfully. "We have hides. Bison, tanned antelope, large deer hides. All from the Plains and distant Shining Mountains. Traded down the Northwestern River from upper river people."

"We'll Trade," the local tells him.

At the arrival, Fire Light and a couple others mosey over.

"Of course," the steersman chirps back, rising and stepping out with the others as they all struggle to pull the heavy vessel up onto the sand.

"So, you're Deer Clan?" the local notes, seeing the Clan symbol on the bow.

The steersman cranes to follow the local's pointing finger. "Oh, that. No. Snapping Turtle Clan, actually." He is grinning from ear to ear. "We, uh, Traded for the canoe. And it was just at the right time. You might say it sort of floated into our laps."

At this I rise, stroll over, and cross my arms. The steersman and his paddlers, mostly men with six women thrown in, are all dressed in Earth Clan's garb, some with Snapping Turtle tattoos, others with Deer Clan, and a single Falcon Clan tattoo on one of the women's faces. They give me a curious look, fixing on the burn scar that mars the left side of my face. Then they notice the Four Winds tattoo on my right and I can see the change in attitude. Two of the women touch their foreheads.

Ah! I am back in civilization.

"What news from Cahokia?" I ask. "We've been upriver. Haven't heard anything since the departure of the expedition."

"Hard times," the steersman tells me, his eyes avoiding mine. "The Houses are in conflict. When we left, Lord Keeper Spotted Wrist had three squadrons and was going to march on Evening Star House."

One of the women adds, "Until someone burned down the River House Palace and in the confusion pushed all the canoes he'd Traded for into the river one night."

I watch several of them glance at the Deer Clan canoe. The others share knowing smiles, as though sharing an amused thought.

There is a story there, but I'm not sure it matters. What does matter is Columella.

"And what of the attack?" I ask. "Do you think Columella survives as Matron?"

"We heard it was hundreds of canoes that were set adrift that night," one of the Deer Clan men tells me. "Columella had her squadrons called up as it was. Last we heard, she was fortifying Evening Star Town. Spotted Wrist sent an entire squadron downriver searching for canoes." He barely hides a smile. "He's not finding many."

"And what about Morning Star?" I ask the question that burns under my scalp.

"According to the stories, he has remained in his palace since Spotted Wrist took the city," the Falcon Clan woman answers. "North Star House was aligned with Horned Serpent House; River House was in chaos after their eternal fire was put out and the palace burned. And Morning Star House . . . well, no one knows what's happening there."

"So, the city was in chaos when you left?"

"Well, not exactly. Mostly it was just the high and mighty . . . um, well, the Houses, you know? Most of us, we just go on with our lives. And then, this opportunity happens."

"And we have a warehouse full of hides that a cousin has just brought down-river from the high plains," one of the men tells me.

"So, it seemed like a good time to go Trading," another finishes.

I reel at the implications.

"What of Wind and Blue Heron?" I ask.

One of the men shrugs. "Tonka'tzi Wind, last we heard, she's sort of Spotted Wrist's prisoner. Some say it's only until Green Chunkey takes her place. And Lady Blue Heron? Spotted Wrist burned her to death in her palace one night."

Blue Heron is dead? The Four Winds Clan clawing at each other's throats? Morning Star unseen?

The sensation is as if the earth shifts and slides beneath my feet. I turn to Fire Light and order, "Go. Find that worm-riddled fool, Canebrake. Tell him we're leaving. Now. And if he's not back within a finger of time, we're taking Trout *and leaving him behind."*

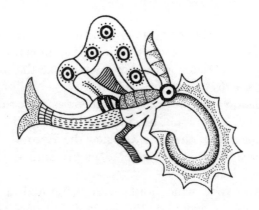

Fifty

The feast that night was a rather somber affair. A Caddo delegation from Yellow Star had been received with great ceremony. Black drink had been prepared and gifts bestowed by both sides.

As Four Winds Clan Matron, Rising Flame had been seated in her usual place of honor just to Morning Star's right and in line with the eternal fire where it crackled and spat sparks. And for once, given the rain outside, the warmth was appreciated.

The feast was to welcome a high-ranking Caddo *kadadokies*, or subchief, who had just arrived at Cahokia. His name was Red Bat, and he was the personal representative of the *kadohadacho*—the supreme chief at Yellow Star Town, the Caddo capital. Accompanying him in the Caddo embassy were ten men and six women. In addition, the usual Cahokian nobility filled the room, packed closely as more of the lower-ranked Earth Clans chiefs and matrons crowded in to avoid the rain and gusty winds outside. The sleeping benches surrounding the walls were also lined, shoulder-to-shoulder, with various Four Winds nobles.

Outside of Morning Star's traditional separation from the others by the eternal fire, the only bare space remaining on the floor was around Spotted Wrist and his little cluster of seated warriors. They didn't just serve as protection, they provided a barrier that set him apart from the rest. A knot of isolation. A thorny island in the midst of Cahokian majesty. It seemed that no one wanted to be anywhere in his vicinity.

Rising Flame considered Spotted Wrist as she watched the interplay in the room. The Clan Keeper, resplendent in a spoonbill-feather cape, looked irritable at times, only to retreat into an expression of distaste that in turn faded to a knowing smile; he seemed to be completely aware, proud in fact, of the wary and often resentful stares he was getting from the Earth Clans nobles. The way they looked at him reminded her of the stories told by the Haudenosaunee up north: like the man might have had poisonous snakes in his hair.

Even the Caddo—despite their treatment as honored guests—were aware. While they'd no doubt been briefed on the political situation by their local ambassador, they, too, treated the Hero of the North with a careful reserve. Polite, they offered empty smiles, their dark eyes guarded.

But then, who knew what stories were being told up and down the river? That Cahokia wavered on the verge of civil war? That the Keeper would have invaded Evening Star Town? And talk of the lost canoes had probably reached the Gulf by now—if not some of the canoes themselves.

The irony wasn't lost on Rising Flame. Her Clan Keeper was supposed to be the one who would report such information to her. Instead, she learned more from her conversations with the Earth Clans chiefs and *Tonka'tzi* Wind than she did from the man in charge of collecting such intelligence. Rather than gathering the news, he was at the center of it.

Along the side wall, Five Fists and his honor guard stood at perfect attention, firelight reflecting off their polished wood and leather armor. And behind them crouched the line of old Mallard's recorders with their beads and strings, the messengers with their staffs, and servants, all waiting for the next command.

Morning Star, dressed immaculately, reclined on his panther hides atop the dais. His hair was done up in a severe bun that supported his crescent-shaped, arrow-studded headdress; the living god's face had been painted white with black forked-eye designs. The familiar shell maskettes covered his ears. His beautiful Itza cloak hung from his shoulders, the white apron with its point dropping between his knees.

Reading Morning Star's expression—never an easy task—was even harder tonight. Rising Flame had made a study, tracking where the living god kept his focus, trying to see the nuances of his expression through the thick paint. If she'd picked up on anything, it was the occasional tightening of the lips and eyes, the sort of pinched expression usually associated with a sudden pain. The expression always seemed to be accompanied by a tensing of his too-thin body, the knotting of his muscles.

Mostly the living god kept his gaze focused on Spotted Wrist; his half-lidded eyes hinted of something dark and brooding.

While four young women Danced to flute music in a line immediately before the Caddo, Rising Flame caught movement at the corner of her eye; the Red Wing slave woman, White Rain, entered through the open double doors. She removed a bark rain hat and slipped a soaked cloak from her shoulders, making sure not to drip on any of the seated nobility as she scanned the room.

Meeting Rising Flame's eyes, she nodded, touched her forehead in respect, and uttering apologies, carefully picked her way across the floor. At Rising Flame's side, she dropped to her knees, head bowed.

Rising Flame noted that Lady Sun Wing watched intently, whispering as she stroked the Tortoise Bundle in her lap with thin fingers.

"Matron," she whispered, "forgive me. My master sends me with news."

"You serve *Tonka'tzi* Wind these days, don't you?"

"Yes, Clan Matron," the Red Wing woman affirmed, barely above a whisper, eyes still averted. "I'm to tell you that the *tonka'tzi* has just been informed that Matron Robin Wing and Lady Feather Worn of Horned Serpent House are dead. The story will be circulated that they both offered themselves as sacrifices to the Sky World as appeasement to Power for the extinguishing of the Sacred Fire. After four days of mourning, Lady Snow Frond, Green Chunkey's oldest daughter, will be named Matron."

"Offered themselves as sacrifices?" Rising Flame wondered as she propped her chin on her fist. "Really?"

"I only report what the *tonka'tzi*—"

"Yes, yes. I understand." Rising Flame arched an eyebrow, aware that from across the room Spotted Wrist was watching the interchange with curious eyes. "How accurate does the *tonka'tzi* consider this information?"

"Very. She wouldn't have sent me here, to this place, at this time, if she had any doubts. She thought you should know as soon as possible."

"Fascinating," Rising Flame mused as she watched the Dancers step and pirouette before the Caddo embassy. "It would seem that High Chief Green Chunkey considers his position to be somewhat tenuous. Somehow, I imagine that Clan Matron Robin Wing and Lady Feather Worn—totally unaware of their magnanimity—discovered their devotion to piety by complete surprise. Even as their traumatized souls are rising to the Road of the Dead, they must be dazed and shocked not only to discover they're dead, but that they 'chose' to be sacrificed."

White Rain's hooded gaze spoke eloquently enough. Wind must have said something similar.

But what did this mean?

Avoiding Spotted Wrist's eyes, she still sensed his smoldering gaze as he watched from behind his small squad of warriors. Could feel his burning curiosity. White Rain was well known to him, Spotted Wrist having destroyed her lineage up at Red Wing Town. That White Rain had been Blue Heron's slave, and now served Wind, would just add to his pique.

"Anything else?" Rising Flame asked.

"No, Matron."

"Tell your master that I am most grateful, and if she should happen across any additional such discoveries, I will be additionally grateful. You may go."

"Yes, Matron."

As White Rain stood, Spotted Wrist leaned over to Cut Weasel, pointing at the slave woman, whispering something. The squadron first was already rising to his feet and began picking his way through the crowd on the way to the door.

"White Rain?" Rising Flame called.

The young woman turned, retraced her steps to crouch down, gaze expectant.

"One moment." Rising Flame beckoned to one of the messengers crouched along the wall.

The young man slipped past Five Fists' honor guard, bent down, his staff of office clutched in his hands. "Yes, Clan Matron?"

"I need you to escort this woman to the Great Sky Wind. She is carrying a private communication between the Four Winds Clan Matron and the *tonka'tzi*. You are authorized to recruit five warriors from the guard outside to accompany you and ensure that no one, I mean *no one*, interferes with her safe delivery to *Tonka'tzi* Wind. And, if they do, your warriors are authorized to take whatever steps necessary." She arched an eyebrow in emphasis. "Even if it means leaving some noble bleeding on the avenue. Understood?"

"Yes, Matron!" the messenger cried with a deep bow as he touched his forehead. To White Rain, he added, "If you will come with me?"

White Rain—her gaze now gone wary and frightened—swallowed hard. Then she meekly followed the messenger as he picked his way around the edge of the crowded room.

On the sleeping bench where she sat, Sun Wing had watched the exchange with an unusual intensity. Rising Flame thought she resembled a predator fixing on her victim.

Rising Flame returned her attention to the Dancers and studiously avoided Spotted Wrist's icy glare.

It might have been a finger of time later when the Dancers finished their performance. The room erupted in calls of approbation, the clapping of hands and stamping of feet. As the Dancers retired, the room broke into conversations, a sign that the evening was drawing to a close.

The Caddo delegation rose, giving the usual closing statements of high praise to Morning Star. Which in turn brought a reply as the living god rose to his feet. Was it her imagination, or did the living god look slightly stooped? His face thinner under the thick coating of face paint?

As the entire room stood, Cut Weasel came easing his way back through the crowd, wet, water dripping from his armor. A look of cold fury filled his face as he stepped close to Spotted Wrist. With corded jaw muscles and lightning behind his eyes, the man spoke curtly. As he did, the Keeper's hot gaze fixed on Rising Flame.

White Rain must have made it, for a moment later the messenger was back, looking half panicked. He still clutched his staff of office—the one that ensured that no one could question him on his business. He glanced her way, nodded, and then shot a meaningful look at Cut Weasel.

"Yes, yes," Rising Flame whispered to herself. "I am way ahead of you."

She kept her place by the fire, waiting as the Caddo filed out into the wet night, and then the others followed. Figured that Spotted Wrist would be stomping up, demanding to know what White Rain had been about. Probably would have, but for Morning Star appearing at her side.

She lowered her head, touching her forehead respectfully. "Yes, Lord?"

"I want you with me this night."

She blinked. "Lord?"

Morning Star, half a head taller than she, gave her a look that burned through her soul. His voice was somehow wounded as he said, "Once you would have raced to my bed. Are you so different now? Less interested in sharing the living god's blankets?"

A quiver ran down her spine, a curious reluctance tightening her stomach. "Of course not, Lord." She offered her arm, let him take it, and walked with him back through the doorway behind his dais and into his private quarters.

She could feel Spotted Wrist's angry gaze, hot on her back like glowing embers as he watched her go.

Fifty-one

Four lamps illuminated Morning Star's personal quarters; the floating wicks were burning low in the hickory oil bowls, casting shadows across the room. The gentle patter of rain on thatch, the musical sound of water cascading down into puddles as it drained from the roof could barely be heard through the thickly plastered wall.

Rising Flame lay propped on Morning Star's bed, her back padded by a thick roll of beaver hides, the hair soft and luxurious against her bare skin. Around her, the familiar room seemed to waver in the dim yellow light as bits of draft played with the flickers of flame.

Morning Star's ornate boxes, his rack of chunkey lances and stones, the holders for his numerous copper, feather, wood, and shell head-dresses, the weapons, and assorted textiles filled one wall. Fine blankets and his neatly folded clothing were stacked nearby, and feather, fur, and woven capes, along with the heavier cloaks, hung at the far end. She let her eyes play over the remarkable wooden carvings above the bed. No doubt about it but that she was in the most opulent room in the world.

She pulled a tangle of disheveled hair back, giving the man beside her a questioning look. Man? Or reincarnated god? Nothing about him had been godlike this night.

Morning Star propped himself in the corner of the bed, back supported by a wadding of wolf hides and stared fixedly into the distance. A frown lined his forehead. The facial paint had smudged, especially the tails of his black forked-eye makeup where they'd been smeared across the white.

Rising Flame suspected that her face had its own splotches from when he'd pressed his cheek against hers during their frantic coupling.

Something's wrong with him.

What had been a growing suspicion over the last couple of moons now felt like a certainty. And it wasn't just the emaciation of his once-toned body.

Who is he? Really?

The first time he had taken her to his bed she had been a wide-eyed girl in her teens. Awed to her bones, almost shivering with excitement—and not a little terrified—she'd crawled onto this same bed. She'd been dazzled by the entire experience. Thought herself possessed by the god. The most memorable coupling of her life.

Over the years, she'd shared his bed often enough. Especially leading up to the Four Winds conference when she was chosen Clan Matron. At the time, she'd thought she had played him well, made her case with logic as well as her willing body as she'd explained why a word from him would place her on the Matron's dais. Why her experience was better for Cahokia than any of the other Four Winds contenders.

Now she wondered. Who had been the player, and who had been the played?

The sex had always been good. Though never with that same tingling anticipation and explosive rapture as that first time. They had locked loins as a man and woman did when they enjoyed the act.

Tonight had been different. He'd frantically ripped the skirt from her hips. Torn out of his own breechcloth and apron in his hurry to get her on the bed. She'd barely settled on her back and raised her thighs before he was on her.

That first coupling had been hard. After he recovered, the second was frantic. And later, the third time was an act of desperation. She'd never joined with a man that way before. She wondered what possessed him.

Steeling herself, she asked, "Are you all right?"

His vacant gaze never shifted. "Do you know what eternity consists of? Ashes, Matron. Dust and ashes."

"I don't understand."

"Ashes are what is left when the joy, passion, and interest have been burned out of life. Ashes cling softly, coat you, stick to your skin with that gritty feel. Then, in the end, they blow away on the wind." A pause. "Just gone. Scattered. Never to be collected in the same place again."

His dull eyes shifted her way. For a long moment he studied her. "I don't know who I am. What I'm supposed to be."

"You are the living god."

He waved a hand around at the room. "All this? This is what godhood comes down to? I am Morning Star, hero of the Beginning Times. My Spirit is supposed to have descended from the Sky, from up there above the clouds, above the realm of the Thunderbirds. All of me that thrived up there in the heavens is missing. When I search my memory all I find is a dark and yawning hole."

He touched the side of his head. "That should all be here. I should be filled with images, memories, sights, sounds, and smells. They should possess me. Be part of me."

Rising Flame shifted, unsettled by such an admission, wondering what it meant. "Lord, whatever is bothering you—"

"It's all this." He waved his hand again. "This is who I was meant to be. And I've tried. I've believed, right down to my souls. I've filled myself with the images. I've lived the chunkey games with the giants. I've imagined every detail of bringing my dead father's head back to life and the journey I took when I carried it into the Sky World and hung it among the stars."

Why was he struggling so, as if desperate to make her believe?

"Lord, I don't pretend—"

"I do," he said softly, his gaze going vacant and distant again. "That's why I wanted you tonight."

"I don't understand."

"Oh, but you do." His laugh was bitter. "How's it feel? Being Clan Matron? You enjoy the constant company of friends? Relish being able to share the little worries? All those private thoughts? The nagging insecurities?"

"Of course not."

"Try being the living god."

She chewed her lips, then asked, "Is that why I'm here tonight? Why you took me so hard?"

His laughter carried no humor. "You are here because you amuse me."

She ground her teeth, hating the honesty in his voice.

"You actually believe that people are inherently interested in bettering their lives, making things work. You thought you could take all these pesky little covetous two-legged rodents and organize their chaos of a city into an orderly and efficient entity like you'd seen in the south."

"You make it sound like I was a fool." She tried to keep the acid from her voice.

His gaze narrowed. "A fool? You tell me. The last time you were in my bed, you outlined the steps you would take. With Spotted Wrist as Keeper, the Houses would be pacified. The old order would be swept away. The Houses would be given new leadership, smarter, cooperative. Like the Pacaha or the Natchez, a unified chiefdom with the living god at the top. Cahokia would become the world. Those chiefdoms you so admired in the south, they would slowly be absorbed into the majesty and grandeur. A northern version of the world the Itza described and just as thunderously glorious."

"If you didn't believe, why did you send Five Fists that day to ask that I be appointed Clan Matron?"

"Maybe I thought it would be entertaining." A flicker of a smile died on his lips.

"You find it funny?"

He sniffed, resettled on the bed. "I find it tragic." A pause. "For both of us."

Rising Flame glanced sidelong at him. Chunkey Boy? Why had that popped into her head? Looking at him, she saw nothing more than a naked young man. His body looked . . . yes, uncomfortably thin. The muscle was gone, his ribs plainly visible. He'd been losing weight, stomach slightly hollow before the rise of his hips. She had the uneasy feeling again. That something was very wrong. That she would be seeing him as only human? That he'd lost some inherent charisma, that godlike . . . what?

"What's the matter with you?" she demanded.

His gaze didn't shift when he said, "I'm tired, Matron. So very, very tired. I can't wait for this to be over."

"What does that mean?" Her heart skipped.

"Just . . . over." And with that he rolled onto his side, pulled a fabric blanket over his too-thin body, and closed his eyes.

Fifty-two

In the Dream, Night Shadow Star walked in the dark caverns of the Underworld. Her pace, along with the slight current pushing against her, caused her long black hair to trail out behind in a sinuous wave that rose, fell, and twirled like opaque smoke. Irregular walls of cracked limestone interbedded with shales created a rough-hewn look; the sides and ceiling were lined with knotted, twisted, and interlocked bunches of roots that made a perverted pattern across the angular stone. Here and there, patches of moss clinging to crevices and outcrops undulated with the current. The floor was sand that puffed up under her feet, the occasional crawfish darting away at her step. Mussels, in clumps, clung together in colonies.

Just ahead, a faint golden glow illuminated the end of the tunnel, and she stepped out into an oval-shaped cavern, its ceiling high overhead and mostly obscured by a mass of giant roots that had woven together into an impenetrable mass.

Even as she entered the chamber, the sand in the middle began to rise and flow, trailing away to the sides as a ridge-backed, humped shell emerged. Snapping Turtle was as big as a sweat lodge, moss-covered, and jagged. As she approached, the blocky head—large as the bow of a Trade canoe—with pointed nose and ragged sharp-jawed mouth, lifted from the cavern floor. Still trailing sand, it turned toward her. Huge round eyes the diameter of seed jars peered at her; the pupils in the weird starburst-pattered irises sent a shiver down her back as they fixed on her.

"Night Shadow Star," the beast rumbled in disgust. "The woman who couldn't. Piasa's endless mistake. Forever incapable of the simplest of tasks. You only needed to kill your brother, and all this would have ended. You kill the abomination, the Thunderbirds blast you, and the balance between Sky World and Underworld is reestablished." He opened his cave-like jaws and wiggled his wormlike tongue at her. "Step closer. Let me end all our pain."

She stopped, swallowed hard. "Lord, I will kill him. He's just hard to catch."

"He didn't seem to have much trouble catching you."

Her heart began thumping against her chest. The massive monster always terrified her. Especially since Snapping Turtle would have devoured her in an instant—and not to be reborn as she had been after Piasa tore her to pieces and swallowed them down into blackness and oblivion.

She said, "Lord, Piasa isn't the only Spirit Power with a hand in this. As you so clearly note, the Thunderbirds are playing their part, seeking to maneuver their tool in place as Piasa plays his. Neither side wants the other to win, though why Sky Power would choose, as you say, an abomination like my brother, I do not understand."

"Then you are as dim and useless as a lump of wet charcoal." He uttered that last with contempt. "A tool is just that. Do you care if the handle on your war club comes from a diseased tree? Or is the only thing that matters is that the grain be strong so it does not break when you smack it into an enemy's head?"

"Given that I know Walking Smoke to be rotten and diseased to the core, I'd say he can only be used sparingly. And, had Power not intervened, I would have killed him that night in Joara."

"Had Power not intervened? Your story shifts like the sands beneath me." He pushed a clawed front foot out, a wave of sand and silt rolling across the floor to tickle and settle over Night Shadow Star's feet.

"I gave my word to Piasa," she insisted. "I will find him. My Lord tells me that Power has shifted. That I must face him in Cahokia."

Snapping Turtle blinked his large round eyes, snapped his jaws for emphasis. "There, you will fail. Again."

She crossed her arms in defiance. "I gave my word."

"As you did when you chose Cahokia over the slave? And yet you crawl under the blankets with him at every chance."

"That does not change my promise to Piasa. I've made my bargain."

"Have you?" Snapping Turtle filled the words with mockery. "Or will you change 'your bargain' again? Hmm? I say you will. I say you don't have the strength to do what you once promised. When the moment comes, you will fail us. Choose your flighty and emotional heart over your word. Give up your precious city, Piasa, and betray Power. All for a man."

"I will not—"

"Oh, yes. I know you too well. And after you do, I will see you here.

In the depths and the darkness. It will be . . . let's say . . . a fitting end for failure."

Night Shadow Star blinked awake, her body shivering and damp with fear sweat. She shifted, set the blankets aside, and slipped away from Fire Cat's sleeping body. To one side, the fire had burned down to low coals. The surrounding sweet gum, oak, and maple loomed dark and ominous against the night sky.

Another wave of shivers played through her, her heart hammering.

As she stared up at the cloud-dotted stars, she told herself, "It's all right. It was only a Dream. I'm here, on the river."

Walking down from the camp they'd made up in the tree line, she felt the night breeze as it drifted down the Tenasee. Alive with the scents of water, mud, vegetation, and late summer flowers, it filled her with a sense of life. Of fertility and hope.

Across the night-silvered water, she could see the dark silhouettes of the floodplain forest, tall treetops humped and rounded against the fainter darkness of the upland forests.

Frogs, crickets, and night birds serenaded her with their disjointed songs.

Rubbing her hands down the backs of her arms, she tried to shake the images from the Dream.

Blood and spit, but she need only close her eyes, and she was back in the Underworld, feeling Snapping Turtle's disdain and contempt. The Spirit Beast had always hated her.

He says I will fail.

Staring up at the patterns of stars, she could see Horned Serpent's constellation in the south where it hung low over the horizon. The great winged and antlered serpent flew up from the Underworld to take his position in the summer sky, guarding the southern entrance to the Road of the Dead.

Now, his tenure was almost over, the coming of equinox marking his descent back into the Underworld.

Otherwise, he, too, might have been there adding his condescension to Snapping Turtle's.

Again that screwbean sensation of fear ran down her back.

"What do they think is going to happen in Cahokia?" she whispered to herself. "I've sworn to kill Walking Smoke. I'll do it before we get there if we can catch up with him."

Or would she?

For a long time, she looked out at the river, heard the soft lapping as it rose and fell on the sand where they'd pulled *Red Reed* up for the night. A fish splashed somewhere in the darkness.

The knowledge that every time she'd believed she had him in the past, every time she'd been on the verge of triumph, something had whisked Walking Smoke out from under her.

What would be different this time? Walking Smoke would have the Thunderbirds to back him.

"The Thunderbirds saved him that time in the Father Water." She frowned. What was it that Sun Wing had said that day as she snugged the Tortoise Bundle to her chest? Something about the lightning saved him, but in the end it had to take him back?

"No," she whispered, the unease still curdling in her gut. "I remember. 'It is up to you. The lightning saved him. You must entice it to take him back.'"

"Lady?" Fire Cat's voice interrupted her thoughts as he stepped out of the trees behind her. "Your sleep is troubled?"

"Spirit Dream. In the Underworld." She turned, stepped into his strong arms. "Snapping Turtle told me that I am going to fail. And when I do, he will be the one to devour my souls in the Underworld." A sense of futility filled her. "Which he thinks is a fitting end to my incompetence."

"What about Piasa? He's your master."

She looked up, meeting his eyes, like holes in the night mask of his face. "If I fail again? My Lord and master may simply wash his hands of me. Turn me loose to whatever fate I might deserve."

"More like wash his talons of you." Fire Cat let his hands stroke her back in reassurance. "We'll catch Walking Smoke, Lady. This time we know where he's going. We know what he's after. And we'll be together, with me at your back when that final moment comes."

She hugged him tighter, as if she could press him inside, stuff him in close to her heart and make this man she loved part of her soul.

"Husband?" she whispered uncertainly, "I don't know what the price will be. It may . . . I mean . . ."

"Shhh!" he soothed her. "Whatever it is, we'll see it through."

"You promise?"

"On my honor as a Red Wing. We've beaten the Itza, conquered the Underworld, and but for a bit of bad luck, you would have already killed the Lightning Witch and we'd be on our way to that farmstead we've been promising ourselves."

It would have been so comforting to let herself believe.

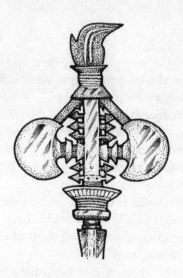

Fifty-three

The man named Mud Foot stood before the fire in Spotted Wrist's palace. The hour was late, the interruption inconvenient. The fellow certainly wasn't much to look at. Average height, skinny build, some kind of poorly rendered tattoos on his hollow cheeks. They might have been spiders or maybe just badly drawn starbursts. To Spotted Wrist's eyes, Mud Foot wasn't much of a specimen when it came to being a man, given his sunken chest and bulging gut with its distended navel.

Either that or the man's belly was just cram-packed with intestinal worms. Spotted Wrist figured he didn't need to know.

Moon Lance—squadron second for Flying Squirrel's North Star Squadron—with Mud Foot in tow, along with two warriors for escort, had arrived just as Spotted Wrist headed to bed. According to Moon Lance, the obsequious individual had information to sell. That is, he would if the Trade was right. And he wanted a lot.

Spotted Wrist leaned back on his litter as he studied the skinny specimen who stood on the other side of the fire. Really? This . . . creature thought his information was worth a couple of plates of beaten copper? Or an engraved whelk-shell drinking cup? Or a skein of cottonwood-down lace?

"You have a pretty high opinion of yourself," Spotted Wrist told the man. "Squadron First Flying Squirrel sent along his own report. You're known as a thief who preys upon unwary Traders at the canoe landing. You broker deals with starving dirt farmers when they're at their lowest. You'll buy their daughters for a sack of moldy corn, and then you sell the girls to Traders for a whole lot more. That is when you're not Trading them for a night in the robes. It seems that people really don't speak highly of you in River City, or anywhere else along the canoe landing."

Scrawny Mud Foot made a face; then he reached up and scratched vigorously at the side of his head, a louse or flea possibly the root of his discomfort. "Well, Keeper. Um, I can call you Keeper, yes?"

"Keeper will be fine." Spotted Wrist spoke without inflection.

That brought a weak smile to Mud Foot's thin lips. "Well, Keeper, I know people. And not just that riffraff that preys on the Traders down at the landing, but real people."

"Real people?" Spotted Wrist cocked an eyebrow, wondering just where the difference might lie when it came to the unreal people in Mud Foot's life.

"You know. Like the high chief. Him and me, we was thick as pitch pine back in the day."

"You mean War Duck?"

"Why, of course. See, the high chief, he's good to those of us as serves him up a portion of the take."

"I don't follow. What's the take?" He glanced at Moon Lance, who shrugged his ignorance.

"You know, what's skimmed off the Trade. So, like you was mentioning, let's say I sell three girls to some Pacaha for six of those head pots they make downriver. I send one of those pots off to War Duck and Matron Round Pot, and they don't come looking should, say, some Tunica Trader show up at their fire hollering that someone made off with a couple of sacks of yaupon or the like."

Mud Foot cast a knowing look from under lowered lids. "You catch my drift there, Keeper?"

"He lets you steal."

"Well, I wouldn't put it quite that way, more it's a matter of redirecting Trade without all the haggling and—"

"Get on with it!" Spotted Wrist snapped. "And if this is not important, I swear you'll—"

"You had a whole mess of canoes, uh, shall we say, redirected off the beach a couple of moons back. Canoes that are gone for good. And I'd bet you'd like to know who was behind that."

"I know. Columella and her little dwarf."

"Oh, to be sure." Mud Foot now seemed to find a bit of backbone, for he stiffened and crossed his arms over his sunken chest. "He had help. On this side of the river. Word was that Evening Star raiders set those warehouses on fire, lured your warriors into fighting with old Broken Stone's. That was a ploy, what we in the game call a sleight. Made to misdirect the gullible into looking one way while we make off with the Trade in the other."

Spotted Wrist's heart began to quicken, and he leaned forward, casting a questioning glance at Moon Lance.

The second arched an eyebrow, saying, "He said he'd only tell you, Keeper. The squadron first thought it was worth the time."

"And who was the help that night, the one who directed the sleight?" Spotted Wrist let the anger in his breast stir.

"Oh, the dwarf and War Duck plotted it." Mud Foot gave Spotted Wrist an oily smile. "But they did it in Crazy Frog's warehouse. And Blue Heron and Seven Skull Shield was in on it. And the person who burned the River House palace that night? Someone who was singing and had a big dog with him? That was Seven Skull Shield, on my honor. And all them other fires? Some of that was War Duck and some of his people. But the others? They was all Crazy Frog's agents who set them."

"Who's Crazy Frog?" Spotted Wrist demanded.

"Part-time Trader," Moon Lance told him. "Bets on chunkey games, or he did back when they were still being played on the River House courts. He's got a big house, bunch of wives, and the stories are that he's a rich man, can get you any kind of Trade you want."

Mud Foot added, "After War Duck, he's the most powerful man in River City. He can get you anything . . . for a price. Used to be he was one of old Blue Heron's biggest spies."

"Then why haven't I ever heard of him?"

"Because, Keeper, there's two Cahokias. The one the Four Winds runs, and the one people like Crazy Frog and me run. We're like the mice, out of sight, scurrying under the benches when you're not looking. Those of us? We nip a bite out of the granaries while the high and mighty are busy with other things." He smiled. "And, of all of us, Crazy Frog is the lord rat, the one who gains the most. Him and his five wives and his chunkey players and his warehouse full of Trade."

"You said that Seven Skull Shield and Blue Heron were involved. Do you know where they're hiding?"

"No, but I know how you can find them. I know all about where they go, who they see. I can give you those names. And when you have those people, they'll give you Seven Skull Shield and Blue Heron. Crazy Frog will give you War Duck and even old Round Pot herself."

"What do you expect in return?"

"Whatever's in Crazy Frog's warehouse after you haul him off. And maybe his wives and kids. Old Mother Otter, she's not worth much, but I can make good Trade out of them younger women, and I can Trade the children for a small fortune."

Spotted Wrist leaned forward, narrowing an eye. "I've got a counter-offer: You give me the names. In return, I'll give you your life . . . and the women and kids to sell into slavery."

"But the Trade in Crazy Frog's—"

"I suggest you take it," Spotted Wrist told him. "If you don't, I'll still get the names. Of course, you'll scream them while you're hanging in a square. Especially after one of my warriors holds a torch under your shaft and balls." Spotted Wrist cocked his head. "I'm told the smell of the burning hair down there is as upsetting as the pain."

Mud Foot swallowed hard, tried to back up a step, but Moon Lance's hard hand slammed into his shoulder.

"The names?" Spotted Wrist asked mildly.

Mud Foot licked his lips, glanced warily around the Keeper's palace, as if in frantic hope of a way out. Finding nothing but the surrounding warriors, he swallowed hard. "Well, there's Black Swallow to start with, but if you really want to get Seven Skull Shield, I'd start with Wooden Doll. She's the only woman he's ever loved. And then there's the cord makers . . ."

Spotted Wrist sat back, feeling vindicated. Mud Foot just kept talking.

There were a lot of names.

But he'd start with Crazy Frog and this Wooden Doll.

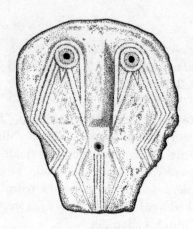

Fifty-four

I sit up in the damp darkness, hearing the sounds of the river, the lower volume of the frogs, and the occasional call of a night bird. We are camped on a gravel bar, the river lapping at the dark shore. The moon is waning and hangs just above the horizon, its glow outlining high cumulus clouds. Thick forest looms along the heights to our immediate south.

Something moves furtively down the beach from where Fire Light and I have made our camp. The high chief snores softly. Just at the edge of my hearing, I detect a whispered command, the tone terse. My questing fingers find the handle of Chief Fire Light's old war club. I lift it from his bedside.

I rise like smoke and creep along the water's edge, gravel crunching faintly under my moccasins.

In the slant of dim moonlight, I can see them. The warriors are loading Trout. One by one they wade out and deposit their rolled bedding, weapons, and gear. Against the moon's sheen on the water, they appear as black blots.

A paddle is shifted, knocks against the hull in a hollow clunk.

"Shhh!" someone whispers.

I smile.

Well, I really can't blame them.

I recognize Canebrake. He stands slightly apart as he always does. Good officer that he is, he oversees the loading and unloading of the canoe, making sure that all details are attended to.

I sigh softly to myself. Test the balance of Chief Fire Light's war club. It's longer than I would prefer, but the stone hafted at the far end was formed of black siltstone and ends in a sharp point.

I've known this was coming ever since the day at Rainbow Town when the reflected sun betrayed the black worm in Canebrake's head. Given the darkness,

I am but one more shadow among the other warriors. I adopt their posture, mimic their stealthy movements, and no one gives me a second glance.

Stepping up behind the squadron second, I brace myself. Judge the distance, and swing.

The sound of his skull being crushed makes a loud pop in the quiet night.

The rest of them freeze, stopped short as Canebrake's body thumps onto the packed gravel.

"The first one of you who moves, or tries to run," *I tell them,* "I will scorch your souls from your body. Pull them out and wind them around my finger."

"Squadron Second?" *Sun Arrow calls, wading back onto the shore, bending down.*

"Leave him!" *I bark.* "He has a black worm eating his brain. And he's not the only one. Or did you think that traveling with a witch came without risks?"

I can sense the rising panic, see the tensing of their bodies.

Now, to reel them in. "Assuming you've paid any attention to High Chief Fire Light, you know how you might end up. But that doesn't mean that you are condemned to suffer his fate. A witch can also reward those who serve him well. Make them rich, get them the woman of their Dreams, ensure that their enemies die in misery."

"I say we leave him," *someone mutters in the back.* "He killed the second. He'll kill all of us."

Rumbles of assent pass among them.

"Go ahead. Leave. You won't feel it until after the sun comes up," *I tell them all reasonably.* "It will start with a nervousness in the stomach. A faint suspicion of guilt and anxiety. You will begin looking over your shoulders, wondering if that twitch of a muscle is the black shadow worm eating at your blood and flesh. Or if that faint feeling of fatigue is my finger winding the souls out of your body. And the knotting in your stomach will get worse, your companions looking at you, trying not to tell you that you look pale, that you're losing color."

"I don't believe this!" *another cries.* "He killed the second. Pick up your war clubs! Let's put an end to this!"

"Oh, that would indeed be smart!" *I cry and do a little Dance.* "Kill the witch's body! Allow his souls to float free, to surround you, to filter in through your nostrils, slip past your lips to be swallowed down into your bodies. Feel those smoke-soft tendrils caress your skin as they wrap around you. Oh, please. Do that. Only then will you be completely and totally mine."

To make my point, I stride up to the closest, who, given the darkness, I think is Ten Man. "Go on," *I tell him.* "Strike me down."

Ten Man backs away, hands held wide. "This wasn't my idea."

"I didn't think it was." *I let the pause sink in.* "But now you have a choice: Do you want to arrive at Cahokia as rich men? Or do I start pulling wisps of your life souls from your bodies?"

From the way they stand, I can read indecision in their postures.

"And yes," I tell them, "a witch always keeps his promises . . . one way or the other."

I know what they will decide long before they do.

They believe every word I've told them. We beat it into them from the time they are children, you see. They start learning the stories as they suckle their mother's milk. Hear them at night when parents want them to sleep. Are warned about what witches will do to them if they are not good, or don't behave. From infancy to the grave, we tell our people what to believe about witches.

It makes my job so much easier.

Fifty-five

To Seven Skull Shield's ears one of the finest sounds in the world was the squeaking that the supporting leather straps made when two bodies were athletically joined on a bed. But an even finer sound was those deep-down moans that issued from a young woman's throat when her loins exploded in spasms of delight.

He was lying on his back, enjoying the view as Yellow Petal rocked her hips back and forth, her head back, the wealth of her thick black hair tumbling down past her animated buttocks to tickle the tops of his thighs. The sight of her arched body, the thrust of her nipples, and those wondrous sounds she made brought him to his own magical moment. His gasping moans mixed with hers.

She was panting when she lowered herself beside him, her callused hand on his chest, perspiration shining on her cheeks and the bridge of her delicate nose. Her large dark eyes studied him warily.

"What?" he asked.

"Why do I let you into my bed?"

"Well . . . is it because you find me irresistible, charming, and roguishly enchanting? Not to mention that Stone String has never taken you seriously. Like today. He's down at the canoe landing laughing and drinking tea with that bunch of Panther Clan relatives down from the Illini River country. Second cousins or some such, aren't they?"

She slapped her hand on his chest. "And no sooner does he amble off than here you are."

"I have this thing about timing."

She closed her eyes, flopped onto her back. "Blood and rot, but you do indeed. And you're just lucky that Amber Plant was able to take the boys on a moment's notice." One of her eyes opened to a slit. "Maybe you've noticed that little Toad has your face?"

"Poor little tyke, no one's as ugly as me."

"Tell me about it. Stone String isn't necessarily the most observant of men, but the day is coming. His sister, mother, and aunt have already noticed that the boy doesn't share his father's thin face, let alone that curved beak of a nose."

"So . . . you're saying . . . ?"

"Oh, don't worry. You're the last man I'd leave Stone String for. You're a roaming weasel, Seven Skull Shield. Wooden Doll was right about you all those years ago. No woman in her right mind would ever think she could make a proper husband out of you."

"But I am charming, roguish, and irresistible."

She was watching him carefully now. "You're going to end badly. I just have that feeling. As it is, I don't know how you've managed to stay ahead of the Keeper's warriors. Except that they're too busy trying to keep Three Fingers in charge here."

He sat up, swung his legs over the side of the bed, and stared down at where Farts lay napping on the mat floor. The big dog's paws were twitching, and as Seven Skull Shield watched, little yips issued from Farts' throat. Then the tail straightened; the sound of flatulence preceded a most remarkable stench.

"Piss in a pot." Yellow Petal pinched her nose and made a face. "What do you feed that dog? Corpses?"

"I think it was a half-cooked pot of mussels from behind Gray Mouse's arrow workshop. Something they threw out."

Yellow Petal used the blanket to fan fresh air into the room.

As the air cleared, Seven Skull Shield said, "Spotted Wrist is a bone-brained incompetent. The miracle is that he's still the Clan Keeper."

Yellow Petal sat up, her hair spilling down her back. "The miracle is that you're still wandering around the city." She took a deep breath after sniffing to be sure it was safe. "Do me a favor?"

"What's that?"

"Wander down to the canoe landing and find a Trader going any direction that is away from here. You're a strong man. Any Trader would be delighted to have your help, be he headed upstream or down. Just go. I don't want to spend the rest of my life looking at my boy and knowing his father died in a square."

"I've never seen the square that could keep me hanging for more than a day. Or was it a couple?"

"The reason you haven't seen it is they'll build it for you special." She pulled her hair back. He'd always loved her hair. "I'm serious, old friend. The net is going to be drawn closed around you before . . ."

The sound of warriors in armor could be heard, their feet pounding in unison.

Farts was immediately up, alert, head cocked. Odd that the dog had learned to recognize warriors as a threat.

They heard shouts after the warriors passed by.

"What are they doing back here in this part of town?" Seven Skull Shield wondered, reaching for his breechcloth. "We're behind the Warehouse district. All packed up with farmsteads and workshops. There's nothing for them here."

From somewhere close behind the house, a voice called, "I just heard. They surrounded Crazy Frog's house. Took all his wives and children. And there's more. Word is that War Duck and Round Pot were there. They're being marched off to the Great Plaza to hang in squares."

"Did they get Crazy Frog?" someone called back.

"No. He wasn't home. But it's just a matter of time."

Seven Skull Shield's heart might have been a stone in his chest.

"Go!" Yellow Petal snapped, dragging her skirt up past her hips and tying it. "If they've taken Crazy Frog and the High Chief, no one is safe anymore."

Seven Skull Shield pulled his old hunting shirt over his head and knotted the rope belt around his waist.

"Come on, dog," he told Farts. "Let's go see what's happening."

"Please," Yellow Petal pleaded as he stepped to the door and set it aside. "Find that canoe, get away from here!"

Seven Skull Shield was already trotting away, taking the winding back ways that would lead him to Wooden Doll's. If there was news, that's where it would be.

Fifty-six

Great White Wolf Village hadn't changed much. The name was still remarkably grandiose for the five bent-pole structures around a small plaza space sporting a couple of log-and-pestle mortars, four ramadas, a few elevated granaries, and a rudimentary charnel hut in the rear. Fire Cat was delighted that the people didn't remember them from the trip upriver in the spring.

As night fell, Fire Cat stood at the landing where *Red Reed* had been pulled up and staked in case the river rose in the night.

He stared across the roiling Tenasee, the water gently churning, its flat surface platinum in the reflected light from the high sunlit thunderheads off to the east. Their tops burned a bright orangish pink, the middles of the puffed clouds lavender trending to bruised blue-black where they were obscured by the tree-thick horizon behind the uplands.

Blood Talon came ambling down the bank, waving at the cloud of mosquitoes that seemed to appear out of nothing just at dusk. The squadron first stopped at Fire Cat's side, followed his gaze to the narrow neck of land still choked with driftwood and beached logs.

"Hard to believe," he told Fire Cat. "This entire trip, from the Fast Wide to here, it's like seeing my life run backward. Each town has its memories of who I was at that one moment in time. Canyon Town, White Chief Town, passing Black Bank Village where I was tortured, and then the spot where you capsized my canoe. Seeing where I humiliated Night Shadow Star at the Rainbow Town landing. And now here, where I first laid eyes on you."

"Quite a journey, Squadron First. But then, for whatever reason, we were chosen for remarkable things."

"I'm still struggling with that, War Leader." Blood Talon leaned his head back, staring up at the colorful clouds.

Fire Cat rubbed the back of his neck, squinted at the distance. "Had I remained war chief of Red Wing Town, I'd have eventually become high chief when Uncle died. I would have raised my children, taken care of my people, and lived my life. All the while I would have thought that I knew who I was, what kind of man I was. Had you asked, I would have told you I understood myself, what I believed, and what all my capabilities were as a man." He paused. Smiled. "And everything I told you would have been wrong."

"Indeed?" Blood Talon shifted, swatted at a mosquito willing to brave the puccoon-and-sassafras root unguent they'd smeared on their skin.

"Blood and rot, Squadron First, I've seen that world destroyed and another built in its place. Consider what's been done to me, and what I've done for myself. I'm still not entirely sure what or who I will be when this is all over, but I desperately wish it could be a simple farmer someplace out of the way. Just me and the woman I love." He gestured back at the village. "The aching irony of it is that these people have everything I want, with no idea of why they're living such a gift."

Blood Talon leaned his head back and sighed. "Power plays us, War Leader." He paused. "But it worries me. Tomorrow we're on the Mother Water. The day after, we'll be in the Father Water, headed for Cahokia. From the reports we've been hearing with each passing canoe, things are anything but settled there."

He shot Fire Cat a dark look. "And Winder and me? We hear just as well as you do. I mean, late at night, when Night Shadow Star is Dreaming."

"She's worried," Fire Cat agreed.

"We're not stupid," Blood Talon told him. "The lady is having Spirit Dreams. Mostly it's mumbles, but she's arguing with Piasa, and the Underwater Panther is slipping into her head more and more often."

"I know." Fire Cat watched a V of ducks winging up the river, their feathers rasping in the air. "She's afraid that there will be a price. That just killing Walking Smoke won't be enough."

"And she's not the only one, War Leader." Blood Talon took a deep breath. "You have nightmares of your own."

Fire Cat sighed. Blood and spit, what could a man do to control his Dreams? It didn't help that in nightmare after nightmare, Walking Smoke would rise from the center of leaping flames, his skin smoking, eyes burning. And each time he did, he was lifting Night Shadow Star by her long hair. Her precious body was savaged, torn, bleeding and abused. The expression on her face was slack in death, mouth gaping and bloody. But it was her grayed, half-slitted eyes, staring at him emptily, that brought whimpers to his lips.

"It's going to be bad, isn't it?" Blood Talon asked softly. "That's what the Power Dreams are telling both of you."

"It is," Fire Cat admitted, his heart pounding just at the admission of it. He took another deep breath. "I'm afraid, Squadron First. Frightened right down to my bones that I'm going to lose her. That there will be a terrible twist at the end of this."

"Want to turn south at the mouth of the Mother Water? Go see the Pacaha and the Tunica?"

"More than anything. So much so I'd give my soul."

"Winder and I, we'll back you."

Fire Cat nodded wistfully. "I know."

"But you won't turn south, will you?"

"No."

Blood Talon—taking a liberty he never had—laid a hand on Fire Cat's shoulder. "Winder and I, we'll still back you."

"I know." Fire Cat blinked as the first bat fluttered past.

"There will be death, and pain, and maybe defeat."

To which Blood Talon simply said, "I know."

Fifty-seven

As if the winds of fortune had changed direction, Spotted Wrist knew things were turning his way. The raid on Crazy Frog's lair had worked. He had War Duck and Round Pot crammed into his bear cage, the one that had once held Seven Skull Shield. The two of them barely had room to breathe. Good thing both the High Chief and the Matron were smaller than the thief had been.

Unfortunately, Crazy Frog—through some sort of foul-up—hadn't been home when Spotted Wrist's warriors came a-calling, but that was neither here nor there. The man's ability to cause mischief was at an end. Three Fingers' people were hunting high and low for him.

Not to mention the wealth, the unbelievable, remarkable, mind-boggling wealth that had been hidden in that ingenious warehouse. Squadron First Flying Squirrel had detailed half the squadron just to pack the whole of it up the Avenue of the Sun to Spotted Wrist's sparsely furnished palace. Just like that, he was now one of the richest men in Cahokia, maybe the richest after Morning Star.

He considered that as he climbed the Great Staircase. With Mud Foot's information, he'd been able to secure River House, and with it, control of the River City Mounds and the canoe landing.

The same with Horned Serpent House down south. What had seemed at the time a catastrophe had played right into his hands. If, as he suspected, that had been Columella's work, she'd handed him Horned Serpent House. Had effectively neutered Green Chunkey, his lineage, and any ability to use the Earth Clans under their control to hamper Spotted Wrist's authority.

Glancing over his shoulder, he could just make out the dark shape of the *tonka'tzi*'s palace. His warriors would be storming up the stairs any moment now.

Have a peaceful night, Tonka'tzi. *Your days of being an asset are over.*

It seemed that—Lady Sun Wing and her addled prophecies aside—the last woman had slipped through his fingers. Now he was tightening his fist around them. Including Rising Flame.

He hadn't had time to think it all through, but the obvious solution to the problem was that once Wind was disposed of, he could put either Wolverine or Slender Fox on the *tonka'tzi*'s high chair. It wasn't like Green Chunkey or River House could object. And who cared if Columella screamed her bloody head off? No one could hear her from way over on her side of the river.

Which left the problem of Morning Star to be dealt with next.

Time to seize the wolf by the nose, and he'd do it in the beast's own den. Today he'd effectively roll up the resistance in central Cahokia. With Morning Star isolated, the town was his to control. But it would have to be done fast, efficiently and quietly. Which meant with force.

Behind him trooped Cut Weasel and a full squad of his warriors. Twenty men in armor, all handpicked. Well, but for a few who were still out on missions, like Nettle Toe and his squad.

For all Spotted Wrist knew, they were on the way, with that paid woman in bonds. And, who knew, maybe they'd run down that pus-licking thief. Nettle Toe and his warriors had their own reasons to search out Seven Skull Shield.

The only uncertainty was whether the warriors accompanying Spotted Wrist would stand with him in the event Morning Star made a scene. These were some of his best and most loyal warriors, but how would they react if the living god pointed his finger at Spotted Wrist and ordered, "Take that traitor to the squares!"

That's when he saw movement above, heard the scuff of feet on the squared-log stairs. The dark forms descending the Great Staircase couldn't be anything but warriors. But why? What were they about in the night?

"Hold," Spotted Wrist called. "Who comes?"

"War Leader Five Fists and Morning Star's guard," came the reply from above. "Clan Keeper? Is that you?"

"It is." Spotted Wrist waited, let Five Fists descend to his step. "What's this about?"

"I could ask you the same," Five Fists replied, his raspy voice sounding irritated. "I'm ordered to make way for you. Morning Star told us to collect our kit and move to the Men's House. That you were not to be interfered with."

"He what?" Spotted Wrist struggled to make sense of it. "No one knew I was coming tonight."

"Morning Star did," Five Fists told him in a voice filled with resentment. "You make some deal? Are you pulling some trick, Keeper? Because if you are . . ."

"No trick." Spotted Wrist felt that prickle of unease he used to get when he knew something wasn't right and he was stepping into the enemy's trap. "Tell me, what were his exact words?"

"To stand down. To remove the guard to the Men's House until someone from his lineage brings us orders. When I protested, he told me to go." Five Fists pulled himself up in the darkness. "And now I find you and your warriors climbing the steps?"

Under his breath, Spotted Wrist wondered, "How could he have known I was coming?"

"He's the living god," Five Fists snapped. "But so help me, if this is some clever plot of yours that gets Morning Star harmed, I will personally hang your pus-dripping corpse in a square."

Spotted Wrist stiffened, heard his warriors shifting angrily behind him. To Five Fists, he said, "You have your orders, War Leader. I suggest you follow them." To his squadron, he called, "Stand aside. Let them pass."

That it was done without shoving, that none of the smoldering warriors on either side got into a name-calling match, was, in retrospect, a miracle. But Spotted Wrist was given the satisfaction of watching the last of Morning Star's guard vanish down the steps and into the darkness on the Council Terrace.

"How did Morning Star know I was coming?" Spotted Wrist asked himself again as he started back up the steps. That eerie sense of premonition continued to send shivers down his spine.

At the top of the Great Staircase, the gate was unguarded. Spotted Wrist shrugged at his squadron first and was reassured by the double lines of North Star Squadron warriors climbing the stairs below.

He ignored the World Tree Pole, though Cut Weasel and the warriors all bowed, touching their foreheads as they passed. That left him wondering. He'd always shown respect as he passed the pole. Tonight, refusing to do so sent thin shivers of nervous jitters down his back.

Power will back me, or it won't, he decided. So emboldened, he strode to the great double doors, with their carving of Morning Star ascending into the Sky World.

Spotted Wrist jerked his head toward the doors. Cut Weasel and his second, Buffalo Horn, muscled the portals aside.

At the head of his warriors, Spotted Wrist entered the Morning Star great room in a strut, his head back, holding his Keeper's staff of office before him.

The eternal fire had burned low. Men and women readied the sleeping benches for the night. The room went quiet, people gaping, stopped short and frozen as they folded blankets, lifted ceramic jugs, or were in the process of packing the boxes on the floor.

"Keep packing!" the call came from the rear.

Spotted Wrist looked to see the living god emerge from his personal quarters in the rear. Morning Star, still dressed in his finery, a split-cloud copper headdress atop his head, face painted white with black forked-eye designs, cloak, and apron, stepped out and walked to his litter atop the dais.

And then, to Spotted Wrist's surprise, Morning Star took a stand atop his litter, raising his arms and calling, "All of you! I want you to leave now. Take what you need for the next few days. Clans people, please return to your respective palaces. The recorders and messengers will reside in their appropriate Society Houses until further notice."

The shock was palpable.

"You have my orders," Morning Star told them. "Leave! Now! You will be told when I want you to return. The Keeper and I have business. Go on, be about it." And he waved a hand in a shooing motion.

By Piasa's balls, this made no sense.

Spotted Wrist felt that familiar stirring of acid in his stomach. He glanced at Cut Weasel, seeing the confusion behind the squadron first's eyes, caught the man's faint shrug. Well, he wasn't the only one.

"I'll go, too," Sun Wing said, slipping a cape over her shoulders before picking the Tortoise Bundle from her sleeping bench. Her wide eyes, half dreamy, contrasted with a happy smile. She walked up to Spotted Wrist, stared up into his face with a quizzical look. "He doesn't have a clue, does he?"

"What?" Spotted Wrist scowled down at her. "Lady, you're talking in riddles."

"Wasn't talking to you." Then her expression shifted the way it did when she was listening to someone. As if in reply, she said, "Wouldn't do any good. He can't hear the copper when he's right on top of it."

Spotted Wrist growled, "Thought you said you were leaving, Lady." He shot a wary glance at Morning Star, hoping he hadn't taken offense. No telling what the relationship was between them.

"Pity, actually," Sun Wing said offhandedly and walked off as if without a care in the world.

For long moments, confusion filled the room, people talking, sharing their unease, but unwilling to demand an explanation.

This was, after all, the living god. Morning Star's Spirit in the flesh.

People with packs and blankets began to file out of the room. They looked confused, dismayed, talking uneasily among themselves as they shot disbelieving glances in Morning Star's direction. They were as stunned as Spotted Wrist.

Cut Weasel, detailing various warriors, said, "Secure the palace. Five of you at the base of the Great Staircase, two at the Council House Gates, two at the palace gates. The rest to monitor the palace walls and bastions. No one gets in without the Keeper's permission."

When the last had left, Spotted Wrist pointed a finger at the double doors. Several of the warriors closed them, shutting out the night beyond.

"It's like you knew I was coming," Spotted Wrist said in amazement.

"Yes, it is." A sliver of a sad smile bent Morning Star's painted lips.

"Kind of you to avoid making a scene," Spotted Wrist told Morning Star, who now slumped on the dais. "This is only a change of administration, Lord. My people will see to your security from here on. Anything you wish will be their command. Any order will be immediately attended to."

As he looked closer, Spotted Wrist would have sworn the man winced, as if in pain and favoring his stomach. Gods, he really didn't look well. The thick paint made it difficult to see, but Morning Star's face had a hollow cast. Was it a trick of the dancing firelight, or were the man's cheeks and eyes sunken?

Then, to Spotted Wrist's surprise, the living god said, "I've been expecting you, Keeper."

"This isn't a surprise?"

Morning Star gave him a dull stare. "You will have no trouble from me. As it happens, your arrival actually comes as a relief."

"But all your retainers, the messengers and recorders?"

"Your people will have to attend to their duties, Keeper. You do understand that, don't you?"

"Of course, Lord." Spotted Wrist bowed his head, touching his forehead. Something about Morning Star bothered him. And it wasn't just that the man looked tired and pained. No, it was a smug sense of accomplishment and triumph.

"Thank you, then, for avoiding an unpleasant scene as your people were dismissed."

"Oh, the pleasure is all mine," Morning Star told him with deadly earnest. "And, as it happens, necessary."

The acid in Spotted Wrist's stomach began to burn.

Fifty-eight

Seven Skull Shield knew this part of River City Mounds better than any other section of Cahokia. Each nook and cranny was as familiar as the pattern of veins on the back of his hand. Now he hurried, almost at a run, dodging the latrines, winding around walls, creeping down the narrow passageways between the workshops, warehouses, and dwellings. Leaping small gardens, he called to familiar faces, slipped into a narrow crack between a potter's workshop and a dye-maker's, and dragged Farts out of the way as a gang of men labored through the labyrinth with a cedar log over their shoulders.

He pressed himself flat against a Duck Clan charnel house wall as an age-bent woman with a pile of sticks on her back taller than she was came waddling down the narrow alley. She gave him a toothless grin of appreciation, her time-wrinkled face cracking with the effort.

At the ancient weaver's dwelling next to Wooden Doll's, Seven Skull Shield found the old lady in her usual place outside. He made the hush gesture with a finger to his lips. The crone was sitting in the shade of her ramada, arthritic fingers plying the warp and weft in her rickety loom. Not that she made great fabrics, but her cloth was always serviceable. Ever since Seven Skull Shield and Flat Stone Pipe had used her house to spy on Horn Lance during the Itza excitement, he had made a habit of cultivating the old bat's goodwill. That he sort of succeeded—given her irascible nature—was one of the crowning successes of his life.

Now she scowled up at him, squinted to make sure who he was, and with a withered arm threw a rock at Farts, hissing, "Don't you let that creature near my box of yarns! Last time, he peed all over it. Soaked the yarn, and everything I wove smelled of piss!"

Farts, out of second nature, ducked the rock. The stone sailed across the yard, hit a decrepit brownware pot, and with a dull *pok!* cracked it down the side. The old woman used it to collect drinking water that ran off the eaves. Seven Skull Shield made a face as liquid began to leak from it.

Fortunately, the hag couldn't see that far these days.

"Just need a look," he told her. "Bring you Trade next time I'm by."

"Didn't you say that last time?" she demanded.

Farts—smart enough to stay out of range—waited while Seven Skull Shield slipped into the old woman's dark house, climbed onto her smelly bed, and, holding his nose, peered through the hole cut into the wattle-and-daub wall.

His heart sank. Through the hole he could see Wooden Doll's yard. One of Spotted Wrist's warriors stood outside the door. At the man's feet sat Whispering Dawn, a rope tied around her ankles. Another around her waist was knotted to the ramada pole. They had left her hands free so she could hold the baby. "One outside. How many inside?" Seven Skull Shield wondered quietly, a weight bearing down on his souls.

Oh, and he knew that warrior guarding Whispering Dawn. One of the Wolverine Squadron men Spotted Wrist had housed in his palace while Seven Skull Shield had been bound and contained in that pus-dripping bear cage.

Drilled Cane. Yes, that was the man's name. A Snapping Turtle Clan warrior from up north at Serpent Woman Town. No way Seven Skull Shield could forget that wide face or the way those fat lips bent into a smile; and the way the squat warrior had broken into weird-sounding giggles each time he smacked Seven Skull Shield in the balls with his war club or jammed the smoldering end of a stick against Seven Skull Shield's naked skin.

A chill, like a skein of ice, began to crystalize along Seven Skull Shield's spine. He hated that warrior. And the man's friends had Wooden Doll? Those men? Those thrice-accursed, brutal, soulless piss-licking human scum?

The howl began inside, rising to his lips by the time he reached the old woman's door. Across the yard, still out of range, Farts had his ears up. The brown-and-blue eyes read Seven Skull Shield's building rage. The Spirit dog shot to his feet, tail out straight.

The old woman kept a weathered pestle and log mortar off to the side. Seven Skull Shield barely heard her angry objection as he grabbed the pestle from its hollow, tested it. As long as his leg, it had been crafted of white ash, with a bulbous end for smashing corn in the mortar's basin. Weathered now, the wood cracked, it still made for a reasonable club.

By the time Seven Skull Shield rounded the side of the old weaver's house, he was at a run. Feet pounding, blood boiling, his vision narrowed. As if Drilled Cane's face—that smug, wide, cruel face—were the entire world.

The warrior was still looking down, telling the cowering Whispering Dawn, "Oh, your time will come, woman. You won't hang in a square. Not like Wooden Doll. Might keep you and that warm sheath of yours all to my . . ." He looked up. His eyes went wide.

As fast as he was moving, Seven Skull Shield's momentum added to the power of his swing.

Drilled Cane got an arm up. Was filling his lungs to scream when the pestle smashed through his guard, caught him square across the face. At the impact, the warrior's head made a sound like a dropped melon, accompanied by the crack of the pestle handle as the wood snapped from the impact.

When Drilled Cane hit the ground, his entire body might have been loose meat. He didn't even bounce.

Whispering Dawn gaped, mouth open, eyes wide. "You?" she whispered.

"How many in there?" Seven Skull Shield asked as Farts trotted up; after sniffing at Drilled Cane's comatose body, the dog lifted his leg to squirt urine on the man's thigh.

"Three," Whispering Dawn told him. "Gods, Skull. Get me away from here."

"Yeah," he said hoarsely.

Three of them. In there. With Wooden Doll. He knew who they'd be. The four of them always ran together. Part of a squad. Their leader, the squadron third, was called Nettle Toe. A real piece of work. He was the one who'd always tried to poke Seven Skull Shield's eyes out. Had left the mostly healed scar just over Seven Skull Shield's right eyebrow.

Seven Skull Shield picked up the war club from where it had fallen from Drilled Cane's limp fingers. Didn't matter if they killed him. No one hurt his Wooden Doll. Not while he was alive. Not when he could save her.

Then he eased the door back, and stepped inside.

Fifty-nine

The worst part for Wooden Doll wasn't the violation; it was being helpless to stop it. Didn't matter that she had her deer bone stiletto hidden in the folds of the buffalo robe. There were three of them. As soon as one groaned, stiffened, and went limp atop her, he was pulled off, and another climbed onto her bed and between her legs. She'd feel his body slam down onto hers. His hard shaft would drive into her. Then he'd be at it.

The noises they uttered, as if each mindless thrust had to be accompanied by a huffing explosion of breath. As if each jabbing of their shafts was some sort of hard labor. And when they ejaculated the cries they made reminded her of coyotes.

It's not about rape. It's theater.

Wooden Doll kept her eyes averted, endured while the squadron third finished with a gasping howl and dropped limp. Dead weight pushing her down into the blankets.

"My turn," Long Cast cried.

Nettle Toe exhaled as if he'd been drained, chuckled to himself, and rolled off her.

Long Cast practically launched himself atop her, heedless of how he hammered himself onto her body.

Oh, she knew this one. The irony of the name Long Cast. He was the one with the short peg, and he was quick. But he'd probably make it appear to the others that he was still at it long after he'd spent his load and gone soft.

She bit her knuckle as Long Shaft started banging his short shaft into her. Stared at the fine beaver fur beside her cheek. Tried to ignore the grunting and squealing next to her ear.

Her first clue anything had changed was the sudden *smack*. Then a guttural croaking, followed by a howl. A weird sort of ululating shriek, high pitched, like that torn from a dying animal's agonized lungs.

Long Cast went rigid atop her body, jerked his head away from her ear. Then he was scrambling off her.

A scream was followed by a beast's snarling, growling, and a heavy thump as bodies hit the floor.

Wooden Doll pulled herself up, clutching for a blanket to cover herself. At first glance the melee made no sense.

Two men were locked in combat at the side of her fire. Nettle Toe and . . . no. Impossible! The maddened shrieking was Seven Skull Shield's as he clawed and pounded at Nettle Toe.

On the floor, Black Beak was wrestling with a big brindle dog that . . .

Gods, it was Farts, and from the savaging the dog was giving the man, this was anything but wrestling. Black Beak kept screaming, the sounds piteous as the furiously snarling Farts caught the man's warding arm, bit down with those huge jaws. The sound of snapping bones could be heard over Black Beak's lung-bursting scream.

"Hurt her?" Seven Skull Shield howled where he battled by the fire. *"Gonna beat you! Stomp your liver!"*

Nettle Toe staggered back, both hands locked on Skull's thick wrists where the thief's big hands were choking the squadron third.

"Gonna rip your balls off, you shit foul piss maggot! Dung! Worm gut pus . . . suck mud . . ."

Nettle Toe broke Seven Skull Shield's hold, back-heeled him, and the two went tumbling to the floor amid Seven Skull Shield's squealing rage and Farts' hideous growling.

To one side, Long Cast was screaming on his own as he rifled through his discarded clothing, found his war club, and straightened. His first blow was aimed at the dog, and glanced off the raging animal's ribs.

Farts let out a pained yip, danced sideways from where he'd been mangling the shrieking Black Beak's face.

"Got you now," Long Cast told the dog. As he raised the club, Wooden Doll scrambled across her bed, ripped up a wolf hide, and tossed it over the warrior's head. Blinded, Long Cast staggered, clawing at the hide.

Which gave Wooden Doll just enough time. She reached down between the buffalo hides, felt through the hair, and gripped her deer bone stiletto.

She caught the barest glance of Seven Skull Shield jerking his head forward with all his might, driving his forehead into Nettle Toe's face with a loud crunch. The warrior's head popped back in a spray of blood, and he tried to twist away.

Long Cast managed to tear the wolf hide from his head, gave the thing an incredulous look, as if wondering where it had come from.

By then Wooden Doll was beside him, smiling.

Long Cast gave her a puzzled look, then gaped as Farts leapt full onto the still-squealing Black Beak's chest.

Wooden Doll drove the stiletto into the warrior's side. She went in low, just under the ribs, angling the length of the weapon up through the right lung. Actually felt it quiver with each beat as it pierced the man's heart.

Long Cast froze, rose on his tiptoe, as if he could rise above the pain. So Wooden Doll pulled her stiletto out and drove it into him again, and again.

"Sort of like what you did to me, don't you think?" she asked him. "But I don't have to grunt with each thrust, and mine doesn't go soft like yours after it's finished."

Long Cast turned, his mouth open, disbelieving eyes on hers. Got a hand on her left wrist. Squeezed, as if that would stop her right as she stepped close, evaded his other hand, and drove her stiletto under the breastbone and into his heart one last time.

She watched his eyes grow dull, saw the consciousness fade. And then he was falling. Landed partially atop Farts, who turned loose of Black Beak's throat, jerked sideways, and bit Long Cast for good measure.

Which left only the hideous screaming at the fire.

"*You fly shit maggot puke! Reach down your throat . . . rip your lungs! You shit puke vomit pus. Think you can rape my woman? I'll eat your tongue. Stomp your maggot shaft. Pop your eyes!*"

As he screamed, Seven Skull Shield was perched full on Nettle Toe's back. He had hold of the squadron third by the ears and hair. With all his weight, he was jamming the warrior's face down into the glowing coals in the fire pit. The squadron third gave one last futile kick, which shattered one of Wooden Doll's favorite lustrous black Four Winds Soul pots.

She winced, made a face at the smell of burning human hair and flesh.

Then she stepped over, laid a hand on the still howling Seven Skull Shield's shoulder.

"It's all right, Skull," she told him. "You can only make him so dead, and I think he's long past that."

The big thief let go, stared absently at his cherry-red fingers. Then he looked up at her, tears in his eyes. "I couldn't let them. Not to you. I had to stop them."

"How's Whispering Dawn?"

"Safe. Outside." Seven Skull Shield climbed wearily to his feet. "We need to go."

"Let me get dressed. Maybe grease those burned hands of yours." She turned to where the big dog continued to savage the corpses on the floor, and added, "Farts, it's all right. You can stop killing them now."

The big brindle dog, jowls dripping frothy blood, looked up, the brown and blue eyes almost wistful. Then the tail whipped back and forth like some sort of perverted club.

Before she could find her skirt, Seven Skull Shield had spun her around, wrapped his arms around her, and whispered, "I'm so sorry. My fault. I should have been here."

She patted him on the shoulders, then pushed back to stare into his eyes. "You did just fine." Then she smiled. "Gods rot, Skull. It's true. You make more noise and less sense than a dying coyote when you fight."

Moments later, dressed, a pack of belongings filled, she took one last look at her house. Black Beak, his face and arms mauled, his throat torn out, was supine beside the bed. Nettle Toe lay on his stomach, facedown and head cooking in the glowing coals. In a spreading pool of blood, Long Cast sprawled flat on his back, his eyes and mouth agape.

Wooden Doll paused only long enough to give the dead warrior's undersized shaft and stones one last hard kick before she headed for the door.

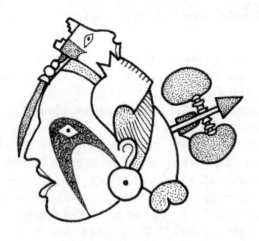

Sixty

The way Blue Heron figured it, not much had changed in the five tens of years she'd been alive. Wind was the oldest, which meant she got to order Blue Heron around whenever their parents weren't looking, back when they were children. Now, here she was, dressed as a servant, working in the *tonka'tzi*'s palace and doing whatever menial task Wind or one of her attendants asked her to.

They were in the *tonka'tzi* palace council room just back from the great room; this was the place where Wind received and occasionally housed foreign embassies, dealt with the lesser matters of Cahokia's governance, and entertained high-ranking Earth Clans high chiefs and matrons. The official and ceremonial acts of state might be carried out in the Council House atop the terrace on Morning Star's Great Mound, but much of Cahokia's business ended up being transacted here, in a much less formal atmosphere.

Better than being out on the street, for sure, and Blue Heron was much better fed than the sometimes-slim pickings from whatever she and the thief could steal.

Of course, when it came to the *tonka'tzi*'s household, White Rain knew Blue Heron's true identity; but White Rain—heretic Red Wing that she was—seemed to be enjoying the whole gods-rotted mess. And, to be sure, the woman played her part to perfection.

Funny how Power twisted the lives of people, lifting them up, beating them down. Blue Heron could almost wonder what she was supposed to learn from all this.

"What's that look?" Wind demanded as Blue Heron bent down to pick up the wooden plate a visiting Quiz Quiz Trader had left by the fire. The day's entertaining was over. Time to clean up and get ready for bed.

"I was thinking."

"That's dubious," Wind muttered from where she sat on her litter behind the eternal fire.

Blue Heron winced as she straightened and pressed a hand to her aching hip. Given that it was just her, White Rain, and Wind, she spoke freely. "I was just thinking that I miss the Trade. More than a bit of excitement in that, especially when I knew that at any second, some passerby might look down, point, and cry, 'There she is! It's Lady Blue Heron!'"

"I wouldn't get too cocky," Wind told her as she leaned forward and braced her chin. "Your own agents report that Spotted Wrist's warriors are still abusing older women across the city, looking for the elusive Blue Heron, though they've begun to tire of it over the last couple of days."

"Not that it does me much good. If Spotted Wrist ever searches your palace with any vigor, I'm right here."

"If he does, he'll be told that you're second cousin Fast Wrist, from over Moon Mound Way."

"*Second* cousin?" Blue Heron cried in mock outrage.

"Would you rather be *third* cousin Fast Wrist?"

White Rain giggled where she was folding blankets on the wall benches.

"You find that funny, Red Wing?"

"Keeper, from my point of view, you could fall a whole lot farther." White Rain folded the last blanket and turned. "I've been in a square once, and I don't want end up there again. It was enough to last me my whole lifetime. I just hope we can all survive this. I know what Spotted Wrist did to my people. What he's capable of."

Wind, her calculating gaze on the young woman, said, "I think we all do. What we don't know . . ."

She stopped short as Clan Matron Rising Flame hurried into the room. The Matron was dressed in a net-weave shawl crafted from buffalo wool. Her hair up, a single copper feather pinned the tight bun at the top of her head. A fine dogbane skirt clung to her hips and fell to her knees.

Wind straightened, lifting a questioning eyebrow. "Matron?"

"Quick, there's not much time." Rising Flame fixed on Wind. "Spotted Wrist is making his move, and his warriors will be right behind me."

Blue Heron kept her gaze averted as she scuttled off to the side with the wooden bowl in her hand. White Rain had bowed her head, retreating to the rear of the room.

"Oh? How?" Wind asked.

"He's placed warriors around the Four Winds Clan House. I suspect that he was figuring to do the same to me that he has done to you. Effectively take me hostage. I just wanted to warn you that . . ." At the sound of shouts from the great room out front, Rising Flame turned, a hand rising to her mouth.

"Quick!" Wind hissed. "Matron, if you want to save yourself, you sidle over by White Rain. Pull that copper feather out of your bun and let your hair fall. White Rain, throw her a blanket. One of the old ones."

Rising Flame had frozen. "What are you . . . ?"

Blue Heron, grumbling under her breath, straightened, grabbed the woman by the arm, and dragged her over to the sleeping benches. As she did, she snapped, "Gods, Matron, are you as dumb as a block of hickory? Do as Wind says."

"You!" Rising Flame's eyes widened. "But you're supposed to be dead! What are you . . . ?"

"Later! Now shut your hole." And with that, Blue Heron reached up and snatched the polished copper feather out of the Matron's bun. The woman's long black hair came tumbling down in a mass. Blue Heron fluffed it over the woman's back. White Rain was there, shaking out an old blanket from under the bench.

"The shawl," Blue Heron barked as she slipped out of her own burlap cape. "Off with it. Now!"

Rising Flame, still confused, let Blue Heron take her shawl, but helped to settle the burlap cape over her shoulders.

As the shouts from the front room grew louder, White Rain pressed the woman down onto the sleeping bench, pausing long enough to thrust the beautiful shawl beneath and out of sight. Thinking quickly, White Rain shoved a roll of buffalo yarn into the Matron's hands, saying, "Look like you're weaving something." She had just settled the worn blanket over the Matron's lap when a squadron second, followed by three warriors, burst into the room.

Meanwhile, Blue Heron had dropped to the floor where she began scraping old food from a brownware bowl and was flinging it into the fire.

"Get out!" Wind snapped. "I heard that Clan Matron Rising Flame ordered you—"

"There's been a change of procedure," the squadron second announced, smacking a fist to his breastbone in an insolent warrior's salute. "From now on, the Clan Keeper will be communicating the Four Winds Clan Matron's orders to you, *Tonka'tzi*."

The man was staring around the room, the other warriors clustering behind him. "Where is the Clan Matron? She was just seen entering your palace."

Blue Heron watched Wind's mild and bewildered expression with envy; piss in a pot, but her sister knew how to adopt a convincing façade when she needed to.

"Look around you, squadron second." Wind gave him an encompassing gesture of the hand. "There's me, my three servants, and an empty room. If your missing Matron entered my palace, I'd say she's still out in the anteroom."

"Or in your personal quarters," the second told her shortly, his eyes on the door in the back wall.

"Well, if Rising Flame's there, I give you my word—on the honor of my clan, House, and Morning Star—she managed to get there without passing through that doorway. I swear to you, she's not there. But you go ahead and look."

She waved him on. "If my word of honor as a Four Winds Clan matron and the *tonka'tzi* is meaningless to you and your vaunted Keeper, go search. Go. Do it so you don't get in trouble."

The squadron second, a man in his late thirties with Fish Clan tattoos on his cheeks, swallowed hard. Glanced uneasily at his three cringing warriors. They looked like they'd rather be chewing cactus pads than facing the *tonka'tzi*, let alone appearing to doubt her sacred honor.

Blue Heron mumbled to herself, keeping her head down as she carried the pot back to the sleeping bench where Rising Flame, head down, was making a fair attempt at fixing a hole in the old, frayed blanket.

"The rest of you, stay here." The second made a face, took a deep breath, and stepped wide as he passed around Wind; she glowered bone daggers at the man from atop her litter.

Blue Heron—a hand on Rising Flame's shoulder just in case the woman was dumber than a sack of rocks—thought the whole thing was marvelously played. The three remaining warriors were trying to look everywhere but at Wind, her servants, or at anything except the soot-covered ceiling so high overhead.

Spotted Wrist's squadron second didn't linger in his inspection of the *tonka'tzi*'s quarters. He was in and out in less than five heartbeats. He touched his forehead respectfully. "My apologies, *Tonka'tzi*. I was only following orders."

And with that he whirled and strode out, his cowed warriors behind him.

"I don't believe this!" Rising Flame sputtered, her expression shocked as she started to rise.

Blue Heron jammed the woman back down on the bench and hissed, "Hold on. Wouldn't put it past that moron to sneak another look through the door once he's assured himself that you're not hiding in the seed jars or under one of the benches in the front room."

"White Rain," Wind ordered, "go see what's happening outside. If they're still in the anteroom or on the veranda."

The Red Wing woman sprang to her feet, rapid steps taking her out the door.

Rising Flame rubbed her face, a slight tremor in her fingers. "His warriors would have seized me. I'm the Clan Matron! The woman who—"

"Just got her comeuppance," Wind growled, her slitted glare fixed on the door where White Rain had vanished. "Welcome to the world you've made."

As quickly, White Rain was back. "On the Keeper's orders, four warriors are to be in the palace at all times. I think they're going to bed down out front in the great room with the recorders, messengers, and household staff."

Rising Flame's gaze was burning. She knotted her fist and snapped, "I explicitly ordered him to leave this place alone. That you were an asset."

"Guess he doesn't listen well."

Sixty-one

Seven Skull Shield figured that his and Wooden Doll's only chance lay in getting across the river to Evening Star Town. Once there, he could place Wooden Doll, Whispering Dawn, and her baby under Columella's protection.

The last place Wooden Doll could go would be back to her house. Not with dead warriors lying all over it. Not to mention that by now Nettle Toe's head was probably cooked to well done, with the flesh falling off the bone and the brain baked to perfection.

Where was a cannibal when you needed one?

As they slipped out from between Gray Mouse's arrow-making work-shop and the adjoining structure that belonged to the shell carver known as Red Nails, it was to find the canoe landing not exactly crawling with warriors, but enough of them were wandering around poking into peo-ple's business that it was apparent that something was going on. Nor were these Spotted Wrist's men, but obviously Earth Clan warriors called up from one of the local squadrons.

"Something's not right," Seven Skull Shield muttered.

"You might say that," Wooden Doll agreed.

"Wait. You said you weren't hurt." Seven Skull Shield gave her a con-cerned look as they stopped on the sandy slope above a Trader's ramada.

"I'll be walking a little stiffly for a couple of days, and sore, if that's what you mean." She gave him a narrow-eyed glance. "But other than that, I was smart enough not to fight them over what they were going to take anyway."

"When they find those dead warriors, they're going to turn River City upside down." Seven Skull Shield studied the lines of canoes and the

Traders drawn up at the water's edge. "I have to get you to the other side. Someplace safe where—"

"And what are you going to do?" Wooden Doll demanded.

"He's going to take the fight to Spotted Wrist," Whispering Dawn told her. The young woman had her baby cradled to her breast, skeptical eyes on Seven Skull Shield. "He never knows when to quit."

Wooden Doll rounded on him, searching his eyes. "You're going to go get yourself killed, aren't you?"

"Listen, Blue Heron's back there. And after what they did to you? I can't just—"

She placed fingers to his lips to stop him. That look she was giving him, it was one he'd never seen from her before. Some mix of love and respect all churned up with resignation. A wry smile bent her lips as she nodded to herself. "Yes, that's my Skull. But not this time."

"What?"

She turned, opened her bag, and pulled out a beautiful ceramic drinking cup. This she handed to Whispering Dawn. "Hide that in the baby's blanket. I need you to go down to the water. A young woman with a baby? You should be able to ask the first canoe making a crossing to take you over to the other side. Once you are there, make your way up to the Evening Star House palace. Ask for Flat Stone Pipe. Tell the guards that you need to give him this cup. When you see him, tell him I asked him to keep you safe."

Whispering Dawn's eyes widened as she took the beautiful cup. "But what about you?"

Wooden Doll's lips curled into a humorless smile. "Maybe I'm no smarter than Skull, here. I was minding my own business, and they used me hard. Told me after they'd finished, they were going to drag me naked to the Keeper and hang me in a square until I told them where to find Skull."

As she spoke, Seven Skull Shield's muscles bunched, the grinding of his teeth loud in his head. "They hurt you to get at me? Wanted you to tell them where to find me?"

"Seems that some people just can't get enough of your company, old lover." She placed a familiar hand on his breast before turning to the young woman. "Now, Whispering Dawn, you be on about it. We'll watch from here. Make sure you get across. No one will be looking for you. Not yet."

Whispering Dawn pursed her lips as she looked down at the cup. "Seems you two are always saving me from disaster."

"We'll be together again," Wooden Doll assured her. "When this is all over. Now, be gone with you."

"I won't forget." Whispering Dawn gave Wooden Doll an awkward hug, maneuvering around the baby. Followed by another for Seven Skull Shield. Only then did she turn and hurry down past the Traders' camps, winding her way to the canoes.

"So, what's with Flat Stone Pipe and the cup?" Seven Skull Shield asked.

"You know his son, Panther Call?"

"Yeah, I pulled him out of the fire back when Walking Smoke got the palace burned."

"The boy needed training on how a man should act under the blankets with a woman. The cup was part of the compensation."

Seven Skull Shield gave her a sidelong glance. "But he's just a boy."

"Not anymore."

"Why are you here? Why aren't you walking down with Whispering Dawn to find that canoe? What I'm going to be storming headlong into . . ."

When he couldn't finish, she glanced up. Fixed those marvelous eyes of hers on his. Told him, "Skull, doesn't matter that we killed them. If they can treat me that way, they'll think they can do it to anyone. Me? I'm tough." She pointed at Whispering Dawn. "What if they'd done that to her? Kid's been hurt enough."

The young woman had approached a couple of upriver Traders; they were nodding, smiling at Whispering Dawn where they stood next to their canoe. "Those maggots we killed would have used that girl just as badly but for the fact she was nursing. Would have if I hadn't made a fuss and told them I'd take it for her."

Seven Skull Shield growled, looked down at where Farts had flopped on the charcoal-stained sand. "Let's go back and kill them all over again."

Wooden Doll had her hard eyes fixed on the canoe as the Traders helped Whispering Dawn in and pushed off. Their paddles flashed as they drove the craft out onto the sparkling water.

Only when they'd reached the other side did Wooden Doll take his hand and say, "All right. Let's go rescue Blue Heron. I'll stick my stiletto into Spotted Wrist's heart, and we'll save the city in the process."

"You sure about this?"

"They humiliated me, Skull. No one does that to me or mine and gets away with it."

Sixty-two

The next morning, in the predawn darkness, as the Earth Clans boys who'd been chosen for the job stirred the hot coals and added firewood to the eternal fire, Blue Heron seated herself on the side of the sleeping bench where Rising Flame had finally succumbed.

"Hey, Matron, wake up." Blue Heron gave the woman's shoulder a shove. "Time to talk."

Rising Flame grunted, started, and blinked. Then she sat up, rubbed her eyes, and stared around as the first flickers of flame illuminated the great room and cast leaping shadows. Like specters they Danced around the great room's decorated walls.

"Where . . . ? Oh yes, the gods-rotted *tonka'tzi's*." The matron chuckled. "I was hoping that was all a bad dream."

"Sorry. You're as deep in it this morning as you were last night."

Rising Flame pulled her thick black hair back. "He'll never get away with it. I'm the Four Winds Clan Matron. He serves at *my* pleasure. As soon as I call the matrons together and tell the high chiefs what he's done—"

"Stop it! You know full well what he's done and why. The only support you've got left is Columella and her brother High Chief Burned Bone from Evening Star House. And, given your history there, I'd call it lukewarm at best. Even if they did decide to back you, though heavens knows why, what good would it do you? They might hold the western bank of the river, but they don't have the strength to take the city back from Spotted Wrist. So forget the bluster. Now let's talk about what is."

Rising Flame studied her in the growing light. From the side, the fire cast the clan matron's profile in dark bronze. The Four Winds and the starburst tattoo on her cheek appeared blacker. Tiny flickers of flame reflected in the matron's dark pupils.

"Then, as you put it, what is?" Rising Flame asked.

"Seven Skull Shield said you were ready to deal. That still true?"

"That was the thief? That night? How'd he get into my quarters?"

"You know? I've asked that question myself. It's what he's good at. Now, are you still ready to deal?"

Rising Flame chuckled mirthlessly. "If Spotted Wrist has really taken my palace, and I'm a fugitive, I may not have anything to deal with, Lady." She paused. "What possessed him? Doesn't he know the Morning Star is going to . . ."

Blue Heron watched Rising Flame's expression fade in response to some revelation. "What?"

Rising Flame uttered the words in a monotone: "Morning Star's not going to act."

"Why?"

"He's sick. I don't know. Losing weight. The last time I was with him, he said crazy things. I got the feeling . . ."

"Yes? Go on."

"The feeling that he has been using me. That somehow I've been his tool. That . . . dripping pus, how do I say this?"

Blue Heron added, "That he used you to put the city in exactly this predicament. That he knew you'd appoint Spotted Wrist, and that knowing exactly how ambitious the war leader was, that we'd end up right here."

Rising Flame closed her eyes, shook her head. "That's impossible. How could he know the canoes would be stolen? That War Duck's palace would be burned, that Green Chunkey would suffer a disaster that effectively neutered his House? That I'd facilitate the . . ." Again the head shake. "No, that can't be."

"Morning Star always plays a deep game," Blue Heron told the woman. "Maybe clear back to the beginning. Him, and Night Shadow Star, and Walking Smoke."

"But what happened with the canoes, the River and Horned Serpent Houses, those were all—"

"We did that," Blue Heron told her. "Well, Flat Stone Pipe had the original plan to set the canoes adrift. Seven Skull Shield burned the River House palace, and I told him to create enough mischief in Horned Serpent Town to ensure that Green Chunkey couldn't replace Wind as *tonka'tzi.*"

"You?" Rising Flame swallowed hard. "And that clanless thief? You *destroyed* two houses?"

"Well," Blue Heron pulled at the wattle under her chin, "Morning Star asked us to work from the shadows. It just seemed . . ." She paused as it hit her. "Pus and spit! It's like we played right into Spotted Wrist's hands. Everything we thought we were doing for ourselves was just making him stronger."

Rising Flame asked, "Do you want to explain that?"

Blue Heron gave her a scathing look. "One by one, we were taking down his potential rivals. River House? Gone. Spotted Wrist's old-time rival, Green Chunkey? He's too busy saving his neck to be a threat. Columella's certainly not going to act on this side of the river. Now the good Lord Keeper can take any action he wants with impunity."

"And I dared to cross him." Rising Flame's expression had gone vacant. "He knew that with Matron Robin Wing's execution, I was as good as on my own." A beat. "I've been such a fool."

Blue Heron continued to pull at her wattle. "What I don't understand is Morning Star's role in all this. He had to know Spotted Wrist would end up right where he's at: taking the city for his own. By why would he choose that? What does he get out of it?"

"Revenge?" Rising Flame asked.

"Revenge for what?" Blue Heron barked. "He's the living god. He can have anything he wants."

"Except out," Rising Flame said softly. "And that finally makes sense."

"Glad you think so."

Rising Flame gave her a knowing sidelong glance. "Don't you see? He's trapped. Imprisoned in that high palace and condemned to endure the sycophants, the whiners, the glassy-eyed worshipers, the fawning nobles, the constant petty trivia. All those endless pleas from people asking him to give them something they can't get for themselves. No wonder he wants to die."

"You think a Spirit Being from the Beginning Times wants to die?"

Rising Flame pursed her lips, nodded. "You said Morning Star always plays a deep game. I think that's what this is all about. It doesn't matter who wins in the end. He's made it so that one way or another, before this is all over, he'll be dead."

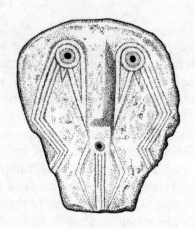

Home Waters

I stand where the rear of the canoe bends up into the high stern. I have set the steering paddle to one side and now spread my arms as Trout *glides across the roiling surface and into the Father Water's wind-chopped stream. Rains upriver have flooded the banks, turning the confluence into a sort of large triangular lake. I know we have made the transition as we round the point of flooded trees, and I can look north up the wide expanse as far as the next bend.*

I know this place, have been here before.

The bluffs rising back of the trees on the east bank are timbered in oak, ash, and hickory. I can see honey locust among the brush in the erosional cuts.

On the eastern bank, the high wall of trees runs back into the lowlands, where, on the occasional ridge, villages eke out a living by some farming, but mostly fishing, collecting, root gathering, and reliance on hunting to keep bellies fed. So many of those people have moved to Cahokia, all desperate to live in the shadow of the reincarnated god.

It warms my heart that within the next moon, they will live in my *shadow.*

I can feel the quickening as Trout *slips out into the Father Water's main channel. This is my last journey, the final leg that began when my accursed brother was consumed by the Spirit of the Living God. That fatal afternoon I was brutally shown my fate and destiny. That it was up to me to become the story. That, as Chunkey Boy had been consumed by Morning Star's Spirit, I must be consumed by Thrown Away Boy's essence. I became the Wild One. I was the balance of Power. The chaos in confrontation to Morning Star's order. And I proved it as soon as I found Night Shadow Star.*

Never had I felt that remarkable shattering of ecstasy as I did in that moment; my entire body convulsed with pounding waves of pleasure as my seed shot into her with each explosive jolt. I was reborn. Power surged through me, bright, burning, and irresistible.

It didn't matter that Morning Star banished me. I understood it was for a reason: I needed to come to grips not only with Power but destiny. In order to destroy Morning Star, I had to learn to be the Wild One in all his phases.

And I understood that as soon as I joined that final time with Night Shadow Star, the Power would be fully mine.

I turn, looking back over my shoulder. I can feel her. She's just back there. Coming as surely as winter. And with just as much Power as my own.

Looking back, I can see how it was all so perfectly orchestrated. Of course she had to foil me back in Joara. Silly me, the time wasn't right yet. She had to whack me in the stones, make me impotent. She had to be taken away so that I could understand my need to return to Cahokia.

Cahokia, it always comes back to Cahokia.

Sixty-three

What do you mean *you can't find her!*" Spotted Wrist's voice thundered in the Great room as he rose from his litter. In his spot behind the eternal fire, Morning Star cast him a curious glance. The living god sat on his panther hide–covered seat atop the raised dais. Lady Sun Wing, who'd appeared sometime in the night, now sat with her feet up on her accustomed sleeping bench against the far wall. She watched with amused eyes, fingers tapping on the Tortoise Bundle.

Despite the fire—now fed by Spotted Wrist's own warriors who'd been tasked with running down, Trading for, and packing the wood all the way up the stairs to Morning Star's palace—the empty room seemed dark, curiously lonely. Didn't matter that Morning Star remained in residence, the big room felt abandoned without the recorders, messengers, servants, cooks, and loitering nobles. Now only five warriors from the squad that provided security for the high palace remained.

Morning Star, for the most part, ignored Spotted Wrist. The living god leaned back on his panther hides, one knee up, and returned his attention to plaiting a heavy string from strands of sinew.

In front of Spotted Wrist, Squadron Second Burning Dog stood at full attention; his knotted fist pressed firmly against his wood-and-leather cuirass in a frozen salute. The second's head tilted back, chin out, his expression hard as hickory. "Lord Keeper, we took possession of the Four Winds Clan House as you ordered. Despite the hostility of the nobles within, we have searched every nook and cranny, inspected the furnishings, boxes, and storage. Even the floor matting down to the separate knots that compose it." He cleared his throat. "Clan Matron Rising Flame was not in the Clan house when we seized it, Lord."

Lady Sun Wing's mocking laughter carried in the still room. Spotted Wrist shot her a hard glance. Piss in a pot, but he *hated* that skinny little bitch.

Refocusing on Burning Dog, Spotted Wrist slapped a hand to his thigh. "What is it with my warriors and these women? Night Shadow Star skips out from under your noses. Blue Heron—who supposedly burned to death—is now reportedly lurking about the city dressed as a dirt farmer. Columella, who's supposed to be dead, laid up in a charnel house and rotting, sits atop her dais in Evening Star Town. And now you tell me that Rising Flame is nowhere to be found?"

The fist Burning Dog held against his chest knotted so tightly the knuckles turned white. "All I can tell the Lord Keeper is that according to her servants, the Lady Rising Flame had gone for a walk."

Spotted Wrist narrowed his eyes to slits. "And then what do you suppose happened, Squadron Second?"

Burning Dog took a deep breath. "As a guess, Lord, I'd say she returned, noticed the warriors surrounding the Four Winds Clan House, and correctly surmised that we had taken possession of it. That, as a result, she ran."

"And?"

"Well, Squadron Second Buffalo Horn thought he saw the Clan Matron entering the *tonka'tzi*'s palace. He was going there to take control of it anyway. Was sure that the woman who was running up the stairs ahead of him was Rising Flame."

"The copper's Power whispers from the shadows," Sun Wing chortled.

Where he reclined on his litter, Morning Star's lips quirked. Given the thick black and white paint the living god insisted on covering his face with, it might have been an amused smile.

"Squadron Second, please use the matron's honorific when you refer to her," Spotted Wrist growled. "You're talking about nobles"—he cast his gaze on Sun Wing—"even if they are a bunch of irritating shits."

"Yes, Lord Keeper!" Burning Dog's jaws knotted, his gaze still fixed high. "Squadron Second Buffalo Horn searched the *tonka'tzi*'s palace from top to bottom and found no such woman as the *lady*." He winced. "Upon reflection, Buffalo Horn thinks he must have seen one of the servant women. After all, it was dark, with the half moon low on the horizon."

Spotted Wrist rubbed a weary hand over his face. "Well, perhaps it doesn't matter. There is nowhere she can run to. Except, perhaps, Columella. If she does, good riddance. With the entire east side of the river under our control, it's a matter of settling in, becoming accepted, and then calling up the Earth Clans squadrons in service to the other Houses. When we're massed, we'll march straight to the canoe landing. This time we'll commandeer whatever craft are there and start our crossing. Load after load as fast as they can be paddled across."

"What of the heights above the landing on the west side?" Burning Dog wondered. "They can overwhelm us on the beach, and then concentrate on each returning canoe."

"Columella will need a couple of days to call up the full strength of her squadrons. We won't give her the time. We'll assemble on the Great Plaza. Call it training to mislead that dwarf's spies. Then order a forced march to the canoe landing and go. Hopefully before Columella expects a thing."

From the look Burning Dog was giving him, the second didn't believe it.

"Oh, trust me." Spotted Wrist made a dismissive gesture. "If I can march an army two moons up the Father Water and take Red Wing Town, I can manage a fast attack across Cahokia."

"Yes, Lord Keeper."

"And, in the meantime, let Rising Flame and Columella plot and plan. They can't move against me."

One of the warriors guarding the palisade gate at the head of the Great Staircase set the door aside. He stepped in, bowed. "Lord Keeper? You asked to be notified. Matron Slender Fox has arrived. Her litter is being carried up from the Council Terrace. Should I bring her straight in when she gets here?"

"Please."

To one of the warriors lounging on the ornate sleeping benches where the recorders used to sit, Spotted Wrist snapped, "I need food for my cousin. Go find something worthy of her."

"Yes, Lord Keeper!" The warrior knocked off a salute, jumped to his feet, and hurried for the door.

That was the way of it for every pus-weeping thing. Water jugs go empty? Got to have a couple of warriors run off down the steps to Cahokia Creek to fill them. Then there was the firewood, the food, the cooking. Sending an order? Got a sack full of refuse that needed disposed of? Or full chamber pots? It took a delegated warrior from his task. Any little thing they needed—assuming it couldn't be found in the palace—meant another trip up and down the stairs.

Sun Wing was Singing some melody under her breath where she fawned over the Tortoise Bundle. Having the woman around was as grating on his souls as fingernails scratching slate. Skinny little witch that she was, the way she looked at him with those half-empty but knowing eyes set his teeth on edge. If she were anyone but Morning Star's little sister, he'd have had her garroted and her body sunk in the Father Water long ago.

On his dais, Morning Star continued to occupy himself with his sinew plaiting.

And that was another annoyance. The living god appeared oblivious. Just sat there during the day, dressed in all his feathered and colorful grandeur, opulent headdress perfect, face painted, and did nothing.

The thought had crossed Spotted Wrist's mind that Morning Star was only biding his time. Waiting. But for what?

Again the door opened, the guard announcing, "Clan Matron Slender Fox, Lord Keeper."

Spotted Wrist got to his feet, walked across the remarkable matting, and gave his cousin a brief hug when she came striding in.

She was dressed in a decorative lace cape, her hair up in a bun and pinned with a series of swan feathers. She wore a bright red skirt adorned with star-shaped pieces of mica and polished copper that caught the light. Several courses of fine shell-bead necklaces hung at her throat. A triumphant smile curled her full lips. Delight Danced in her eyes.

"Good to see you, Lord Keeper," she told him. "Especially when it's for such a momentous occasion. Hard to believe."

Then she pulled away, stepping to a spot before the eternal fire, where she dropped to her knees. Bowing, she touched her forehead to the matting, calling, "Greetings, Lord. I hope you are well."

Morning Star really did smile this time, the action bending the points of his forked-eye design where they extended down his cheeks. "Matron, I hear you shall be the city's new *tonka'tzi*. Knowing your reputation, your position as the Great Sky will allow you to spread your abilities wide and open your most notable assets to those who can satisfy you. Given your already considerable experience, I would expect you to call upon your brother, High Chief Wolverine. I am familiar with the service he has rendered you in the past, and he does have considerable genius when it comes to satisfying the more familiar needs of politics. Not to mention discretion. Therefore, I would encourage you to rely on his talents when you find yourself in need."

"Thank you, Lord." Slender Fox touched her forehead, rose, and cast nervous glances at Morning Star and Sun Wing as she strode over to his litter. "So, Lord Keeper, what happens next?"

Spotted Wrist dismissed Burning Dog with a flick of the wrist and watched the second trot for the doors, no doubt delighted to be finished with a most uncomfortable grilling.

He gave Slender Fox a crafty grin. "I don't know what's been reported to you up in Serpent Woman Town, but I have Clan Matron Rising Flame on the run, the *tonka'tzi* is captive in her palace, Horned Serpent House is paralyzed, and Green Chunkey has sacrificed his sister and a wife and fears murder in the night. I have War Duck and Round Pot in a bear cage in my palace, while Three Fingers has his hands full trying to rebuild River House. Columella is bottled up on the other side of the river."

He hesitated, glanced suggestively toward Morning Star, and said, "And some appear to have no side in this, but accept what is as what will be."

Slender Fox gave him a sly smile. "Who would have thought? When do I become *tonka'tzi*?"

"I think tomorrow morning will be fine. I've sent for food. Once you've eaten and had a chance to wash up, you can search through the storage boxes for the finest cloak, headdress, and skirt. Tonight we'll find you appropriate dress for the occasion. Then, in the morning, we'll paint you in white with yellow and blue accents indicative of wisdom and serenity."

"You know my favorite color is bright red," she told him with amusement.

Spotted Wrist shared her secret smile. "Cousin, I know your appetites. For the present I would ask you to limit your bed to your husband, Cut Weasel. At least keep up the appearance of propriety until the city is firmly ours. After that, we can rotate the old *tonka'tzi*'s servants and staff out and your people in. After that you can sate your appetites with whomever and however you please." A beat. "Do you understand?"

She nodded. "Of course, cousin." She gave him a conspiratorial wink. "If it means being *tonka'tzi*, I'll stitch my sheath closed with buffalo sinew."

"No need to go that far. Just restrict your horizontal relaxation to your husband for the time being."

Slender Fox arched an eyebrow. "Seriously, is that all you have to tell me?"

"No. I just need you, as *tonka'tzi*, to back me. There may be an outcry from some of the Four Winds Clan nobles, but with the leadership in crisis, we can ignore it. As to the rest of the city? The Earth Clans are concerned and watching warily, but as long as they're not threatened, they'll keep out of it. They don't want the pot kicked over, or the chaos that would follow. I've assured them that once the Houses are reorganized and new leadership is chosen, my warriors will ensure that everything remains orderly and that life will go on."

"What about the dirt farmers?"

"All they care about is that we've got a productive growing season, crops are bountiful, the weather is good, and everyone is happily reveling in the reflected glow of the reincarnated god. Same with the Traders and artisans. Goods are flowing into and out of Cahokia, people are keeping their bellies full, weddings and funerals are taking place, babies are being born. And, but for the constant misery of flies and mosquitoes, no one is being pestered. As long as that happens, they couldn't give a moldy acorn about what's going on between the high rulers of the Four Winds Clan."

Slender Fox braced a hand on her round hip. "Then all we have to do is not rile them up."

"Correct."

Yes, indeed. He glanced at where Morning Star had engrossed himself in the plaiting of his cord. Who would have guessed that it would be this easy?

The warrior guarding the door set it aside for Squadron Second Ten Throws from North Star Squadron. The second, wearing his full armor, looking hot and sweaty, panting from his long climb up the Great Staircase, crossed the room at a trot. Pulling up beside Slender Fox—who was giving him a distasteful inspection—the second slammed a fist to his chest, declaring, "Lord Keeper! Squadron First Flying Squirrel sends his regards. It is my unhappy duty to report that the paid woman, Wooden Doll, has escaped. Further, the four warriors sent to capture her, including Squadron Third Red Thorn, are dead. Murdered at the paid woman's dwelling. We're searching all of River City Mounds for her and her accomplices now."

Spotted Wrist blinked. "A woman, a *paid* woman, killed four of my warriors?"

Ten Throws made a face filled with distaste. "Well, Keeper, it may be a bit more complicated than that. We don't think it was just the woman. From her reputation, she wasn't the kind to cook a man's head in the fire hearth. Or bash a warrior's skull with a pestle. Given the wounds, maybe she might have stabbed Long Cast. But Black Beak was mauled. Some say by a bear. Others say it was a Spirit wolf."

Spotted Wrist slumped back onto his litter, mystified. It was all going so well. And then to discover that Wooden Doll is missing?

"You are ordered to *find this Wooden Doll* and bring her to me!"

Again Ten Throws slammed a fist to his chest, barking, "Yes, Clan Keeper." He swallowed, the corners of his lips quivering. "Given the manner in which our people were killed, our warriors are taking this most seriously, Keeper. We'll find Wooden Doll if we have to take River City apart stick by stick."

"Do whatever you need to. Just *find her!*"

Across from Spotted Wrist, Morning Star was smiling. He seemed to have finished plaiting his cord, and now studied it in the firelight.

Spotted Wrist shot a questioning glance at Slender Fox. "What is it with my warriors and these women?"

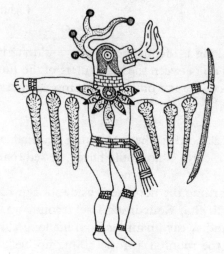

Sixty-four

From where Matron Columella stood on the edge of the high bluff overlooking the Father Water, she had a good view of River City Mounds on the other side of the roiling Father Water. Despite the distance, she could hear faint shouts, even detect an occasional scream.

Standing to her right, her younger brother, High Chief Burned Bone, had his gaze fixed on the far bank, his arms crossed. Clustered around her were several of the war chiefs who led various Earth Clans squadrons, most of which had been stood down from full alert, the warriors rotating back to their home farmsteads and villages to see to crops, fulfill family obligations, and attend to chores.

Up until now, keeping the balance had been precarious, hoping that she and Burned Bone retained just enough warriors that Evening Star Town could respond if Spotted Wrist made a move yet allow enough of her people to go on about their daily lives.

Now she wondered as she counted the number of fires that had broken out back in the warehouse district. A couple even sent gray-white columns of smoke into the hazy air around the River City plaza, with its high-pitched roofs and towering World Tree pole.

At the canoe landing, a constant exodus was taking place. Traders and locals were packing their possessions, carrying them down to canoes or away from the landing. Most of the ramadas were now empty. Up and down the waterfront canoes were being put out, the paddlers stroking in unison as they fled.

Though some headed north—paralleling the banks where the current wasn't as strong—most were fleeing to the Evening Star side, pulling up onto the sand below the bluff. About half of them so far. And more were coming. There they unloaded, the refugees standing in knots discussing what was happening back in River City Mounds. At the same time, other canoes headed off downriver, perhaps to the landing below Horned Serpent Town.

Just in the hand of time she'd stood here, most of the canoes had fled. Another six or seven fires had started back among the tightly packed buildings, a billow of smoke marking the spot. If there was any upside to this, it would be in the thunderheads building to the southwest. From her experience, they were going to see hard late-summer afternoon rain showers with concomitant lightning and high winds. Hopefully they'd bring enough rain to put out the fires the winds would inevitably spread.

"What are they thinking over there?" Burned Bone asked in bewilderment.

"About those four dead warriors at Wooden Doll's," she told him, having been briefed by Flat Stone Pipe's agents. "Someone has to pay, right? I heard that Spotted Wrist ordered Wooden Doll to be found, no matter what. After the murder of those four warriors, they wanted to turn the city upside down." She paused. "Looks like they've done it."

That Seven Skull Shield was somehow at the bottom of every major upsetting event in the city never ceased to amaze her. Whispering Dawn had told the whole story.

Not that Columella blamed the thief. Most everyone knew that despite the peculiar way his relationship with Wooden Doll worked, *Hunga Ahuito* help anyone foolish enough to hurt the woman.

"But River City's a tinderbox," Burned Bone told her. "They've borne the brunt of Spotted Wrist's occupation. They've had their canoes stolen, their warehouses emptied, their palace burned, and had to feed all those arrogant northern warriors."

"More like a tightly sealed pot on the flames," Columella said, squinting as another puff of smoke rose from back by the Avenue of the Sun. "As the steam builds inside, it's only a matter of time before it explodes. Three Fingers is demanding they build him a new palace, forcing people to give him Trade for logs, thatch, plaster, vines, and rope. Then to have Crazy Frog's raided, War Duck and Round Pot hauled off, their bodies hanging from poles like war captives . . . ?" She shook her head. "People loved and cherished Crazy Frog and his wives. That they took the children? Gave them to Mud Foot to sell?"

"Bad news, that." Behind her, Squadron First Falcon Sky crossed his muscled arms. "The chunkey players have their own authority and charisma, you know. Not just from being blessed by the game, but people look up to them. I have a cousin over there who idolizes the chunkey players. He told me that Skull Thrower, and a lot of the others, have been calling for people to take their city back."

Her brother gave her a sidelong look. "What do you think we should do about this?"

Columella fingered the thick layers of shell necklaces at her throat. "Brother, open the warehouses. I want food rations delivered to the people who've fled to our side of the river. Offer the Traders down there shelter for their packs and Trade. Tell them they can put it in our warehouses. I want to keep them, and more importantly, their canoes, on this side of the river."

"And the rest of us?" Falcon Sky asked.

She laid a hand on his shoulder, smiled. "Old friend, I think we should recall every warrior who's on leave. If what's happening over there goes from bad to worse, we're going to have our hands full."

She turned, looking back at the pillars of smoke rising to mix with the brown haze above River City. Another chorus of faint screams carried from across the distance.

Did she dare intervene?

The problem with sticking one's nose into the middle of a civil war was that not only might you get it bitten but you might get the rest of your head chewed off in the process.

Sixty-five

The way Mud Foot saw it, each and every one of the pus-licking Four Winds lords in Cahokia could waste away with gut-rot, and the whole world would be better off. What did the exalted Four Winds Clan do for anyone but themselves? Seated in their high palaces, feasting, throwing their weight around, giving orders to the Earth Clans, Trading for precious shell, copper, black drink, and the finest fabrics? How was that good for anyone?

It was the common folk who did the hard work. They were the ones who sweated rivers under the burning sun. While digging sticks raised blisters on their hands, they were the ones who levered thick black clay from the deep pits. They were the ones who packed it on their backs up and out of sweltering barrow pits, toiled up to dump it by the basket load to build the high mounds those selfsame lords would live on. Then, exhausted, they finished their too-long day by weeding their gardens, packing water, shucking corn, pounding acorns, parching knotweed, cutting thatch, checking trotlines, and mucking for crawfish.

All that . . . and then what happened? The maggot-choking chiefs and matrons demanded tribute. Took half of a farmer's crop or a fisherman's catch. To add insult to injury, the lords made the poor barefoot fools pack it off to the matron's warehouse on his or her own backs.

Not that Mud Foot had ever been one of those people, mind you. He'd assiduously avoided anything that smacked of hard physical labor since he was a boy.

That didn't mean he couldn't still hate Cahokia's rulers for the injustice they imposed on others. Mud Foot considered his outrage on their behalf to be most charitable on his part.

I should have been one of the richest men in the city, he thought. When had he ever felt this bitter? His left eye was twitching, as it did when he was upset.

Helpless to intercede, he'd stood and watched all the remarkable Trade that had been in Crazy Frog's warehouse as it was packed off to central Cahokia. Deposited—he'd been told—in the Keeper's palace, where it was guarded by a full squad of warriors.

Which left Mud Foot hurrying through the back warrens of River City, a blanket over his bowed head to keep from being recognized.

A couple of houses over, a woman screamed in fear. Then came the sound of angry shouts, the crash of breaking crockery. He could hear a dog's squealing yip as it cried out in pain. Terror everywhere.

The whole city had come undone. It had just exploded in an instant like a too-wet pot in a kiln. Gone crazy. People mobbing warriors, warriors beating people. Fires here and there. Madness. It was all madness. His eyes burned from the smoke, wraiths of it blowing in streamers through the labyrinth. He could hear people yelling. Sometimes the muffled sounds of fighting.

Hurry. Just hurry. Anything to keep from being noticed in a city gone insane.

Ducking between a potter's workshop and a basket maker's, he found both closed up tight. The whole city was that way. Doors barricaded, people hiding. Or running. Or roaming in bands looking to take their frustration out on the Keeper's warriors.

Almost to his warehouse now.

"By Piasa's swinging balls, tell me they're still there."

For the price of a brownware pot, he'd hired a dirt farmer—a big strapping fellow—to keep an eye on his warehouse, such as it was. With the constant noise and confusion, the incipient violence, he had to hope the man hadn't run.

True, that piss-dripping shaft of a Keeper had made off with all Crazy Frog's Trade, but the snot-sucking "Hero of the North" had kept his word and handed over Crazy Frog's five wives and the nine children. They'd been tied at the neck, hands bound behind them, looking shocked and broken. The squadron third had even detailed warriors to escort them to Mud Foot's rickety warehouse at the northern edge of the canoe landing.

Neither had Mud Foot anticipated a riot. He'd been watching the last of the Trade being hauled out of Crazy Frog's warehouse when word came that four warriors had been hideously murdered at Wooden Doll's. He'd seen the moment when Squadron Second Marten Hide had declared, "Someone's going to pay for this! Find that accursed woman if you have to tear this city into pieces!"

He'd watched as the warriors left to do just that, breaking into houses, demanding to search the council houses, the shrines, and word was they'd even ripped up the altar in Old-Woman-Who-Never-Dies' temple. Tearing things apart, spilling and breaking pots, shredding bedding. Frightening children, clubbing dogs, and smacking the adults. And then they'd started setting dwellings and crops on fire.

Mud Foot had been well on his way to the canoe landing by the time the first of the locals picked up digging sticks, pestles, chunkey lances, lengths of firewood, war clubs, and fishing gigs. The city had had enough.

Except that at the canoe landing, the Quiz Quiz Trader Mud Foot had been dickering with in hopes of Trading for his captives was gone. A narrow groove in the charcoal-stained sand showed where the man's heavy Trade canoe had been pushed out into the river. In frustration, Mud Foot had kicked and stomped the groove flat. Shouted imprecations at the roiling water and the flood of canoes joining the mass departure from the beach.

It was all going wrong. His Quiz Quiz Trader—willing to give a fortune for Crazy Frog's wives and children—was gone. The city was devouring itself, and Mud Foot had a warehouse full of newly made slaves whom he was going to have to protect, feed, and keep from escaping—and for whom he now had to find a buyer. Fast!

Crazy Frog was still out there somewhere. Chances were good that he was going to find out sooner or later who gave his name to the Keeper. Who took his wives and children slaves.

And Mud Foot wanted to be long gone before that happened.

He ducked around the flintknapper's workshop, relieved to see the hulking dirt farmer he'd hired to guard the place.

"Any trouble?" Mud Foot asked as he trotted up.

"Just a snoopy dog. Big thing. Came around and peed on the corner of the building. It ran when I threw a rock at it." The man looked past him. "Where's your Trader come to take the slaves?"

"Yes, well, that's sort of a problem. You heard all the commotion?"

"Yep. You got my Trade? You said you'd give me a nice brownware bowl for making sure none of the women or kids escaped."

"That's part of the problem. My Trader has left. Afraid of the violence. As soon as he's back . . ."

The big dirt farmer reached out, grabbed Mud Foot by the throat. "He told me you wouldn't have the pot. Told me you'd say to just let it go for now, but to collect later. Told me to ask for two pots since you didn't have one now. You'll do that? Give me two pots later instead of one now?"

Given the pressure on Mud Foot's throat, and the fact that if he wanted, the gnarled old dirt farmer could have lifted him off the ground with one hand, Mud Foot squeaked, "Yes!"

"I know where to find you. You owe me. You pay."

Mud Foot clawed the man's callused hand loose, backed a step, rubbing his throat. "You'll get it. My word on that."

"Then I'm leaving. Got my own family to look to." The dirt farmer stuck a thick finger against Mud Foot's nose. "You pay, or I hurt you."

"Sure. Of course. I promise."

Mud Foot rubbed his neck, watching as the big man ambled back the way he'd come and vanished between the buildings.

"He said you wouldn't have the pot? He told you? Who is this 'he'?"

But then who knew how the dirt farmers thought? Barbarians, all of them. And crazy.

Mud Foot took a deep breath. Wished he was in that Quiz Quiz Trader's canoe, headed downriver with a bulging sack of Trade.

Lifting the plank door to the side, he winced at the sounds of someone screaming back in the warehouses up on the levee.

Heart beating against his ribs, he stepped inside. In the dim light he could see the five women and all the children where they crouched in a line in the back. Crazy Frog's high-and-mighty wives along with their spoiled offspring. They didn't look so full of themselves now, all huddled on the floor. They followed his entry with worried eyes, looking nervous.

Behind him, from the shadowed corner of the room, a familiar voice said, "Didn't have the pot to pay him with, huh? You really are a stupid bit of shit."

And as Mud Foot turned, a blurred object came hissing out of nowhere. It hit so hard that lightning blasted through his head. And then he was falling . . .

The next thing that registered was pain, like his head was splitting in two. Something kept puffing air against his face, caused his eyes to flutter open. He tried to make sense of what he was seeing . . . but his swimming vision—and the pain—made it so difficult to . . .

He blinked against the air puffing on his eyes and realized it was a nose. A big dog's nose that was sniffing in his face.

Looking past the block of nose, he stared into one brown eye, one blue. Gods, that was a big dog standing over him.

A child's bare feet pattered past behind the dog.

Piasa take him for a fool, where was he? What was a dog doing drooling so close to his face? How had . . . ?

His fractured thoughts came together as someone said, "Get them out of here. Veer wide around the north end of town. Follow the Cahokia Creek trail until you can cut across to the Avenue of the Sun."

Mud Foot knew that voice. And with a cold shiver, realized it was Crazy Frog. Which was when the rest of the pieces dropped out of his scrambled thoughts: His warehouse. The slaves. The blow that had come whistling out of the dark.

He swallowed hard. Tried to get up.

Couldn't.

His hands were tied behind him.

"I wouldn't try that." A human face bent down past the dog's. Oh yes, that was Seven Skull Shield.

The big thief said, "Crazy Frog let me whack you a good one. Lay you out like a stunned fish while we untied the women and kids. That was Crazy Frog's little gift to me, seeing as how Wooden Doll and I can't be here to really pay you back in kind. Seems we have to get the family to safety."

"How?" Mud Foot rasped through his pain-filled head.

"That Third who was abusing Wooden Doll couldn't help but brag while he thought he had the upper hand. Told her everything, exactly who gave us up. Thought that telling her that it was you, you walking bit of garbage, was going to humiliate her even more."

"And he humiliated me enough," a woman's voice said sharply.

Mud Foot craned his neck just in time to see Wooden Doll pull her foot back. She kicked him hard enough in the side to blast the air from his lungs in a whoosh. It hurt. Really hurt. Left him gasping.

"Now," Seven Skull Shield told him, "we have to be going. Have to leave you here with Crazy Frog and Black Swallow. They're going to spend some time with you." Seven Skull Shield cocked his head, listening. "With all the screaming and crying in the city, who will notice a little more from you, huh?"

Seven Skull Shield straightened, leaving the huge dog to stare down at Mud Foot. Spit and blood, the thief wouldn't sic the dog on him? Have the beast maul him like had been done to that warrior at Wooden Doll's?

"I'm so sorry. I can explain. Just don't . . ."

Crazy Frog loomed over him, a stone-headed war club in his hand. "And explain you will. But slowly. And in a way I can really appreciate." He looked at Seven Skull Shield. "You have the shell gorget?"

The big thief lifted a beautifully carved gorget; four overlapping sides creating an open square. "When I get Mother Otter and the rest to Wind or Blue Heron, I give them the gorget. It's Night Shadow Star's promise of protection. But you know they've got their own—"

"I know." Crazy Frog slapped a hand to the thief's slab of a shoulder. "But I think the lady knew that when she gave it to me."

"You got it."

"Be careful," Crazy Frog insisted.

"You, too." The thief turned. "Make him suffer for all of us."

"Oh, he will," Crazy Frog promised.

As the thief's bulk filled the door, partially blocking the light, the big dog turned, lifted his leg.

Mud Foot gasped as urine pattered hot and wet on his bare skin; then the beast loped out the door into the light.

As the liquid cooled and trickled down Mud Foot's side, Crazy Frog leaned close, a smile beaming from his ever-so-average-looking face. "Smart dog, that Farts. But as dumb as you are, that's the least of your problems."

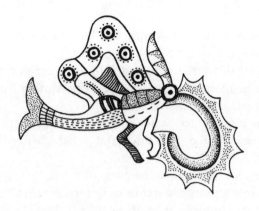

Sixty-six

By the time Spotted Wrist was ready to see to Slender Fox's installation as *tonka'tzi*, most of the day had vanished into a flurry of other concerns. From where the sun was sinking on the western horizon, the Keeper didn't need the Great Observatory to tell him that the fall equinox was looming. The shadows at sunset were barely canted to the south. It wouldn't be more than a quarter moon before the priests would be up at sunrise, watching the sun crest the horizon due east on the high bluffs, and then sink due west over distant Evening Star Town.

And no arrogant Morning Star House nobles are giving me orders to prepare for the feast, the ceremonials, or organization of the celebration.

No, indeed. He would now delegate that responsibility, and he had just the person for the job.

Spotted Wrist glanced across at Slender Fox. His cousin, now dressed in splendor such as even she had never donned before, climbed onto her litter. She wore Morning Star's quetzal-hide cloak: the famous gift from the Itza, borrowed for the occasion and given with a faint wave of the living god's limp hand.

A headdress of beaten, polished, radiant copper topped her head, the bun drawn tightly forward, pinned, and supporting a Spirit Bundle in a small carved wooden box. Behind it, a splay of swan feathers spread in a radial burst.

Slender Fox had painted her face in an intricate design of delicate blue starbursts, swirls, and the Four Winds Clan design on the cheeks, all against a white background. In contrast, her mouth and nose were done in a black triangle. Smaller black forked-eye designs were painted around her eyes to represent the Sky World, and her place within it. She was, after all, becoming the Great Sky.

Thick necklaces of white marine shell beads hung down between her breasts, and a large mother-of-pearl gorget with Mother Spider engraved on the shining surface dominated it all.

Her skirt was a gossamer weave of almost transparent cottonwood-down lace that shimmered with mica and polished silver nuggets from the far north.

All well and good. She looked the part.

And—after the alarming reports he'd been receiving all morning from River City and River House—it was time for a little celebration. Yes, he'd have to deal with the unrest. Call up his squadron, march down the Avenue of the Sun, and break some heads while he restored order.

Reports were muddled, but somewhere between thirteen and twenty-two of his warriors were supposedly murdered by the locals. Another thirty-some were wounded, being cared for at the Four Winds Clan House on the River City Mounds plaza. The rest of his squadron, backed up by a couple of River House Earth Clans squadrons, had retreated to the plaza, set up a defensive perimeter, and essentially abandoned the rest of River City to the rabble.

And even then, the Earth Clans squadrons were supposedly under strength, the chiefs having called them up only to have but a fraction of their warriors answer the summons.

What in Piasa's name was Flying Squirrel doing over there? How had he let this get so out of control?

"Enough," he muttered, taking one last look at himself. He indeed looked the part, dressed as he was in his finest. A cloak of spoonbill feathers hung down his back; he wore a white apron, spotless and decorated with shell and copper, the long point hanging down between his knees. On his head, he'd placed an eagle-feather crown, the pin feathers sticking straight up in a high cylinder of white tipped in black.

He asked Slender Fox, "Are you ready to become *tonka'tzi?*"

"Oh, indeed, Cousin." She gave him her signature wink. "Let's put North Star House in charge of Cahokia once and for all."

He raised his staff of office—a copper-clad hickory stick as long as his arm—and warriors rushed forward to lift his litter.

Behind the eternal fire, elevated on the dais, Morning Star watched with a bemused expression, his thickly painted face looking somehow hollow. He did, however, flick his hand in dismissal, a gesture like shaking water from the fingertips.

Spotted Wrist was borne through the double doors and out into the slanting light of the palace courtyard. To his dismay, so much of the day had been wasted over that nasty business in River City that he'd be making his speech from the *tonka'tzi*'s palace steps in twilight.

The journey through the various gates and down the Great Staircase was made without mishap. His honor guard—who'd been waiting for most of the day—formed a box around him and Slender Fox. They marched smartly, slapping their armor, clapping war clubs against their shields. Cut Weasel marched out front, calling for the crowd to "Make way for the Keeper and *tonka'tzi*!"

To make such an announcement had to be a thrill for the squadron first. Granted, being married to Slender Fox came with its disadvantages. Fortunately for the sake of their marriage, Cut Weasel had spent most of it away. Various campaigns had taken him east to fight the Shawnee, north to wage war on Red Wing Town and then the forest tribes. And since the return to Cahokia, he'd been gainfully employed dealing with the Keeper's various problems. All of which had left Slender Fox's bed open to be filled by her various lovers. Most of whom—especially her most secret one—she was discreet about.

What mattered to the squadron first was that, as of this evening, he was the *tonka'tzi*'s husband. An honor that elevated him above all but a handful of Cahokians, symbolically at least.

The small entourage rounded the northwest corner of the Great Plaza and marched south down the avenue to the *tonka'tzi*'s sprawling mound and palace. Though not as imposing as Morning Star's soaring abode, it still was the largest structure in the city.

At the foot of the stairs, Spotted Wrist called a halt. After he lowered his staff of office in the signal to set him and Slender Fox down, his litter was placed on the beaten avenue.

Surrounded by their phalanx of warriors, he rose, stepped back, and took his cousin's hand in his. Then, with a smaller escort of warriors, he and Slender Fox climbed to the head of the stairs in matched step.

And yes, rot it, they stood half hidden in the great building's shadow as Spotted Wrist turned at the top of the stairs. There, flanked by the *Hunga Ahuito* guarding posts, they faced the plaza.

A mere crowd of fifty or sixty had gathered, all standing back from his warriors.

Raising his voice, Spotted Wrist called, "People of Cahokia. It is with great joy that I inform you that a new leader ascends the *tonka'tzi*'s high chair. I present to you, Matron Slender Fox, of the North Star House of the Four Winds Clan. She replaces Lady Wind who, for reasons of health, has abdicated her position. It is with anticipation and delight that Wind passes the staff of office to *Tonka'tzi* Slender Fox!"

He hadn't thought of that twist, but, shadowed and elevated as they were, none of the rabble could see the details, even if they knew the *tonka'tzi*'s staff in the first place. So he handed Slender Fox his staff of office, muttering from the corner of his mouth, "I want that back, by the way."

While a bellowing hurrah came from his ranked warriors, only a couple of desultory shouts came from the crowd. Most, with burden baskets on their backs, just continued on their way as if they'd been interrupted in the midst of their daily drudgery. A few others shrugged, turning to talk among themselves.

Doesn't matter. Slender Fox is tonka'tzi.

"Hardly a stirring celebration," she mused as she studied the intricate repoussé on the copper cladding. "You sure you want this back? It's nice workmanship."

"You'll have the right one in a matter of moments, Cousin." He turned, took her arm. To the warriors, he ordered, "Let's be about this."

In formation, Cut Weasel and his warriors led the way. Finding the big double doors open, they all trooped into the great room where sleeping benches, a fire surrounded by pots of food, and most of the jars, boxes, and ritual paraphernalia were kept. Here visiting dignitaries and their entourages were often housed, cared for, and hosted. Spotted Wrist ignored the looks from both foreigners and Wind's attendants and servants.

His warriors—the ones he left to keep an eye on Wind and her visitors—snapped to their feet, beating out hard salutes as they slapped fists to their chests. Even as they did, the squadron third gave Spotted Wrist a nod that all was well.

Spotted Wrist's warriors marched straight to the entrance leading back to the *tonka'tzi*'s council room. There, they threw the doors wide and filed in.

According to instruction, they were supposed to immediately surround Wind, ensure that she was restrained, gagged, and bound. The same with any of her servants who might be present. No one was to make a sound.

Slender Fox would take her place on the panther hide–covered litter. Wind would be carried back to her personal quarters, and the announcement would be made in the front room for everyone to come and make their obeisance to the freshly installed *Tonka'tzi* Slender Fox.

But the room was empty. Nothing moved but the smoke from the smoldering eternal fire in the center.

"Her personal quarters in back," Spotted Wrist ordered his warriors. "Go secure her."

As the warriors hurried back through the door in the rear, Slender

Fox, in all her splendor, stepped lightly forward. She didn't hesitate but climbed up on the elevated litter chair, seated herself, and reclined with her slim arms braced on the chair's arms. Then she crossed her legs, fingered his Keeper's staff, and asked, "Well?"

"You look born for it," Spotted Wrist told her. "Cahokia is now ours."

Even as he spoke, the first of the warriors emerged from Wind's personal quarters, a confused look on his face. "Lord Keeper?"

"Got her? Good work. I didn't hear a sound."

"Um, your pardon, Lord. But, well, there's no one here. The place is empty."

Sixty-seven

From where Blue Heron stood, leaning against the door frame in High Chief Six Strikes' Raccoon Clan palace, things looked pretty pathetic. Sheltered by the palace veranda, she let her gaze rove over the vista, such as it was. She'd never liked the land up here above the Eastern Bluffs, though she had to admit the air wasn't quite as muggy.

To call the building a "palace" was something of a stretch. The structure was constructed of four set-post walls, the uprights tied together with vine, then daubed with thick clay and fire-hardened before the thatch roof had been added.

However, for the prairie zone east of the bluffs, it was not that bad. From the front door—elevated as the building was on a low rise—she could see the Avenue of the Sun where it ran straight as a stretched cord to the Moon Mound complex. A day's walk to the east, that was where the lunar observatory and ceremonial site lay. At that juncture, the road turned to the southeast, following the line of sight across a quarter moon's travel across forest and hills to Moon Rise Town, which was being built on the north shore of the Mother Water.

The entire lunar complex was oriented toward moonrise during the lunar maximum on the northwestern horizon. That event occurred only once every eighteen and a sixth years. The mound site itself was a large earthen pyramid with a wide ramp oriented at right angles to the lunar maximum moonrise. Conical mounds marked Spirit Avenue, down which pilgrims would watch on that sacred occasion.

"I tell you, this is intolerable," Blue Heron muttered as she stared out at the endless spread of farmsteads. This was dirt farmer territory. The breadbasket of Cahokia, the uplands were packed with immigrant farms. Each had its World Tree Pole, rudimentary chunkey courts, council house, and temple complex dedicated to *Hunga Ahuito*, Old-Woman-Who-Never-Dies, and Morning Star.

"I couldn't agree with you more." Rising Flame paced before the line of benches built into the western wall. She stopped to scowl at the plaster where a spiderweb of cracks was running down the wall and needed repair; Raccoon Clan—with ties to the Underworld and its Spirit Helper a messenger of the dead—was neither prestigious nor influential. Let alone numerous. What they were was loyal to Four Winds Morning Star House.

Settled around on the opposite side of the room, Mother Otter, Wild Rice, Blanket, Flower Reed, and the youngest of Crazy Frog's wives, Sweet Bulb, along with all the wide-eyed children, were making the best of the limited accommodation.

"Had to take them in, huh?" White Rain asked as she worked on altering an old blanket into a cape. With equinox so close, the evenings had taken on a bit of chill.

Blue Heron pulled what she called the "Four Plank" gorget from her belt pouch, rubbing her thumb over the smooth shell carving. "The thief says that Night Shadow Star gave this to Crazy Frog in case he needed our assistance. Not that I wouldn't have granted it in any case, Crazy Frog being who he is, but this, as the saying goes, 'seals the pot with pitch.'"

"Huh!" Rising Flame grunted. With a nod of the head toward Wooden Doll, she said, "What about her? Of all the women I'd never so much as—"

"Careful, Matron," Blue Heron warned, voice dropping an octave in threat. "Back when the biggest problem in your life was divorcing Tapping Wood, that woman was placing her life on the line and saving this very city."

"Why have I never heard of it?"

"There's a lot you don't know. Things that went on with the Itza, the Natchez, and Lord Horn Lance." She gestured to include the room. "These people, including Crazy Frog, all played a part to bring the Itza down. You might think it was all the Red Wing and Night Shadow Star, but like so much, there was a deeper level to that whole fight."

Rising Flame stepped close, crossed her arms. Her voice low, she said, "This entire bunch are nothing more than clanless two-footed vermin. And her? She's a *paid* woman that no clan would take. These women and children, clanless, homeless, the spawn of a gambler and who knows what sort of unsavory—"

"Stop it." Blue Heron gave her a scathing glare. "I was like you once.

See, the thing you have to understand is that Cahokia is their city, too. Maybe this is why Morning Star set you up as Clan Matron. He knew you were going to have the unholy piss slapped out of you. That you were going to have to deal with me, with the reality of how Cahokia works, because by Piasa's swinging balls, it doesn't run on the will and pleasure of the vaunted Four Winds Clan and their snotty Houses."

"You think it's here?" Rising Flame almost squeaked. "With these . . . these . . ."

"Bits of flotsam?" Blue Heron supplied mildly. "A big part of it, yes."

White Rain laid her half-finished blanket cloak on her lap, gestured with the sewing awl to make her point. "If Seven Skull Shield hadn't slipped in and told you Spotted Wrist was coming with warriors to replace Wind as *tonka'tzi*, where would you be right now?"

"In even more of a fix if Wind hadn't had that secret door built into the wall when she had all those repairs made this summer." Blue Heron gave the slave woman a sly smile.

Rising Flame didn't answer, her expression stormy but concerned as she glanced at the refugees. Her gaze lingered on Wooden Doll. The paid woman was deep in conversation with Mother Otter.

Blue Heron told her, "You'd have been right there in the *tonka'tzi*'s chambers, waiting to be snatched up by Spotted Wrist. Instead of here, you'd be under his guard. Totally at his mercy."

"Now I'm in a lowly Raccoon Clan palace at the edge of the bluffs, hiding with a bunch of . . ."

"And free," White Rain added sourly. "You should try captivity sometime. Being turned into a slave? Trust me, Matron, you wouldn't like it."

Something moved in the doorway, shadowed against the deepening evening beyond. First into the room was Farts, bounding, his big paws slapping on the cane matting. The children exploded in cries of delight as they mobbed the oversized mongrel. Farts twisted and cavorted, knocking the smaller ones off their feet in the process. They began to howl and bawl their fear and surprise.

As mothers raced forward to save their little ones, the older children were climbing all over the beast, laughing, hugging, being dragged this way and that or lashed by that relentless tail.

Into the chaos came Seven Skull Shield, and behind him, *Tonka'tzi* Wind. Seven Skull Shield, as usual, looked like a bit of human debris, his shirt dirty, soot-stained, and showing the occasional hole. His homely face split into a grin as he watched the antics of Farts and the children.

At least until the big dog fixed his attention on the glowering Mother Otter as she came to stand over him, her arms crossed. At sight of the woman, Farts shook the kids off. Head lowered, tail down, he raced for the door, almost bowled Wind off her feet, and vanished into the night.

"Must be a story behind that," Blue Heron mused, figuring she'd corner Mother Otter for the details when she got a chance. Spit and blood, if there was a trick to making that cur disappear, she needed to know it.

"Well," Wind announced as she lowered a burden basket filled with twigs from her sloped shoulder, "it's official. Spotted Wrist just declared Slender Fox as the new *tonka'tzi*. According to him, I have stepped aside for 'reasons of health.'"

"Uh-huh," Seven Skull Shield grunted as he plodded over to Wooden Doll's side. "As in, if they'd a caught you in there, you'd be dead right now. That's about as unhealthy as you could be."

"He *can't* do that!" Rising Flame cried, spinning around and walking up to Wind. "That's a *Clan* decision! He's just the Keeper! Wind, you outrank him. As do I."

A subtle humor lay behind Wind's eyes. "Matron, no matter how you spin it, I don't outrank a full squadron of warriors. Unless the living god were to intervene, who's going to listen? Hmm? Clan Matron, do you have the Houses behind you? Perhaps ready to call up their squadrons and roust Spotted Wrist from his new lair atop Morning Star's great mound?"

Rising Flame seemed to deflate.

"Yes, I thought so." Wind removed a threadbare cape from around her shoulders, gave it a critical inspection, and walked over to extend her hands to the fire burning in the puddled-clay hearth. "Fascinating opportunity, this," she noted. "Seeing life from this perspective. Spotted Wrist stood up there on the landing, gave his speech, and looked me right the eyes. He never saw me. Looked right through me, in fact. I was just some old dirt farmer woman."

"Means the city is his," Blue Heron carped. "And unless Morning Star has a problem with it, we're stopped cold."

"But we're still free." Rising Flame seemed to be trying to find a bright side.

"For the time being," Mother Otter called from the other side of the room. The woman stepped up to Wind. A head taller, she studied the *tonka'tzi*. "As I and mine just found out, you're free until someone decides to sell you out for something they want in Trade. Just how well do you know this Raccoon Clan chief? Even more to the point, how well do you know his clan kin, and so on down the line? How long before one of them sidles up next to a North Star House warrior, the way Mud Foot did, and says, 'For the price of a whelk-shell cup, I can tell you where Lady Blue Heron, Matron Rising Flame, and Wind are hiding'?"

Wooden Doll added, "The smart thing would be to get you all out of Morning Star House territory and into Matron Columella's protection."

Mother Otter, her expression thoughtful, said, "We didn't know the Keeper would be moving against the *tonka'tzi*. Crazy Frog was under the assumption that she could protect us better than Columella. It was risky enough getting here, but to go back all the way across Cahokia, let alone find a way across the river?"

Rising Flame's brow furrowed. "Columella still recognizes our authority. Beyond that, Evening Star House is the only thing standing between Spotted Wrist and domination of all Cahokia. She has enough warriors to move against him."

That's when Seven Skull Shield said, "Forget moving against the Keeper. Columella won't."

"And you know this?" Blue Heron asked. "How?"

"Because she's a smart woman," the thief replied. "Her strength for the time being is in keeping Evening Star House together. She's not going to march on Spotted Wrist in some insane campaign to free the rest of Cahokia. It would cost her too much; open fighting would destroy the city."

"Assuming the chaos in River City doesn't spread," Mother Otter replied, all the while giving Seven Skull Shield a probing stare. Sort of like he was somehow surprising her.

"How did that happen?" Rising Flame demanded. "What's possessing those people?"

Mother Otter snapped, "We're tired of being played with and jerked around like fish on a string by the Four Winds Clan. And it doesn't matter if it's War Duck or Spotted Wrist. We've fed them, given them tribute, let them lose our canoes, take a portion of Trade—"

"And you've lived in peace!" Rising Flame shot back. "We've kept order. Made sure that barbarians didn't raid, steal your children, and murder you in your beds. We've ensured the Trade, made it so that goods from all over the—"

"*Enough!*" Seven Skull Shield roared as he stepped between the two incensed women. "Up until now, it all worked. And don't forget Morning Star. He's the reason for all this. Not the Four Winds Clan, not the Traders or the squadrons."

"So?" Wooden Doll asked. "Where's his interest? How come he isn't intervening? He could stop all this nonsense and restore order with a single appearance. From what I've heard, he hasn't left the Great Mound since his souls were rescued from the Underworld."

"No." Rising Flame rubbed a hand over her face, took a breath as if to still her anger at the still-recalcitrant Mother Otter. "If you ask me, he's lost all interest. I think he wants out. Says he's tired. The only subject he ever reacts to is that accursed Koroa copper."

"What is Koroa copper?" Mother Otter asked.

If Blue Heron hadn't been watching Seven Skull Shield at exactly that moment, she'd have missed the subtle tic of his lips.

Could that be the key to this whole thing?

Blue Heron cocked her head. "He sent me and the thief a message. Asked us to work from the shadows. And all this started when the Koroa copper was stolen way back when."

"That gods'-rotted copper?" Rising Flame asked. "It's an obsession with him. And maybe more so with Lady Sun Wing."

Blue Heron kept her gaze fixed on the thief's face as she said, "How do we get a message to Morning Star?"

"To ask him what?" Wind demanded.

"What he'd give to find that copper." Blue Heron pulled at her wattle, correctly reading the expression Seven Skull Shield tried so hard to hide.

Sixty-eight

The river ran smooth and fast over the stony bottom, the outcrops only noticeable when the river was low and the water clear. Here the eastern bluffs rose sheer and close to the water's edge, separated only by a narrow floodplain filled with cottonwoods, willows, and oaks.

The sandy shore beneath the bluffs made for a favored camp spot a day's travel down from Horned Serpent Town's canoe landing, or two days' travel upstream when battling the current.

Within a bow shot both up and down the river from Night Shadow Star and Fire Cat's camp, other Traders had pulled in for the night. Earlier in the season, wood was generally plentiful. But this was late, just days away from equinox. The fire this night was a scant potful of twigs. Just barely enough to heat a bowl of little barley stew. Meat would be jerked duck: hard and chewy until soaked in said lukewarm stew.

The day had been unseasonably warm and clear. From long experience Night Shadow Star figured that by tomorrow the wind would pick up. That a major storm was blowing in from the north.

She walked down to the beach where *Red Reed* was pulled up; a rope ran to a stake driven deep to anchor the craft in case the river rose. There she looked out over the mighty expanse of roiling water, watched as the last of the sunset faded from the western horizon.

But what did it mean? And more to the point, where was Walking Smoke?

"*Close,*" Piasa whispered in her ear. "*Just up ahead.*"

"Can we catch him before he reaches Cahokia?"

"*No.*"

She made a face. There went any chance of paddling up beside the war canoe; river gossip said it was called *Trout*. Had they been able to do that, she could have grabbed up the slender bow she'd Traded in exchange for Summer Ice's. As Walking Smoke stood to see who it was, she could have shot him through the heart.

"*Power won't let you,*" Piasa chided.

"So it has to be the hard way, Lord?"

"*Yes. All those moons ago, Sun Wing saw the truth of it. You and he . . . and the lightning.*"

"But you will be there, right, Lord? Your Power against that of the Thunderbirds?"

"*I will give you everything I can at that final moment.*"

"That's reassuring." She leaned her head back, feeling the spill of dark hair as it tumbled down her back. It didn't seem worth it. All that way to Cofitachequi, to come so close to success, only to have it whisked away by the barest of chance. Then to travel across half the world back to Cahokia. So much effort, so many lives, and all the while Power played her and Fire Cat for fools.

She told Piasa, "When I kill my brother, Fire Cat and I are finished, you understand? We're leaving. Going away someplace where we're not important. Not you, nor Morning Star, nor Snapping Turtle need call upon us again. I will have fulfilled my bargain."

"*When your bargain is fulfilled, once Walking Smoke's Power is broken, and balance is achieved, I will have no hold over you.*" The Spirit Beast might have been whispering into her ear, so close did the voice sound.

She took a deep breath, exhaled. "Thank you."

Once balance is achieved. Underworld and Sky World, red Power and white, order and chaos, male and female. Balance, balance, always balance. And Walking Smoke had sent it all awry.

She needed but to put it right, and she and Fire Cat could walk away. Still . . .

"If I do this, Lord, I will be free. I will no longer be your pawn. You swear that, don't you?"

"*Of course.*" A pause. "*But you know it comes at a cost.*"

"And once I pay, that's it. I am no longer your creature."

"*You will be free.*"

Laughter sounded from up the beach, and in the light of the next Trader's camp, she saw Winder stand. The big Trader wished the men and women seated around the fire a good night and came slowly—head down and lost in thought—along the narrow strip of wave-washed sand.

He glanced up, discerned her form, and walked up to stare at what was left of the sunset. "More news from Cahokia."

They'd heard plenty from the canoes heading downriver who'd called,

"Going to Cahokia? River City's a mess." And "Just heard! Three Fingers, who called himself High Chief, was murdered last night. War Duck's son, Fringed Smoke, ran a spear through Three Fingers' chest. Said he was taking the high chair. Then he had to run when Spotted Wrist's warriors came looking to hang him in a square."

Night Shadow Star rubbed the back of her neck where she'd pulled off a tick the day before. "What did they say?"

"The Keeper's warriors, what's left of North Star Squadron, are in defensive formation in River City plaza. They don't dare march anywhere unless they're in strength. And if they get into the maze of warehouses, any place where they can't defend themselves, the people start tossing rocks at them. An entire squad was caught in an alley that way and almost burned to death when the people set fire to the two warehouses pinning them in."

Winder stuck his thick fingers into his rope belt. "If we can trust the Traders, a lot of the Keeper's warriors are fading away rather than standing to fight. Especially since they don't see the honor in it. I guess, from what I just heard, they're losing faith in the 'Hero of the North.' That fighting weavers, fishermen, Earth Clans folk, potters, and stone grinders isn't quite like crushing enemy warriors in a line of battle."

Her brow lined as she said, "I don't understand. What's Morning Star doing? Why is he letting this happen? No one seems to know."

"Neither do these Casqui Traders. Like everyone else we talk to, they say Morning Star hasn't been seen in moons. That the Keeper now lives in the Great Palace, and he's put all his people, including *Tonka'tzi* Slender Fox, in charge of Cahokia."

Tonka'tzi Slender Fox? What had happened to her aunt, Wind?

"It doesn't make sense!" she cried. "Everything Morning Star has ever done has been calculating and . . ." She chuckled. "Well, *maybe* except for letting that Chicaza girl poison him." Then she frowned. "Or *maybe* letting Sacred Moth carry his souls to the Underworld."

She paused, thinking it through. "Or was it? Fire Cat thinks the poisoning was an elaborate ruse. Some sort of manipulation. But what purpose could it possibly serve? I don't understand."

"Maybe it was to unleash chaos so that Spotted Wrist could take control? Break the authority of the Houses? I was there, remember? I watched it all start to fall apart with the Quiz Quiz excitement. The Houses barely avoided war while they waited to see if Morning Star was going to die."

"But why take the chance that the city would break out in civil war? This is Cahokia!"

"Oh, it's Cahokia, all right," Fire Cat's voice called from the gathering gloom as he walked out to join them. "I just came from that camp downstream. You know all those stories we've been hearing about Forest Squadron and their futile canoe hunt? The Traders tell me that the last of what's left of Forest Squadron put in at the Horned Serpent canoe landing today. Over the last couple of days, as they've arrived in dribs and drabs, they've disembarked and have been marching piecemeal on Horned Serpent Town."

"That being the case, we don't want to put in there." Winder was rubbing his chin, staring out at the now-dark river. "But what does it mean for us? Sounds like it's ensuring another part of the city isn't going to rise in rebellion."

"Not our problem," Night Shadow Star insisted. "I have to deal with Walking Smoke, and Piasa tells me that we can't catch him." She glanced sidelong at Fire Cat's shadowy form. "It will happen in Cahokia. And, if I know Power, it will either be on the river where he escaped last time, or in Morning Star's palace."

"And just how do we do this?" Fire Cat asked. "Blood Talon and me? Can we just kill him outright?"

She laughed bitterly. "I must face him, husband. As I have always had to face him. Him and me. The two of us. And only the two of us. Sun Wing said I had to 'entice the lightning.'"

"What does that mean?" Winder wondered.

She gave the big Trader an awkward shrug. "I have no idea, only that lightning is his Spirit Helper, granted to him by the Thunderbirds."

"Lady," Fire Cat said softly, "if I have the chance—"

"No!" she cried, turning, placing her hands on his chest as she searched his night-shadowed face. "You know the rules. When Piasa tells me the only way I can be free is to defeat Walking Smoke on my own, what does that mean? Tell me."

Fire Cat trembled under her touch, lowered his head to place his cheek against her hair. "I can't lose you."

"He's not going to win. I only need to kill him, and Piasa will no longer own my souls. He has promised me this."

"That doesn't mean that if I get the opportunity—"

"No." She winced, ground her teeth. "You once gave me your word as a Red Wing that you would serve me. That you would follow any order. Is that vow still binding?"

As Fire Cat hesitated, Winder had backed away, turned, and faced the high bluffs to the east, now inky against the night sky.

"On my honor as a Red Wing, I will do as you say." Fire Cat made it sound like the words were torn out of his very heart.

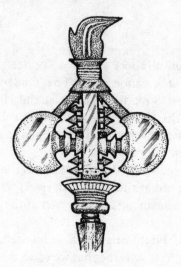

Sixty-nine

If Morning Star's body didn't look so pathetic, Spotted Wrist wouldn't have had to fight a constant battle to show his respect. Wouldn't have had to remind himself that, yes, this was the living god. That Morning Star's Spirit had been reincarnated in that particular young man's body.

But, pus and rot, it was hard to look at the fragile figure curled in fetal position atop the high dais behind the eternal fire.

Adding to the effect were the occasional gasps, the tensing of the man's body. He is in constant pain, Spotted Wrist thought.

And it didn't help that Morning Star rarely ate, and what he did consume was fed to him by lady Sun Wing. She would show up with a bowl of something, the Tortoise Bundle hanging from her back. The guards would let her in, and she'd walk across the mat floor, around the fire, and climb up next to the living god.

Her arrival seemed to be a balm to him. Morning Star would straighten, a smile barely visible through the thick layer of face paint. A spark would return to his normally lusterless eyes, and he'd resettle his stunning regalia.

In the beginning, Spotted Wrist had listened in on their conversations, but given the totally trivial content about what Traders were offering on the Great Plaza, or which stickball team was beating another, or how Lord so-and-so was doing on the chunkey courts, he'd found it a waste of time.

A god should have more pressing concerns.

Spotted Wrist had just finished his own breakfast of baked yellow lotus root, groundnuts, sunflower seed bread, and squash blossom tea when Cut Weasel ushered Lady Sun Wing into the great room. Singing softly to herself about threaded clouds and Dancing rain, the soul-addled woman crossed the room, a simple brownware bowl under one stick-thin arm. But then, given her broken souls, who knew what Dancing rain might be?

Spotted Wrist watched her cross to where Morning Star had just limped his way out from his personal quarters, dressed as usual in all his finery, with a copper split-cloud headdress, his quetzal cape, and white apron. As thick as the grease paint on his face was, Spotted Wrist wondered if it would melt and drip should Morning Star stand too close to the fire.

"Greetings, Lord," Lady Sun Wing called in that vacuous voice of hers, her gaze seeming to drift absently around the room, flitting from one wall hanging, carved relief, and textile to another.

She slung the Tortoise Bundle from her shoulder and laid it on the bottom of the litter. As she did, Morning Star let out a sigh, as if in relief. The hint of a smile bent his lips, his body relaxing.

"Shadows and smoke are floating on the Father Water," Sun Wing chattered in some half-witted comment. "Smoke drifts closest, finding foot in the sand as the shadow paddles closer. Lit by the flashing clouds, brother. Lightning will twist and join, guided by the World Tree. And in the end, you'll be free, free, free."

Spotted Wrist shot them an annoyed look, drank down the last of his squash blossom tea, and stood.

"Here's the sister who will Dance . . ." Sun Wing's voice seemed to fade, as if she couldn't remember what she was saying, her eyes going vacant.

Setting the brownware bowl on the step, she reached into the bag where she carried the Tortoise Bundle and removed a small jar. About the size of a woman's fist, and burnished to a gleaming finish, the incised jar was stoppered with wax. She handed it to Morning Star who clutched it to his chest as though it were something precious.

Then she retrieved the brownware bowl and climbed up on the dais. She offered Morning Star the bowl, saying, "Goose and duck stewed in little barley with stirred-in knotweed seeds."

Morning Star took the bowl, tilted it to his lips and sipped.

Spotted Wrist forgot them as Squadron Second Moon Lance entered the room, bent his head in a ritual greeting to the living god who was slurping from the brownware bowl in a most ungodlike manner.

Stepping up to Spotted Wrist, he bent his head lower, snapping a fist to his chest. "Squadron First Flying Squirrel sends his regards, Lord Keeper. I'm to inform you that we've managed to drive this Fringed Smoke into hiding for the time being. We've made sure that he can't profit from the murder of High Chief Three Fingers. We still control the plaza, the Four Winds Clan House, and the Men's, Women's, and society houses along with the major Earth Clans high chiefs and matrons, most of whom are more or less under our protection."

"Protection?" Spotted Wrist asked.

Moon Lance's expression warmed. "Yes, Lord. That's what we're calling it. By keeping them under guard, Squadron First Flying Squirrel can ensure that no unwanted support will be given to the upstart, Fringed Smoke. When things settle down, we're sure the Lord Keeper will have appointed an appropriate Four Winds Clan replacement for Three Fingers as High Chief for the River House."

"Assuming the Lord Keeper can find the time to do so," Spotted Wrist muttered. "The first few detachments from Forest Squadron are settling themselves in Horned Serpent Town. Word is that Green Chunkey has bid them welcome . . . and he has even sent me a runner to the effect. Squadron First Heart Warrior, however, sends me a runner expressing additional concerns. He informs me that while no overt moves have been made against the first squads to get there, the mood of the people is anything but welcoming."

Moon Lance frowned slightly, but nodded, as if appreciative of being included in the sharing of such important information.

Spotted Wrist narrowed an eye. "In addition, Flying Squirrel's report is also less than encouraging. He's missing about a third of his squadron. He reported last night that not only was he unable to contact all the squads he had out searching for the canoes but his command is spread out, coming upriver squad by squad as they can. And some, he fears, may not have received the order at all."

"So, what are they going to do? Keep heading on down the river?"

"Who knows?" Spotted Wrist said dryly. "I didn't know the lure of southern lands and nations had such a seductive call to a true warrior's heart."

He cocked his head, glaring into the squadron second's stoic face. "How about your squadron? How many have we lost in the last couple of days? What's your true strength?"

Moon Lance stiffened, worked his lips. "We're down to about half, Lord Keeper. Given the ones killed in the rioting, not to mention the wounded, and well, others just keep drifting away. I left before the morning count."

"Half?"

Moon Lance kept working his lips. His eyes fixed uncomfortably on the far back wall, with its Four Winds Clan carvings.

"Squadron Second?" Spotted Wrist prompted.

"Maybe a third might be a more accurate representation of what Squadron First Flying Squirrel can call into formation."

Spotted Wrist stepped over, sank onto one of the ornately carved sleeping benches. "A third? Maybe, what, forty or fifty warriors?"

Glancing up, he saw the hesitation in Moon Lance's eyes, told the second, "Give it to me straight."

"Before you make a judgment, Lord Keeper, I want you to know that Squadron First Flying Squirrel has never failed in his—"

"Yes, yes, I know!" Spotted Wrist felt the first curdling in his stomach. "What's the rest?"

Moon Lance looked like the admission might make him sick. "There is a reluctance among the warriors to leave the plaza, Lord Keeper. They don't want to make patrols out into the city. And if they're so ordered, they trot out of sight, hunker down, and wait it out before returning to report that all's well."

"And is all well in River City Mounds?"

Moon Lance nodded. "Yes, Lord Keeper. It is. As long as our warriors stay on the plaza and don't venture out into the warehouse district, the canoe landing, or the workshops. As long as we stay out of the way, the city couldn't care less. They just go on about their business."

"And Columella?"

"She's carrying on an active Trade, moving goods across the river by the canoe load. The Traders land on the upper part of the canoe landing. Follow the northern trail along Cahokia Creek, and cut over to the Avenue of the Sun. The good news there, Lord Keeper, is that the Traders and Columella pretty much ignore us. Acts like she couldn't care less what we're doing as long as we don't bother her or her people."

"And if she tried to take River City?"

Moon Lance was back to sucking on his lips. "If she made a concerted push, landed a couple of squadrons, given how the people feel about her versus us? Understrength as we are, she'd roll right over us."

"Cut Weasel!" Spotted Wrist bellowed.

At his call, one of the great double doors was set aside and the squadron first appeared. The man's armor was freshly polished, his cuirass looking a little tight since he'd been eating so lavishly and exercising so little. Cut Weasel stepped smartly across the matting and saluted. "Lord Keeper."

"What's your take on the situation here?"

"Nothing to report, Keeper. If anything, we're getting lazy. And still no sign of Rising Flame, Wind, or any of the rest of the troublemakers. Five Fists and his officers seem to have settled in at the Men's House. They constantly drill and train, but that's about it."

"Could we spare Long Wrist and three squads? Send them to reinforce Flying Squirrel?" Spotted Wrist fingered his chin, a speculative eye on Cut Weasel.

The first squinted in thought. "You dispatched Buffalo Horn with three squads to Horned Serpent House last night. As thinly spread as what's left of us are—"

"Have you or your warriors seen anything that might suggest anyone in Morning Star House or central Cahokia might cause trouble here that you couldn't put down with a small force?"

"Not to date, Keeper. Even my wife . . . um, the *tonka'tzi* remarked that she's dismissed the old Great Sky's staff, has almost entirely replaced it with her own servants from Serpent Woman Town. She's preparing a feast for when High Chief Wolverine comes down to discuss House business."

"Then send them," Spotted Wrist decided. He glanced up at Moon Lance. "That should shore up your defenses. But if you see anything that suggests that Columella might be making a move, send me a runner immediately." He smiled. "She's the only possible threat to us, and if for the moment she's willing to ignore us, we'll offer her the same courtesy."

"For the moment?" Moon Lance asked.

"For the moment." The smile Spotted Wrist gave the man leaked satisfaction.

To Cut Wrist, he added, "Send Long Wrist with the second, here."

"We'll have to strip half the guard from the Great Mound," Cut Wrist told him.

"As if there's a need for them," Spotted Wrist half growled. "They just stand around, bored stiff, with aching feet. If they're in River City Mounds, it's that much less water, food, and supplies that we have to haul up the stairs. Besides, this is the home of the living god. Who'd dare attack it?"

He pointed at where Morning Star was, leaning close to Sun Wing. While she stroked the Tortoise Bundle, he kept whispering something into the Power-touched woman's ear. As he did, she was smiling and singing some nonsense song about brothers and trails, and "mounds of dirt raised on hurt."

Spotted Wrist gave his warriors a knowing smile. "Who's going to mess with him?"

Seventy

After all the things War Leader Five Fists had endured in Morning Star's service, he'd figured that he had seen and done just about everything. That nothing could surprise him anymore. Or he'd believed that right up to the moment Morning Star had ordered him, his warriors, the recorders and messengers, and the rest of the household staff out of the Great Palace.

That morning he stood in the doorway of the Men's House where it fronted the Great Plaza's eastern side. One arm braced on the heavy frame post, he looked out at the sunbaked, trampled plaza. The portal was set aside to allow what breeze there was to blow through the building. From the shade of the covered veranda, he watched two men's teams battling on the stickball field just across the avenue. They were drenched in sweat and panting hard, some staggering in the heat. But the brutal game went on, as if the stifling humidity made the players even more aggressive.

"Not good to have a day this hot, especially coming up on equinox," he told the warriors lounging on the veranda porch. That usually meant one hell of a storm was going to roll out of the north or west tomorrow or the next day. But then he'd never understood weather.

Behind him and to either side, his Morning Star Squadron warriors had laid out their armor and adornments. Just because Morning Star had stood them down didn't mean that the finest military unit in the known world would allow themselves to stagnate.

In fact, for Five Fists and War Chief War Claw, this was an opportunity to exercise and train his warriors in a way he'd never been able to while they were standing guard or escorting Morning Star or his various

356 W. Michael Gear and Kathleen O'Neal Gear

high and exalted guests. Someone was always on duty, which meant only portions of the squadron could train together, and it had always been haphazard.

With all of them stood down, Morning Star Squadron had already made two forced marches around the city, had drilled with shields and war clubs, practiced formation assaults, coordinated movement, and worked on defensive maneuvers behind a shield wall as blunt-tipped arrows rained down on them.

Chosen from the finest veteran warriors in Cahokia, Morning Star Squadron was now at its peak operating efficiency.

Yes, the vaunted Wolverine Squadron strutted around the Great Plaza, and yes, under Blood Talon's command, they'd taken Red Wing Town. And yes, they'd fought in the north.

Five Fists, however, knew warriors. All the Keeper's squadrons had been tight when they returned to Cahokia. Blooded from battles with barbarian forest chiefs up north. But they hadn't stood against truly trained warriors.

For all the upset and soul-searching that had been caused by the Itza massacre of Cahokian warriors at Lady Night Shadow Star's wedding, Five Fists and War Claw had taken the lesson to heart. Death in combat was an unforgiving teacher. That it had been so humiliating meant it could never be allowed to happen again.

Five Fists watched as four of Spotted Wrist's warriors trotted past, helmets hanging behind them due to the heat, their shields and war clubs dangling, sweat staining their leather-and-wood cuirasses. As they passed by, they shot dismissive glances his way. Nothing overtly offensive, just those hints of mocking smiles on their faces.

But he caught the implication, their sense of superiority.

And so, too, did the rest of his Morning Star warriors where they lounged around in the shade, cleaning their kit.

Five Fists could see it in their postures, the fixing of their eyes, and the working of their jaws. It didn't matter that these were Cahokians. Morning Star Squadron wanted to mix it up. And he'd crush Spotted Wrist's vaunted veterans like a poorly fired and crumbling pot.

This whole situation was intolerable.

"What could you have been thinking?" Five Fists whispered under his breath as he glanced sidelong at Morning Star's high palace atop the Great Mound. The palace, its thatched roof steep behind the high palisade, the World Tree Pole shooting up into the sky, it all seemed to waver in the heat and humidity.

In answer to his own question, Five Fists said, "Morning Star plays a deep game."

Blood and spit, but he hoped that was what this was all about.

Not that Morning Star had been quite right since his return from the Underworld and that insane business with Sacred Moth and that Chicaza girl.

That was another time when it had taken every bit of Five Fists' integrity, discipline, and resolve to follow the living god's orders.

"You will not interfere," he growled loudly enough that Half Moon glanced up from where he was waxing his cuirass until the wood and leather gleamed.

"War Leader?" the warrior asked.

"Just talking to myself."

"You heard that Spotted Wrist"—no one called him Keeper in Morning Star Squadron unless they were in public—"sent a full third of his strength to River City this morning?"

"I did. On top of the third he sent to Horned Serpent Town last night."

Half Moon squinted across the plaza at the Great Staircase where it led up to Morning Star's high palace. "He's got hardly enough warriors left to man the posts, not enough if they've got other duties."

"And they do." Five Fists pointed across the Great Plaza, past the soaring World Tree Pole to where a knot of people crowded in front of the *tonka'tzi*'s earthen pyramid with its sprawling palace. "With Morning Star doing whatever Morning Star is doing—and he's seeing no one but Spotted Wrist—the good Lady Slender Fox has shifted all functions from the Council Terrace to the *tonka'tzi*'s palace. All those embassies, the Earth Clans chiefs and matrons, the entire focus of Cahokia is now in her front room and council chamber. That slick sheath has to love every moment of it. It's made her the center of the city."

"I take it you don't like her very much." Half Moon was staring at the crowd that, from his vantage, looked to be choking the bottom of the staircase.

"You never heard me say that, warrior."

"Of course not." Half Moon pointed at his right ear. "I ever tell you that I'm hard of hearing? I think my mother let a cricket climb into my ear one night when I was a baby."

Five Fists grinned his lop-jawed grin.

From somewhere overhead, a red-tailed hawk screamed a shrill *keeraw*.

As if it were an announcement of her arrival, Five Fists saw Lady Sun Wing strolling down the avenue, passing in front of the Recorders' Society House. She wore a milkweed fiber skirt and a thin textile cape to block the sun, and carried the Tortoise Bundle in its sack slung over her shoulder.

Just the sight of her sent a nervous quiver through Five Fists' stomach.

Touched by Power as she was, her souls broken and shattered by her brother's insanity, she always made him anxious. Not that he blamed her. Walking Smoke had stripped her naked, had her held upside down over a pot to catch her blood, and had even placed a blade against her throat to sacrifice her. Lady Night Shadow Star had saved the young woman within an instant of having her throat slit.

That would make a gibbering idiot out of anyone.

Right up until Sun Wing had taken the Tortoise Bundle as her own and become its keeper. Something of her had come back, but she was still spooky, vacant-eyed, and unpredictable.

Too much Power was concentrated in that whole family.

To Five Fists' consternation, she turned off the avenue, crossed the packed-dirt yard, and stepped up on the veranda. This was followed by a rapid scattering of warriors unwilling to be anywhere close to the demented and Spirit-possessed Sun Wing.

"Lady Sun Wing." Five Fists, unable to flee despite his most fervent desire, bowed and touched his forehead respectfully.

Her gaze went vague, as though unable to fix on anything. That or she was seeing something from the Spirit World that was hovering around like a wounded bumblebee.

"You remember my brother's last order?"

"I'm sure I do, Lady. But, just to be clear, that would be . . . ?"

"Do nothing until you hear from someone in my lineage," she repeated Morning Star's last words, and giggled as if that was amusing. "Lineage is a funny word, isn't it? What does having grown in the same womb inside a woman's body or having been squirted out of the same man's hard shaft as a milky fluid have to do with lines? Lines are straight. From here to there. Like a string pulled tight."

"Lady?" The sensation—like crawling ant feet—in Five Fists' stomach started to unnerve him.

She finally fixed her gaze on his, emptiness looming behind her large black pupils. "It's time."

"Time for what, Lady?"

She smiled absently, head cocked, squinting slightly. He knew that look. She did that when the Tortoise Bundle was whispering in her ear, or souls, or wherever.

Five Fists never heard anything, just had that cold chill run down the back of his neck. The one that made his hair stand on end.

"Time to bring it all to an end." She sounded so sure of herself.

"Bring what to an end?"

"Can't have a beginning without an end. It's time. Some die. Some live. Endings and beginnings. Takes us right back to that womb and the milky white fluid. Everything starts there. With that beginning moment. That's the key, isn't it? Everyone's born to die. Without death there would be no need for that squirting semen. If it weren't for the semen and the womb, there would be no need for death. They are one and the same, you know."

The cold shiver had run clear down from his scalp to the small of his back. "Lady, does this have a point?"

She blinked. Seemed confused, then her expression came back into focus. "Should be obvious, don't you think? Morning Star wants you to go capture Blue Heron, Wind, Rising Flame, and the thief. He wants you to take them up to the palace."

She turned, stepped off the porch, was singing that same Song she always did. The one about dead brothers, and drought, and fire, and some man and woman married on high.

"Wait!" he cried. "How can I go capture them? I don't even know where to find them."

She frowned, as if puzzled by his ignorance. "Why, the Raccoon Clan palace. You know, the one up on the Eastern Bluff just off the Avenue of the Sun. Where High Chief Six Strikes governs the dirt farmers up there."

"How do you know that?"

She shrugged as if it were nothing. "Seems obvious, don't you think?" She turned, made two more steps, and whirled back. "Oh, and you can bring the dog. Morning Star doesn't care if he pees on the door frame or the World Tree Pole. He won't be there for much longer anyway."

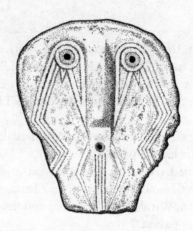

Where the Serpent Eats His Tail

I *brace myself as* Trout *is driven onto the charcoal-stained beach at the canoe landing below River City. As always, the sharp bow slices a furrow into the wet sand.*

I am perched in the canoe's rear, braced, as the vessel comes to a stop.

But there is no joy, no shouts of delight. Instead, the warriors turn, paddles in their hands, and stare at me with wary and uncertain eyes. I can see the worry in their tattooed faces, the thin set of their lips.

They are waiting.

All but High Chief Fire Light, who bends his head and begins to weep.

For the warriors' benefit, I reach into my belt pouch, remove the lightning shell mask, and slip it over my face. Through the eye slots, I enjoy the sudden terror as the warriors recoil.

In the accented Muskogee tongue used at Cofitachequi, I cry, "Begone, you little worms and useless bits of flesh. Go live your miserable and meaningless existences! Couple with your homely women and beget a pack of sniveling, snot-nosed children so that the world must endure another generation of pointless lives that do nothing but produce yet more sniveling and pitiful brats."

Then I remove the mask, and, in Cahokian so they understand, say, "You are free to go. Don't eat fish, deer, turtle, or turkey for a half moon. Avoid any copulation with either a woman or black-spotted dogs. Such foods and activities interfere with the souls' ability to attach firmly back in your bodies."

I make a shooing gesture. "Now, go. Away. Be off with you. Go find your clans."

Like passenger pigeons before a sharp shinned hawk, they scramble out of the canoe. I see a flurry of arms grabbing blankets and packs, and they scatter like quail.

This leaves me and Fire Light. The high chief still weeps, as if some part of his damaged souls is either relieved or saddened to have once again returned to Cahokia.

I climb out, wishing I'd had the forethought to have the warriors drag Trout farther up on the sand. But what do I care if the canoe drifts away?

I look at the boxes and stacks of beaded messages; all those reports compiled with such diligence by the various chiefs and matrons. All waiting to be carried up to the Council House and brought to the tonka'tzi's attention.

Water splashes as I wade ashore. As is my habit, I reach down and clutch a handful of sand. Placing it to my nose, I inhale the musk of mud and decomposition. Then I press it to my chest and close my eyes before rubbing it into my breastbone above my heart.

Cahokia. I am home.

"Yes!" the voice whispers behind my ear.

I straighten. Unlike the last time I arrived here, there is no throng of Traders and gawkers coming to greet me. Instead, though there are plenty of canoes— and even Traders occupying the ramadas higher on the beach—no one appears to pay me much attention. In fact, if anything, it seems as if the only activity is from canoes landing after crossing from Evening Star Town. The occupants, mostly men, lift wrapped bundles from the hulls and carry them up and into the warehouse district higher on the levee.

Something, however, isn't right. The skyline should have more roofs. It looks like there are buildings missing. And here and there, I can see burned structures where only black ash and charred posts remain.

The word on the river was that River House was on the verge of war.

When I look back at Evening Star Town across the river, the skyline is familiar. The mounds, roofs, and World Tree Poles are like I last saw them. Not that I looked back at Columella's fiery palace that day.

And right out there, just downstream, is the place where Night Shadow Star almost got me killed. The place she capsized our canoe and dragged me down to Piasa's lair.

I finger the scar on my cheek, wondering what happened that day when the lightning saved me, and where it took my body for those missing moons until I walked out of a burning temple in far-off Cofitachequi.

Then I turn back to the canoe and order Fire Light, "Get up, chief. We're here. You have the thing you wanted more than life itself. You are home. And I,

Walking Smoke, heir to the Four Winds Clan, the Wild One, do hereby grant you forgiveness for whatever misbehavior got you banished in the first place."

Not to mention that doing so might put me in good favor with his sister, Rising Flame, who is now Four Winds Clan Matron. I remember her as an attractive girl. But that was years ago, before her father took her with him down south.

Fire Light clambers slowly out of the canoe, collects his blanket, and gives me a dull "what now" look. Something about the man reminds me of a faithful dog. The kind that just waits for you to tell him what to do.

Retrieving one of the pointed paddles, I set off up the beach. Fire Light follows along, his half-empty eyes looking this way and that as if he's slightly confused. There is no telling what thoughts fill his blocky head. But then, I don't need him for his ability to think.

The day is unaccountably hot for this late in the season. The sky brassy, the air sweltering.

For the moment, I need an abandoned building. And, even more to the point, someplace where no one will come looking if Fire Light lets out a scream or two.

Seventy-one

Seven Skull Shield figured he was better than this. Well, all right, except for those times when he was caught by surprise in Meander's shell-carving workshop, or when he was plumbing the depths of some willing woman's ever-so-inviting sheath. To his embarrassment, the time when Spotted Wrist's warriors had separated him from Willow Blossom's cunning and too-clinging embrace came to mind.

Well, that time didn't count—seeing as how she had plotted his capture from the very beginning and was purposely distracting him with her enthusiastic charms.

This time, he should have sensed the coming trap; might have, but he and Farts were on the floor playing with Scoot, Tick, and Lumpy while Crazy Frog's girls, Sky and Tight Hair, laughed from the side.

Wooden Doll, legs kicked out and crossed at the ankles, had been watching him with an evaluative gaze that he wasn't used to. Usually when she was giving him a look, it was the hard one that she adopted when she was picturing how his life was going to end. How he'd be dying on a square. And how short and painful it would be.

This appraisal was softer, as though she was seeing him in an entirely different light.

Seven Skull Shield was as surprised as everyone else when Five Fists opened the door, set it aside, and led an entire squad of Morning Star warriors dressed in battle armor into the room. At the same time the warriors entered, Farts sent children tumbling as he broke loose of their hold. The dog took one look with his blue and brown eyes. In a most athletic leap, the beast crashed through the lattice-covered window in the palace wall and vanished.

Seven Skull Shield, caught flat-bottomed on the floor, gaped first at the splintered window, then at Five Fists and his warriors.

The grizzled war leader barked, "You are all under guard. I have orders to take you to Morning Star."

Matron Rising Flame had shot to her feet, demanding, "Do you know who you are talking to?"

Five Fists, his jaw even more crooked, if that were possible, dryly said, "Four Winds Clan Matron Rising Flame, if I'm not mistaken. Charming outfit. Even with the holes, stains, and frayed fabric." He pointed, "And there, despite their equally tawdry dress, I see Ladies Wind and Blue Heron of Morning Star House."

Then he'd given Seven Skull Shield a disgusted look. "Ah, it's my old friend Tow Rope. What a surprise. As to you, you bit of human garbage—"

"I can go?" Seven Skull Shield suggested as he stood and started for the door. "Got to find my dog."

Smart dog, that Farts, but how had he known so quickly?

"If the thief takes one more step, brain him!" Five Fists snapped. The homely war leader gave Seven Skull Shield his best grin, which wasn't all that pretty given his broken jaw. Then he added, "No one said anything about either conscious or alive."

"What about the rest of them?" another of the warriors asked as he shot an uncertain glance at the terrified children scrambling across the floor toward their mothers' arms. Crazy Frog's wives had retreated to a corner, where they cowered.

Five Fists stepped up to Wooden Doll, who'd also stood up, and met his questioning gaze with her own steady stare. "I don't know you."

"No, you don't."

"Bring her, too," Five Fists muttered. "She's dressed too well to be riffraff."

He took in Crazy Frog's wives, all of them, including Mother Otter, where they crouched in the corner. The children reminded Seven Skull Shield of mice caught in the bottom of a seed jar with nowhere to go.

"You live here?" Five Fists demanded.

Mother Otter just nodded, trying to keep her chin from quivering.

"They belong to High Chief Six Strikes." Blue Heron stepped forward, scowling at the nearest warrior as she did. "Don't hold our presence here against him. He was only following my orders, and these women and children had nothing to do with it."

Five Fists said, "I'll take your word for it, Keeper. Now, let's go. Morning Star gave me an order. You know this is nothing personal, and if it had come from anyone but the living god . . ."

Blue Heron reached out and laid a reassuring hand on the war leader's shoulder. "You and I made our peace long ago, old friend. Before we're hanging in squares, is there anything I should know?"

"Only that Lady Sun Wing brought me Morning Star's order. And yes, I know it came from him and not Spotted Wrist." He gave her a pained look. "Otherwise I'd have told the 'Hero of the North' to go blow air up his anus."

"But you don't have a clue?" Rising Flame asked.

"No, Clan Matron." To the warriors, Five Fists gestured. "Let's go. It's going to be after dark before we get there as it is."

Then the old warrior fixed Seven Skull Shield with a narrow-eyed glare. "And keep a close eye on this one. In fact, tie a couple of ropes around his neck. Slippery as he is, I don't want him disappearing before we get there."

As the ropes were fastened around his neck, Seven Skull Shield cast one last longing look at the broken window. "I am so misunderstood."

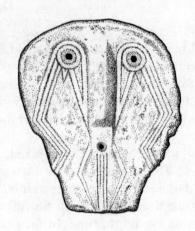

Vision

*I*t is to my good fortune that River City, with its packed warehouse and work-shop district, is in a state of turmoil. I have arrived at exactly the right time. Call it perfect. No one gave me so much as a sidelong glance as Fire Light and I searched among the thickly packed buildings atop the levee.

I see the locals battening down, sealing themselves in their houses, or helping warriors as small parties they trickle through the maze that is River City, all filtering their way down toward the plaza. Looks to me like a fight is brewing, but that is the least of my concerns.

I find what I am looking for on the north end—an abandoned dwelling with a Fish Clan marking over the door. Inside is a mess, with leaf-filled corners, a rickety pole sleeping bench along one wall, and some old rags in one corner. The closest buildings have been burned, which supplies me with lengths of charred wood for a fire.

When Fire Light steps down onto the semi-subterranean floor, he stops. Looks puzzled for the first time since we were pulled from the water below the Suck and Rage.

I hesitate for the moment, amazed to see the light come back to his eyes. His face bends into a frown, which pulls the Four Winds tattoos on his cheeks tight. He cocks his head, asks, "Where are we?"

"A house," I tell him. "On the north end of River City just before the levee drops off to Cahokia Creek."

"What are we doing here?"

"We're in search of a vision," I tell him.

He opens his mouth to ask the next question; I put all my weight behind the *canoe paddle. My swing is perfect. The edge catches Fire Light in the back of the neck, right at the base of the skull.*

He drops like a sack of meat.

I step over him and, using the point on the end of the paddle blade, drive it down with all my force. The point spears into the high chief's throat just below the angle of the jaw. I can hear snapping and cracking, and the man's eyes pop wide.

I wait as he twitches, gasps, and dies. From my pouch I take a sharp chert flake.

"Now you will do me one last favor, High Chief."

Then I bend down and use the razor-sharp stone to cut from Fire Light's breastbone down to the top of his pubis.

As I study the way his ropy intestines are wrapped around, I begin to see the pattern.

But then, this is the most important divination I have ever attempted. I will need to see everything, read the future as I never have. This time I have to be perfect.

I will take my time.

After all, I have all night.

In the distance I hear the unmistakable sound of fighting, the clatter of war clubs on shields. The occasional shout and scream.

And then the rising wind from the north carries them away.

A storm is coming. In more ways than one.

Seventy-two

Thankfully, gnarled old Five Fists had a humane streak. Blue Heron could tell by his glances in her direction and Wind's that he was uncomfortable with the entire operation. When it had become achingly apparent that she couldn't keep the pace because of her hip, and that Wind was going to flag as well, Five Fists had his warriors round up a couple of litters. As a result, both women rode in comfort as they were carried down between the mounds at the top of the bluffs.

Here the Avenue of the Sun had been cut into the loess at the top, and the fill used to create a ramp that eased the gradient for people descending to the floodplain or climbing to the heights.

As they hit the bottom, the sun was already sinking on the western horizon; with equinox on the morrow, it was directly in their eyes. Given the low-hanging smoke and mist, there was no way she could make out Evening Star Town in the far distance.

Wish I was there right now.

Five Fists and his warriors were traveling as fast as Rising Flame and Wooden Doll's pace would allow. And no matter what the war leader's orders required he was unwilling to whip, beat, or prod the Four Winds Clan Matron to get her to move faster. Not that it mattered, but Rising Flame and Wooden Doll, who were both young, were panting, sweating, much more accustomed to a life of leisure.

Blue Heron knew that look on Seven Skull Shield's face: It was the amiable smile, the almost happy twinkle of the eyes that he adopted to allay any suspicion that he was anything but the most affable of characters. Which meant deep down, he was desperate for any opportunity to escape. How he was going to do that with two warriors holding ropes tied to his neck would be quite a trick. Even for him.

When she was carried past one of the Duck Clan's charnel houses atop its mound, she caught the stench of decomposing human flesh and wondered how long it would be before, she, too, smelled like that.

Five Fists picked that moment to drop back, asking, "How are you doing, Keeper?"

"I'm not Keeper any longer."

"You are to me. Much more so than that idiot Rising Flame appointed." His attempt at a smile didn't really work given the wreckage of his jaws. "Wonder how the Clan Matron is feeling about that decision these days?"

"I think she's wishing she could go back and pour water hemlock into his tea. I sure am." She shot Five Fists a sidelong look. "What's this about?"

"No clue. I told you. Sun Wing came to give me the living god's order, and she did it in the way the living god told me it would happen. So, yes, I know it's from him. But whether it was of Morning Star's own free will, I can't tell you."

"How'd you find us? We were hidden. Looking like we just stepped off a dirt farmer's field." She made a face. "One of Six Strikes' people sell us out?"

"Got me." He gave a shrug. "Sun Wing acted like everyone should know."

"Huh!" Blue Heron rubbed her hot face. "What happens when you get us up to the palace?"

"No clue. I was just sent to find and bring you back." He glanced up. "You know that if it wasn't Morning Star . . ."

"I know your oath." She lowered her voice, hating that the six warriors carrying her litter could hear the entire conversation. "You know whose side we're on, here, right?"

"Keeper, I do." He knotted a fist, shook it, and made a throwing away motion with it. "Sorry."

She sighed, fixed her eyes on the avenue ahead where it ran straight as a tight thread toward the distant Great Mound. People passed, packing all manner of burdens. Like the blood in the very body of the city, they carried food, fuel, Trade, and the supplies that fed the sprawling wonder of Cahokia. As Five Fists' party approached, people made way for the warriors, casting curious glances, backs bent to their burdens, and wondering who the plain-dressed women were atop the litters, and the tall thief led by two ropes.

Fact is, next time you see us, it will probably be hanging in squares as Spotted Wrist's warriors torture us to death.

She asked the war leader, "How long has Morning Star been up there alone with Spotted Wrist?"

"Almost a moon, Keeper." He paused. "That's a lot of time to work on someone. Even a living god. Time to slowly influence, bend him to one's will. And there's no telling what the 'Hero of the North' has been telling Morning Star. He could be feeding him any kind of lies he likes."

Five Fists looked around at the palaces, temples, society houses, and council lodges they were passing. Overhead the sky was turning purple with the evening. A storm was definitely coming down from the blackening north. "As to why Morning Star sent me? Could be because Spotted Wrist has so few warriors left after sending so many to prop up River House and Horned Serpent House that he doesn't have the necessary bodies."

Blue Heron glanced over the heads of the warriors carrying her litter. "You sure you won't just let us go?"

Five Fists pursed his lips. "I would like nothing better. But I can only be what and who I am."

She grunted. "Rising Flame says Morning Star's not healthy. That the last time she saw him, he looked sick."

"He looked frail when he ordered all of us out." Five Fists paced uneasily beside the litter. "Don't know why he'd be feeling poorly. He's in Chunkey Boy's body. It's what, no more than twenty-five years old?"

"But if he was ill?" she wondered. "Maybe fading? That's a reason to order people out of the palace, isn't it? And you can bet that if Chunkey Boy's body is dying, Spotted Wrist would never call Rides-the-Lightning. Blood and spit! No, he'd want the living god preoccupied with health issues for as long as he could. Less likely that Morning Star could issue some order he didn't like."

"And, for all we know, Keeper," Five Fists said, "maybe Morning Star is so feeble he'll do anything Spotted Wrist asks."

She twisted in the litter, looking longingly at the bluffs in the dim light behind them. Wishing she was headed back toward the safety of the bluff top.

Then she saw the dog. Farts was following along in the growing shadows as they merged with the night.

Well, it looked like the mangy beast wasn't any smarter than the rest of them.

"I guess, if I'm going to die, I can do so," she told Five Fists. "But if I could ask for one last favor?"

"Of course, Keeper."

"Don't let me linger? Even if I'm ordered to hang in a square. You'll make it quick, won't you?"

Five Fists nodded. "I will." A beat. "Assuming I'm not hanging in a square beside you."

"What?"

He shrugged in the gathering gloom. "I think none of this is going to work out well for us, Keeper. I think we're all about to die."

Seventy-three

With the last rays of light bleeding out of the western sky, White Mat used his paddle, turning *Red Reed* in toward Cahokia's canoe landing. On the western bluff, Evening Star Town made the faintest silhouette, just a black shadow against the darkening heavens and the wall of inky cloud that rode down from the north.

The first fingers of wind pushed a light chop down the darkening river.

Night Shadow Star, filled with images that stirred and teased her imagination, bent to her paddle, driving it deep in the rhythm she and the rest had turned into a smooth poetry of motion during their time together on the river.

Winder and Blood Talon hopped over the side, holding *Red Reed* against the shore as Night Shadow Star, Fire Cat, White Mat, and Shedding Bird climbed out. Taking hold of the gunwales, they dragged the slim Trade canoe up onto the beach.

"*Yes, you are home, woman. This is the end,*" Piasa's voice hissed behind her ear.

Fires burned in the camps dotting the canoe landing and before the ramadas, the flames bending and snapping with the increasing breeze. For the number of canoes present, there didn't seem to be the expected number of people camped or tending the vessels.

Cocking her head, Night Shadow Star stood listening as Fire Cat and the rest began unloading their bedding and packs.

Mixed in between the lulls in gusts, she thought she could hear the sound of fighting coming from over by the plaza.

"How are you doing?" Fire Cat asked as he brought her pack with its weapons and blankets. Her cape she wrapped around her shoulders, then slung the heavy pack.

"I'm filled with dark thoughts," she told him. "I keep catching glimpses of Piasa, just flickers at the corner of my eyes. It's the feeling I'm getting: ominous and threatening. Walking Smoke is here. A storm is coming." She laid a hand on his shoulder. "I've never felt this sure. It's coming to an end, Fire Cat. Him and me. Like we're tied with some cord that is drawing us closer and closer."

"*The worlds are coming together.*" Piasa flickered at the edge of her vision. "*Feel the Power.*"

Fire Cat glanced uneasily at the surrounding canoes, studied the closest camps where low fires burned. Then he reached into his pack and pulled out his war club. "Just in case," he told her. "Think I need my armor?"

"Not yet." She felt the correctness of that. "If I didn't meet him on the river, where he and I were last in conflict, it will be at Morning Star's."

"*Yes,*" Piasa whispered in her ear.

She glanced around as White Mat, Shedding Bird, Winder, and Blood Talon finished their duties and stood waiting.

"White Mat? Shedding Bird?" she asked. "I need you to stay here. All the Trade in my box is yours on the off chance I don't make it back. Otherwise, Fire Cat and I want you here, ready go at a moment's notice."

She walked over to White Mat, laid a hand on his arm. "You have been a good friend." Then to Shedding Bird, she added, "It is a privilege to have shared such a journey with you."

"Lady," White Mat asked, "are you sure you don't want us to go with you?"

"No, this is Power. Just my brother and me. But I want you ready to go. When I finish this thing, Fire Cat and I are free. We're leaving Cahokia. We'll bring Trade, more than enough, and you will carry us downriver. Or maybe up the Tenasee. Someplace where they have never heard of Night Shadow Star or Fire Cat."

"And what then?" Shedding Bird asked.

"We disappear," Fire Cat told him before taking Night Shadow Star's hand and raising it to his lips. "Then we farm, perhaps Trade a little. We will raise our children and grow old together. Maybe someplace like Maygrass Town. That's where you will take us. A place like that."

The brothers both bowed, touching their foreheads. In unison, they said, "We'll be waiting."

White Mat added, "And even if half of Cahokia is chasing after you, they'll never catch *Red Reed*."

"Be ready," Night Shadow Star insisted. "We'll look for you here." Then she turned, and headed up the beach. It sent slivers of fear up her back. She could feel Piasa pacing right behind her. Could almost hear his clawed feet on the shifting sand.

Beside her, Fire Cat said, "I liked Maygrass Town. Abandoned, but with good soil. Mussels and fish in the Sand River. Good hunting."

She liked the way he said it, as if it would really happen. She needed to hear that, especially as lightning flashed in the distant north and lit up the clouds.

"What's the plan for us?" Blood Talon asked as he and Winder followed.

"Morning Star's palace," Night Shadow Star told him, seeing a faint blue glow at the edge of her vision where Piasa now stalked among the pulled-up canoes.

"And then?" Winder asked.

"That will depend on Walking Smoke." She glanced uneasily toward the north and the gathering storm. A prickling of concern grew in her chest, a tightness that made it impossible to draw a full breath.

She could feel the moment Walking Smoke's presence loomed in the darkness, and she gasped.

"What is it?" Fire Cat asked, raising his war club, head craning as he searched this way and that for a threat.

"He's watching us," she told him, a chill like a miasmic breeze nauseating her souls.

"Where?" Blood Talon asked, his bow in hand, an arrow nocked.

"Not here," she told the squadron first. "No . . . He's . . . Don't you feel it? He's seeing us as a vision . . . one reflected in blood. From somewhere here." A pause. "In the city."

"What do you mean?" Winder asked as he turned this way and that, arms bent the way they would if he were about to grapple with an assailant.

"Power," Fire Cat grunted. "He sees the future by murdering someone and gutting their body, remember?"

"Perverting the uses of Power," Blood Talon agreed. "Wonder what poor fool crossed his path this time?"

"High Chief Fire Light," Night Shadow Star said softly. "He's using Four Winds blood to track me. A relative. That's why he kept him alive all this time. For this."

"What does it mean?" Fire Cat asked her.

She hated the feeling of eerie chill, that sensation of eyes watching her from the darkness. Knowing that Walking Smoke knew exactly where she was, what she was doing.

She fought a sudden shiver, as if black tendrils were reaching out of the wind-blown night to trace across her skin.

"Got to change this," she told herself, desperately trying to shake off the growing realization that she was going to fail.

"How?" Winder asked.

"Got to play it differently." She started up the beach, muscles driven by her growing desperation. As she did, it was all she could do to keep from curling against Fire Cat's reassuring side. Asking him to hold her close and safe.

And then she caught sight of Piasa slipping between two of the ramadas just at the edge of the buildings. As if the Underwater Panther were leading the way. And it hit her.

"He's always waited for me. Just like that first time when he raped me. As he was at Evening Star Town. And again at Joara. This time, I'll be waiting for him."

"How do you know where he'll be?" Fire Cat asked.

"Like a snake devouring his tail, everything goes back to its beginning. The place it all started."

"And where's that?" Winder asked.

"Morning Star's palace," she answered. "We have to beat him to the Great Mound."

"And then?" Fire Cat asked.

"And then I kill him," she said with false assurance.

In the night, Piasa laughed, the hollow echo sending tremors through her bones.

Seventy-four

Rising Flame had never been so humiliated—or as physically exhausted—as she was when she was half-carried up the Great Staircase. She wasn't used to walking far or fast, let alone at a forced pace. After the trek from the bluff, she could not have climbed those steps without collapsing. As it was, her legs barely supported her, muscles trembling and half-flaccid. Her feet ached as if they'd been bent backward.

She glanced over her shoulder, seeing the thief, still on the end of ropes, sweep the exhausted Wooden Doll off her feet when she could go no farther. The paid woman—equally used to being transported by litter—hadn't fared any better. As they started up the final stairs, the thief carried Wooden Doll as if she were a feather weight.

Not only was Rising Flame a stumbling-weary prisoner but she was dressed like a common farm woman. A mere laborer in the fields. Or a grinder of corn. Not that she'd minded such ignominy when—as a scared fugitive—she'd passed unnoticed by Spotted Wrist's warriors. Essentially invisible to them. But that they now raised torches to illuminate her half-staggering and panting shame, and called out names, made it intolerable.

"Hey, dirt farmer! Where's the Clan Matron?" one short, swarthy North Star warrior called as she stumbled over the top step and onto the head of the Council Terrace stairs. "Steal that filthy skirt from a corpse in some dirt farmer's charnel house, did you?"

The Morning Star House warriors assisting her didn't respond, just kept their faces ahead as they helped her through the Council Terrace Gate and across the plaza. But she did hear one of the Morning Star warriors say, "And they're bragging? Didn't notice them finding the Matron or the *tonka'tzi.*"

"And how does that make you feel?" Rising Flame asked the warrior who'd spoken. "You're the ones doing their dirty work. You understand, don't you, if we get up there and Spotted Wrist is giving the orders, this might be the last night your city will be run by Morning Star House."

"How's that?" one of the warriors asked.

"After he kills me, Wind, and Blue Heron, it will be Spotted Wrist's city. His warriors will be the elite. You all will serve him. Take his orders."

"The living god won't allow it," another said. "You'll see."

"Oh?" she wondered. "You been counting the number of Spotted Wrists' warriors who are guarding the Great Mound? Only four at the foot of the stairs? That maggot that just insulted me at the Council Gate? He was alone. And now, look. Here we are at the foot of the stairs leading up to Morning Star's palace, and there's no one."

It proved to be the same at the top, the high palisade gate unguarded, and only a single warrior stood before the carved double doors leading into Morning Star's palace.

"Who comes?" he demanded. "How did you pass the guard below?"

Five Fists strode forward at the head of his procession. "I am War Leader Five Fists. I come on Morning Star's orders. I was asked to find, detain, and deliver *Tonka'tzi* Wind, Clan Matron Rising Flame, the lady Blue Heron, the thief, and anyone I considered part of their group."

From her angle, Rising Flame couldn't see Five Fists' face, but he laid a war club on the guard's armored shoulder, and said, "Step aside," in a deadly voice. "Or I will knock you out of the way."

With a full squad of Morning Star House warriors backing the war leader, the guard moved rapidly, even saluting in the process.

Cued by a nod of Five Fists' head, two of his warriors set the double doors aside. A formation of five warriors led the way inside.

Rising Flame hobbled into the great room where Spotted Wrist was climbing to his feet. Apparently, he'd taken her accustomed position to the right of Morning Star's raised dais. They'd caught the man in the middle of his evening meal, given the steaming bowl and wooden plate before him.

"What is the meaning of this?" he bellowed. "Guard!"

"He's outside," Five Fists muttered from the side of his mouth. Then he stopped in front of the eternal fire. Dropping to his knees before Morning Star, he touched his forehead to the matting, calling, "Lord, according to your orders, I have delivered the people you asked for. I give you *Tonka'tzi* Wind, Four Winds Clan Matron Rising Flame, Lady Blue Heron, the thief, and a paid woman who was in their company."

Behind him, the rest of the Morning Star warriors had taken a knee, heads bowed.

To Rising Flame's surprise, Morning Star was curled on his side atop the panther hides on the litter. Knees tucked to his chest, arms bent, he looked somehow broken, pathetic. Anything but a living god. How had this happened? What had the Keeper done to him?

"I didn't order this!" Spotted Wrist barked.

"No, you didn't." Morning Star's voice was hoarse. He carefully uncurled from his pained fetal position. The way he did reminded Rising Flame of a moth rising from a cocoon. The living god looked frail and thin as he straightened.

The living god was dressed in his usual finery: burnished copper headdress with a radial eagle-feather splay, the gorgeous quetzal-feather cape, a stunning white apron with scalp locks and a Spirit Bundle sewn on the front.

Instead of his polished copper mace—the symbol of his office—he held a small fist-sized ceramic jar with a narrow neck. Into this, he dipped his index finger, then touched it to his tongue, apparently tasting the contents.

Morning Star's face wore its traditional paint: white background and black forked eyes with the two tails running down his cheeks. The human-head maskettes covered his ears. To Rising Flame's practiced eye, the paint was thicker, not applied with the usual intricate attention to detail. Despite the makeup, the living god's features looked hollow, almost drawn. And yes, his body was almost skeletal.

What's wrong with him?

Morning Star then stood, descended to the top step of his dais; his dress left him resplendent in the firelight. He turned half-lidded eyes on Spotted Wrist. "The War Leader is following my orders. Doing what you seem unable to do."

Again Morning Star reached into the small jar, dipped a finger, and touched it to his tongue. "I thought we should bring this unsettled situation to its logical conclusion. Keeper, you can't assume control of the city while Wind, Rising Flame, and Blue Heron are loose and creating discord. It is your desire to have them eliminated. I have brought them to you."

Rising Flame wondered what was in the jar. Morning Star's very appearance unnerved her. The man looked . . . fragile. But what did that mean for her? If only she had some idea of how to turn this.

Spotted Wrist frowned, actually appearing surprised by Morning Star's apparent vigor. "But I thought—"

"Did you?" Morning Star interrupted. Then he turned to where Five Fists remained bowed. "War Leader, given your successful delivery of the Keeper's most-sought-after fugitives, I now have need of Squadron First Cut Weasel. From what I heard earlier, he is commanding the warriors guarding *Tonka'tzi* Slender Fox's palace steps. If you could have someone bring him, I would appreciate it."

"Yes, Lord." Five Fists rose, turned, and pointed at one of the warriors. The man leapt to his feet, sprinting for the door.

Morning Star then fixed his gaze on Blue Heron and the thief where they were standing to the side. "I hear that Lady Slender Fox is entertaining her brother tonight. Some intimate House business of theirs. They are not to be disturbed."

To Rising Flame's surprise, Blue Heron frowned, glanced sidelong at the thief with a knowing but satisfied look. The thief just gave her his most bland smile.

What was that all about?

Morning Star then turned his attention to Rising Flame. Something burned and smoldered there, almost feverish in its intensity. It sent a spear of panic through her. "Clan Matron, you honor me with the most flattering attire. I take it that you didn't go to such extremes and care merely to impress me with your dazzling apparel. Or was this some clever and well thought out statement you were trying to make?"

She cringed, burning inside with humiliation and shame. To appear here, dressed in a cast-off rag? If she could have melted through the floor, she would have.

Spotted Wrist was chuckling, fingering his chin, as he studied her through narrowed eyes.

Rising Flame swallowed hard, her heart beginning to pound. "Lord, I . . ." And she couldn't find the words. So desperately tired, aching, and numb she could barely stand, she wanted only to sag onto the matting and weep. "I didn't mean any offense, Lord. We were just trying to keep from . . ."

When she couldn't finish, Morning Star snickered grimly, his burning gaze still fixed on her. In a lowered voice he asked, "Where now is your vaunted pride, Matron? Where is that arrogant superiority?"

"I was . . ." Her legs had begun to tremble, all the Dreams and plans like so much ash. The last of her resistance crumbled. "I was only trying to do the best for Cahokia, Lord. And for you."

"By rummaging around like a dirt farmer, Matron? By rubbing elbows with the lowest among us? Did you find Cahokia's greatness there?"

Rising Flame shook her head wearily, all the while thinking, *I'm as good as dead.* "What I found?" She glanced at Wind and Blue Heron, and then at half-panicked Wooden Doll. She thought of Mother Otter and her children, desperately grateful that Blue Heron had talked Five Fists out of bringing them to face this. "I'm not sure you'd understand what I found, Lord."

"Ah, understanding. That fickle fleeting illumination of the souls." His sharp laugh stung like a lash. "I can only imagine the kind of Clan Matron you would make after you've come to such understanding. As if you've had a taste of the whole of Cahokia, instead of your limited and exalted lineage. I suppose even you might now begin to glimpse another reality. What it feels like to be a bottom feeder."

Rising Flame swallowed hard, the urge to throw up tickling her empty stomach.

He turned his attention to Wind. "I see that in my honor you, too, have dressed in your finest, *Tonka'tzi*. Must have been some remarkable circumstance that the War Leader discovered you in. Settling in among the migrant dirt farmers up there on the bluff top, perhaps? A change of occupation? A way to leave all that dreadful responsibility of office behind?"

Wind bowed, touched her forehead in respect. "No, Lord. Just doing whatever seemed to be the smartest move at the moment. I didn't think that allowing the Keeper here"—she pointed at Spotted Wrist—"to take me, the Clan Matron, or Blue Heron, and hang us in a square was in Cahokia's best interest."

A triumphant gleam lay behind Spotted Wrist's eyes as he softly said, "Yet here you are."

Morning Star cocked an eyebrow in agreement. "Indeed, *Tonka'tzi*. Looks like you ended up in front of the Keeper despite your best planning and plotting, and I imagine he's still figuring that you will hang in a square."

Spotted Wrist said, "Oh, you can count on it. Cut Weasel will get the order before he leaves here tonight." Spotted Wrist glanced from one to the next. "Let's see, I need a square for the Matron, one for Wind, another for the incredibly still-alive Blue Heron, a big one for the thief, and one for . . . Who are you?"

Wooden Doll, despite her fatigue, crossed her arms defiantly, the terror receding as she met his stare. "I'm more than you'll ever be able to handle, pus-dripping worm."

Rising Flame noted that everyone but Morning Star gasped.

"What are you doing?" Seven Skull Shield almost wheezed as he tried to take a step in Wooden Doll's direction.

"She's making sure she screams for a long time," Spotted Wrist promised, stepping forward and glaring into Wooden Doll's face. "I don't know you, but you're—"

"You know of her," Morning Star said. "Or her work, at least. She's the woman who killed your Willow Blossom. Left her maggot-ridden body dead and rotting."

Spotted Wrist cocked his head, inspecting Wooden Doll with new curiosity. "Why?"

When Wooden Doll's expression hardened, and it became apparent that she was going to say nothing more, Morning Star said, "Because Willow Blossom betrayed the thief."

He dipped his finger into the jar again, tasted it. "You still don't understand, do you, Lord Keeper? This is Wooden Doll. Who killed the warriors you sent to rape and capture her. Whose wealth you've carted off to your palace and now detail a full squad of warriors to guard."

"You?" Spotted Wrist asked. "You're Wooden Doll? By Piasa's swinging balls, I'm going to make you pay!"

"Yes, make her pay," Morning Star declared. "There should be some terrible price for love and loyalty. How dare she kill the woman who betrayed the man she loves? A man you tortured in a cage. How dare she strike back at the warriors who were raping her? Take a close look, Keeper. Stare into her eyes. See that strength. And tell me how a despicable *paid* woman could have that kind of courage and character."

Rising Flame watched Wooden Doll's flicker of a smile; it goaded Spotted Wrist as surely as if she'd spat in his face.

"Look at them!" Morning Star insisted. "Look at them all. Dressed in rags, broken. Can't you see the humor in this?"

Spotted Wrist turned on his heel and glowered at Morning Star. "What humor? People are dead! My people!"

"And these people are alive." Morning Star made a dismissive gesture. "At least for the moment. Even Blue Heron."

Blue Heron gave Spotted Wrist the same disgusted look she'd give green slime.

He thrust his face in hers, spitting out, "You should have *burned* in your palace. My people were talking to you up until the last. How did you get away?"

When Blue Heron just chuckled and crossed her arms, Spotted Wrist slapped her hard across the face, sending her staggering back.

Despite the ropes around his neck, Seven Skull Shield bulled forward, growling, "Strike her again, you shit-dripping maggot, and I'll reach down your throat and rip your lungs out. I got her out through the roof."

Spotted Wrist jacked a hard knee into Seven Skull Shield's crotch, staggering the thief, almost dropping him. The warriors who held his ropes stepped closer, supporting him.

Rising Flame thought that if looks could burn, Wooden Doll and Blue Heron both would have been searing the flesh from Spotted Wrist's bones.

Over the rising tension, Morning Star's bored voice said, "There's your answer to so many things, Lord Keeper. A thief, a paid woman, and an old Morning Star House lady you dismissed as dead. They've been under your feet the whole time. Blue Heron sat in this very room, dressed as she is now, ignored by you and your agents. She listened to your plans, and then wrecked them. Time after time."

When Morning Star turned his eyes on Rising Flame, it was all she could do to keep from wilting. "As Blue Heron did while acting as a servant in your palace, Clan Matron. And the entire time she was in touch with Columella and *Tonka'tzi* Wind, plotting against you and the Keeper. Well, until the Keeper finally came to realize that you were about to betray him. Quite the change of fortune, don't you think?"

Rising Flame lowered her head. Gods, this couldn't get any worse.

"*They* were behind my trouble?" Spotted Wrist cried incredulously.

"Well, they and the Koroa copper." Morning Star dipped his finger into the jar again, touched the end of his finger to his lips. "Blue Heron and the thief plotted with Columella to steal your canoes. It was the thief who made the distraction work when he tricked Broken Stone into sending warriors to fight yours and burned down the River House palace. It was he who set one fire in the Horned Serpent Town plaza and put another out in Green Chunkey's palace. He was slipping in and out of Wind's palace, well, until she had that secret door installed in the rear. Or don't you remember when the *tonka'tzi* had those repairs made just before the Busk?" Morning Star smiled in what appeared true amusement. "Probably much more dignified than loosening thatch to crawl through the roof."

Rising Flame gaped, reading the truth of Morning Star's words on Blue Heron's and the thief's faces. Even Wooden Doll was staring at them in amazement. Wind seemed to take it for granted.

But Spotted Wrist was trembling, his jaw knotting and jumping; the man's hard-clenched fists resembled rocks. He took a step closer to the thief, who hunched waiting for the blow.

"So now, amusing as this has all been, it comes to an end. In return for one small favor, you can have them, Keeper," Morning Star's voice called. "Do with them as you will."

Rising Flame's heart dropped, the sensation as if she'd gone empty inside. She closed her eyes, almost to the point of tears.

"Anything!" Spotted Wrist cried, spinning around to stare at Morning Star.

Rising Flame herself was amazed at the transition: Morning Star was no longer the same emaciated figure she'd seen rise from the dais. Thin, yes, but he now radiated energy and Power. His face possessed an animated glow. Looking indeed like the living embodiment of Morning Star's Spirit, he gave Spotted Wrist a conspiratorial grin.

He said, "I'll give you everything you've ever desired . . . in return for the Koroa copper. That was the only thing I specifically tasked you with. The only demand I made upon you."

Spotted Wrist's smile faded. The acid was back, churning in his stomach. Why did it always have to come back to that thrice-accursed Koroa copper?

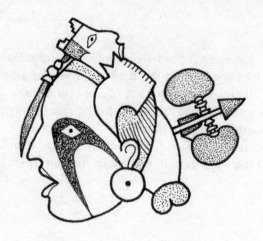

Seventy-five

In her day, Blue Heron had seen more than the occasional stunned expression. When Morning Star made his demand, Spotted Wrist stopped short. A look of astonished disbelief filled his face. The man's hands reached out, half imploring, half questing.

"But Lord . . ." He struggled for words. Then cried, "Blood and pus, what is it with that thrice-accursed copper? They were just some plates, and not all that valuable compared to other pieces. On my honor, Lord, I'll *give* you twenty plates in place of these idiotic Koroa ones."

Blue Heron shot a quick glance Wooden Doll's way as the woman muttered, "Twenty copper plates stolen from me and Crazy Frog, you mean."

It might have been an illusion cast by the eternal fire's flames, but Morning Star seemed to swell, expand, and glow where he stood on the dais. He dipped his finger in the small jar again, tasting whatever its contents were.

Five Fists kept fingering his jaw, giving his squadron of warriors signals with his fingers. The subtle cues and excitement shown by the Morning Star guard warriors radiated satisfaction as they shifted ever so casually to cover the few of Spotted Wrist's warriors who remained in the room.

As if it were the simplest of questions, Morning Star asked, "Are you telling me that you do not have the copper?"

"Lord," Spotted Wrist spread his hands wide, "I have been preoccupied with a huge number of—"

"I *ordered* you to find that copper. You told me from the beginning that you were turning the city upside down. You promised me over and over that it was your highest concern. That you were doing everything in your Power to locate the copper and whomever might possess it."

Morning Star's voice rose, thundering, "That was your only duty to me!"

Spotted Wrist, instead of cringing, lifted his chin and declared, "If it were in the city, I would have found it."

"You give me your word that it is no longer in the city?"

"Yes, Lord. Whoever took it knew we were closing in. If I had to guess, the copper is now somewhere in the south. Perhaps among the Kaskinampo, or the Tunica. Maybe among the Quiz Quiz. They have their own reasons for—"

"What would you do to the person who possessed that copper, Keeper?" Morning Star's gaze had taken on a singular burning intensity.

"I'd have the foul miscreant tied in a square. Then I'd break his bones so that he hung by his meat alone. After he'd hung thus for a couple of days, I'd have my people start slowly flaying him alive, each bit of skin burned before his eyes. Only then would I char his shaft and stones away with a slow fire."

"That is your will?" Morning Star took another dip from his ceramic pot.

"That and making a small slit in his belly so I could pull out a finger-length of his intestines each day." Spotted Wrist crossed his arms. "And I would have already done so, given the irritation that foul copper has caused me."

"Oh, it's far from foul," Morning Star told him. "And you have no idea where it is? This is the last time I will ask."

"By Piasa's swinging balls, Lord," Spotted Wrist cried angrily. "I have no idea where it might be! Do you understand? It's *gone*! Vanished!"

In the silence that followed, Blue Heron watched the almost sultry look in Morning Star's eyes.

"Ahem," Seven Skull Shield cleared his throat, head down, scuffing at the matting with a moccasined toe.

"Thief?" Morning Star asked mildly, voice carrying over the fire's crackling flames. "Did you have something to add?"

"Well, um, you know how it is with warriors?" Seven Skull Shield's voice was laced with hesitance.

Blue Heron cringed. She knew that expression, that self-deprecating slope of his shoulders.

"How is it with warriors?" Morning Star cocked his head, the elaborate headdress catching the firelight.

Every head in the room turned Seven Skull Shield's way, every eye on his blocky face. Wooden Doll looked as if whatever he was going to say, it would make her throw up.

"Well, Lord Morning Star, your godship, I . . . uh, was held in a bear cage in the Hero of the North's palace. You know that creaky building he built on Lady Lace's old haunts?"

"I might have a passing familiarity with the location," Morning Star agreed.

Spotted Wrist, his face red and near bursting with anger, took a step forward, raising a fist. Blue Heron could see murder in the Keeper's face, the veins in his neck bulging.

"Hold!" Morning Star snapped. "War Leader Five Fists? Please ensure that the thief may speak freely."

The old war leader promptly stepped next to Spotted Wrist, saying, "You heard Morning Star. Let him speak."

Spotted Wrist's three warriors had taken on a sweaty sheen in the firelight as they glanced nervously at the warriors boxing them on each side.

"Yes, well . . ." Seven Skull Shield kept scuffing the matting with his toe, eyes downcast. "You see, being in a cage, there's not much to do but keep from getting blinded by burning sticks and trying to keep from being whacked in the stones by sadistic warriors. Not that I was bored or anything. Far from it, but—"

Blue Heron cried in exasperation, "Pus and blood, Thief! We don't have all night to listen to your stories. Just once, will you get to the gods-rotted *point*!"

Seven Skull Shield blinked, shrugged. "Well, you know how it is when warriors don't have anything to do? They really like to brag. It's . . . well, I guess you'd call it a sort of entertainment, warriors not having a whole lot of imagination and all. And it wasn't like there was anyone but the Keeper's people to overhear. And the Keeper never came right out and said, but that one night he was laying it on thick to Willow Blossom that he had the copper."

"I what?" Spotted Wrist started forward, only to have Five Fists straight-arm him into a stop.

Seven Skull Shield gave the man his most disarming, wide and innocent smile. "Not that I ever heard him say it outright, mind you, but I sort of got the idea those missing copper plates were tied to the strapping under the Keeper's bed."

"*Impossible!*" Spotted Wrist was sputtering. "When I get you in a square . . ."

Seven Skull Shield gave an indifferent shrug of his thick shoulders. "It was, well, I guess, one of those things. You know. They were hidden in a place no one would ever look."

Spotted Wrist broke out in insane laughter. "I'm actually glad that I've made room in that bear cage. By tonight, you bit of walking human filth, after I've gouged the eyes out of your head, you're going to be right back in that cage."

Seven Skull Shield—that infuriating mild grin that Blue Heron knew so well still pasted on his lips—glanced at Morning Star. "Sorry. I know the Hero of the North is sort of supposed to be on your side and all. Hope hearing this doesn't put him in too bad with you."

Spotted Wrist—held at bay by Five Fists—made strangling sounds, his fingers clawing at the air.

The living god, one eyebrow cocked, said, "War Leader, take as many of your warriors as you think necessary to search the Keeper's palace. In the process, take these few North Star House warriors with you. They can act as guides. If any of the Keeper's people try to stand in your way, remove them by whatever means are necessary."

"Yes, Morning Star!" Five Fists smacked a hard fist against his cuirass with a loud thump. The smile on his lop-jawed face reflected pure delight. He gestured as he glanced at Spotted Wrist's outnumbered few warriors; the North Star warriors moved like scared rabbits. Then he was out the door on their heels, taking ten warriors with him.

Blue Heron cast a wary eye at the thief. Seven Skull Shield still had that innocuous look, practically beamed it. It had taken her years to figure out that he was guilty as sin when he looked that way.

"He's *not* going to find any accursed copper under my bed!" Spotted Wrist bellowed, stomping over to face Morning Star. "What is it? Why is that insipid copper of such a concern? I don't understand."

Morning Star took another taste from his jar. Blue Heron could see what looked like paste on the tip of his finger.

To Spotted Wrist, the living god said, "It's not just 'insipid copper.' The plates have been imbued with a special Power. Red Power, I suppose, since it's female by nature."

"Excuse me?" Spotted Wrist crossed his arms, tapping a foot in displeasure. The looks he was shooting Seven Skull Shield's way promised mayhem.

Morning Star gave him a dismissive look. "He who has possession of the copper will be unable to keep or control women. Any woman he's interested in will flee, vanish, disappear, or be taken from him."

"That's the most ridiculous thing I've ever heard!" Spotted Wrist bellowed, so enraged spittle flew from his lips.

"Is it?" Morning Star shot a knowing glance at the women in the room. "The only way you will convince me otherwise is if that copper isn't under your bed. Because I'd say it works."

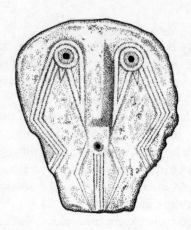

A Spider in the Storm

*I*n the glow of the firelight, I study the image reflected from the blood forming two pools in Fire Light's empty rib cage. I have oriented his body north-to-south. Directions have Power. Divided by the man's spine where the vertebrae stick up like a ridge, that leaves one pool on the east, or the direction of the morning sun and birth and renewal. The other is now on the west, the side of night, darkness, and death.

I have used all my skills, called upon all my Power. I am the Wild One, the Spirit Being called Thrown Away Boy. The chaotic and discarded Twin.

I add another chunk of wood to the fire, and then another, building it up so that the flames leap and send flashes of yellow Dancing around the interior of the room. Overhead I hear the strengthening wind as it tears at the moldering thatch.

The important thing now is to watch the patterns that form as the blood in Fire Light's chest and abdomen cools and starts to dry.

To do that, I place the Lightning Shell mask on my face, and stare through the slitted eyes. Shell carries its own magic, coming as it does from the depths. As a result, it seeks Underworld Power. And tonight, in Cahokia, that is Night Shadow Star and Piasa.

No doubt about it. The sensation is electric, like rubbing dry fox fur. It crackles and prickles down my back the moment I see Night Shadow Star's image in Fire Light's still pooling blood.

She was here, on the canoe landing. Not more than four or five bow shots south of the abandoned house where I hunch over Fire Light's body.

Not that I was ready to move. Not then. The time wasn't right. I saw that in the patterns of Fire Light's intestines as they squirmed warm and squishy in my *fingers. That vision told me how this would end: Me, lowering myself onto my sister's defeated body as lightning flashed and banged around me.*

I could tell it wouldn't be on the canoe landing. It felt all wrong for that. No, this would happen in a place of Power.

And where but Morning Star's high mound top had that kind of Spirit Power?

So now I wait. First, however, I check. Fire Light's heart has cooled enough after cooking in the fire. I lift a strip and begin to chew. Never would I have guessed my cousin had such a tough heart, but then he was always a rather callous sort. Lacked any kind of empathy.

As I chew, I stare down into the drying blood. Looking toward the east, I see the faintest of images forming in the drying surface where the blood looks slightly matted. In contrast, areas of shine make a square. In the reflection I see Night Shadow Star walking alone past a pole, and in that instant I know where she's headed. Morning Star's palace. And, better yet, from the flashes of light cast by the fire, I can recognize patterns of lightning illuminating the high plaza.

Very well, I will find her waiting for me in Morning Star's high plaza. Like a spider in the storm, I shall tuck her into my web.

"And then, dear sister, I will pay you back for the pain and humiliation you caused me at Joara." Thanks to Fire Light's sacrifice, that part at least is clear.

But my biggest surprise comes when I turn my attention to the west side. There the blood is still shiny, with little matting except around the indentations made by the ribs.

"Where are you, brother?" I ask.

And then I see.

But at first, I don't understand. I am seeking Morning Star. Nowhere in Cahokia should there be such a concentration of Spirit Power. My brother's body should be pulsing with it, almost like concentric circles in Fire Light's blood.

Instead, I see but a pinpoint of a ripple.

Stunned, I drop to a seat on the old sleeping bench and feel the wood creak under my weight.

I can think of only one reason Morning Star's Power would reflect so poorly. He knows I'm coming for him. He's doing this deliberately to hide his essence.

How remarkably cunning. When it comes to killing Morning Star, I am essentially blind.

Seventy-six

While they waited, Spotted Wrist stepped up to the thief, let his gaze burn into the man's unnaturally mild stare.

He had never hated a human being as much as he did this one. It was all he could do to keep from reaching out to grab the thief by the sides of his head and use both thumbs to gouge the man's knowing eyes from their sockets.

But I will. On my honor, I swear it.

Around him, the room had gone quiet, though Rising Flame and Wind were talking off to the side. Both women, along with Wooden Doll, had taken seats on the wall benches. Blue Heron, however, kept her place beside Seven Skull Shield, arms crossed, a poisonous hatred boiling behind her black eyes.

"You know, Thief," Spotted Wrist told the man, "I really am going to make you wish that you'd died at childbirth. The sheer stone-balled stupidity of accusing me? Do you know what I'm going to do to you?"

He hooked a thumb toward where the woman called Wooden Doll was watching through wary eyes. "First off, I'm going to make sure you witness every painful moment of her death. I want you to live with the responsibility and knowledge—short though it will be—that you were the cause of her suffering, degradation, and pain."

"You're not doing so well," Blue Heron told him before Seven Skull Shield could answer. "You really are a disaster going someplace to happen. The city is going to be so much better off once you're in a square."

He laughed. "Me?"

She nodded, sucking her lips in over her brown teeth. "Knowing Morning Star like I do, he's going to make sure it happens just like you said it should. Five Fists will hang you in a square. Probably one of the ones facing the Great Plaza. Break your arms and legs so that you dangle by the meat and tendons for a couple of days. Then start with the flaying. Oh, and don't forget that bit about pulling out a little intestine at a time. That was how you lined it out, wasn't it?"

"Old woman, are you as dense as a hickory block?" Spotted Wrist leaned down to thrust his face into hers. "My squadrons control the city. Nothing is going to happen here that I don't approve. For someone who used to be a Keeper, are you that much of a simpleminded dolt? My warriors follow me."

Blue Heron cocked her head toward Morning Star. "But the city follows him."

"He's sick. Just lies on that dais of his. Wouldn't surprise me if we didn't have to have another requickening ceremony in the next few months. Wonder who I'll pick to serve as a host body this time?"

"Doesn't look sick to me," Blue Heron murmured, casting a gaze at the resplendent Morning Star, who stood straight-backed on the dais step.

"It's a sham," Spotted Wrist told her. "I've seen illness like this before. All he does is sit on the high chair braiding rope and cord. In fact, I used one he'd made of sinew to strangle War Duck and Round Pot." He narrowed a deadly eye in Seven Skull Shield's direction. "That's how your cage came to be empty and waiting for you."

"Murdered them both, eh? Then I guess River House is really going to Fringed Smoke." Blue Heron nodded. "He'll be a good High Chief. I'll lobby for Lady West Song for House Matron. She's got sense. I think Rising Flame will back that."

Spotted Wrist broke out in guffaws. "Old woman like you? You'll be dead by sunset tomorrow! You won't last in a square." He leaned forward, again thrusting his face into hers. "You've made your last escape, old woman. You're going right from here to a square if I have to detail an entire squad to make sure it happens."

Something about the return look she gave him sent a premonition down his back.

"Lord Keeper?"

Spotted Wrist turned to see Cut Weasel, escorted by two Morning Star House warriors, enter. The squadron first paused only long enough to drop to a knee and touch his forehead to the matting in obeisance to Morning Star, then he hurried across the matting, a look of almost panic on his thin face.

"Squadron First, I want you to find me—"

Cut Weasel cut him off, crying, "I just received a message from Flying

392 W. Michael Gear and Kathleen O'Neal Gear

Squirrel! He's surrounded. Columella is making her move, Lord Keeper. The slick sheath has been slipping her people into River City Mounds for days now. Disguising them as farmers, Traders, fishermen, you name it. As it grew dark, they formed up squadrons, started to close the net around what's left of our warriors in the plaza."

"How?" Spotted Wrist demanded. "We've had patrols out—"

"It's the *people*." Cut Weasel spread his hands wide. "They've been hiding Columella's warriors. That man Crazy Frog, he's been working with Flat Stone Pipe and Columella. At the same time the usurper, Fringed Smoke, has been subverting the Earth Clans matrons and chiefs, laying the groundwork for their defection."

"That's impossible!"

"Lord Keeper," Cut Weasel told him, "we have to assemble the squadron. I've already sent the orders out. We're understrength, only about a third of us are still—"

"Yes, and send a runner to Heart Warrior. I need him to march in support immediately. Reinforced with Forest Squadron, we'll hit them from behind. Like crushing a walnut between two stones. Be ready to march at full light. If we're fast enough, they will have no clue that we're coming until we're in the middle of them. With surprise on our side, confusion and fear will do the rest."

Blue Heron had started laughing halfway through. Now he turned on her. "Like I said, you'll never . . ."

She was pointing toward the door.

Spotted Wrist followed her gnarled finger to where a hard-faced Five Fists marched in from the darkness, his warriors in two lines behind him.

But it wasn't the battle armor, so finely polished that it shone in the light of the eternal fire, or the immaculately formed ranks of warriors marching in step that caught his eye. Rather it was the two pieces of rectangular copper the war leader held so reverently before him.

In that instant, Spotted Wrist could only gape. "What? Where did you . . . ?"

He wasn't even aware of Morning Star's cocked brow, or the way the warriors shoved Cut Weasel aside. He could vaguely hear his squadron first's protests, but his gaze remained fixed on that thrice-accursed copper that Five Fists laid at Morning Star's feet.

Seventy-seven

Rising Flame leaped to her feet when Five Fists triumphantly carried what she assumed was the Koroa copper into the room. Not that she'd ever seen the stuff, but from the look on Spotted Wrist's face, and the almost sublime satisfaction on Morning Star's, she was pretty sure that this was the famous missing copper.

She stepped forward on her tired legs, having recovered enough not to wobble. But on the morrow, she was going to be stiff and sore enough to plead for willow bark tea.

As she stared down at the two copper plates, they gleamed a bloody red in the leaping flames.

By the time she looked up, Morning Star's warriors were escorting Spotted Wrist toward the door—and acting none too kind in the process. Squadron First Cut Weasel kept trying to interfere, calling, "Wait, that's the Lord Keeper!"

"Stand down, Squadron First." Morning Star didn't need to raise his voice. The Deer Clan man stopped, turned, gazing at the living god with confusion.

"War Leader?" Morning Star asked.

"Yes, Lord?" Five Fists bowed his head.

"You remember the Keeper's words? What should be done with the miscreant who had the copper?"

"Yes, Lord. My people have already been given instructions. Everything will be done just as the Keeper so eloquently described."

Cut Weasel kept shifting back and forth, as if hopping from foot to foot. "What about Columella? What's happening here?"

Rising Flame raised a hand to still the squadron first's anxiety. "You have a choice to make. Do you serve the Hero of the North, or the living god?"

Cut Weasel gulped, turned to Morning Star, and dropped to his knees. "We all serve Morning Star!"

From where he stood on the dais, the living god seemed to swell, raising his arms. In the firelight he looked as if he might sprout wings and fly, as did his image in the carvings on the doors. "Then it would appear we have a few things left to attend to."

Morning Star glanced at Wind, who for the most part had remained silent. "It is my understanding that you were never replaced as *tonka'tzi* by the Four Winds Clan."

"That is correct, Morning Star." Wind touched her forehead respectfully.

"Then I assume you can resume your duties as soon as Slender Fox is removed from the *tonka'tzi*'s palace." Morning Star turned his attention to Rising Flame. "And I fear we need a new Keeper."

"That is also correct," she told him.

"Have you any suggestions?" Morning Star glanced suggestively at Blue Heron, who was patting the big thief on the back in a congratulatory gesture.

Rising Flame bit off a bitter laugh, asking, "Lady Blue Heron, would you have any objection to assuming the mantle of Clan Keeper once again?"

Blue Heron considered her, and for a moment Rising Flame thought the woman would flatly turn her down.

"Oh, take it!" Seven Skull Shield chided. "Or I'll end up owing the shell carvers a whole basket of whelk shells."

"Why's that?" Blue Heron gave the thief a skeptical look.

"Made them a bet."

Blue Heron waved him away with a pained look. One that promptly turned crafty as she asked Rising Flame, "Why now?"

Rising Flame glanced unsurely at Morning Star, wondering if this was some sort of trap. But then, tired as she was, maybe her inhibitions and cleverness had all drained away. "For one thing, you have the network of spies. If, as we've heard, Columella is in the act of capturing River House, you can broker an agreement with her. The two of you seem to see eye-to-eye about things. Working from the shadows you've stayed a step ahead of Spotted Wrist, and to an extent, me. To be honest, I think we need your wisdom as we tackle the uncertainty among the Houses."

"But?" Blue Heron asked, crossing her arms.

"But I'd like you to take someone younger into your confidence. Someone you can train who will learn the finer arts of your craft."

"Putting this all together again won't be easy." Blue Heron was pulling at the wattle under her chin as she considered.

"Sure it will," the thief told her. "You've got me to help. And Crazy Frog owes us for once."

Wind was making a face. "What about Slender Fox? She's over in the palace right now." She glanced at Cut Weasel. "And she's got a detachment of warriors who will back her, correct?"

Cut Weasel—looking as uncomfortable as if he had cactus thorns poking into his flesh—nodded. "She and High Chief Wolverine have retired to her personal quarters in the back. She asked not to be disturbed. That they had serious decisions to make about the future of North Star House and how some of the Serpent Woman Town Earth Clans were going to be—"

"At least that's not going to be a problem," Seven Skull Shield interrupted. He shot a look at Blue Heron. "You thinking what I'm thinking?"

Blue Heron—giving the thief a gap-toothed grin—replied, "With that hidden door, they'll never know until it's too late. I'd say use a net this time."

"Me too." Seven Skull Shield was frowning as he fingered his chin.

"What do you mean 'use a net'?'" Wind asked.

Seven Skull Shield—that irritating grin back on his face—turned to Five Fists, who had adopted a disapproving scowl. "You got a net, War Leader?"

"I can find one, Thief."

Wooden Doll had walked up bedside him. "Skull? I know that look. Whatever it is, I don't think you should—"

"Shhh!" He put fingers against her lips, glancing sidelong at Five Fists. "War Leader, I'd take at least ten warriors." He paused, thinking, then added, "Oh, and good old Cut Weasel here, too. You need to climb up the back of the *tonka'tzi*'s mound. Don't let anyone see you. You'll find the secret door Wind had put in on the southwest corner. Jigger the latch next to the corner post and lift what looks like the plaster wall back. Puts you right in the personal quarters. But move fast and toss that net right on top of them before they can get out of bed. Once you catch them, I'd walk right out the front. They'll be squealing and screaming, and making threats, but I promise, this night will be talked about for years."

Five Fists glanced curiously at Morning Star, who told him, "Do as the thief says." A pause. "And take all your warriors."

"What about your—"

"All of them, War Leader. I need to speak with *Tonka'tzi* Wind and Clan Matron Rising Flame. Alone." He paused again, sticking his finger into the small pot and touching it to his tongue. "You have your orders,

War Leader. Be about them. Oh, and hang Slender Fox and Wolverine next to Spotted Wrist. Incest should be punished. Even when it's among the nobles."

Rising Flame shook her head as Five Fists gathered his warriors, took one last uncertain look back at Morning Star, and followed the rest out.

Seven Skull Shield took Wooden Doll's hand, saying, "That poor Cut Weasel. I bet that boy's going to be wishing he'd gone hunting them missing canoes all the way to the Gulf."

"What's this about?" Rising Flame demanded.

Blue Heron told her, "Wolverine likes slipping his shaft into Slender Fox's ready sheath. We've used it against them before. How else do you think we got North Star House to send all that food to Columella last winter?"

Rising Flame shook her head. *How could she have ever been so stupid as to replace Blue Heron with Spotted Wrist?*

In the silence that followed, Morning Star climbed back up to his panther-covered perch and seated himself. In that moment, he seemed to fade, body deflating like a punctured bladder. Again he dipped a finger into his little pot.

"What is that, Lord?" Rising Flame asked, stepping closer.

"A mixture Rides-the-Lightning prepared. Bear grease filled with Sister Datura." The living god looked down at the little pot. "I don't have much time."

"Lord?" Wind asked, stepping over to peer at him with narrowed eyes. "What's this all about?"

"Storm is coming." Morning Star tilted his head. "Hear the wind in the thatch?"

Rising Flame nodded warily. "None of this is a surprise to you, is it?"

He smiled faintly, crinkling the thick paint on his cheeks and lips. "It's all Power, Matron. Sky World and Underworld. Red Power and White, chaos and order, pain and bliss. Everything is balance. Even Night Shadow Star and me. The Thunderbirds and Piasa. From the beginning. Though the story has taken some twists and turns we hadn't expected."

At that moment, Sun Wing slipped through the double doors, leaving them open a crack. And in her wake came the thief's big dog, Farts. The beast paused, staring warily around. Only after sniffing did it slink over to Spotted Wrist's forgotten supper. Tail slapping back and forth, it began lapping up the last of the Lord Keeper's meal.

Sun Wing walked quietly across the matting, the cape on her shoulders woven in diamond designs and decorated with occasional staring eyes. The pack in which she carried the Tortoise Bundle hung over her shoulder. Heedless of convention, she crossed behind the fire and settled on the lowest step of Morning Star's dais.

"Everything all right?" Morning Star asked.

"The lightning comes, Brother."

"What are you talking about?" Rising Flame demanded.

Morning Star, looking wan and fatigued, said, "Earth, hey Earth, from it spread. Raise the Underworld of the Dead."

"What's that supposed to mean?" *Tonka'tzi* Wind asked.

It was Sun Wing who replied, "One must live and one must die. See the souls rise to the sky."

Morning Star, eyes closed, breathing deeply, said, "We're done here. *Tonka'tzi*, you will order my war leader not to interfere. He and his guard are to stand their positions at the bottom of the stairs. He is not, under any circumstances, to allow anyone but my sister and those with her to ascend the Grand Staircase. Do you understand?"

"No, Lord. I—"

"Only Night Shadow Star and those with her." Morning Star opened his eyes, staring at them all one by one. The pain of all Creation might have lurked behind that gaze. "Now go!"

Seventy-eight

As a dark wind blew out of the north, Seven Skull Shield led the way up Night Shadow Star's stairway. While he kept a hand on Blue Heron's arm to steady her, Wooden Doll had a hold of the Keeper's other arm.

Just as they reached the top of the steps, the thumping of big feet could be heard on the squared logs behind them.

Seven Skull Shield turned, squinted against the wind, and called, "Farts! There you are!"

"Oh, piss in a pot! Figures," Blue Heron muttered.

Seven Skull Shield thought it better not to mention where he'd seen Farts lift his leg when no one was looking up in Morning Star's palace. Four Winds nobles could be incensed by the most insignificant of things.

The big dog stopped long enough to bang his insistent nose into Seven Skull Shield's hand, then trotted over to lift his leg on the glowering statue of Piasa. The artfully carved guardian post ignored the insult and continued to glare down at the Avenue of the Sun below.

"You sure this is all right?" Wooden Doll asked as they plodded across the unkempt grass and stepped up on the veranda.

"Lady Night Shadow Star left me in charge," Seven Skull Shield told her. Then cried, "Farts! Don't pee on that!" as the big dog lifted his leg on what looked like a roll of blankets against the palace wall.

Blue Heron shook her head. "I'm just as glad Spotted Wrist burned my palace down. Wasn't any other way I was going to get the odor of dog piss out of the floor."

"Hadn't thought of burning," Wooden Doll told her. "But after the bodies we left at my house, the idea is sounding better and better."

Seven Skull Shield set the door aside. Farts went barreling into the dark room with a happy bound.

"What the . . . ?" Then, "Is there a dog in here?" a voice called. Slurping could be heard from the direction of a large ceramic pot near the eternal fire. The faint glow was barely enough to illuminate the room.

"Green Stick? That you?" Seven Skull Shield called. "Clay String? Winter Leaf?"

"Yes. Who is . . . Oh, pus and rot, no! It's the thief!"

Groans came from the back.

Someone shouted, "Get that accursed disaster of a dog out of the stewpot! That's our breakfast!"

"Oh, come on," Seven Skull Shield answered, "a little dog spit never hurt anyone."

"Blood and maggots, Thief, if you don't leave, we're going straight to Spotted Wrist. We'll tell him—"

"It'll be a waste of effort," Blue Heron barked as she hobbled into the room. "Morning Star's hung him in a square. I'm Clan Keeper again, and my niece left this place under Seven Skull Shield's care. Now, we need beds."

Farts continued to gulp down the contents of the stewpot, his tail slashing back and forth in delight.

Wooden Doll took Seven Skull Shield's hand and asked, "Is it always like this around you?"

"Actually," Blue Heron told her dryly, "today is rather mild compared to most."

In the dim glow of the coals, Seven Skull Shield saw Wooden Doll's eyebrow arch as she asked, "Got a sleeping bench in here big enough for two?"

"In the back," Seven Skull Shield told her.

"That's Lady Night Shadow Star's bed," Wooden Doll hissed as she gave his thick arm a disciplinary slap.

"Hey, she said I could use it."

Blue Heron poked the thief in the back. "Oh, go on. Exhausted as you both are, you're going to be asleep before you hit the covers."

Seven Skull Shield put an arm around Wooden Doll's shoulders, leading the way. In the darkness in the rear, he helped her onto the covers. He was too tired to worry that the blankets and furs smelled dusty.

Snuggling himself against her body, he told her, "You know, now that the Keeper's back in charge, I've been thinking about making some changes."

"Like what, Skull? You think you could ever give up the chase? The excitement of the game?"

"Well, I don't know. The Keeper's going to need our help. It's as if . . . well . . ."

"Spit it out, Skull."

"Maybe we could do it together. On the way down the stairs, *Tonka'tzi* Wind said you could have all your wealth back. And it's not the same as the old days. Maybe we could try something different? Something we did together. You and me."

"Maybe," she told him with a yawn. "That's for tomorrow." She sounded muzzy as she added, "I like thinking about tomorrow. Has . . . possibilities . . ."

And then she was asleep.

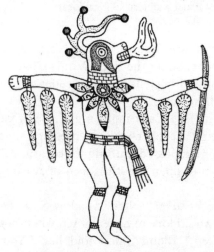

Seventy-nine

The scent of rain carried on the night wind that came gusting out of the north. Enough distant flashes of lightning lit the Avenue of the Sun that Fire Cat could have traveled it at a run.

They had managed to make their way through the warrens of River City, having run into but a single squad of Columella's warriors. Interested only in hunting down North Star House enemies, they had let them pass with hardly a sidelong glance at the weapons they carried or the packs on their backs.

Besides, Fire Cat thought he and his party looked like anything but warriors. Even Blood Talon—whom Fire Cat had once thought cast from such an inflexible mold that he could never be mistaken for anything but a battle-toughened warrior. Now the fire-scarred squadron first looked like any other river Trader, right down to the somewhat awkward walk caused by endless days of crouching in a canoe.

As to Winder, well, of them all, he was totally authentic, right down to the beguiling smile. The big man had kept the pace, thumping along on his stumplike legs, his pack swinging on his back.

"So, I'm home?" he'd asked Night Shadow Star. "Forgiven for all my ill deeds?"

"I so declare," she told him. "If anyone questions that, tell them you are under my protection and in my service."

Winder laughed at the irony. "And to think that I once told Seven Skull Shield he was crazy for involving himself in Four Winds politics."

"It's a different Cahokia now," Blood Talon told him. "Consider what we just saw in River City. Columella's squadrons, allied with the new high chief of River House, hunting down North Star House warriors. Who would have ever thought the Four Winds Clan would allow that?"

Fire Cat said, "Something tells me the Keeper's got way more than his share of problems these days."

Even as he said it, Fire Cat caught a glimpse of yet another runner trotting toward them, a copper-covered message shaft clutched in his hand. As the young man passed, huffing for breath, a flicker of lightning illuminated him in full: open mouth, sheen of sweat, the design on the copper-clad staff.

"That's from the *tonka'tzi*." Night Shadow Star shot a look after his retreating form. "I would love to have known what message he carries."

"Could have asked," Blood Talon told her. "You are Lady Night Shadow Star."

Her response was a nervous chuckle as she forced herself to a faster pace. "I'm a river Trader dressed in burlap with a disfigured face and a pack on my back. Lady Night Shadow Star would be traveling on a litter, wearing her finery."

"Who do you think the messenger was headed for?" Fire Cat wondered. "Columella? With orders to stand down? Or Squadron First Flying Squirrel with orders to fight on?"

"Guess we'll find out when we get to the Great Plaza," Blood Talon told him. "This whole notion of Slender Fox as *tonka'tzi* still leaves me reeling. Never liked that woman."

"Save your breath for the road," Night Shadow Star told them. "We are running out of time."

Fire Cat followed her lead as she broke into a trot.

As they pounded their way around the bend at Black Tail's tomb, the wind caught them full force. Tearing at them, sending cold fingers to wick away perspiration.

A high bolt of lightning shot white-hot through the clouds. In the frozen image of the tortured heavens, Fire Cat could see the twisting turbulence. Couldn't help but compare it to the worry and fear he saw reflected on Night Shadow Star's face.

"Are you all right?" he asked between breaths.

"When we get there . . . I need you . . . to do as I ask," she managed through huffing breaths.

"Of course."

"No . . . I mean it." She shot him a questioning look during the next flash of lightning. "Don't argue with me."

He kept the rhythm, could hear Winder and Blood Talon's feet thumping on the avenue behind him.

"Lady, I gave my word."

"Good," she told him. Then she somehow found her old stickball-playing stride, and despite all that time in a canoe, started to pull ahead.

"Got to . . . slow down," Winder finally called from behind.

"Lady?" Fire Cat called.

He could see the frustration in her expression as she slowed; bolts of lightning flickered and flashed through the northern heavens. The wind kept beating at them. Strong enough now to pick up bits of trash and send sections of loose matting fluttering and flopping across the avenue. The smell of latrines, the occasional whiff of a charnel house, and smoke from banked fires mixed with the wet smells from Marsh Elder Lake. A stronger gust pelted them with driven sand.

Conditions turned worse as they headed east, passing the Great Observatory, the Four Winds Clan House, the plaza where the Natchez had beaten and humiliated Fire Cat at chunkey. Then Night Shadow Star's palace, dark now, the faint smell of smoke blowing down and across the Avenue of the Sun.

A sudden flash of chain lightning laced the cloud-tattered heavens with a web of light that stretched from horizon to horizon; it illuminated Piasa and Horned Serpent at the top of Night Shadow Star's stairs. Both Spirit guardians might have been alive, ready to leap down upon them.

"How do you think the thief is doing these days?" Fire Cat asked, hoping the question would lighten the strain, fear, and determination in Night Shadow Star's expression.

"One way, he's up there in my palace," she said stiffly, her eyes fixed on the road ahead. "In another, he died horribly in a square, blinded, burned, beaten, and slowly gutted."

If her palace—home to her and Makes Three, the place where she'd been subjected to the Itza, and later had seen him vanquished—meant anything, she didn't bother to pause. From what Fire Cat could see, she barely spared the place so much as a glance.

Instead, she kept muttering under her breath. Though the words were unintelligible, the tone was the one she used when Piasa took possession of her souls.

Night Shadow Star's attention was fixed on the base of Morning Star's earthen pyramid; at the foot of the Great Staircase flickers of lightning illuminated a full squad of warriors. Heads covered with blankets for protection from the violent wind, they huddled together.

Fire Cat asked, "Lady? Should I don my armor?"

"You won't need it, Red Wing," she told him in a clipped voice and walked straight up to the humped shape that a blast of white light from above exposed as War Claw himself.

"War Chief," Night Shadow Star greeted through the rolling of distant thunder. "I am Lady Night Shadow Star, of Morning Star House of the Four Winds Clan, returned from the east. I have need of seeing Morning Star. Now."

The war chief pulled back his blanket, squinted. "Lady? That really you?" And at the flicker of lightning, asked, "What happened to your face?"

"Fighting for my life in the east. Yes, it's me. If you will recall, you held the blanket the day I married Makes Three. Offered it to Morning Star when he was ready to place it around our shoulders. To your eternal embarrassment, you handed it to him inside out. I forgave you then, I forgive you now."

"It is you." He peered at her as thunder continued to roll down from the blackness above. "Are you sure you want to go up dressed as you—"

"Now! Blood rot it!" Night Shadow Star snapped. "And spread your warriors around. Walking Smoke is right behind me. He'll try the stairs first, but with the storm, there's no telling how he'll try to get up to Morning Star's palace."

And with that, she pushed past him, through the knot of warriors, and tackled the steps. In tight formation Fire Cat, Winder, and Blood Talon followed. He glanced back as they started up. The warriors were gaping as War Claw started barking orders.

"If he doubted she was Four Winds," Blood Talon said as they climbed, "that set him straight."

"That's my lady," Winder blurted with pride. "Tough as hickory and sharp as obsidian."

Fire Cat frowned as they passed the Council Terrace Gate, asking, "Where are the guards?"

They hurried across the Council Terrace plaza and started up the long steps to the high palisade. Here, the wind—angry and violent—sought to topple them off their feet.

At the palace gate the portals were swung open, gaping like an invitation.

"What's wrong here?" Blood Talon asked.

The tall palisade walls blocked the worst of the wind's blasting gusts as they passed the World Tree. The gale moaned and roared in the high-thatched roof and whistled around the World Tree. Fire Cat and Blood Talon lifted the double doors aside.

Night Shadow Star was first into the Great Room, where the eternal fire snapped and crackled, sending its sparks up toward the high roof. They could hear the howl and wail as the bitter storm worried the thatch.

Fire Cat stopped short, staring around the Great Room. No guards, no staff, no retainers. No one but Sun Wing, perched on the bottom step of the dais. Not even surly old Five Fists, which made no sense.

"Where is everybody?" Blood Talon asked.

Winder—gaping as he slowly turned on his heel—let out a low whistle. "By Piasa's swinging balls, would you look at this place? The carvings? The copper plate? The textiles? All the wealth in the world. Who'd have thought?"

Night Shadow Star marched straight past the fire, stopping where Sun Wing looked up with scared eyes, the Tortoise Bundle cradled lovingly in her arms.

Thunder boomed and rumbled around the palace like a cascade of doom.

Fire Cat stepped up behind Night Shadow Star, half of his attention on the room. He kept expecting Walking Smoke to come shooting out of the shadows, enraged, wearing his famed shell mask.

That's when he finally noticed the figure hunched in a fetal position on the high dais. He'd mistaken the man for a mere pile of clothing. Thin, wasted, and frail looking, the individual wore the living god's best finery.

"Who's that?" he asked, pointing.

"Morning Star," Sun Wing told him, glancing up from where she stroked the Tortoise Bundle. "He's dying."

Night Shadow Star barely hesitated, climbing up onto the dais and bending over Chunkey Boy's curled figure. "Can you hear me? I'm back. I wasn't able to kill Walking Smoke in Cofitachequi. But then I guess you know that." She smiled down into Chunkey Boy's face as he turned and looked up at her with hollow-set eyes.

"I know," he whispered as thunder crashed overhead, almost drowning his words. "Long shot, that."

"He's on the way here. Probably tonight." She took his hand, adding, "And you don't look like you're in any condition to face him."

"No . . . suppose not."

Fire Cat watched the man pull out a small brownware pot that he'd tucked next to his belly and dip his finger inside. Placing the paste-smeared fingertip in his mouth, he sucked it clean.

"Sister Datura?" Night Shadow Star asked.

"It stops the pain," Sun Wing told her from below. "And it keeps his Spirit out of Walking Smoke's vision." The woman's eyes went vacant as she said, "He's been searching for us. Eyes all over the room, looking out from a pool of blood. Peering here and there, but with the help of Sister Datura and the Tortoise Bundle, they just keep sliding off my brother and me."

Night Shadow Star laid a hand to her brother's brow, frowned. "No fever. Where does it hurt?"

"Stomach. Like a cactus pad is swelling and throbbing, driving its spines into my insides. There, just below my ribs."

A thunderous bang sounded just overhead, lightning flashing white through the half-open palace doors.

Night Shadow Star reached down below where the quetzal-feather cloak was wrapped around Chunkey Boy's chest and pressed. Chunkey Boy cried out, the sound almost a screech.

"I have to get you to Rides-the-Lightning." She smiled down at him again. "But you knew that, didn't you?"

"You and I had a bargain, Sister," he told her. "Sky Power and Underworld Power. I'm ready for this to be finished."

She sucked in her lips as her brow lined in thought. "I have promised my lord that it ends here. And then we'll both be free."

The first sounds of rain could be heard outside, the beating of it overhead muffled by the thatch. Moments later, it came down in a torrent.

Night Shadow Star pulled the pins that released the heavy copper headdress, setting it to one side. Next she removed his quetzal-feather cloak. She turned, fixed her haunted gaze on Fire Cat. "Husband, I need you, Winder, and Blood Talon to get Morning Star to the soul flier. With the storm, on the wet steps, and with the wind tearing at you, it will take all three of you."

"Of course, Lady," Winder said, stepping forward. The burly Trader winced as another thunderbolt rent the sky outside with enough force to shake the palace.

Blood Talon was right behind him, looking askance. "The man's litter is more than the three of us can carry. Takes six at least."

"Not to mention the wind." Winder rubbed his jaw. "We'll do it the old-fashioned way. You and Fire Cat get his arms. I've got his feet."

"Wait!" Fire Cat turned to Night Shadow Star. "I'm *not* leaving you. Not with Walking Smoke hunting us."

She stepped up, placing her palms on his chest as she looked into his eyes. "Piasa has told me how this has to happen. I need you to get Morning Star to the healer. Do you understand? If there is no Morning Star, the city will fall. Everything we have done, endured, and sacrificed will be meaningless. You have to take him to Rides-the-Lightning immediately, or we're going to lose it all."

"But I—"

"I *need* you to do this for me. Please." Her eyes searched his, desperate. "It is your responsibility to save Morning Star. Make sure, no matter what it costs, that you *keep Morning Star alive!*"

He exhaled his anxiety, a tearing anguish in his chest. "Lady, I do this under protest."

She smiled, wrapped her arms around him in a frantic hug. "We see this through, and we're free. Back on *Red Reed* and headed south. Away from Cahokia."

"It will be you and me," he promised. "And I'll never let you go."

"What's important is that Morning Star continues to rule in Cahokia." She stepped back, eyes dewy, her lip trembling.

Fire Cat shot a calculating glance at Chunkey Boy where Winder and Blood Talon stood ready to lift the man. He could be back in less than a hand of time. Just get the man to Rides-the-Lightning and run back. Nothing to it.

As if to mock him, the wind howled through the thatch as though to rip it loose.

"Close the doors behind us," he told Night Shadow Star. "You've got your bow and war club."

Fire Cat took Morning Star's right arm, lifted it over his shoulder as Blood Talon did the left. Though the footing was awkward on the panther hides and high dais, the three of them lifted the sick god down.

They all looked up as another terrible gust of wind shook the roof, pummeling the thatch. Bits of soot, dust, and old grass fluttered down.

"Hope that holds," Winder muttered.

Blood Talon said, "Going to be a miserable trip down those stairs. And to think it's the living god we're carrying."

"So we'd best not drop him," Winder agreed. "Hate to make him mad. I've been in a square before. Don't want to go back."

"Me either," Blood Talon agreed. "Be sure you have a good grip."

"Makes it unanimous all the way around." Fire Cat figured everyone knew his story when it came to squares. He gave Night Shadow Star one last longing look. "Love you," he added, and together, he, Winder, and Blood Talon started for the door.

As soon as they stepped out into the storm, Fire Cat knew it was a mistake. A feeling, like his heart tearing in two, almost sent him staggering.

The rain—partly mixed with hail—pounded down in lashing waves, drenching them to the skin before they could cross the small plaza; the steps would be dangerous enough. Flashes of white light flickered on the carvings that decorated the World Tree Pole, creating a Dance of light that made it seem as if the figures were moving.

Lightning blasted tortured patterns across the sky, silvering vicious drops of rain and little balls of hail.

"I'm going to regret this," Fire Cat uttered under his breath as the storm battered him with water and ice. It beat on his skull, ran down his head, sent cold fingers of water through his cape to chill his skin.

Struggling to keep their hold on Morning Star's weak body, they passed through the gates, slipping and sliding on the slick wooden steps as wind blasted them this way and that.

Eighty

In the flash of lightning, Night Shadow Star caught that last glimpse as Fire Cat and the others maneuvered Morning Star's limp body through the palisade gate.

The strobe-white flashes showed her an empty plaza. The ferocity of the rain increased until it savaged the small courtyard, already puddling in the trampled grass.

Lightning accompanied another blast of thunder; little waterfalls were spitting off the carvings on the great bald cypress World Tree Pole. A representation of Creation, it towered in the center of the plaza. Its high tip shot up into the Sky World, its symbolic roots extending to the depths of the Underworld all the way down to where Old-Woman-Who-Never-Dies had her lair. The link that held all of Creation together. Lightning-silvered threads of water poured down its sides like a fountain to splash and pool at the giant pole's base.

Night Shadow Star let her breath out, slapped the carved relief on the door with a callused palm, and turned back into the room. Grief tightened under her tongue, wouldn't let her swallow.

"I shouldn't have let him go," she cried.

Sun Wing watched her from across the fire, large eyes reflecting the flames. "I was that selfish, once." Her fingers played over the Tortoise Bundle. "And people paid terribly for my greed. All I could think about was what I would do to make myself great. My wishes. My ambition. And I did terrible things. To Father, to Lace, to people I thought I loved."

Night Shadow Star—her feelings a confusion of fear, loss, and heartache—walked back to the fire. Paused long enough to throw another couple of logs on the flames, then took a seat on the dais next to her sister.

"It's not about, me, Sister. It's about the man I love. And I don't want any of this. I just want to vanish. Be left alone. Is sharing my life with Fire Cat, bearing our children, and growing old together selfish? Well, so be it. But you and I have different definitions for the word."

From her pack she pulled her bow, the quiver of arrows, and her war club with its copper-bitted ax. This time, there would be no Underworld Power imparted to the copper to make it more deadly.

Sun Wing lifted her hand, spread her thin fingers, and frowned as she studied them. "I want you to know, I'm sorry for what's going to happen. What I have to . . ." She bit off the words, looking away.

Night Shadow Star told her, "That day in Columella's palace. You came within an instant of paying with your life. If I hadn't arrived when I did, in another heartbeat, Walking Smoke would have cut your throat."

Sun Wing tucked the Tortoise Bundle under her chin, caressing it as if it were a beloved child. As she did, Night Shadow Star heard the familiar whispering of the Bundle's voices. Like feathers stroking her souls.

Lightning banged and sundered the night; rain pounded down harder.

Sun Wing gave her a pained sidelong glance. "It should be me, you know. I should be the one who faces him. My price to pay."

Night Shadow Star shook her head. "You know what your job is. Remember? You told me it was all about enticing the lightning."

"I don't think you understand what that means."

Night Shadow Star set the vicious war club aside and reached out to resettle her sister's hair the way she used to when they were little. "Sun Wing, you know why it has to be me."

A howl of wind, like shrieking voices, shook the high roof overhead.

"Incest, Power, and destiny. All twined together." Night Shadow Star stared into the infinity of her souls. "Because we come from a family of monsters, Sister, we should not be surprised to discover that trait in ourselves."

"So, what are you going to do?" Sun Wing asked, her eyes on the storm just beyond the door.

"I'm killing him. Tonight. It ends here, Sister. I have to restore the balance."

"How?" Sun Wing glanced uneasily at her. "He's a man, strong. And you, you're just—"

"He's soft, Sister. I, on the other hand, am as tough as buffalo sinew." Night Shadow Star lifted an arm and flexed her biceps. "In Joara, I would have killed him with my war club if Fire Light's warriors hadn't interceded."

"And you think he doesn't know this? Won't plan a way around it?"

"Sun Wing, our twisted brother is vain, filled with his own importance. He thinks the Thunderbirds will protect him in the final moment. Just like last time when they pulled him from the river."

"I . . . we have to make it different this time."

Night Shadow Star felt the Bundle's Power flowing into Sun Wing; her hair began to prickle, rising like rubbed fox fur.

As if in accompaniment, fresh bangs and flashes were followed by another pounding deluge in the furious night.

"I understand." Sun Wing's voice had gone hollow as she spoke to the Bundle. Then she turned terrified eyes on Night Shadow Star. "It just told me how to bring this all to an end."

"Then do it."

"But I don't want to. Not if I have to . . ." She winced, averted her stricken expression.

"Whatever it takes," Night Shadow Star insisted. "There was a reason the Tortoise Bundle called to you. A reason that you and I ended up here. Tonight. Together. I want to be free. Do you understand?"

Sun Wing blinked at tears, sniffed, and nodded.

"Good," Night Shadow Star said softly. "Tonight we restore the balance. Sky and Underworld. Piasa, too, wants this finished. Fire Cat and I have a canoe waiting for us."

Piasa's image flickered, ghostly and blue at the edge of Night Shadow Star's vision.

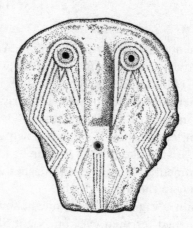

To Split the Night Sky

I *Dance in the rain, driven by the Power of the storm. Overhead the Thunderbirds own the sky! I am ecstatic.*

It doesn't matter that the Tie Snakes called the downpour. That Piasa controls the Tie Snakes. The Underwater Panther and his minions might have conjured the intensity of the pouring rain, but the Sky World is reacting in kind.

This is not a night for Piasa, for anything Underworld. Not while thunder and lightning rule the clouds and unleash their wrath.

I don't feel the cold as I trot down the Avenue of the Sun. Instead, my body is fevered, and I revel as I continue to chew on strips of Fire Light's liver. With each swallow, I sense his life soul and energy flowing through my gut and into my charged limbs.

With my route storm lit, I pass the Great Observatory, splash my way past the Four Winds Clan plaza, and shoot a wary glance up at the guardian posts atop Night Shadow Star's stairway.

I pause long enough to give Piasa's rain-dripping image a low and insolent bow. Then I spit in his direction. As I do a web of lightning threads its way across the sky. Is it my imagination? Or did Piasa just cringe and shiver?

Howling with glee, I Dance my way, skipping, stomping in puddles as the rain spatters on my bare head. Water from the sky! Power from the Sky World, the blood and flesh of a sacrifice filling my gut!

Nothing will stop me now. I live the feeling of victory!

In the afterflash of a lightning bolt, I see a knot of warriors crowded around the base of the Great Staircase. That is a problem.

A flickering of white through the brooding clouds shows me water cascading down a rivulet on the sloping west side of the mound. The deluge is so Powerful, runoff has eaten a channel in the packed black clay. I slop through the delta of spreading clay, set my toes in the runnel, and with hands and feet, start my climb. Water sloshes over my skin with each grip and questing foot, but it is as if the irregularities make the steps.

It takes me not even a finger of time to reach the Council Terrace flat. I make my way along the base of the palisade and am shocked to find no guard at the terrace gate.

Inside, perhaps?

But when I crouch low and peek around the heavy door, I find an empty Council Terrace; the rain-stippled pools gleam, silvered in the constantly strobing light.

I race across the terrace accompanied by a rolling drumming of thunder. Still finding no guards, I sprint up the long staircase to its head, expecting to find at least one guard. I have been planning on how to step close, grab him by the armor, and pitch him headlong down the long slope.

Nothing. No one.

I can almost believe the way has been cleared for me.

I slip past the high palisade gate and scuttle to the closest bastion. Crouched in the recess, water dripping through the floor above, I wait until the next white bolt of lightning blasts its way down from the ripped and torn clouds.

A string of thunderbolts boom and roar, drowning the gusting wind that tears at the steep thatched roof.

In the flashes of light, I see no one. The door to Morning Star's palace hangs open. And, for the first time, my heart skips with anxiety.

No guards? The gates and finally the palace door open?

"So, Morning Star, is this why I couldn't see you reflected in Fire Light's blood? Have you somehow masked your souls, dimmed your Power?"

I close my eyes, sending my souls out of my body, seeking, sensing. And to my surprise, I only detect my sister. But there is another Power here, something hazy and indistinct. A Power I cannot quite place.

Is that the trap?

When I think back, I realize that the huddle of people, the stacked and waiting litters, the fawning servants and attendants at the bottom of the stairs were missing.

"It's like the whole Great Mound is abandoned," I whisper.

Coming to a conclusion, I rise, walk boldly through the torrent of endless rain, each step accompanied by a peal of thunder while a thousand jagged and throbbing flashes fill the Sky World.

As I reach the double doors, a relentless wind slams into the palisade, whistling, roaring through the thatch above and shaking the very building.

Eyes slitted against the gale and driven rain, I see sections of thatch tearing loose.

For the first time, the pelting rain begins to sting.

Another bundle of thatch is torn away.

The gale roars around the towering World Tree Pole, and I wonder if it will be uprooted from the ground.

Night Shadow Star stands in the doorway. I glimpse her surprised eyes reflecting distant lightning. See her start to raise the war club she holds in her right hand.

I hear her say, "You ready to die?"

Hot white lightning blinds me, the crack painful like an impact to my now shivering skin. I am deafened and blinded, the Power of the bolt charging my body.

I leap back as she swings, steps into the pounding rain, and slashes again. I trip, claw for balance, and then I am falling. Lightning arcs and fills the tormented clouds with white. I kick, knocking her foot from under her as she takes a step.

She slips in the mud, tumbles beside me.

Then we are wrestling for the war club. I can feel the Underworld Power; it still lingers in the wood. It sends prickles through my fingers as I try to wrest it away from Night Shadow Star's grip.

Underworld Power. Working against me.

Fear lends me strength, but as I grab her free hand, she twists.

In a flicker of distant white light, I catch the image of her face. The long scar running through the Four Winds tattoo on her cheek, the mangled ear, shock me.

Who is this woman?

And in that instant, like a she-cougar, she rips out of my grasp. Spins in the pouring rain, and in the blackness between flashes from the Sky, drives an unforgiving knee into my stomach.

I double over, air whooshing from my throat.

As I gasp, trying to get a breath despite the rain beating on my face, she rises.

"All you've left me with is hatred, Brother," she tells me as she straddles my chest and rises on her knees. "But now, you're going to set me free."

In a white flicker from the Sky, I see her raise the copper-headed war club.

Where's the lightning? Where are the Thunderbirds?

Another flash shows me Sun Wing, her face contorted where she stands in the doorway behind Night Shadow Star.

Sun Wing's arms are already in midswing, holding something. A long piece of wood? The hoe handle catches Night Shadow Star full in the back of the head. Makes a sodden crack.

Before I can catch my breath, Night Shadow Star collapses on my breast.

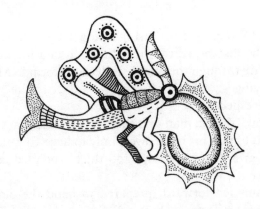

Eighty-one

Staggering and splashing in the rain, Fire Cat, Winder, and Blood Talon had managed to carry Chunkey Boy's limp and shivering body across the Great Plaza. Then they struggled up the steep staircase to Rides-the-Lightning's mound-top temple. Fire Cat didn't bother to pound on the door. Releasing Chunkey Boy to Winder and Blood Talon's grip, he muscled the carved portal to the side.

As they carried the dying man into the healer's temple, Fire Cat was surprised to find the fire crackling brightly, spitting sparks at the high ceiling. As always, the decorations in the place sent shivers down his spine. The various masks hanging on the walls, the painted bones, the carved wooden boxes with their hidden magics, and the hanging Spirit plants all cast a tingle of Power across his already shivering skin.

Rides-the-Lightning, the blind soul flier, was waiting behind the fire. A smile bent the old man's thin lips and exposed toothless gums. All the Earth Clans healer's acolytes stood dressed and waiting.

"I knew you would come," Rides-the-Lightning called. "Bring Morning Star here. Lay him on the pallet."

Blood Talon and Winder cast nervous glances in all directions as the priests made way for them.

As they laid him on what looked like an elk hide–covered pad, Morning Star gasped in pain, water trickling down his body. Blood Talon and Winder beat a fast retreat to the door, glancing up as thunder cracked so loudly overhead that the temple shook.

When Fire Cat tried to step back, Chunkey Boy grabbed onto his hand with a death grip. "No. Please. Don't leave me."

"I have to get back to my lady."

"Not yet, Red Wing." Rides-the-Lightning hobbled forward, his white eyes fixed on the distance. From the direction and intensity, he might have been looking through the temple walls and storm to Morning Star's high palace. Seeing . . . what?

"Elder, with respect—"

"He needs you," the old man said simply. "He has always needed you."

Fire Cat tried to pull his hand away, only to have Chunkey Boy groan and tighten his grip. Chunkey Boy's too-thickly-painted face stared up, his eyes plaintive.

The priests hurried forward, prepared to hand the old man any of the various herbs, artifacts, sucking tubes, or divining rods the old man might require as he bent over Chunkey Boy's body.

"Please, Red Wing," Chunkey Boy rasped as the Healer slowly waved an eagle feather across the man's rock-hard stomach. "Stay with me."

"I have to get back," Fire Cat told him.

"If you leave," Chunkey Boy managed to say despite a pained contortion as the old man softly probed with stiff fingers, "I won't last another finger of time."

The full wrath of the storm beyond the walls seemed to affirm it. Fire Cat had never heard such thunder, a constant rolling bang, crash, and boom that alternately deafened, echoed, and faded in the tempest.

"If you leave, he dies," Rides-the-Lightning affirmed, then glanced at Fire Cat with those soul-shivering white-blind eyes. "This is Power, Red Wing. You are his only hope."

"I am no one's hope," Fire Cat protested. "I don't even think he's Morning Star. Do you understand? *I don't believe.*"

"Opposites crossed," one of the priests said.

"Power Dances on the night," another replied. "Equinox Power. When Sun and the seasons seek balance."

"They can't take me while you're here," Chunkey Boy insisted weakly.

"They who?" Fire Cat asked.

"The Thunderbirds." Chunkey Boy swallowed hard, sweat beading on his chest and arms. "You remember the river? The day you saved Night Shadow Star? If I die, she's . . . lost."

"I have to get back!" Fire Cat cried. "Walking Smoke's coming."

"He can't win." Chunkey Boy gazed up expectantly. "Not as long as you are here. You're the Power. Don't you understand? You hold Cahokia's future in your hands."

"He's raving." Fire Cat tried to tug his hand free, only to feel Chunkey Boy's grip tighten. The man's tortured eyes went bright with panic.

"If he dies, she's lost," Rides-the-Lightning repeated as one of the priests handed him a sucking tube. Then the old man bent down, placing it on Chunkey Boy's stomach just below the ribs. He sucked on the tube for twenty heartbeats, then turned and spat something bloody into the fire. It hissed and burned brightly as it hit the flames.

A shiver raced down Fire Cat's back.

Meanwhile, Winder and Blood Talon had hunkered down by the door, apparently happy enough to enjoy the snug temple's warmth while the storm lashed the outside with rain, wind, and occasional hail.

If he dies, she's lost.

He was tired of Spirit Power.

Eighty-two

Pain. Blasting behind Night Shadow Star's eyes.

Rain beat on her head and shoulders. Felt it running cold down her body. Wind kept tearing at her hair. She could feel someone's body squirming beneath her. Whose?

Too much to think.

Where was she?

Blinking water from her eyes, she looked up to see a high palace roof in the flicker of storm light. Wind, roaring and howling through the palace roof, was ripping away thatch and whistling around the carvings on the World Tree Pole.

Morning Star's palace.

She'd been fighting with Walking Smoke.

And then the impact to the back of her head, the stars bursting through her skull and vision.

Rain kept beating on the backs of her thighs and calves, her shoulders, neck, and head. The pain . . . a spear of fire . . . burned through her brain.

Sun Wing's voice—out of place—shouting over the howl of the storm: "Take her to the World Tree Pole. That's where you have to do this!"

"Do what?" Walking Smoke bellowed back; Night Shadow Star felt him slipping out from under her. Her vision was blurry, her body felt like it was falling, sick and plunging. The urge to vomit tickled the bottom of her throat.

Everything was spinning.

She felt someone grab her arms. Pull them up over her head. Then she was jerked, pulled through the mud and water, her arms straining painfully in their sockets. Thoughts still scrambled, she stared up, found her wrists bound where Walking Smoke was tugging them.

When had that happened?

White flashes of lightning illuminated the towering World Tree Pole in gleaming, actinic light. The carvings cast black shadows, outlining the story of Morning Star's twin birth with the Wild One. Their exploits as boys. She couldn't see higher on the pole where the sculpted relief showed them playing chunkey with the giants, or their various exploits during the Beginning Times, or even the resurrection of their dead father's head. And then she was dropped at the base of the pole. Was allowed to flop loosely on her back in the puddled water.

The rain beating on her face just made the agony and nausea worse. Flashes of white lightning burned through her vision like soul fire.

"Not your night for Power." Walking Smoke leaned down, partially blocking the rain. "I *am* the lightning!"

Night Shadow Star blinked against the water spattering on her face, tried to pull her arms down, and found them still tied. She felt her skirt being stripped from her hips, the wind-blown rain impacting on her abdomen and pelvis before trickling down between her legs.

"Piasa," she whispered, desperate for the sound of his voice, for his presence. "I gave you everything. Help me."

Even as she whispered her plea, the flickering heavens turned the clouds into white lanterns. Walking Smoke was peeling off his breechcloth. An ecstatic glow seemed to radiate from his scarred face as he donned his whelk-shell mask. Its opalescent surface glowed eerily in the strobing white light.

A staccato of thunderous flashes and bangs lit Morning Star's plaza, illuminating the palisade walls, the soaring World Tree Pole, and Walking Smoke as he stepped between her legs. She turned her head away as light danced on his hardened penis.

"No!" She tried to thrash as his weight crushed her into the mud.

Casting one last desperate glance to the side, she saw Sun Wing, her rain-washed face tilted to the heavens. She held the Tortoise Bundle lifted on high.

In the outline of the palisade gates, Piasa glowed a mystical blue, his barred wings spread; eagle-talon feet clutched the wet ground. Gaudy red light shone from his antlers, and the cougar's mighty jaws parted in a snarl.

Night Shadow Star bucked and struggled as Walking Smoke lowered himself onto her. Felt his probing shaft. She was looking up into the heart of the storm when the lightning gathered. It wove a web of pulsing and knotting light across the sky. The torn and sundered depths of the clouds formed the image of great winged beings as the bolts of lightning met overhead. The instant he violated her, she saw the great bolt snap down, blindingly fast. Saw it sear its way down the World Tree Pole, wood exploding in fiery splinters . . .

Eighty-three

Equinox dawn arrived with a remarkable sunrise of searing yellow that became flaming orange before rippling its way west in patterns of red that burned the bellies of the clouds.

Fire Cat pounded across the Great Plaza, splashing through pools of water and leaping over bits of thatch and cane matting torn loose in the worst of the tempest. He could only grind his teeth and clutch his bow. Nothing in that storm-ridden night had been reassuring.

After holding Chunkey Boy's hand through a series of sucking cures, smoke baths, and purifications, the man had fallen into a troubled sleep. Only then, as if through some understanding, Rides-the-Lightning had said, "Go now, Red Wing."

Fire Cat had slipped past the sleeping Winder and Blood Talon, opened the heavy door, and stepped outside to discover the pink of pre-dawn casting the eastern bluffs in black silhouette.

Despite the wreckage left in the storm's wake, people were already out and about as he sprinted across the stickball field, past the World Tree Pole, between the chunkey courts.

At the base of the Great Mound, he slowed, nodded at Five Fists.

The steely-eyed war leader asked, "How's Morning Star?"

"Asleep but alive."

"Did he send you with any orders for me?" Five Fists kept glancing up at the high mound. "I'm tired of waiting, of following orders I don't understand. What's he doing? What's this all about?"

"No orders." Fire Cat shook his head. Paused long enough to say, "Any sign of Walking Smoke?"

"In that storm?" War Claw asked as he stepped up. "Not even frogs wanted to be out in that. As it is, we're soaked, tired, and shivering."

"Then, War Leader," Fire Cat told the warrior, "I'd take whatever measures you think best. My lady is up there. I've done enough for other people. Especially your beloved Morning Star."

Then he started up the Great Staircase, feet slapping the wet wood as he climbed.

To his surprise, he was winded by the time he made the high gate. Paused long enough to look around.

Cahokia was remarkably clear in the wake of the storm. For once the haze was missing, blown away, half the fires in the city probably drowned. He could see from the thickly populated eastern bluffs all the way south past the lakes and Rattlesnake Mound, then southwest toward Horned Serpent Town. To the east, he let his eye travel over the dense clusters of houses, farmsteads, palaces, and temples, mixed as they were with marshes, barrow pits, and lakes all filled to brimming after such a heavy rain. Evening Star Town, clearly visible as pinpricks on the western bluffs, had a pinkish tone. From here, he had no view of the north or Marsh Elder Lake, let alone Serpent Woman Town.

Cahokia had been cleansed by the torment of the night and ready for a fresh start. Fire Cat could sense the city coming alive, as though in rebirth.

"When did I ever come to care for a place such as this?"

He was, after all, still a slave in the eyes of these people.

Them and their fake god.

That dying man, whose hand he'd held through the night, most assuredly had not been divine.

With that he turned, slapped the wooden frame at the palisade gate, and stepped into the courtyard. Water pooled everywhere, maybe a quarter of the thatch bundles had been torn off the pole framework that supported the high-pitched roof. But what caught his eye was the reddish-pale streak blasted out of the towering World Tree Pole; a giant's gouge might have ripped that sinuous channel out of the intricately carved bald cypress trunk. The various reliefs from the top down had been defaced by the blast, leading all the way down to . . .

For a couple of heartbeats, Fire Cat tried to make sense of what he was seeing. At first glance he thought it some mythical eight-legged creature with its limbs outstretched. But this was two-headed. A caricature of human copulation that . . .

He took a couple of steps toward the gruesome remains. Stopped short, disbelieving.

The male sprawled atop the woman's body, legs and arms shock-stiff and straight. A whelk-shell mask, its surface discolored and the left side of it heat-browned and burned, lay in the mud to one side.

Weird patterns of burns marked the conjoined bodies, like someone had laid burning fern leaves across their swollen and blistered skin. A great cracked circle had been scorched in the middle of the man's back. His head was craned back, face in a hideous grimace, eyes popped from the skull. White foam, like a perverted tongue, protruded from his mouth and nostrils.

"She's free." The voice came from the side.

Fire Cat turned, saw Sun Wing walk out from the palace's gaping doors. The woman wore a light fabric cape and a textile skirt woven in chevron and square designs. The Tortoise Bundle was cradled like a baby in her arms.

"Free?" Fire Cat tried to understand, blinked, and with a cry stumbled toward the ghastly burned bodies.

"No!" The scream tore from Fire Cat's throat as he bent down, seized the man's wrist, and pulled the stiff body from atop the woman.

She lay spread-eagled; death-gray eyes protruded from her skull. That same white foam clogged her throat and nostrils from when her lungs had boiled. The long black hair was singed, mud-clotted, and burned away in clumps despite the damp ground on which she lay. The intricate burn lines left by the lightning made a lace-like design over her breasts, stomach, pelvis, and thighs.

No! This isn't her.

But the scar running along her cheek to the mangled ear left no doubt.

"Lady?" Fire Cat whispered as he pulled her stiff corpse loose from the mud, fought against the board-stiffness in her wide-spread limbs.

"*Gods, no!*" he screamed, holding her cold body tight. He settled onto the wet clay, pulled her close.

"Underworld Power has no hold on her now," Sun Wing told him softly.

His beating heart fell away.

Into some deep and lightless place.

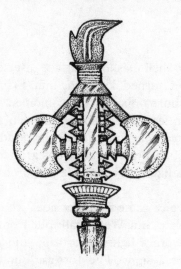

Eighty-four

Seven Skull Shield stood in the back of Morning Star's magnificent palace and looked up at where the storm had ripped entire chunks of thatch away from the pole frame. It seemed so odd to see blue sky. And then he could lower his gaze, and in the daylight, really get a good look at Morning Star's palace. Remarkable how beautiful and intricate the hand-carved sleeping benches were. How bright the dye in the exotic textiles that hung from the walls. Not to mention how the copper repoussé artwork shimmered and shone. Even the matting under his feet, having been woven exclusively for Morning Star, proved mesmerizing.

"Pus-rotted place has always been a cave when I've been here."

Wooden Doll, standing beside him, shot him a censorious look.

"Well, it has," Seven Skull Shield said in defense. "That or I've been so scared that I was going to die at any second that I couldn't really appreciate the surroundings."

"Don't you have a single feeling in your body? Or are you as insensitive as a rock? She was your friend." Wooden Doll indicated where Fire Cat crouched on the floor, back wedged in the angle created by the sleeping benches in the southwest corner; he still cradled Night Shadow Star's body. The Red Wing had pulled her corpse onto his lap. Kept stroking her singed and muddy hair. Seemed unaware when brittle clumps of it continued to come loose in his fingers. Lips close to her bloody ears, he whispered to her. Almost mumbling. As he did, his entire body quivered and his face contorted.

Sometimes the sobbing catch of breath could be heard clear across the room.

"Gods and blood, Skull," Wooden Doll told him, "but that man really loved her."

"She was a remarkable lady." Seven Skull Shield met Wooden Doll's haunted eyes. "She was never anything but respectful. And me, just a clanless thief. Spooky as a pot full of water moccasins, maybe, especially when Piasa was possessing her, but she never treated me like I was some menial. I'll weep when I can." He paused. "But not here. Not now. She'd understand."

Blue Heron stepped away from where she'd been standing with Wind and Rising Flame at the eternal fire. Their talk had been too low to overhear, but the worried glances the women cast in Fire Cat's direction had been eloquent enough.

"Bad business this," Blue Heron said, then glanced at where Sun Wing sat, vacant-eyed, on one of the sleeping benches against the east wall. She had her feet drawn up, heedless of the dried mud that cracked off onto the exotic blankets. The young woman kept the Tortoise Bundle tucked tightly to her chest as she Sang to it in a soft crooning voice.

"What's she say?" Seven Skull Shield asked.

"Just keeps Singing that same song," Blue Heron told him. "It's eerie, starting to get on my nerves. All that business about dead brothers, piles of dirt, and water trickling in ditches. The light and black brothers? That I get. Reminds me of Chunkey Boy and Walking Smoke."

"That hideous thing out there by the World Tree Pole really is Walking Smoke's body?" Wooden Doll asked.

Blue Heron pulled at her wattle. "I took a good look. I know those tattoos on his right cheek: Four Winds Clan." She pointed at her own wrinkled face. "Same as mine. Ride-the-Lightning's work, though he did mine when he could still see. That's what's left of Walking Smoke lying there. Stiff as an old board and twice as splintered."

Wooden Doll asked, "What were they doing? Copulating? Out in the storm? You saw the impression in the mud."

Blue Heron rubbed her brow, as if to relieve a headache. "Winder and Blood Talon tell me he thought taking his sister by force would make him the most Powerful witch alive." She grunted her disgust. "No wonder the Thunderbirds blasted him in the back as an abomination."

"How sick and twisted can a person . . ." Wooden Doll stopped short as forms darkened the doorway and Five Fists entered, followed by a litter born by Winder, Blood Talon, War Claw, and additional warriors.

Atop it rode Morning Star, sitting erect, all his finery on display. In an instant, everyone in the room dropped, prostrating themselves on the matting. Seven Skull Shield, knowing the protocol, grabbed Wooden Doll by the arm, dragging her down with him.

Though, when Seven Skull Shield shot a glance from the corner of his eye, Fire Cat remained as he'd been, seemingly unaware of Morning Star's arrival or the change in the room.

Seven Skull Shield watched the warriors and porters lower the litter before the dais. Morning Star rose, ascended the steps, and settled himself on the panther hides atop his high chair.

No one seemed to notice when Farts peeked around the double doors, sniffed, and darted in. Then, in his slinking sneak, head and tail low, he slipped over to where Fire Cat cradled Night Shadow Star's body. Ears back, the big dog dropped, nose working, eyes fixed on the dead woman. Then he lowered his blocky muzzle between his front paws.

"War Chief War Claw." Morning Star's voice carried in the stillness. "You will take my warriors and alert the engineers. My roof is in need of repair. After that, you will ensure that no one ascends the Great Staircase until ordered otherwise by myself or War Leader Five Fists."

"Yes, Morning Star!" War Claw slapped a hard fist to his armored chest—shot a concerned glance at where Fire Cat cradled Night Shadow Star's body—and with his warriors, trooped out into the daylight.

No sooner had he departed than Morning Star sagged. Seemed to wilt onto his high perch. In a weak voice, he called, "Rise."

"Lord?" Wind asked, climbing to her feet. "Are you all right?"

Morning Star smiled weakly. "Anything but, *Tonka'tzi*. That aside, we have more pressing concerns for the time being."

To Five Fists, he said, "War Leader? Could you ensure that my sister's body is carried in state to Rides-the-Lightning's for proper care in the Earth Clans charnel house? Her souls are no longer Piasa's but are free. Once her flesh is stripped away and her bones cleaned and bundled, she is to be laid in a shallow open pit at the top of the burial mound. Halfway between Sky and Underworld. The choice is hers as to whether she ascends to the Sky World with her ancestors or seeks the Underworld where she also has ties."

"Yes, Morning Star," Five Fists barked, his skeptical eyes taking in the shrunken figure on the dais.

The grizzled old warrior turned, walked across the room, and—after giving Farts the evil eye—bent down. "Red Wing, I need to take her now."

The man looked up, tears streaming down his cheeks. "I can't let her go. If she goes . . . Nothing left . . . not for me."

Five Fists' voice remained firm. "I have my orders."

"You strangle me first. Lay my corpse beside hers in the charnel house. She needs me . . . *Gods,* I *can't* let her go!" He clamped his eyes shut.

Seven Skull Shield realized wetness was welling at the corner of his own eyes.

He walked over, told Five Fists, "Let me try."

Seven Skull Shield gave Farts the "back off" sign. Bent down and laid a hand on the man's shoulder. He'd seen the like in Fire Cat's eyes before. On the day Night Shadow Star had married the Itza. But not like this. Not this gutted look.

"Fire Cat? Let us help you. She has to be prepared. We'll do it together. Send her off with the honor the lady deserves."

Fire Cat tried to swallow, couldn't, as if the grief knot under his tongue was choking him. Gaze empty, face expressionless, he kept stroking Night Shadow Star's filthy hair.

Seven Skull Shield pulled one of the fancy blankets off the sleeping bench, unfolded it. "Come. Let's wrap her in this for the trip. Then, at the foot of the stairs, you and I will place her on a litter. With Five Fists and some others, we'll carry her to the soul flier."

He tried to smile reassurance. "All of us who loved her. Caring for her. She'd have liked that."

"Without her . . ." Fire Cat's eyes had lost focus. "Promised . . . to serve her."

Seven Skull Shield glanced up at Five Fists. The old warrior's eyes had gone misty. "Help me wrap her."

The war leader bent down, and though Fire Cat remained listless, he didn't hinder their actions as they managed to fold the blanket around Night Shadow Star's stiff corpse.

Together they lifted, Seven Skull Shield helping Fire Cat up with one hand. The Red Wing wavered, eyes glazed and lost. Farts, as if in support, followed at the Red Wing's side. The big dog kept looking up, worry in his blue and brown eyes.

Supporting most of her weight, Seven Skull Shield led the way as they started for the door. Fire Cat had taken the woman's legs, seemed to be floundering.

Thinking of love, and what the Red Wing was enduring, Seven Skull Shield shot a glance back at Wooden Doll. Saw the deep and aching sympathy in her gaze.

Never had she looked so beautiful.

As terrible as it was to be carrying Night Shadow Star, what if it they were bearing Wooden Doll's body to the charnel house? What would it mean for him?

Eighty-five

The caricature of a man hung in the wooden frame. Arms, tied to each upper corner, were too long to be normal. The legs, swollen, misshapen, with spears of bone blackened with old dried blood sticking through the bruised skin. Where the ankles were tied in each lower corner, the feet looked overinflated, like old bladders.

The man's head hung down over his chest, most of the scalp cut away to leave stained and darkened skull, the sutures like squirming dark lines. It swarmed with flies, the surrounding scalp alive with wiggling maggots. Below the sunken ribs, the man's belly was swollen, the navel protruding.

A man?

Yes, the clotted wound where his shaft and stones had once hung was that of a male.

Blood Talon closed his eyes, almost swaying on his feet. He glanced to the side, seeing the two guards who stood to either side, away from the swarming flies.

Behind him, Morning Star's great earthen pyramid rose against the evening sky. The high palace roof shooting up like a sheer wedge against the sky. The high guardian posts of *Hunga Ahuito*, Ivory Billed Woodpecker, and Sky Eagle, stuck up like silhouettes.

Blood Talon swallowed hard, shook his head.

The misshapen thing hanging in the square moved, lifted its maimed head.

Blood Talon slitted his eyes. "Gods and rot, War Leader, is that you?"

"Who's there?" the voice sounded hoarse, weak.

"Squadron First Blood Talon. I have returned to Cahokia, War Leader.

I came with Night Shadow Star. So, in a perverted sense, I fulfilled the terms of my orders, if not the intent."

"Who are you?" What was left of Spotted Wrist blinked, seemed to have trouble focusing.

"I have asked myself that same question, War Leader. The answer is complicated. And I suspect it will change with time, and life, and the challenges I must face. Even with the choices I will make."

"What?" the cracked voice said.

"Do you remember that you sent Squadron First Blood Talon to bring Night Shadow Star back to Cahokia? So that you could marry her?"

The pain-racked face twitched, the lips working slowly. "Yes. Marry her . . . put my child in her . . . and Cahokia's . . . mine . . ."

"She had a different fate, War Leader." Blood Talon took a deep breath, looked to the west where the sun was sinking behind the distant horizon. Equinox. Its golden light slipped down the angle of the Great Mound's northern side. The black clay, battered by the storm, was no longer smooth.

Blood Talon vented a bitter laugh. "I suppose we all do. None of us could have foreseen this day. Who we would become. How we would end up."

"What are you doing?" Spotted Wrist mumbled through his misery.

"Waiting for dark, War Leader," Blood Talon said as he turned away. Searching the slope above, he saw just the place he was looking for. Yes, there.

"Help . . . me . . ." Spotted Wrist's head dropped, the weight of it on his already too-stretched arms pulling the torn muscles and tendons. A pitiful yip from the pain broke the man's dry, cracked lips.

"I will," Blood Talon promised. "Night Shadow Star brought one arrow back with her. No one will recognize it. It can't be traced. The design is different, being made in far-off Cofitachequi as it was." He glanced at the distant guard. "I'll have to wait until full dark, War Leader. But then it will all be over."

"Why?" Spotted Wrist whimpered.

Whether the War Leader was in his right mind, Blood Talon couldn't know. He told him, "Because it is my last service to you, Keeper. Because I owe it to myself to end your misery. Because, as a man, it is the right thing to do."

And he would. Just as soon as it was dark enough he would creep up on the side of the mound. Then, this done, he would go and stand watch for Fire Cat.

The last service for an old leader, the continuing service for a new one.

Eighty-six

The dog's nose brought Fire Cat back from the Dreams. In them, he and Night Shadow Star had been hidden. Lost somewhere in the endless forest. They had a farmstead in a clearing; corn, beans, squash, and goosefoot grew in riotous splendor. Their house was a trench-wall structure with a split-cane roof and had a thatched ramada attached to the western side. Not that they got much sun given the high canopy of oaks, maple, ash, and hickory on all sides. A giant mulberry stood out front, heavy with its bounty of berries. The small yard with a log-and-pestle mortar was just right for the children to tear about.

Two boys and a little girl. And always a handful.

In the Dream, Fire Cat and Night Shadow Star stood side by side, arms around each other as they surveyed the splendor that was theirs. A culmination, a perfect ending filled with . . .

The nose pressed into Fire Cat's face again, sniffing; puffs of foul breath tickled his nose and cheeks. Then the insult of a sloppy wet tongue brought Fire Cat fully awake.

The cloying stench wasn't all the dog's breath. Even as Fire Cat blinked awake, the hollow grief came crashing back.

He sat on the hard dirt floor, back braced against the bench that supported Night Shadow Star's corpse. What was left of it. Around him the thick odor of decomposing human flesh permeated the dark air.

Fire Cat had grown used the smell, used to death. The priests insisted it was both the ending and the beginning of things.

He couldn't have cared less. His desperate wish was to escape to the Dream. To be with Night Shadow Star, walking across sunlit meadows, netting fish in the river, laughing, running his fingers through her thick black hair. In the Dream he could stare into her bottomless eyes, revel in her smile. There, he and she could hold each other. Enjoy slow and endless sexual unions as a warm fire crackled nearby.

Love lived in the Dream.

Grief sucked away the awful endless wakefulness.

Rides-the-Lightning's acolytes had done most of the de-fleshing of Night Shadow Star's body. They'd carefully skinned her—at least as well as they could given the burn patterns. Then they'd sliced away the muscles, removed her cooked and burst organs.

And I endured every moment of it.

Through it all, the dog, Farts, had stayed. And no one, not even Rides-the-Lighting, had given the beast a sidelong look, let alone tried to drive him out.

When it became too much to bear, Fire Cat would pull Farts close, wrap his arms around the shoulders, and weep with his face buried in the brindle dog's neck.

As if some solace was shared between them. Didn't matter that Fire Cat had tried to kill himself when others refused, the dog was always there. Understanding. Sharing the empty, pointless process of breathing.

Farts tried to nuzzle him again; Fire Cat pushed the dog away. The big dog resisted as it snuffled at his face. And given his position on the floor, Fire Cat couldn't get the leverage to dislodge the heavy animal.

"Pus and spit, dog, why are you bothering me?"

Farts—delighted to have spurred a response—panted foul breath into Fire Cat's face while the thick tail thumped against Night Shadow Star's bench with enough force to shake it. In the charnel house's dim light, he could barely see the peculiar blue and brown eyes fill with delight.

"Came to get you," a familiar voice told him.

Fire Cat blinked up to see Seven Skull Shield and Winder. "Go away."

"How are the cuts on your wrist?" Seven Skull Shield asked.

"Healing," Fire Cat told him, looking down at the scabs. "When Five Fists, Rides-the-Lightning, and you refused to strangle me, it seemed like the only way I'd be able to go with her."

Winder—standing behind Seven Skull Shield—crossed his arms. "Wherever she is, she's irritated with you." The big Trader bent down. "You know why that smelly dog's stayed with you? Why you couldn't kill yourself? It's because her souls are hanging in the air around you. Telling you that you're still in her service."

"If I were in her service, I'd be dead. My souls would be with her. Protecting her in death as I failed in life."

"Then stop acting like a child," Winder said curtly.

"Ah," Seven Skull Shield said, giving Farts a knowing glance. "That's it."

Fire Cat dully said, "I said, go away."

Winder gave Seven Skull Shield a weary look. "And these nobles think they're so smart, being chiefs and all."

Seven Skull Shield told Fire Cat, "For a man who's been living with Power for so long, you don't seem to have learned anything about it. Go back to the beginning. Think, Red Wing. She and her brother. They were supposed to die in the river that day. Might have, if you hadn't pulled Night Shadow Star out of the water. Maybe that's why the Thunderbirds kept Walking Smoke alive. Because you interfered. You kept Night Shadow Star from dying. So to keep the balance, the Thunderbirds deposited Walking Smoke's sick and twisted carcass way out in Cofitachequi. Night Shadow Star never had a choice. Piasa and the Thunderbirds knew that. And so did Morning Star."

"Which is why we're here." Winder hooked a thumb at Seven Skull Shield. "Skull here asked Five Fists for the chance to talk you out before he barges in here with a bunch of warriors and drags you out."

"What for?" Fire Cat reached up, wrapping an arm around the big dog's neck, fingers scratching the warm fur. Farts leaned against him, happy for the attention.

"Morning Star has ordered you to be brought to him." Seven Skull Shield dropped to a crouch, hands between his knees. "Says you've had plenty of time, while he's run out of it. One way or another, you're coming."

"Tell him no. White Mat and Shedding Bird have *Red Reed* waiting at the canoe landing. If I can't die with my lady, I'm going with them."

Winder told him, "They've been here already. Came and showed their devotion to our lady. I saw to it that they were amply rewarded and that they left as heroes. By now they've made it to the confluence of the Mother Water."

"There are other Traders." Fire Cat hugged the dog tighter, fought tears. Realized how he'd been keeping *Red Reed* in the back of his mind. How the river had come to represent escape from the pain and futility.

"Let's go," Winder told him as he extended a hand. "Oh, and Five Fists says you can bring that mongrel mutt with you, too."

"He's a Spirit dog," Seven Skull Shield reminded.

Winder looked at the dog. Made a face.

Fire Cat shook his head in defeat and climbed stiffly to his feet. "I'll do it. I'll see Chunkey Boy." He shot a hard look at Winder. "Maybe see my mother and sisters. And then I'm gone. This place . . . Everywhere I go, anything I see . . . as long as I'm in Cahokia, she's going to be here. I can't stand that."

"No," Winder agreed. "I guess not." His gaze narrowed. "With a load of Trade, there's a profit to be made down among the Tunica."

"Now you're talking." Fire Cat managed a smile.

Yes. He could live now. Maybe find a place.

Far from Cahokia.

Turning, he brushed his fingers over Night Shadow Star's desiccated face, whispering, "I'll see you again. Someday. In the Spirit World."

He turned and, Farts walking by his side, followed the thief and the Trader from the room.

The Dead—whom he had once so feared in that dark cave in the Underworld—now stroked his side and arms in a token of their affection and compassion as he passed.

Eighty-seven

Fire Cat, with Farts still at his side, stepped through the high palace gate and stopped. In the slanting afternoon light, the new lightning scar was glaring and pale where it had blasted weathered wood from the intricately carved World Tree Pole.

And there, at the bottom, he had to look away. Too afraid he'd still see the imprint of her body.

That would be too much to bear.

Anything but that.

So he looked up, surprised to see that the entire palace roof had been replaced. It hadn't been that long. Had it?

But then, he'd lost track of time in the charnel house, and this was Morning Star's palace. The living god need only make a request and thousands would spring to comply. For all he knew, a swarm of workers could have replaced the roof in a matter of days.

"What do you think, Farts?" Fire Cat asked, wryly amused that these days he sounded like the thief.

The big brindled dog looked up, his odd eyes alight, mouth agape and panting while the thick tail switched back and forth.

"Let's get this over with."

He had paused only long enough to recover his weapons and chunkey gear. A couple of changes of clothing and cold-weather dress given that they were into fall. Now the pack hung on his back. Everything he had left.

The palace door remained unguarded—a fact that sent a quiver through him. Inside the ornate Great Room, the eternal fire burned brightly, crackling and sending sparks toward the high ceiling.

Still smelling of death, his hair matted, the Trader's shirt he wore bloodstained and spattered with fluids from his time in the charnel house, he walked up to the eternal fire and dropped his pack.

Farts entertained himself by gulping down a half a fish someone had left on a wooden trencher; then he commenced to lick the trencher spotless.

Atop the dais, Chunkey Boy sat. For the first time, Fire Cat saw him without makeup. The Four Winds Clan tattoos looked curiously out of place in the hollows of his sunken cheeks. No headdress covered his now-loose hair. The man only wore a simple breechcloth. His body was propped up by rolled buffalo hides; every bone was sticking out in his chest, ribs, and thin legs. The knee joints looked oversized given his emaciation. Now the deep-set eyes—as if they peered out of a skull—fixed on Fire Cat.

"Have you finally let her go?" Chunkey Boy asked in a weak voice.

Fire Cat touched his chest. "No. I'll keep her here. With me. Until my souls find hers in the afterlife."

He glanced around. The only other occupants of the room were Sun Wing—who was cradling the Tortoise Bundle—Rising Flame, Columella, *Tonka'tzi* Wind, Blue Heron, and Five Fists. They all watched with curious eyes, expressions worried, wary.

Doesn't matter, he thought. And a sense of relief came with it. Knowledge that he no longer had a stake in the game.

After this, I'm gone.

Chunkey Boy seemed to read his thoughts and smiled knowingly before adding, "Not yet, Red Wing."

"Oh, yes. My time here is up, Chunkey Boy." He chuckled, reached down and scratched the dog's head. "The man you knew as Fire Cat is dead. His only oath was to serve his lady. Beyond that, whoever I am now, I'm going Trading in the south."

"Tell me what you saw on the Tenasee." Chunkey Boy's voice rasped like a faltering breath.

The order caught Fire Cat by surprise. It took him a moment to organize his thoughts. "Your expedition is proceeding. The colonies are thriving; by now you have control of the Tenasee all the way to the Wide Fast and then east to Cofitachequi. War Leader Tall Dancer is doing an excellent, if ruthless, job of managing such a huge operation. Your alliance with the Yuchi is intact, the smaller nations that have been colonized may not be happy about a Cahokian presence, but there's not much they can do about it given Cahokian strength."

He frowned. "I think Winder said it best: 'The Tenasee is a Cahokian stream from the Wide Fast all the way to the Father Water.'"

Chunkey Boy studied him thoughtfully. "So, given your history as an enemy, tell me, Red Wing, do you think that's good or bad?"

"A little of both, but given our experience in the Upper Tenasee, the areas controlled by Cahokia are safer for travel. For the subjugated peoples, ultimately it's hard to say. They lose their autonomy; their stories and beliefs make way for Cahokia's. They have a club to their heads when it comes to accepting whether or not to believe in Morning Star's miraculous return from the heavens. And a square awaits those who choose to resist. Whatever happens, your empire is going to change the Southeast forever. The same with the new colonies you're building in the north. It's all being bound together by Trade and the Morning Star story. As a result, the chunkey courts are in a lot better shape in that part of the world."

Chunkey Boy's smile barely bent his lips. "And what happens if Morning Star goes back to the Sky World? If this palace at the center of it is occupied by, oh, say, High Chief Burned Bone from Evening Star House?"

Fire Cat glanced sidelong at Columella, seeing panic flash across her face. For whatever reason, the notion terrified her.

"Cahokia will dry up and vanish within a generation," Fire Cat told him. "The myth holds it together. But you, or your heirs, can always perform another Requickening ceremony. Just like last time, the masses will buy the whole charade. The pomp and ritual, the spectacle of a couple hundred young men and women being sacrificed and interred as you build a new ridge mound. All the Dancing and praying, the offerings burned. Morning Star's Spirit can, what do you call it? *Devour* another young man's souls and possess his body?"

Chunkey Boy's half-lidded stare burned into Fire Cat's. "I won't do it again."

"I don't understand."

"You've never believed, Red Wing."

"If you're worried about me heading south, preaching the heresy of the living god, don't. People *need* to believe in the miracle. Black Tail changed the world with his hoax. His presence enticed countless towns and villages to come here, to make this giant city. First Morning Star changed Cahokia, now it's changing the rest of our world."

"What was my sister's last wish, Red Wing? What did she ask of you?"

"To take care of you. To see you to the soul flier's. To keep you from dying."

"Will you still do that?"

"Take you to the soul flier's? Of course. But after that—"

"Will you keep me from dying?"

Fire Cat laughed at the absurdity. "Me? How can I do that?"

Chunkey Boy studied his bone-thin hands as he raised them. "Night Shadow Star's last command was that you keep Morning Star alive. Once, I told you that through the most cunning of means I was preparing you to do me some terrible service." He chuckled hollowly. "Like my sister, I am asking you to keep Morning Star alive."

The man's gaze intensified, almost burning, and for the moment, Fire Cat could almost believe Chunkey Boy was indeed Morning Star.

In a weary voice, Chunkey Boy said, "I am not asking you to serve me. I'm asking you to serve Cahokia."

"How?"

"Here, on this dais. For the sake of the city, I want you to take my place."

Eighty-eight

At Morning Star's announcement, Blue Heron could only gasp as she sat, paralyzed, on the sleeping bench. The first to react was Wind; the *tonka'tzi* scrambled to her feet, paced over to the dais where she gaped, first at Morning Star, and then the stunned Fire Cat.

"Are you out of your mind?" she asked, heedless of the effrontery.

"Impossible!" Five Fists declared, also stalking forward. "Lord, this man's a heretic! He doesn't believe you're really you!"

Columella, too, had stood and headed over, which Blue Heron figured was her cue. If Morning Star was going to order any of them into the squares, it would be all of them.

"Would you rather have the thief?" Morning Star turned his head, a wan smile on his sallow face as he read their expressions. "The time has come to bring balance back to Creation."

Columella cried, "What does the Red Wing have to do with it? Isn't he a slave? A heretic? A . . . A . . ."

"An Unbeliever!" Five Fists finished. "He's not even one of us."

Fire Cat's expression reminded Blue Heron of a man condemned as he watched the exchange with growing horror. "I'm going south to Trade."

Morning Star raised a calming hand, saying, "Everything I have done was to prepare you for my return to the Sky World. I needed you to understand that the city is more than just Four Winds Clan and its trivial politics. Rising Flame is correct about unifying the city. But first, Spotted Wrist had to rise and then fall as a lesson about authority and ambition."

"A lesson that almost devoured us, you mean," Wind muttered.

"Those are the most Powerful of lessons," Morning Star agreed. "But the Red Wing has paid the most, risked the most, and learned the most.

All of you are here—knowing the truth—to help him govern when he takes the High Chair and becomes Morning Star."

"Not a chance," Fire Cat declared. "I'm leaving on the next canoe south."

Sun Wing stepped up to him, staring into his eyes. "Are you the man my sister loved? That man served her, and she served Cahokia. She asked you to keep Morning Star alive. Will you turn your back on her now?"

Blue Heron watched the conflict play over the Red Wing's face. Then, clamping his eyes shut, he shook his head. "Without my lady . . . I can't stand the pain."

And with that, he turned, hitched his pack on his back, and walked through the open doors and into the light beyond. The big brindled dog glanced sadly at Morning Star, uttered a sad whimper.

Blue Heron would have sworn some subtle communication passed between them; Morning Star flicked his hand in a dismissive gesture, and the dog—head and tail drooping—walked wearily from the room.

"What now?" Rising Flame asked.

"Eventually," Sun Wing told her, "the city dies. The people leave. Everything you know will be gone. Grass and trees will grow on the mounds. Where children now play, and people laugh, only the wind will blow. The Dead will sleep, and even memories will fade and vanish."

Eighty-nine

Of all the impossible, outlandish, and insane ideas Fire Cat had ever heard, nothing had prepared him for the shock. As he strode out the carved double doors and into the plaza, he glanced back over his shoulder at Morning Star's great palace.

"Don't you know who I am? I'm the last Red Wing. My people never believed."

He stomped harder as he passed the soaring World Tree Pole, refusing to glance at the spot where Night Shadow Star died. Looked instead at the heights where the lightning had blasted the pale scar through the intricately carved story of Morning Star's life.

That brought a chuckle to Fire Cat's lips. Looked to him like the Sky World, too, rejected the whole absurd farce. The heretics in Red Wing Town had been right from the beginning.

But what a price to pay for vindication.

On a whim, he dropped his pack, crossed over to the bastion on the southwest corner of the palisade, and climbed the ladder. There—on the heights from which Morning Star used to gaze out at the city—Fire Cat braced his hands on the clay-plastered wall. Rain had damaged it. Something that would need to be fixed.

And then he looked out at the city, stunned by the enormity of it. From this height, he could see distant Evening Star Town, the urban sprawl that followed the Avenue of the Sun from River City Mounds, past Black Tail's tomb. The circle of the Great Observatory was perfectly clear from this height. As was Four Winds Plaza, and of course, Night Shadow Star's palace with its Piasa and Horned Serpent guardian posts.

For a long time, he gazed at her palace. Remembered his first night there, his only wish having been to die. So many memories. He and his lady. The shared pain and challenge, how their desperate hatred had faded into an equally desperate love.

Just follow my orders.

As the words rolled around in his head, he let his gaze wander over the great city. *"No matter how preposterous they may sound."*

His gaze returned to the west, past Black Tail's tomb, to the distant River City Mounds. There, behind that cluster of buildings, temples, and palaces, Winder would be preparing to head south. To follow the river.

"I can be finished with the pain, the heartache." He closed his eyes, imagining the river, the surface roiling, sucking, flowing ever south toward a new life. His paddle dipping into the murky water and propelling the canoe—like a thing alive—across the smooth surface.

With the memory of Night Shadow Star's smile breaking his heart, he climbed down. Farts was standing before the palace door, head up, expression anxious as if waiting for his decision. The tail switched back and forth, the dog's eyes pleading.

"Sorry, old friend. Some wounds are just too deep to heal."

Picking up his pack, he walked through the palisade gate and started down the steps to where Blood Talon waited.

By this time tomorrow, he would be on the river. Headed south in search of a way to forget that he would never love again.

Ninety

Fire Cat tilted his head back, letting the sun bathe his face. In the cool fall air the warmth was a relief. Maybe even a reminder that something might be worth living for somewhere in the south. Downriver. In some as yet undiscovered place.

He sat on the Trade canoe's gunwale. The story was that the vessel was called *Water Strider*, and that it had been one of Spotted Wrist's "lost" canoes. Winder, eyes averted, voice low, had hinted that where the deeply carved image of a water strider was now incised in the bow, a Fish Clan insignia had once been.

Winder had just slapped Seven Skull Shield on the back, had said his goodbyes and watched as the thief went stalking up toward the warehouses on the levee. Said he needed to collect on a basket of whelk shells from some bead carvers. The big dog, Farts, had given Fire Cat one last, longing look, then reluctantly followed the thief until he disappeared among the ramadas and stalls.

"Spirit dog," Fire Cat whispered, and wondered how he could have made it through those first wretched days when his souls had died and his heart had beat with nothing but loss.

Fire Cat ran a thoughtful finger across the long scabs on his wrists. Wondered if it wouldn't have been better to have died in that charnel house. He'd used an obsidian blade. Looking back now, he wondered if he'd been the one to stop just short of severing the arteries and tendons, or if it had been Night Shadow Star's hand reaching out from the Spirit World to restrain him.

Funny thing about grief. It would have been so much easier to have died. Living the rest of his life, thinking of her every day, aching over her death, and wishing he'd stayed to keep her safe would be a relentless torture.

"My penance for failing her," he told himself. The longer he lived, the longer he had to mourn and grieve. Maybe that was the balance.

Up and down the canoe landing, life went on. Traders coming and going, farmers in dugouts paddling in from outlying farmsteads, arriving with canoes piled high with harvested corn, beans and squash and sacks of goosefoot, knotweed, little barley, and maygrass. The nut harvest was in full swing upriver. So was the fall hunt; the loads of smoked and jerked meat were arriving by the boatload. So, too, were rafts of bark, thatch, cane, firewood, and other forest products. Cahokia's insatiable needs were being met.

The canoe landing reminded him of a hive.

Fire Cat looked up as Winder tossed a heavy pack of Trade into *Water Strider*'s midsection. There it lay, the last of the load, filling the last hole in the packs.

"You ready?" The big Trader was rubbing the backs of his muscular arms. Staring thoughtfully up to where the new roof was being raised over River House palace. Across the distance, the Earth Clans workers looked like ants as they swarmed the pole frame that would support the thatch.

Fire Cat stood, took a deep breath as he gave the place one last inspection. "I have nothing left here." He glanced at Blood Talon. "What about you, Squadron First?"

The fire-scarred warrior gave him a crooked smile. "Me? I've done what my honor demanded of me. As you served your lady I will serve you, War Leader. Wherever you go, whatever you do, I'll have your back."

The way Winder kept looking at them, it was as if he were expecting something.

Fire Cat asked, "Got something on your mind, Trader?"

"You think you'll ever come back?" Winder's gaze had narrowed.

"Too much pain here," Fire Cat told him. "What about you?"

"I've made my peace with Keeper Blue Heron, had my laughs with Skull, and seen our lady laid to rest. It's time for me to go visit my wives. Make the most of my newfound fame before the world forgets." Winder glanced around. "But Cahokia's the center of the world. I'll always return."

Fire Cat slapped the man on the back. "Then let's be about it."

Winder, Fire Cat, Blood Talon, and the two other Traders they'd joined bent to the task of shoving and dragging *Water Strider* out into the river, each leaping aboard and grabbing their paddles.

As they turned the long canoe to ride the current's thread, Fire Cat threw a last look over his shoulder at the canoe landing and River City Mounds.

In the clouds hanging over Cahokia's haze, he thought he could see Night Shadow Star's smile: sad, as if her heart were breaking. He'd seen that look the day she had retrieved his clothing from the Natchez.

"Bless you, Lady," he whispered. "I wish I . . ."

He blinked away a tear, reached for his paddle, and drove it deep into the roiling water.

With each stroke, the ache in his heart grew stronger, more painful.

He wouldn't look back.

He couldn't.

Ahead, somewhere down that immense and Powerful river, lay the future.

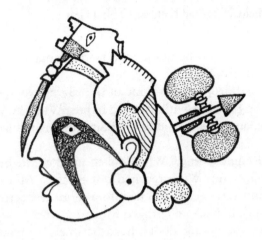

Ninety-one

The earthly body that held Morning Star's Spirit only lasted a day after the Red Wing walked out through the palace doors. The moment Chunkey Boy's body died, Blue Heron saw the shaft of light—as if the sun burned down through the high thatch roof for just an instant. And in the aftermath, only a wasted corpse remained; limp and lifeless meat and bone slumped on the panther hide–covered litter.

"He's gone," Sun Wing called softly, her dark gaze emotionless. She lifted her finger from where she'd been monitoring the living god's breathing. "Morning Star has returned to his place in the sky."

When Morning Star's Spirit left, it took the last of Blue Heron's hope. Now what? She looked around the room. The only occupants were Five Fists, Columella, Rising Flame, Wind, and—as incongruous as could be—Seven Skull Shield and his big brindled dog. The thief had come to report that Fire Cat, true to his word, was headed south on a Trade canoe.

The eternal fire crackled and spat sparks that Danced and leaped toward the new roof. Wind bent down on her old knees and threw a fistful of charred yaupon leaves into a pot of boiling water to make black drink.

Gods knew, they needed it.

Rising Flame perched straight-armed on the sleeping bench beside Blue Heron, her gaze fixed on an eternity that only she could see. She began shaking her head from side to side in some silent negation, then asked, "So, what do we do now?"

"We'll think of something." Columella stood, arms crossed, and paced nervously before the eternal fire, her head back, lost in thought. "And no,

Burned Bone is out of the question. Trying to make him Morning Star would be a catastrophe."

Five Fists had dropped onto one of the carved wooden storage boxes and was rubbing his face with callused hands. When he looked up, it was to fix his gaze on the corpse atop the dais. He might have been willing it back to life.

"Another Requickening." Wind looked up from the black drink pot.

"He said no." Sun Wing reached out to close Morning Star's half-lidded eyes and arrange his hands into a more respectful position. "Or do you want to call back an enraged Morning Star?"

Farts lay by the double doors, head between his paws, ears up, as if attentively following the conversation.

Sun Wing—having retreated back to the other side of the room—tucked the Tortoise Bundle between her pulled-up knees and chest. Something about the woman set Blue Heron's teeth on edge. Or at least what was left of them.

Rising Flame tilted her head in Sun Wing's direction, asking, "You think she's right? Morning Star's death means the death of Cahokia? Nothing but grass-and-tree-covered mounds? Wind and wildflowers where we're sitting now?"

Blue Heron gave the woman an appraising sidelong glance. "Just because the living god says we can't hold another reincarnation, doesn't mean—"

"Yes," Sun Wing's voice caught her by surprise, "it does, Aunt. You cannot conjure what Power does not allow. A bargain has been made. Night Shadow Star and Walking Smoke. And now Piasa and Morning Star, everything has been brought back in balance."

"And how would a fake Morning Star have changed that?" Wind demanded as the pot began to foam a rich brown. Using rags, she pulled it back from the fire where it would cool.

"It wouldn't," Rising Flame replied. "Not if you didn't believe in the miracle of Morning Star's reincarnation. We just have to find someone to step into Morning Star's shoes now that he, um, went back to the Sky World."

Nice mincing of words, Blue Heron thought.

Aloud she said, "Got someone in mind?"

"No . . . but let me put my mind to it." Rising Flame frowned, eyes slitted in thought. "Have to be someone we could control. Maybe from one of the outlying . . ."

"We have the Houses by the balls," Wind burst out, straightening from the pot of steeping black drink. "Five Fists? With the Morning Star squadrons and Columella's squadrons, we can pretty much maintain order, can't we?"

"Order's not the problem," Blue Heron replied. "When word gets out that Morning Star's Spirit has gone back to the sky? What then? The dirt farmers will be the first to go. A trickle in the beginning will turn into a rush. My call? A fourth of them will be gone by winter solstice, most of the rest by spring equinox so that they can be home in their old territories before planting season."

"And the Trade will vanish over the next year as word is carried down the rivers," Columella finished.

Five Fists had recovered enough to stand and pull a blanket from the engraved box he'd been sitting on. It was a beautiful piece with its rendering of Cosmic Spider. Blue Heron studied the cross on Cosmic Spider's back and Soul Bundles on her abdomen as she carried them across the night sky. Part of her wished she, too, was being borne away from the coming disaster. "As fast as the city was born, you'll be amazed at how much faster it will die."

Five Fists carried the blanket over, laying it across his sleeping bench. He added, "Oh, people will continue to come here for a time. Make pilgrimages to the old sacred sites, make offerings to the Spirits and ancestors. In the beginning, the priests will stay. Trying to keep the Power alive. But without Morning Star to believe in, the city and the empire are doomed."

Columella said, "You can bet that all those forest chiefs up north among the Oneota will be looking our way. They'll be sending raiding parties downriver as soon as they hear Morning Star has returned to the Sky World."

"So will the Shawnee," Wind added. "Come to pick the bones clean as Cahokia withers and dies."

Rising Flame fingered her chin, eyes slitted. "Without dirt farmers to grow enough surplus to keep the squadrons fed, we'll have no full-time warriors."

"Don't remind us." Blue Heron shot her a dirty look. "Spotted Wrist's shadow still hangs over us."

Five Fists snorted his displeasure. "Full-time warrior though he might have been, there's not enough of him left to cast a shadow. Some slinking cur shot him dead with an arrow in the middle of the night." He glanced at Blue Heron. "Keeper? Any word on the culprit?"

"Funny thing that," Blue Heron told him. "Don't have a clue about the arrow. Foreign. And none of my spies have heard any of Spotted Wrist's warriors bragging about the deed."

"That doesn't solve the problem," Wind reminded. "How do we keep the city from dying?"

"All cities die," Columella shot back. "Some sooner than others. Cahokia will slowly dry up, blow away, and the grass, the trees, or the river will take it back."

Blue Heron pointed a gnarled finger. "It's the sooner part that's at issue here. How do we save that later part until after our grandchildren's grandchildren's grandchildren are dead?"

"I'll do it," Seven Skull Shield called from where he was seated on a bench in the corner.

Every eye in the room turned to him. Even Farts gave the burly thief a curious look.

"Of all the insane notions. You? You're a . . . a . . ." Rising Flame couldn't finish.

Blue Heron threw her head back and laughed. "I can only imagine the kind of Morning Star you'd make, Thief."

Seven Skull Shield stood, hands spread wide. "It's not like anyone would miss me. And no one knows the city better than I do. The way I see it, all I have to do is sit on that dais, dressed in fancy stuff. If I dressed even fancier, who'd know the difference? Then there's the paint. Morning Star wore lots of it. Really thick there at the end. If no one got close, who'd know?"

Columella was fingering her chin, studying Seven Skull Shield. "Shoulders and arms are too thick, but covered with the cloak . . . ? I don't know. We'd have to do something about that face. And the nose? Pus and blood, how do we hide a nose like that?"

Tonka'tzi Wind, with a gesture of disbelief, cried, "We're *not* seriously considering this, are we? He's a . . . a *thief*! Clanless! A bit of human flotsam who—"

"Saved your life," Blue Heron reminded.

"Not that I'm buying into this, but no one will believe he's Morning Star," Five Fists thundered, raising a gnarled finger to make his point. "People know Morning Star. All the women he slept with. My guard. The recorders. Everyone. The thief doesn't even look like Morning Star."

Seven Skull Shield—that mild and innocent look on his face—asked, "And what have people seen? Hey, I hear what people are saying down in the plaza. For the last year—ever since that Sacred Moth business—he kept to himself. People said, 'After being poisoned by the Chicaza girl, he only beds select women.' And most of them, so I hear, are from outlying areas. For almost a year, no one but those of you here, and of course the soul flier, has seen him up close. And Rides-the-Lightning knows what's at stake."

"The thick face paint?" Rising Flame said softly. "That aloof manner? What we thought was disengagement? He was keeping his distance, only letting people see the mask."

Five Fists was still scowling. He shot Blue Heron a disbelieving glance, hooking a thumb in Seven Skull Shield's direction. "What makes you think—even if people didn't recognize him—that this bit of two-footed trash could pull it off? A clanless thief, take the place of the living god?"

That was when Sun Wing rose from her sleeping bench, striding across the floor. "That's what Morning Star meant when he asked if we'd rather have the thief. Opposites crossed. Don't you see the brilliance?"

"No, I don't," Rising Flame declared hotly.

The young woman glanced from face to face with her eerily empty eyes. "We just need enough time. People have to be told that Morning Star fought a Spirit battle . . . that he needs to recover. Later, when they see the scars, they will be told that Morning Star got them battling Piasa for his sister's life."

"And you expect me, as Four Winds Clan Matron, to be part of this?" Rising Flame muttered angrily.

"There are ways," Wind said thoughtfully. "I can have different stories told. Each more fantastic than the last. The thing is, people *will* believe."

"Why?" Five Fists demanded.

"Because they *want* to," Wind replied.

Sun Wing stated, "The foreign embassies won't know the difference. For the last couple of moons, Spotted Wrist always kept them at arm's length."

Five Fists was fingering his broken jaw. "You're forgetting the recorders and messengers. Mostly they're kept to the side room, but they'd know in a moment that the thief was a fake."

Seven Skull Shield now looked like he'd swallowed something moldy. He had to be figuring out what this would cost him.

Yes, thief, Blue Heron thought. *Next time, keep your big mouth closed.*

Rising Flame seemed to be reconsidering; she stepped close to stare thoughtfully at Seven Skull Shield. "He's got the same jaw. Nose is a lot flatter and wider after being broken so many times."

"We could fiddle with the face paint," Columella added. "Change it slowly over time so that people got used to it."

"Mostly they just see the headdress, cape, and apron," Wind said thoughtfully. "And with the maskettes covering his ears, no one will notice. But most of all, the eyes and brow are almost the same. That's the most important thing."

"No!" Five Fists smacked a fist in his palm. "Do you hear what you're saying? Do you know what kind of man he is? Keeper, you were the one who first called him Tow Rope! The notion of putting Seven Skull Shield on the High Chair makes me gag. He's got the manners of a camp dog and the morals of a weasel. And even if I went along with this insanity, how would we control him? Be more like him to break wind and belch the first time he had to—"

"And I thought we'd become friends," Seven Skull Shield told Five Fists in his fraudulently pained voice. "You don't want me? Fine. I said I'd do it because no one will miss me. And I know what's at stake. Who else can we call on? One of the Four Winds nobles?"

Rising Flame burst out in half-crazed laughter. "No. Five Fists is right. We're out of our minds to even think like this." She gave Seven Skull Shield a smile. "Sorry, Thief. But you're just not . . ."

When she didn't finish, Seven Skull Shield said, "So, if not me, who? And what happens to the city? If you've learned anything about me, it's that I'm not stupid. I'm pretty good at being tricky and pretending I'm someone else when I have to."

Blue Heron walked over, laid a hand on the thief's shoulder, and looked at the others. "Without a Morning Star, the city dies, and the empire with it. Someone has to take a seat on that panther-hide litter. Maybe for a couple of moons? Or until we can find a better solution? No one says it has to be permanent."

Five Fists made a strangling sound. "You're *serious*?"

"A few moons?" Rising Flame asked. "Right. What could go wrong?"

Seven Skull Shield was grinning in a way that made Blue Heron cringe. Piss and spit, even knowing the enormity of the stakes, the fool was still willing to take the risks?

"Someone will find out," Wind muttered as she checked the temperature of the black drink. "We'll only end up in the squares, but they'll tear the thief limb from limb. Cut him open and string his intestines all over the Great Plaza while he screams. Rip that famous shaft of his from his hips like it was a deeply rooted weed."

Blue Heron thought Seven Skull Shield had taken on a green pallor, his ears reddening. "Okay, so maybe . . ." She didn't finish. What was a little risk when it came to the survival of the city?

Over at the door, Farts let out a low whine, his tail flipping back and forth.

To Blue Heron's surprise, it was Fire Cat who stepped in the door, his pack hanging from one hand. The Red Wing was followed by an armed and armored Blood Talon. The squadron second glanced uncertainly around the room, staying a step behind the Red Wing.

Fire Cat smiled down wearily at Farts as the big dog nuzzled his hand.

Then he dropped his pack with a clanking thud, walked up to the fire, and said, "I'll play the charade. For my lady. Because she asked me."

Blue Heron walked over to stare into the man's tortured face. "Thought you headed south with Winder."

"Made it as far as Horned Serpent canoe landing." Fire Cat stared down at the muscles in his forearms as he knotted his fingers into fists. "That's when I understood what she meant. What she wanted me to do. The last order."

Five Fists uttered a huge sigh as if he'd just avoided a catastrophe. He shook his head in unfeigned relief as Seven Skull Shield gave him a mocking grin.

"Chunkey Boy?" Fire Cat asked, his haunted gaze fixed on the empty dais.

"He's gone," Sun Wing said, not that Morning Star's boneless slump could be mistaken for anything but a corpse.

Fire Cat's jaw muscles twitched. A glittering of despair grew in his eyes. "My lady and I, we never had a chance, did we?"

Sun Wing told him, "Power chose you for this from the start."

Blue Heron watched the Red Wing walk over to the corner where he'd held Night Shadow Star's body. There, he sank to the floor and dropped his head into his hands. Farts settled himself at the man's side, tail thumping the matting as he laid his massive head in Fire Cat's lap.

Seven Skull Shield placed his thick arm over Blue Heron's shoulder, whispering, "Looks like I barely dodged a close one."

"Are you kidding? You never stood a chance." She jabbed him in the ribs with an elbow.

Ninety-two

For Clan Keeper Blue Heron, it had been a snowy, cold, and very busy winter. With the countdown to spring equinox, the weather had finally broken. Given that the sun was setting a mere finger's width south of due west, even she would have known equinox was upon them without having to ask the Sky Priests. Though the mavens at the Great Observatory could have told her to the exact hand of time how long it would be before that blessed sunrise.

In appreciation of the balmy weather, Blue Heron had left the palace veranda, walked along the edge of the earthen pyramid, and settled with her back to the clay-plastered palace wall. Below her, the Avenue of the Sun was alive with people, children, and dogs packing all sorts of goods into and out of central Cahokia. The city, more than ever, was thriving. And part of it was a new optimism. One she couldn't quite put her finger on.

She suspected, however, that a lot of the buoyancy and enthusiasm came from the top. A new energy had come to rest in the Houses with their carefully picked high chiefs and matrons. These were younger people, chosen from outside the old House lineages. In taking the high chairs, rebuilding Horned Serpent House, River House, and North Star House, they had imparted a vigor as well as a sense of rebirth. Part of that, Blue Heron liked to believe, was her doing, since her spies monitored all manner of changes.

Lessons learned and all that.

Another source of optimism came from the reports that had trickled in over the winter. Tall Dancer had reached Cofitachequi, reinforcing the once-lost colony there. Again, communications had been restored all along the route down the Tenasee. Morning Star's priests were traveling far and wide, and even in the dead of winter, pilgrims had been arriving to view the miracle of the living god. And, having seen Morning Star in the flesh, they had gone back, most of them, to add their witness to the legend.

She leaned back, lifting her old stone pipe to her lips and inhaling the aromatic smoke. Let Sister Tobacco Dance through her lungs and blood. Gods and rot, but she enjoyed a good smoke.

If she looked north, she could see the back wall of the new palace that had been built atop the ruins of her old one. Sun Wing lived there now.

Blue Heron had been given Night Shadow Star's palace for her base of operations. Not that she relished it. The location was too public—the ramp and stairs visible to the entire plaza. Made it outright impossible for her spies to slip in unobserved. Right up until the thief had suggested a second, less visible stairway of half-sunken steps that led up the mound's northwest corner.

She took another puff on her pipe, letting the sun warm her face and chest. Even with her eyes closed, the blinding orb turned the backs of her eyelids blaze red. Summer couldn't get there fast enough.

Which was when a shadow blocked the light.

"This had better be good," she growled, opening her right eye to a baleful slit.

"Smells like good tobacco," the thief told her as he stepped around and seated himself beside her. "I haven't had a good smoke in days."

From inside the palace—despite the thick wall—Smooth Pebble could be heard shouting, "Get that foul beast out of the stewpot!" It was followed by a crash of a thrown pot as it shattered on something hard.

A moment later, Blue Heron caught sight of Farts as he dashed into view down below, scattering people as he raced west on the Avenue of the Sun.

"Thrown pot. Good trick I learned from Mother Otter," she told him. "Works like magic when it comes to getting that mongrel out of the stew."

"Hard on pots, though." Seven Skull Shield reached for her pipe.

"I might hit you with more than a thrown pot. You take chances, Thief. Asking the Clan Keeper for her personal pipe? You never seem to remember that I can have you hung in a square with a single word. Can't you steal your own pipe from some unlucky dirt farmer who looks at you the wrong way?"

"Somehow, it keeps slipping my mind," Seven Skull Shield told her. He took a puff, expanded his chest, and exhaled the smoke through his nose with a sigh. "And even if you did, I'd just ask Morning Star for clemency. He thinks kindly of me for some reason."

She shot him a warning glance. "You know we don't talk about that."

"'Course not." The thief couldn't suppress a smile as Farts came sneaking warily back, floppy ears pricked, nose quivering as he slunk his way back toward the stairs. "I figure another finger of time, another pot."

"One of these days Smooth Pebble will hit him."

"I think she just likes breaking your pots."

"She does have a soft spot for you and that dog." Blue Heron shot him a disdainful stare. "What is it with you, anyway?"

"I grow on people." He took another draw on her pipe and handed it back. "You heard about that new chunkey player down at River City? Calls himself Red Wing Black, paints his entire body in secret before he steps out onto the court? It's a guy with a lot of scars. Looks like he fought an Itza or something. Wins with uncanny frequency."

"Huh. Thought Five Fists and Blood Talon were putting a stop to that."

"I think they tried. Gave it up as a lost cause. That, and well, what're they supposed to do when the living god gives them an order?"

She pointed the pipe at him in a warning gesture. "You're to keep your mouth shut. No one—"

"Crazy Frog knows."

"Pus, rot, and spit! I thought it was too good to last. By the end of the quarter moon, half the city will—"

"Not a word is being said." Seven Skull Shield pulled his knobby knee up, clasping it with his callused hands. "For one thing, Crazy Frog owes you and Wind for saving his family. For another, he's as anxious as anyone to keep Cahokia's prosperity and peace. He's winning a lot of bets when Red Wing Black plays. And, if the day ever comes when Morning Star is found out, it will bring even greater fame to the River City chunkey courts. Crazy Frog's no one's fool."

"Haven't seen you for a couple of days. Where you been?"

"Canoe landing. Around. Had to do something sneaky for Lady Sun Wing. She needed someone . . . um, discreet."

Blue Heron felt her heart skip and sink. "Don't tell me you've been sneaking into Sun Wing's bed and—"

"Pus and snot, no!" Seven Skull Shield gave her a disgusted look. "The lady asked me to get her to the canoe landing without anyone knowing. Wanted to meet up with some people Winder brought upriver. A holy man and woman. Names are Spots and Cactus Flower, from down south, or out west, or whatever. Bundle business. That's all."

He grinned. "Not that the lady is without charms, assuming you might be into all those empty-eyed spooky stares and the real chance that she'd wind the souls out of your body just as you slid your—"

"That's more than I need to hear. Or even want to try and imagine, thank you."

"Besides—" Seven Skull Shield gave her a shrug—"it's different these days. Wooden Doll and me, something's changed. Maybe it was seeing how the Red Wing was with Night Shadow Star. I realized something about myself, about what I wanted."

"Not supposed to use my niece's name. You could call her Spirit from whichever afterlife she's in."

"You know I don't believe that stuff the priests spew out." He nodded as he squinted into the setting sun. "Besides, of all the people I've ever known, she was the most remarkable. Soul possession and all. If I could go back . . ."

When he couldn't finish, she shot him an evaluative look. "Yes?"

"Nothing. It's silly." Then he gave her a saucy wink. "Actually, I had too much fun spending time with you." He sighed. "And it was fun, wasn't it? Outfoxing all those dangerous foes, rescuing friends, defeating enemies, all the sneaking, and thieving, and burning palaces? The howling fights, the—"

"Gods, if I never have to hear you fight again, it'll be a plea to the Spirits of Earth, Sky, and Underworld come true."

He tugged on his uplifted knee, then reached over for her pipe. After drawing and puffing out a blue cloud, he studied the stone tube. "Maybe you're right. My fighting days are over. But I can still Sing. I was down at Meander's while I was at the canoe landing, had him and his people weeping just with the Power of my voice."

"No surprise there. Your Singing would bring a rock to tears."

He knocked out the dottle, pinched up tobacco from her little bowl, and repacked the pipe. Then, lifting the pot of glowing embers, he bent down, sucked, and managed to light the pipe. This, he handed to her.

At that moment, calls broke out, screams followed by curses.

Blue Heron craned her neck, staring down at the Avenue of the Sun where people were diving out of the way. Farts went charging through them like a thrown boulder, ears flapping, big paws hammering on the packed sand. The dog was stretched out in full flight; a catfish was clamped in his massive jaws, the fish's head and tail flipping up and down with each bound as if it were still alive.

"Someone!" a Deer Clan fish Trader called as he pounded past in pursuit. "Stop that foul dog! He stole my fish!"

"Guess he didn't try for Smooth Pebble's stew. Saves you another pot." Seven Skull Shield leaned back to grab his knee again and bask in the setting sun. "That Deer Clan fellow doesn't have a chance."

"Might as well save his effort," Blue Heron agreed.

"Spirit dog, don't you know?" Seven Skull Shield told her.

She lifted the pipe, drew, and exhaled. "Thanks for refilling my pipe."

The thief shrugged his thick shoulders. "What are friends for?"

Ninety-three

The equinox sun seemed to peer out from beneath the thick blanket of clouds that cloaked the sky. All through the day, people had worried that the overcast would obscure the yellow orb as it illuminated the Avenue of the Sun and marked the beginning of spring.

Then, at the last minute, it burned free on the western horizon to illuminate the bottoms of the clouds in fiery yellows, shimmering orange, iridescent crimson, glowing blue and purple.

Dressed in finery, wearing the quetzal-feather cloak he'd seen the Itza present Morning Star, his hair pulled up in a severe bun and supporting a heavy burnished-copper headdress, Fire Cat stood at the head of the Council Terrace stairs overlooking the Great Plaza. He lifted Morning Star's heavy copper mace high in his right hand as if in benediction to the dying light.

Four Winds Clan Matron Rising Flame and *Tonka'tzi* Wind—wearing their finest ceremonial robes—stood to either side and a step behind.

A half year had passed, and the irony remained just as biting and acidic as it had that day he had agreed to take Morning Star's place. He, who had doubted and fought the Morning Star myth all his life, now perpetuated the hoax.

I become the lie.

He raised his arms to the sunset, mace held up to reflect the hot red light. The roar that began with the crowd in the Great Plaza stretched out on the Avenue of the Sun; it hit him like a physical wave. Almost made him step back in shock, but he held his ground, staring into the setting sun where it dropped behind the distant silhouette of Evening Star Town.

"It's not for you, you know," Wind—who seemed to read his discomfort—said just loud enough to be heard over the roar of the crowd. "It's for them."

"No," he answered. "It's for my lady."

As the last sliver of sun vanished behind the far western horizon, he turned to face the crowd, arms still spread wide. He then slowly drew his arms closed, as if personally embracing the thousands upon thousands who crowded the Great Plaza. As a final gesture, he bowed as low as he dared with the heavy headdress and touched his forehead with the mace.

The resulting roar must have been heard in the Underworld, for it surely shook the Sky World.

"You are so much better at this than he was," Rising Flame told him. "It's as if you *own* them."

Fire Cat turned and—Wind and Rising Flame following—walked back through the double gate and into the relative sanctuary of the Council Terrace. The Earth Clans high chiefs and matrons stood packed shoulder-to-shoulder to either side, held back by Blood Talon's warriors. No one who might have known Morning Star from the old days got within so much as four paces of Fire Cat. Even with the thick makeup and face paint.

At the foot of the stairs, Blood Talon and Five Fists—each in their polished armor—stepped in behind, climbing the high stairs. The crowds below Sang and Danced; bonfires were set here and there, and feasts were laid out to mark the end of equinox.

Fire Cat stepped to the side as the rest filed through the high palisade gate, saying, "Give me a moment. I'll be right in."

Only Blood Talon hesitated, standing in the recess of the gate to keep an eye on Fire Cat. "Are you all right?"

Fire Cat smiled, feeling the resistance of the thick face paint. "Squadron First, I doubt I'll ever be all right again."

He looked out over the masses who now Danced to the sound of pot drums, saw the flicking fires, and extended his left hand. He could feel the Power radiating from the crowd.

What he believed didn't matter. It was what they did. And they had changed the world. Would continue to change the world. More than even Morning Star, he had lived it from the North to the far East. And here, in this central place where the Underworld and Sky World met, he had found magic.

"I still serve you, Lady."

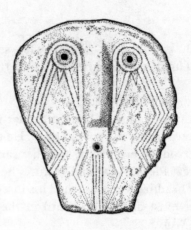

Epilogue

All across the Great Plaza, people burst into cheers as those who stood on the Avenue of the Sun and those gathered behind the posts in the Great Observatory marked the location of the setting sun. The celebration culminated the seven-day countdown to Spring Equinox.

Where she stood at the foot of the Great Staircase, Sun Wing turned, looking up to see Morning Star at the head of the stairs. Standing before the double gates that led into the Council Terrace, the living god faced west. In the rays of golden, glowing light, he lifted his arms, the action spreading an eagle-wing cloak as if to take flight. Sunset burned red-gold as it reflected from the polished copper headdress. And even from where she stood, Sun Wing could make out the black forked-eye design contrasting with the white face paint.

The crowd erupted into a frenzy of applause, whistles, and shouts. Behind her on the Great Plaza, the thumping of drums, the rising lilt of the flutes, and the shuffling of thousands of feet marked the beginning of the Dance. As the sun dipped behind the uplands on the far side of the river, the great bonfires were being lit.

On all sides, the Traders and vendors were doing a booming business in food, trinkets, drinks, and Trade.

"I've never even imagined such a place could exist," the gray-haired man beside her said in heavily accented Cahokian. His name was Spots—a holy man from the far Southwest who had known the legendary Nightshade. His wife, a spare woman called Cactus Flower, had pulled her white hair back in a severe bun, the foreign design of her zig-zag black-and-white blanket standing out in the crowd.

Sun Wing—a curious throbbing in her chest—turned. "The Bundle tells me the time has come. I must let it go." She steeled herself. "Power is a terrible master. I have done things, horrible things. Some I have atoned for. But the others? Some debts cannot be repaid, and I have to live with the memory."

Spots studied her in the growing twilight. "We have a saying in our land: 'No one wants to become a Dreamer.'"

With a quavering smile, she handed the Bundle across, felt its Song change as Spots took it.

"Take it home." She closed her eyes, swayed on her feet, a confusion of grief, guilt, and relief filling her. A part of her suddenly went missing, opening a gaping hole within her. The sensation was akin to half of her souls vanishing in an instant. She was no longer whole.

"Are you all right?" Cactus Flower reached out and steadied her.

Sun Wing swallowed hard, the welling emptiness expanding below her heart. Memories, like bats, came fluttering up from deep down in the eye of her souls. Images of her mutilated sister, Lace, and the dissected remains of the fetus she had carried. Fragments of her madness, of the despair. The endless remorse and self-disgust. Memories of the battle she'd fought for her souls, and how the Tortoise Bundle had absorbed her pain and granted her peace. All for a price. One that had to be paid the night she'd hit Night Shadow Star in the back of the head with a hoe handle.

Power used me for its own purposes.

The knowledge struck her like a physical blow. And again, Cactus Flower kept her from staggering.

"I am so sorry, sister," she whispered, blinked at tears, and stared up at where Morning Star still stood at the head of the Great Staircase, arms outstretched to the glow that burned along the bottoms of the low clouds.

Spots and Cactus Flower were watching her with knowing eyes. He told her, "Lady of Cahokia, Power wouldn't have chosen you if you couldn't bear the burden."

She smiled weakly. "I have the rest of my life to try to come to terms with the things I did." She gestured at where Morning Star lowered his arms and turned, surveying the crowd that called his name, Dancing, and celebrating in the miracle of his reincarnation on Earth. "And as he served my sister, I shall serve him. I owe him nothing less."

She took a breath, stiffening her resolve. "And what about you? Will you stay in the city for a while?"

"Off tomorrow," Cactus Flower told her, those knowing eyes shifting from Sun Wing to Spots. "Winder said he'd leave by midday. Something about spending time with a wife among the Quiz Quiz. From there we can Trade for transportation to Yellow Star Mounds. After that we will make the crossing to our lands."

"And the Bundle?" Sun Wing asked. Not that she needed to. The Bundle would ensure that no mishap befell them.

Spots lifted it, staring hard at the blue wolf Sun Wing had painted on the worn leather. "Yes, I know," he said in response to something the Bundle had asked.

Then he gave Sun Wing a weary smile. Told her, "The Bundle tells me we have a cannibal to kill and a soul to set free."

Cactus Flower wrapped her black-and-white blanket tighter around her shoulders, and bowed in the Cahokian fashion, touching her forehead. "It has been an honor, Lady."

"Mine, too," Sun Wing replied, with a bow of her own. "Now, you'd better be going. The bonfires will light your way to River City Mounds. They'll be feasting and Dancing all night at the canoe landing as it is."

She watched them turn and thread their way through the jostling crowds to vanish in the growing gloom.

"Gods and rot, I am so alone," she whispered. Then taking a deep breath, she turned and started up the steps. Morning Star would need her. Tomorrow morning he would be receiving an embassy from the Koroa.

She would have to tell him why the Koroa were so important, and why they would be interested in what happened regarding the theft of some of their copper.

If she was lucky, Farts and the thief might even be in the palace at the same time. The story was always so much more interesting to tell when they were present.

Bibliography

In addition to below, we refer the reader to the extensive bibliography on Cahokia and the Mississippian world included in *People of the Morning Star*. Please consult that source for the nonfiction information we relied upon during the writing of the People of Cahokia series.

Since the publication of *People of the Morning Star*, remarkable research has been conducted at Cahokia. The following titles should be read as an introduction to the latest Cahokian archaeology by anyone interested in understanding Cahokia, its religion and culture.

Alt, Susan M. *Cahokia's Complexities: Ceremonies and Politics of the First Mississippian Farmers*. Tuscaloosa: University of Alabama Press, 2018.

Baires, Sarah E. *Land of Water, City of the Dead: Religion and Cahokia's Emergence*. Tuscaloosa: University of Alabama Press, 2017.

Deter-Wolf, Aaron, and Carol Diaz-Granados. *Drawing with Great Needles: Ancient Tattoo Traditions of North America*. Austin: University of Texas Press, 2013.

Diaz-Granados, Carol, James R. Duncan, and Kent F. Reilly III. *Picture Cave: Unraveling the Mysteries of the Mississippian Cosmos*. Austin: University of Texas Press, 2015.

Emerson, Thomas E., Brad H. Koldehoff, and Tamira K. Brennan. *Revealing Greater Cahokia, North America's First Native City: Rediscovery and Large-Scale Excavations of the East St. Louis Precinct*. Illinois State Archaeology Survey, Prairie Research Institute; Illinois Department of Transportation, University of Illinois at Urbana-Champaign, 2018.

Fritz, Gayle J. *Feeding Cahokia: Early Agriculture in the North American Heartland*. Tuscaloosa: University of Alabama Press, 2019.

McNutt, Charles H., and Ryan M. Parish, eds. *Cahokia in Context: Hegemony and Diaspora*. Gainesville: University of Florida Press, 2020.

Pauketat, Timothy R. *An Archaeology of the Cosmos*. London: Routledge, 2013.

Pauketat, Timothy R., and Susan Alt. *Medieval Mississippians: The Cahokian World*. Santa Fe, NM: School for Advanced Research Press, 2015.

Acknowledgments

With special appreciation for the Chamberlain Inn in scenic Cody, Wyoming, for providing our getaway when we need to brainstorm plot twists, character motivation, and "what happens next." Our thanks to Elizabeth Scaccia for keeping our glasses full and pizza warm. The Chamberlain is a true jewel when it comes to creativity.